LIESMITH

First printing 2019.
Copyright © 2014 by Alis Franklin.
All rights reserved.

ISBN: 978-0-6450882-0-5 (paperback)

"Chibi Lain" © 2015 Kim Koskamp

https://alis.me

Praise for *Liesmith*

"In this wildly entertaining debut novel, Australian author [Alis] Franklin has kicked off what's sure to be a popular series. Fractured, funny, and fast-paced, this book is guaranteed to resonate with fans of mythopoeic fantasy from the likes of J.R.R. Tolkien, George R. R. Martin, and Neil Gaiman."
—*Library Journal*

"A very entertaining yet touching read."
—Popcorn Reads

"A fabulous start to a new series."
—The Blogger Girls

"Cinematic with page-turning action sequences."
—Blogger's Bookshelf

"*Liesmith* is a delightful, refreshing story with some unlikely characters and a plot filled with mythology and adventure that will keep you guessing."
—Bookwinked

"Exciting and filled with danger . . . Fans of mythology will enjoy this urban fantasy story."
—Inside of a Dog

Books of the Wyrd

Liesmith
Stormbringer
Bad Meme

Wyrdverse: Tales from the Wyrd

Other Works

The Dragon of Rosemont High
Unnatural Order

ALIS FRANKLIN

LIESMITH

BOOK 1 OF THE WYRD

Everything is true, especially the lies. That's the trick.

Every tale ever told, every whisper, every song, every single string of words ever uttered by mortal mouths or carved in rocks or scrawled on paper. It's the ultimate human trait, this endless urge to speak and name and label. To attach sounds to things and meaning to sounds. To make language.

Sometimes, when a sound refers to nothing, something comes in to take its place. Pulled up from the black void behind the world, shaped into form and given story.

This is the thing we call the Wyrd, and it's the place where gods are born. Well. Gods and monsters, and sometimes the line between the two is thin.

Humans might not believe in the old gods much anymore—they don't venerate our deeds or perform our bloody rituals—but that doesn't mean that we're forgotten. Not with our tales recorded in bestsellers and played out on film and collected in the bits and bytes of libraries that span the globe. That sort of repetition ensures our survival more readily than any sacrifice or prayer, and with less effort on our part, too.

It's good to be retired, even for a god.

Not that we're all living the life of worship-free leisure. More humans and more *things* mean more gods and more monsters; and for every gnarled, thousand-year-old sky father, twenty bright young memes spring up in his place: the Liberal Media, the Wisdom of Crowds, the Random Number Gods.

The Start-Up CEO.

Some of us don't fully retire, don't pack our things and drool out our dotages in some eternal old folks' home. We go consulting instead. Pick new roles, part-time gigs, a little extra belief to trickle in over the top of our stagnating day jobs. The New World is crawling with us, and not just the United States.

Stop me if you've heard this one before, set not long ago on an isle far, far away. A wild place of danger and mystery; of deadly beasts and rugged men; of old clichés and biting irony.

This island called Australia.

A little over two hundred years ago—and much to the consternation of the locals—white men from Europe arrived and didn't leave. They turned the land into a prison, the place to send the chaff they didn't want back home—the poor and the Irish, the whores and the thieves—crammed onto stinking boats and abandoned in a hell of endless, burning deserts.

I heard someone once say that a country founded in the gutter has nowhere to go but up. And Australia did, more or less, dragging itself kicking and screaming into the twenty-first century. When it went, we came with it.

Because mortals weren't the only ones to make the long voyage across the sea into the present. The old gods have always been here, of course. Ngalyod, the Rainbow Serpent, drives cross-country in a battered Land Rover. Waa and Bunjil make trouble down in Melbourne. And the *kurdaitcha* and *illapurinja* roam the sands, nursing old wounds beneath the blistering sun. A thousand gods from a thousand peoples, all fighting for space in the crowded cities and rural ghost towns of this new century. When they fight, they fight us, the exiled gods of Europe, come to languish in a new prison, one fitted out with shining beaches and reasonable Internet.

In Sydney, a fallen angel makes deals with politicians, promising good front-page press in exchange for souls. In Perth, the wife of a bound titan runs open-cut mines that dig deep beneath red earth, searching for a way to free her imprisoned in-laws. And, somewhere in between, an old trickster hides from death by crafting little altars in aluminum and glass.

That's the country. Pinch and zoom, and end up in a city.

Its name is Pandemonium, but the locals call it Panda. It's inland, temperate, surrounded by mountains and bush, its population three hundred thousand or so. Back in the 1800s, it was founded on dreams of gold. By the 1950s, it'd settled on mining coal instead. Nowadays, it oversees a global web of technology. Cell phones, computers, video games. That sort of thing.

This is where we start. There's a house here, an unassuming white-collar relic from the 1970s, located in a suburb that's largely the same.

Inside the house is a boy, standing just beyond the threshold of adulthood, metaphorically speaking. Literally speaking, he's standing in his bedroom, wearing faded black briefs and not much else. He's staring at a pair of crisp brown slacks, and his mind is thinking of the tattered jeans he's only just kicked off, left in a pile on the floor, atop a T-shirt that threatens darkness with the spell of *magic missile*.

Stop me if you know this reference.

The boy does, and knowing that he does will tell you almost everything you need to know about him. These are the other things: He's twenty-two; his skin and hair and eyes are cast in shades of brown; he wears glasses; no one would ever call him handsome; he's somewhat overweight. If you asked him his greatest talent, he'd laugh nervously and tell you it was slaying dragons. On the Internet.

No one ever asks. Which is why the boy never mentions the final detail. It's about lying—or rather the lack thereof—and, if squinted at in bright light, it could be considered a kind of magic. We'll get back to it later.

For now, know that the date is late December, and the time is evening. It's a Friday. Tonight, the boy has his first official Office Christmas Party.

He doesn't want to go.

His father, David, says he has to. Both father and son work for the same company, Lokabrenna, Inc., nowadays mostly re-branded as just LB. Once upon a time, Lokabrenna mined for coal. Now, LB's computers sit on every desk, its smartphones in every purse and pocket.

The boy's father is an accountant, the boy works in IT. In-ternal IT, of the have-you-tried-turning-it-off-and-on variety. His father believes in old-fashioned corporate progression, of starting in the mail room and working up the ziggurat with sweat and dedication. The boy knows this idea is a rusted rel-ic of the past, a scratched record in an era of MP3s and online streaming. Because privilege is born, not made, and talent is scouted from abroad, not recruited from the basement. If the boy ever gets his name in the credits for any Great New Thing, it will be buried down at the end of a very, very long list.

He doesn't want to shake hands and make small talk at the party. He's young, has posters of dragons on his walls, and would rather spend his Friday playing games on the Internet with his friends. He resents the crisp brown slacks and nice new shirt, and he resents his father, just a little, for buying them. Mostly, he resents the arguments and awkward silences that won over his acceptance of David's secondhand aspirations.

The boy dresses and heads downstairs. His father gushes and tries in vain to smooth his son's hair down into something fit for corporate consumption. In the end, he gives up, but pretends he's satisfied with the results. He is so, so proud of his boy, for whom he dreams great things.

He has no idea.

David drives them to the party. It's outside, in the center of the city, in a place called Osko Park. The gleaming edifice of LB's corporate temple looms large across the street, the grandest and most imposing building in the state.

It's hot, and bright, because that's what December evenings mean in this part of the world. The boy nurses an imported beer—a Corona—and worries that his sweat stains will show on his new shirt.

After an hour or so of misery and too many small spring rolls, the boy detaches himself from his father's watch and retreats behind a large and ugly piece of public art. He sits down on the grass, fends off mosquitoes as best he can, and pulls something from his pocket.

It's a Spark, a handheld gaming console made by Pyre Computers, a subsidiary of LB. The boy uses it to work on a game played by only two other people in all the world. Those two others are his friends, and the game is a project the trio makes together. One does art, one writes. The boy cuts code.

They have the first half of a level for an isometric dark fantasy RPG. The boy knows every part of it and also knows how progress has been stalled for over a year. Knows that, soon, the console in his hands will be obsolete, taking with it both their game and their hope for breakthrough indie success.

Being adults got in the way of crafting dreams. It happens.

The boy plays his game. As he does, he's transformed in the way of mortals inspired by love and art. His lips purse, his brow furrows. He's not handsome but, in that moment, someone might imagine that he was.

Someone almost does and, lost in concentration, the boy misses the approach of soft footsteps. He doesn't miss the voice.

"Fucking Christ."

The boy looks up.

"Um . . ."

For one terrible, ceaseless moment, the Wyrd—fate—turns upon its gyre.

Then: "Shit, man. Didn't see you. You escaping, too?"

The boy blinks. He suddenly feels foolish, sitting in the dirt in ill-fitting slacks and a sweat-stained shirt.

Looming over him is a stranger, wearing jeans and an LB tee beneath a trendy-ugly jacket. The boy is jealous of the casual attire. He's not so jealous of the unlit cigarette hanging from the stranger's mouth.

"Yeah," says the boy. "Yeah, it's a bit much."

"It is, isn't it? Mind if I smoke?"

"Actually, yeah. Kinda. Sorry." The boy winces, but the stranger shrugs.

"Shitty habit. Picked it up before public health became a thing, now just can't seem to drop it." He tucks the cigarette behind his ear and takes a sip from the glass in his other hand, wine swirling rich and dark and red. Then the stranger leans forward, pointing toward the Spark. "There's a new one of those coming out in April, you know."

"Yeah, so I've heard." April. The boy figures that's when childhood truly ends.

"What're you playing?"

The boy looks down, then looks up. The stranger is peering at him, all odd green eyes and chin-length hair. His skin is olive; his hair is black. He has a goatee. He is very, very handsome.

"Uh." The boy knows he's blushing. He hopes the stranger doesn't notice in the dusk. "It's, uh. Nothing really. Just . . . something I made. With my friends."

The stranger's eyebrows hike. "You made it? Cool! Can I see?" And he sits down on the grass.

The boy panics, just for a moment. He doesn't want the stranger to see his game. It's his heart, his soul. Not something he can give to someone he only just met, someone he doesn't trust. What if they don't like it?

"Sure, man."

He hands over the Spark.

"What's it called?"

"Well. Um. We kinda hadn't decided. Em—she's our writer—she wants to call it *Gangleri*."

The stranger looks up. For a moment, his green eyes burn brightly in the gloom. " '*Gangleri*'?" He has a strange emphasis on the word. An accent.

The boy nods. "It's, um. It's one of the names of Odin. Y'know, the Viking god?"

The stranger nods, just once.

"He's, uh . . . man. I don't want to spoil the plot." The boy tries a laugh, realizing how foolish he must sound.

But the stranger asks, "And what do you call it?"

The boy bites his lip. "Um, well. *Gangleri*'s cool but it's a bit of a mouthful, you know? Not very marketable. So I was thinking something simple. So, like. Um. *Saga*?"

"*Saga*," says the stranger.

The boy laughs, or tries to. "Too simple?"

The stranger looks down at the glowing screen. "Show me how to play," he says.

The boy does.

That's how his father finds him, over an hour later. Lost deep in conversation with his odd new friend. (Despite *Saga*'s flaws, the stranger loves it. If that doesn't make him friend material, the boy doesn't know what could.)

"Sigmund! There you— What are you doing back here? I've been looking all over for you."

The boy winces at his father's voice; the stranger sees it.

"Sigmund, this is Mai Vo. She works in the CFO's office, and—"

The boy tries not to die. He's sure Mai is a lovely woman. He's sure he has absolutely no desire at all to meet her.

The stranger stands.

"I was telling her about your accounting degree. She says they're always looking for— Oh."

Because the stranger extends his hand, and the boy's father has seen his face. He's recognized it, in fact, in exactly the way his son did not.

"Hale," says the stranger. "Travis Cameron Hale, CEO. But I'm sure you know that already."

"S-sir . . . Uh. David, sir. David Sussman. It's an—"

"Is this your son? He's been showing me the game he's made. It's pretty cool."

The boy's name is Sigmund. Sigmund Sussman. Right now, sitting on the grass, Corona in one hand, Spark in the other, he wants to die. Wants to die because he's just spent the last hour showing the CEO of *the fucking company that he works for*—the CEO he *didn't fucking recognize*, despite the fact that the man's *fucking face* is splashed on *every fucking magazine*—his shitty little two-bit game.

Sigmund's life, welcome to it.

This is his story. And mine.
Stick around. You'll see.

SIGMUND

There sits Sigyn,
but much happiness
she doesn't have.

—"Völuspá," stanza 35

ONE

H{OLY SHIT, YOU} are such a *dork*.”
"I know.”
"You were talking to him for like an *hour*.”
"I was.”
"And you didn't *recognize* him.”
"I did not.”
"Holy shit, man.”
"Yeah.”
"Holy motherfucking *shit*.”
"Yup.”
Once upon a yesterday, there lived a boy called Sigmund.
"Holy . . . You *showed him our game!*”
And a girl called Em.
"Yeah.”
"Dude!”
"Yeah.”
"*Dude!*”
It wasn't like Sigmund didn't know he'd been in the run-

ning for World's Most Influential Loser since circa 1990. He'd been himself for over twenty years now; things like that weren't exactly a surprise.

"So, like. What did he *say*?"

Monday. First day back at work after Christmas break. Outside was hot and bright and humid. Inside, Sigmund was getting the third degree from his best friend. One of them, at any rate.

"Um. He was pretty cool, I guess."

"You *guess*?"

Sigmund shrugged. That was the best he had. Hale had been nice. Personable, talkative. Polished. The guy was a god-damn CEO for Christ's sake. Sigmund figured he probably knew how to make small talk with the plebes.

"Dude. He's like the richest man on *the planet*. How did you not recognize him?"

Third richest. Sigmund had looked it up.

"I dunno, man," he said. "He was wearing jeans and a T-shirt. And was, like, talking to me. It's not exactly some-thing you expect, y'know?"

"Dude. I swear . . ."

Sigmund held up his hands to stop whatever felt like com-ing next. "I know, I know," he said. "Believe me, there's noth-ing you can tell me I haven't already told myself."

A litany of excuses: It was twilight, he'd been drinking, Hale looked younger in person. And taller. And spoke with a slightly different voice. And what it all really boiled down to was the fact that guys like Sigmund didn't get accidentally chatted up by guys like Hale. Didn't sit in the grass for an hour, nursing lukewarm beer and getting their nerd on over shitty hobby RPGs. Not with the owner of *Utgard fucking Entertainment* (among other things), one of the most awesom-est game development studios on the planet.

In the car, on the way home from the party, Sigmund's dad had been oddly silent. Sigmund had expected him to freak, to hassle Sigmund over not, like, getting Hale to be his buddy on LinkedIn or whatever. (Not that it would help, given Sigmund's stunning lack of a profile on said service.) Or maybe he'd been expecting Dad to be angry, yell at him for wasting the CEO's time and getting them both fired for his trouble. But Dad hadn't done any of that. He'd just been quiet, and they'd driven home and gone to bed, and by Saturday it had been as if the whole party had never happened. Dad hadn't mentioned it, and neither had Sigmund, and now here he was. Back at the office. Not fired, not noticed. Not even gossiped about, at least not until he'd opened his big mouth to blab to Em. Just another average day in the Basement.

It wasn't the literal basement, of course: It was the seventh floor. But it was where IT lived, so Sigmund figured it was going to end up being called the Basement no matter how high it was above sea level.

Not that the seventh floor was very high, particularly not compared to the exec offices, sitting way up above the skyline. LB was not a modest building: a thing of status and towering glass, one that seemed to get rebuilt every few years, get a new look and new floors. Sigmund figured that must cost LB a fortune, but the company was like that. Sigmund could hardly complain. Not when he got to spend most of his day nestled in the enormous expanse of light and glass and green. Lots of green: It was impossible to sneeze in LB without blowing snot all over indoor plants or "living walls." Or whole actual gardens, trees and all, on the lower levels. Some environmental initiative, staff health or whatever.

LB loved things like that. Break rooms full of hammocks and beanbags and Inferno consoles. A gym. Even a day care in one of the annex buildings. And a chef in the cafeteria, responsible for at least ten percent of Sigmund's body weight. (Because seriously: Best. Burgers. In town.)

It was a pretty sweet place to work, even for go-nowhere plebes like Sigmund Sussman.

Sigmund, who worked in IT ops. Third-level support stuff, when turning it off and on the first two times wasn't enough.

It was a job. Not what he'd imagined doing as a kid, maybe, but money was money, and money turned into comic books and video games. Particularly given they were located, like, five seconds' walk from Torr Mall, right smack bang in the heart of Pandemonium City.

Pandemonium. People got used to the name, growing up there. Some mining accident from the 1920s or whatever, back when there'd actually been a mine. Back before LB had taken over the place, like some enormous silicon cancer, gobbling up council and economy alike. Now everything Panda was LB, and everything LB was Panda. Anyone who wasn't employed by the company itself was in some kind of support industry, like baristas at the coffee shops, pulling lattes for executives. Or barristers, pulling lawsuits for the same.

And Sigmund, turning things off and on.

—

Mornings were spent talking to Em, and then, when the boss emerged, flicking through the help desk system, looking for easy wins. Tickets Sigmund could send back to first or second level. That the monkeys could do, and should do, and would do, if they weren't all a bunch of part-time kids who didn't give a shit. Mailbox restores, profile resets, distribution-list creations, desktop reimages. Jobs that Sigmund would rather send back with a snarky thousand-word how-to guide in the comments field than touch himself.

That was all maybe an hour's work, and fifteen percent of the overnight queue. The rest of the morning was the

ten-minute stuff: anything Sigmund could knock off without
a phone call to a customer. Server reboots and process kills.
Log checking and clearing. Reporting. Un-fucking fuckups
made by the *n*-minus teams.

Low-hanging fruit. It was Sigmund's system, and it worked.
So long as anything more difficult—anything involving talking
to anyone, or thinking about anything—could hold over until
after lunch. Or, preferably, tomorrow.

Or, today, after the team meeting. Not one of their usuals,
something New and Exciting, which left Sigmund grabbing
his phone off the desk when his calendar started chiming.
Team meetings always sucked. He figured he could at least
get some *Minecraft* in while pretending to check emails.

The meeting room was down at the other end of the floor,
near the kitchen. It was round, and made of glass, and Sigmund supposed the intent was to be "creative" and "hip."
Everyone on the floor called it The Box, said it was where
the supervillains were kept after hours. A life-sized cardboard
cutout of Darth Vader lived in the room when it wasn't used.

The half a dozen people of Sigmund's team were already
assembled: Chewie and Boogs, Van and Steph, Michael and
Divya. Plus Harrison, their boss.

And, today, someone else.

"Okay, so as you can probably already tell, we've got a new
starter coming on board," Harrison, standing in one half of
the glass cylinder, said new starter at his side.

The rest of them were sitting on the seats ringing the opposite side of the circumference. From his left, Sigmund heard
Van mutter, "I didn't think we were hiring."

"This is Lain," Harrison continued. "Lain, uh—"

"Laufeyjarson," Lain finished, patient and smiling like he
got people stumbling over his name a lot.

Tall, skinny. Coppery hair hanging in loose waves down to

his chin. Freckles, attractively understated piercings, bright green eyes, and the edge of a tattoo peeking above his collar. Sigmund heard Steph whistle under her breath.

"Right," Harrison said. "Lain's got a background in ops, same as the rest of you, but he'll need some help getting on his feet in the company. He's gonna need a buddy."

Hands shot up, accompanied by giggling. Most of said hands had long slender fingers and brightly manicured nails. Sigmund got it. Lain was hot, this was IT. The women would take what they could get.

He flipped out his phone, checked it was on mute, and launched *Minecraft*.

Which was about when Harrison said, "Sussman. There's a free desk next to you, right?"

Sigmund looked up. Everyone was staring at him, new guy included.

Crap.

"Uh . . . yeah. I guess."

Crap. That was *his* desk. Except, well. Obviously not *his* his desk. Just . . . the desk between him and anyone else. The Buffer. Window on one side, no one on the other. Meaning no one to see Sigmund playing *Minecraft*, or watching Let's Plays on YouTube, or reading comics. Or programming *Saga*, line by painful line.

Not that Sigmund would be doing that sort of thing. Not on company time.

"That's settled then," Harrison said, and it was. "Lain, you're with Sussman. He'll show you the ropes. Now, for the rest of you . . ."

Team meetings. Lain sat himself down on the edge of the circle. Sigmund tried not to make eye contact.

"So, um. This is a pretty nice desk."

Half an hour later, after the too-long, too-boring trip 'round the team, everyone spewing out as much as they could think of to try and impress Harrison with their corporate indispensability.

Lain had a satchel. Some hip distressed thing in army green. That described a lot of Lain, really: hip and distressed, from his skinny jeans to his unseasonal scarf. All he was missing were the nerd glasses.

Sigmund, at least, wore the latter because he *had* to.

"Yeah. It's okay." It overlooked Osko Park, the faintest smudge of lake glimmering just beyond. Then, because silence was awkward and small talk was coming whether he liked it or not: "Where were you before this?"

Lain waved a hand, something halfway between two gestures. "Around," he said. "I kinda . . . went traveling for a while after uni, you know how it is."

No, Sigmund didn't. And neither did Lain.

Because that was the other thing, Sigmund's Real Actual Talent. The thing he never got to mention. The one thing that maybe, just maybe, made him special. Just a little.

Sigmund was never fooled by lies, and could pick them, every time. Like now. Nothing in Lain's voice or in his posture. Just a scratching at the back of Sigmund's mind. Something prickly. Something wrong.

"Oh. Cool. I never did any of that." Calling the new guy a liar within moments of meeting him? Probably career limiting. Sigmund decided to lay off.

"Never got the urge to see the world?" There was something loaded in that question, maybe. Something sharp in Lain's strange green gaze. It was hard to meet that gaze. Like Lain was always focused somewhere two inches behind where he should be, beneath the skin and bone.

Sigmund looked away, throwing himself down into his

chair, watching Lain unpack the requisite minimalist hipster office possessions from his bag: a tablet, a phone, a charger, some headphones.

"Nah, not really. I mean, it's so fucking far away, you know?" And, yeah. Maybe not so cool to swear in front of the new guy either. But Lain didn't look like he minded, so: "Some guys from high school did the whole Contiki tour thing. Saw the photos on Facebook, never really appealed."

"Hm." Lain spun his headphones around on his finger. "I guess I traveled a lot when I was younger. With my brother, mostly. It does get old." And that, at least, was true.

Sigmund couldn't help himself: "Brothers or traveling?"

Lain barked laughter, a single sharp snap. "Both," he said. When he grinned like that, his canines hung over his bottom lip. Just a little.

"Well . . . I wouldn't know about that, either." Sigmund's own grin was apologetic. "Only child."

Lain flicked his eyes up, then back down. Bit his lip then finally said, "Me too, at first. But I, ah. I ran away from home pretty young. My 'brother' . . . we weren't related, you know? He was older, and looked after me."

"That's . . . nice?" said Sigmund. Except it wasn't. He could tell it wasn't. Something in Lain's voice, in his posture. Some awkward stiffness.

"Yeah," said Lain, running a hand through loose curls. "We had fun. Maybe too much fun. And sometimes, too much fun . . . We were always gonna end up dead or in jail. And, well. I'm not the one who's dead, am I?"

"Oh, man," said Sigmund. "That's harsh, man." Because what else were you supposed to say when some guy you'd met only five minutes ago confessed to being an orphaned ex con?

Lain must have picked up on the hesitation, huffing laughter and looking away. "Sorry to dump," he said. "It's just this is an office. People talk. I just . . . wanted someone to know the real story first."

Sigmund pushed his glasses up his nose, blinking and trying to focus on anything but Lain.

Lain, who added, "But, look. Hey. I did my time, did my cert, got snapped up by LB on the outreach. So"—he grinned, gesturing broadly—"here I am."

"Yeah," said Sigmund. "Here you are."

Oddly, only that last part had been a lie.

TWO

THIS PART I piece together only later, dredged up from the fragments of memories and broken bodies left behind. That means some of it is lies. But, maybe, they're entertaining lies.

And what are entertaining lies if not a story?

So. It starts within a cave, dark and foul, stinking of piss and shit and hatred. For one thousand years this cave has heard exactly two sounds and two alone. The first, that of an endless liquid drip, is incessant. A clock that marks the countdown till the end of time itself.

The liquid is not water. It's venom, falling from the ever-open jaws of a snake, hung high up in the cave. Beneath the drips lies the body of a man. He's rotting and wasted, as dead as any living thing can be, chained to three great rocky slabs by the enchanted entrails of his murdered son. When the venom drips, it falls into his face, and the man screams.

That's the second sound, and the mortals say his agony is the cause of earthquakes.

It's lucky, then, that his screaming isn't endless. Most of the time the venom is caught in a bowl, held up by a woman's shaking hands. She isn't much better kept than her near-dead husband, a puppet made from bones and brittle skin, blue eyes faded into dullness and blond hair matted into clumps. Once upon a time, she used to be a goddess. Now she waits.

One day, the dripping stops. And the woman knows her time has come.

—

She leaves her husband in the cave, freed of his chains and from his exile. According to a story written a thousand years before, today is the day he marches off to war. His wife has other plans, starting with whacking him across the head with the bowl she's holding.

He won't wake up for a while.

His wife leaves him, walking from the cave, step by painful, shaking step. If she stumbles, no one in the dark is there to see it.

At the mouth of the cave, an army waits. A swarming sea of monsters, all vicious teeth and scything claws, and of the dead, with rotting skin and rusting steel. At the front of the horde is a woman. Standing at least a head higher than her army, she's dressed in black robes that hide her eyes and hands, leaving only a lipless rictus grin and feet like the talons of a raven.

The woman has wings, small and flightless, and horns, twisted and huge. Her name is Hel, and once upon a time she was banished from the realm of gods, cursed to watch over the dishonored dead. Thieves and murderers, oath-breakers and cowards.

She is their queen, and she's also the bound god's daughter.

The woman who stumbles from the dark is not Hel's mother, but Hel loves her all the same. She gestures, and hollow-eyed serving girls come forth to clean the woman's skin and peel off her stinking rags. The girls re-dress her in a man's tunic and trousers. Gray-skinned page boys bring forth food, dead warriors produce a chair. Thus does the woman eat her first meal in an aeon. Her first, and her last.

The dead honor her, for today she honors them.

Today, she dies.

—

There's a ship called *Naglfari,* made from the nails of the dead. It sets sail carrying Hel's forsaken army, the bound god's wife standing at the helm.

Dressed in heavy armor fit to hide her sunken cheeks, she leads them into battle.

The prophecy says this place is her husband's, that he should ride the dead ship off to war, should clash with gods until he falls. This is the Wyrd his wife would break. At her side, a huge beast not unlike a wolf sits waiting, blood dripping from its eager jaws. It too knows this is the day they die.

The ship lurches and groans, water spraying on the deck. The seas beneath it roil, churning in an endless, white-capped swell. Every now and then something breaks the cold black surface; a fin, a claw, an enormous, staring eye.

The woman sees this, and she smiles.

She goes to war, and she has monsters at her side.

—

Three armies rise. From the sea, the dead wait upon their ship. From the south, the lands burn black as a roaring fire eats the ground. From the east, ice and snow blanket all in unending, silent cold.

This is the way the world ends. In pestilence, in flame, and in frost. Three great calamities, marching forth to meet the gods.

When they clash, the whole world beneath them bleeds.

—

Everyone has a fate, even the sun and the moon, devoured by the wolves that chase them.

The gods fall too, as their Wyrd would have it. Kings and warriors, broken and torn, until the ground is frozen mud and the sky is black with the ash of burning corpses. Ravens circle overhead, barely waiting for souls to die before beaks like razors tear out guts and eyes.

This is war, and today the only victors are the birds.

—

The woman's ax drips red with blood. She howls as she faces another foe. He's one of the chosen dead, a warrior plucked from Hel's domain and trained by gods to fight this futile war. Shields of living meat their masters throw against the hordes in endless waves, hoping to delay their own ends for moments more.

The woman hates them. She hates *all* of them. For herself and for her husband. For Hel and for the Wolf and for the Serpent. For her own children, and the dead she fights beside.

The gods will *burn* for what they've done. And the woman? In death, she will have her victory.

—

Some things the woman changes. Other things she doesn't. Her husband may not die this day but, to keep her ruse, the woman must fight his final battle for him.

Across the field, she sees her target, standing tall and bright, armor barely dented by the filth and blood around.

The sight of it sends hate burning through her gut and she launches herself toward him. He turns, and, through his armor, the woman sees a smile.

Today, he thinks he slays a foe.

He is wrong, and the knowledge makes the woman grin, hidden behind steel and runes that let no one see she is not who they think.

Fools. Her husband would never wield an ax to war.

Her foe, meanwhile, wields a sword and wields it well, sharp blade slicing even as he brings his buckler up to stop the woman's ax.

They both know how this will go. Yet neither wants to be the first to fall.

—

The battle is a necessary lie. Perhaps the woman draws first blood, grinning as she smells it on her blade. Perhaps her foe trips her on the bloodied ground, sending her sprawling even as he hefts his sword. She kicks him and he bends double, hands grabbing between his legs as he curses someone who still dreams beneath the Tree.

The woman howls with laughter and with rage, long since taken by the red mist of the berzerk. She scrambles to her feet, raising her ax once more. This time, her foe is not so fast in the raising of his shield, catching the blade against his shoulder. He cries out, stumbling backward, and the woman lunges forward to finish what was started.

She doesn't feel the sword when it slips between her ribs.

She does feel the resistance as her weapon kisses bone. It's not a clean cut, and she raises her arms for a final strike, this time severing sinew and spine alike.

Her foe's body falls, his head bouncing as it hits the ground a moment later.

The woman gives one final laugh before she feels the pain of steel, feels the hot-slick oozing of her blood.

Perhaps she fights on, or tries to. Perhaps not. Either way, like all casualties in this pointless, foretold war, she ends up sinking in the mud, eyes turned toward the sky.

Perhaps the last things she sees are two ravens, landing by her side. They whisper secrets in her ear, and the woman does not die alone.

Perhaps. It's a nice thought, anyway.

THREE

So there's me, halfway up this hill in the middle of bloody nowhere, trying to wrangle this ancient wheezing ox we've got, pulling this enormous wagon."

Strike one: It wasn't an ox.

"And you can see what comes next, right?" Lain's voice, floating over the cubicle partition. "Shitty little gravel path, overburdened cart—"

"Oh, no." That was Divya, leaning against Sigmund's desk, listening to Lain's stories.

"Oh, yes," Lain said. "And my brother and his mate, charging ahead on their scooters"—strike two: They were not on scooters—"and taunting me all, like, 'Lain, Lain. Glaciers move faster. We'll be dead before we get there.'" Strike three: They hadn't called him Lain. "And finally I'm, like, 'Right. Screw you guys.'"

"Uh-oh . . ."

If nothing else, Lain knew how to play an audience, Divya rocking back and forth in her anticipation for the tale. Sigmund wouldn't mind but for the fact that she bumped his desk on every oscillation.

Divya was nice, really. In small doses. At a distance. Which made Sigmund feel like the world's biggest jerk, because it wasn't Divya's fault she had a voice like a banshee and was followed by miasma of cheap shampoo strong enough to cause complaints from two states away. She tried hard, and was nice.

And irritating. Really, really irritating. And Lain was new, and Divya was talkative, and so she came over and Lain told her stories that were mostly lies and scratched the inside of Sigmund's head, and Divya shrieked laughter like a fire alarm and the whole thing just made Sigmund want to scream.

"So I lean forward, and slap this ox, right on the rump—"

"No, you didn't! Poor thing!"

"*Whack!* Hard enough to be heard in Norway. And the ox, which has been half asleep the entire bloody time, just flips its shit."

"That serves you right! You shouldn't hit animals."

"Well, it gets its revenge, right? Because the cart, it's, like— the ox starts to buck, rodeo style, and the cart's just, like"— some action Sigmund couldn't see, which had Divya make a sound loud enough to evacuate the building—"and I'm, like, 'Ffffuuuu—!' And then there's this horrible crack of snapping wood, and the next thing I know, I'm rolling head over heels, dodging broken cart, all the way down the hill."

Divya gasped, a whole body motion that sent Sigmund's desk slamming against the window. "Oh, oh no! Were you okay?"

"Nothing broken," Lain said, which was strike four. "But the barrels on the cart smash, and by the time my brother and Homer"—five: Not the friend's name any more than Lain's was Lain—"find me down at the bottom, I'm bleeding and groaning in a pile of wood and rocks and wine."

"That's terrible!"

"No, the earful I got from my brother was terrible, for smashing all the barrels. And the fact we're all still stuck on this damn hill, with this ox we have to get to the next town. Except the cart's gone, so we end up with me walking the rest of the way, dragging the thing behind us on a rope."

Sigmund scowled. "They didn't let you ride on the, uh. To ride?" he asked.

Lain's head appeared over the partition, as if surprised that Sigmund had been listening. Surprised, but not displeased, judging from his expression. "Nah," he said. "My brother said it was 'punishment' "—Lain made air quotes—"for the wine. Hell of a thing, though. I mean, ox hair plus full-body gravel rash? Infection. Central. I swear I was oozing pus for weeks."

"Oh, gross. That's so awful," Divya said.

Sigmund thought that was an understatement. He scowled at his keyboard, picking old crumbs from between the keys and reminding himself Lain's unnamed brother—whomever he had been—was dead.

There was comfort in that thought, something dark and vicious Sigmund wasn't used to. So much resentment against a guy he'd never known. A guy whose name he didn't even know. Because this wasn't the first story Lain had told about his brother: It was only Wednesday, but Sigmund must've heard half a dozen by now, always by eavesdropping over the partition while Lain narrated to someone else.

They were all the same, the stories. Lain and his brother in some ridiculous situation, Lain doing something foolish, then being punished by the universe for his act.

Then getting the same again from his brother.

They would've been funny, if not for the latter part. And maybe Lain was right, and he did bring things on himself, and maybe there were a million other stories he didn't tell that ended happily ever after. Maybe. Sigmund liked to think so, if only because it made the odd black ball of hate sit lighter in his gut.

Divya hung around for a while after Lain was done talking, too-loud voice grating through Sigmund's mind. He tried to tune it out, head down and headphones on, working through an email archive recovery. Mindless stuff, watching blue bars fill while deep below in the depths of some cold, dark server room, tape drives spun up and down.

———

A week passed, more or less. As far as cubicle mates went, Lain turned out to be not the worst Sigmund had ever had. He was funny when he spoke and unobtrusive when he didn't, and, according to initial tests, was not a raging douchebag. A bit of a magnet for the women on the floor, which meant Sigmund's corner got a lot more visitors than usual.

"It won't last," Lain confessed to Sigmund on Thursday. "They're just here for the enormous hands"—he wiggled his fingers in demonstration, and, yeah, they were pretty big, now that he mentioned it—"and cheekbones like razor blades. They'll move on in a few weeks. When they realize what an asshole lives beneath."

That sounded like another story—like a lifetime of stories, maybe—so Sigmund decided not to ask. Lain was nice enough, but there was that whole thing about the dead brother and the jail time and maybe Sigmund didn't want to push too hard.

The brother and the jail and the fact that "Lain" was an absolute, utter, pathological liar. Scare quotes not optional because, go figure, *Lain* wasn't Lain's actual name. He used it, and he answered to it, but he hadn't been born with it.

People asked him about the name all the time. Because it sounded foreign, Sigmund supposed, and not in the usually identifiable ways. Lain said it was Icelandic, except that was a lie, too, even if Lain really had been to Iceland. He hadn't been born there, though, and neither had his parents. Nor had he gone to school . . . anywhere, as far as Sigmund could tell. Lain was pretty good at tailoring his life history to his audience, but listening to it still left Sigmund with a head full of itching.

Lain's alleged IT credentials were, in Sigmund's opinion, also suspect. Lain had a story for it, of course: how everything at TAFE had been based on the wrong architecture, in the wrong areas, thirty years behind current corporate practice. Except that was a lie, too, and not just because Lain had never actually been to TAFE. He was wicked smart, and didn't need telling twice, but he did need telling once, even for things he maybe should have needed telling nonce at all.

Still. He was an okay guy, despite everything. Sigmund figured there were worse things.

FOUR

So here's the deal.

You know what you can get away with doing, being the world's third richest man? Being CEO of the world's largest fucking technology company?

Fucking. *Anything*.

Power. Money. It comes with the territory. Everyone has a price; everything can be bought.

Every day, a thousand mortal souls come to pray within my temple. Come to lay their sacrifices—their minds, their toil, their money—at my feet. Every day, millions more carry my idols in their pockets, have them hold pride of place within their homes. Billions of hours, spent in supplication at my altars.

When they share secrets—wicked prayers, tapped through keyboards or whispered into mikes—they share them all with me. Wishes, hope, fantasies. Revenge. All dark words uttered in my name.

This is power. This is the way that gods are made.

This is me. Now.

But it wasn't always.

Stop me if you've heard this one before.

—

Tuesday morning, I get in early and make a call. It has some very, very specific instructions. The sort only a CEO can make without any awkward questions.

After the call, I get in the elevator.

Upstairs, in the foyer of the executive suites, it'd been Travis Hale who stepped through shiny chrome doors. On the seventh floor, it's Lain Laufeyjarson who steps out.

See where this is going?

This isn't the first time I've played King Incognito among my own unwashed masses, but I admit it's been a good decade between cons. And the previous ones were mostly corporate-development-type stuff, making sure managers weren't assholes and the staff were happy with the hamburgers, that sort of thing. This time, it's personal.

Because sure, the desks are nice and ergonomic and the windows let in plenty of light (when people haven't pulled the blinds down), but I'm only halfheartedly making an index of that stuff. Mostly, what I'm here for is—

"Lain!"

—that.

I turn, ensuring my grin is bright and open and my slouch is appropriately apologetic for my height. I'm tall compared to Sigmund. I don't want to loom.

And here he is, rounding one of the partitions, Sigmund Gregor Sussman de Deus himself. Father, David Sussman, born in Sydney, son of post–World War II Jewish migrants. Mother, Lynne Sussman, *née* Maria Madalena Silva de Deus. Born in Brazil, immigrated in the '70s. Died when Sussman was a toddler. Father never remarried, because the Wyrd is a bitter spiral.

Sigmund was born right here and never left. Unremarkable at school, unremarkable at university. Computer Science/Accounting, the former for himself, the latter for his father. Grades were better in the latter, because life is never fair.

Scraped into LB on the grad program last intake. Competent, unambitious, liked well enough by his peers. Might make it into middle management in a decade or two if he's lucky.

Two main associates: Evdokia "Emily" Ivanovich and Wayne Kalinda Murphy. Both women, the latter cursed with the legacy of 1980s unisex parenting. Both very fond of black and spikes, judging from their Tumblrs. Sigmund and Ivanovich went to school together, Murphy met them at university. Ivanovich works in the Basement, doing INFOSEC. Murphy pulls part time at a comic shop while studying at the Computer Arts Academy, an LB talent funnel.

All the background information money can buy, hidden in a file in my drawer upstairs. Shit. At least I hope it's in the drawer. If I left it on the desk, I'm kinda screwed.

"Dude. Harrison's looking for us."

"Oh?"

I follow Sigmund into his boss's office. James Harrison is a hulking meat slab of a man, ex-infantry, with a tendency to shout at office politics rather than work around them. He'll never be anything but what he is, but his staff like him and, sometimes, that's enough.

"Sussman. Lain." Harrison gestures at us. "Come in."

He gives the briefing, mostly for Sigmund's benefit. I know the story because I invented it, filtered down through managers and subordinates until it reached the Basement.

"You're needed upstairs, right now."

"Upstairs?" Sigmund shifts from foot to foot, fingers twitching and flexing. I know he's thinking of his run-in with me—with Hale—back at the Christmas party.

"Right up," Harrison says, confirming Sigmund's fears. "To the Big Boy rooms. Our Fearless Leader needs someone to fix his printer." He holds out a small white card, and Sigmund takes it.

"Don't we have other guys for this?" I say. I mean VIP Support, neat assholes in suits, trained more in babysitting execs than dealing with IT. Everyone fucking hates them, myself included.

"VIP sent someone up already," Harrison says. "Hale threw him out. Allegedly his words were 'I need a geek, not an MBA.' " This is technically a lie, but it is a dutiful recitation of the events people have been told to tell. And, to be fair, it's only a lie for this particular instance. When I say I hate dealing with VIP, the feeling is definitely mutual.

"Jesus." Sigmund, also not a fan of the office babysitters, is trying not to laugh.

It gets a smirk out of Harrison, too. "VIP is fuming. I said we'd handle it. And guess who happens to look the part?"

Somewhere, beneath dark skin, Sigmund blushes. He knows what he looks like, all ratty jeans and *Game of Thrones*/*Pulp Fiction* mashup T-shirt. Plus the nerd glasses and explosive pile of wiry hair. If I'm the Hollywood version of a TV-acceptable geek, Sigmund's very much the real deal.

The option for us to decline Harrison's task is illusory at best, so, a minute or two later, Sigmund and I are riding up in the elevator. There are only two that go to the exec floor, and only one that goes all the way to the penthouse above that.

It's a long trip up. Sigmund is jittery, watching the numbers on the screen slowly increment by one. When we reach twelve he says, "This is my dad's floor. I've never actually been above it."

Fuck. He's just so *adorable*. "You know you can just, like, press the buttons randomly, right? Go wherever you want?

There's a balcony on thirty-two that has a really good view of the lake." It occurs to me, as soon as I say this, that it's information new staff-member Lain really shouldn't know.

Fortunately for said new staff member, Sigmund is too busy being nervous to notice the discrepancy. His anxiety oozes out of him, thick and yellow in the enclosed space of the lift. Worried he'll run into Hale again after the mortification that was the party.

That one wasn't his fault. Meeting Sigmund was an accident, but once I saw him . . . Christ. All I could feel was cold winter sun on my skin, and all I could smell was the blood and ash and death of war. Old memories from a forgotten life, a debt paid in blood, lost and buried.

Not my blood, though. So maybe *paid* is an exaggeration. Maybe the word I'm looking for is *transferred*.

I had to *know*. So I got close, made sure he wouldn't recognize me in the dark, and listened to him pour his heart out over a dream that's going nowhere.

Sigmund is never going to be the designer behind a breakout indie video game. His Wyrd has something much, much better in store for him.

With a chime and a cheerful recitation of the floor, the doors open.

"Wow." Sigmund stops so abruptly outside the elevator that I almost run right into him. "This is . . . posh," he says.

"I guess?" It's designed to be impressive, all the plushest carpet and richest wood money can buy.

There are exactly two offices on this level. A set of eyes watches us from the second.

"The card, please."

Sigmund startles at the voice, and at the fact that he didn't hear the owner as she approached. Nicole Anne Arin, LB's senior vice president, as cold and sharp and thin as the circuit board I found her in, all those years ago.

She's also giving me the dirtiest look over Sigmund's shoulder. I give her a wink, and the corresponding drop in the room's temperature is literal as well as figurative, given Nic's connection to the HVAC. Not to mention everything else in the building.

"I'm, uh. I'm Sigmund," Sigmund starts. "This is Lain. We're from—"

"I know who you are." This is directed at me, over Sigmund's head. So *maybe* I've been obsessing over the guy a bit since Christmas, and *maybe* Nic is the only other one up here to hear. Maybe. Nic continues: "Mr. Hale's office is that way. His tablet won't print to the printer, and this is what you're here to fix. You will not touch anything in Mr. Hale's office, other than the desktop, printer, and his tablet. A document is open for you to test. You will not close it or attempt to open any other application."

Sigmund is going grayer by the minute, so I make *Cut it out, Jesus* motions to Nic behind his back. She does stop talking, but only with a withering glare that leaves me under no illusions re getting it in the neck from her later. She hates the idea of me chasing ghosts. And Sigmund? He's about as ghostly as someone can get while still breathing.

Quite literally, at the moment. So I come to the rescue with a "Don't worry, Ms. Arin. We're professionals. We won't disrupt Mr. Hale's day any more than it's already been."

I think I actually feel the cables in the floor shift beneath the carpet. I'm astounded they don't rip through the wool and strangle me where I stand.

Nic is great at a lot of things, like PR and predicting the stock market. She's not so great at dealing with people in the one-on-one. Sooner or later, she'll always fail the Turing test.

Sigmund is still fixed in Nic's glare like dead pixels on a monitor, so I clap him on the shoulders and say, "C'mon!" Then walk across the floor toward my office.

The doors are currently closed, two huge things made from a Huon pine older than I am. The LB logo is inlaid in the front in brass: three big upright pillars, a hole in each and an indentation in the top. As I go to push them open, Sigmund says:

"You know, I walk past the statue every day, and I never did manage to figure out the logo."

He's talking about the enormous monstrosity downstairs, just outside the foyer. The original set of three stones I had shipped here from Iceland, and on which the LB brand is based.

I could tell Sigmund what it means, but I don't. It isn't a nice thing, and I suspect he'll remember that trauma soon enough.

We walk into the office.

"Wooow. It's good to be the CEO." Sigmund laughs nervously, shooting a glance over his shoulder to see if Nic's still listening (she is).

I give a huff of laughter but, well, my office is my office. What am I supposed to say about it? Of course it's impressive. The point of it is to impress people. Why else would it have an enormous picture window looking out over the city and, if that weren't enough, a fucking fireplace?

My desk is at the far end of the room, in front of the window. I walk over to it, getting there first mostly to ensure that I did, in fact, put Sigmund's file away the night before. (The answer turns out to be yes.)

"Holy shit."

Behind me, Sigmund has discovered Boots.

"There's a *snake*!"

A large area in the wall to the right of the desk is taken up by a herpetarium. It's full of plants and branches and UV lamps, and is inhabited by exactly one enormous, aging snake, the aforementioned Boots.

"I'm sure she won't bite you," I say. This is true. I found Boots curled up miserably in the same place from where I hauled the LB "statue." The name is indicative of my initial plans for her, but, well, things change. And now she guards my office from anyone stupid enough to be here without permission. Three deaths-by-snakebite later, and LB hasn't had a problem with corporate espionage since.

I hear a crash from the far side of the room. Sigmund, colliding first with the desk and then with the floor.

"Holy shit, it can *get out!*"

Boots's tank has no glass. Yeah. I've had this reaction before.

"Uh, are you okay?"

Sigmund is on the floor, surrounded by a stapler, an upturned cup of pens, and a scattered pile of P&L reports.

"What is going on in here?"

Sigmund leaps upright at Nic's voice, looking from her to the tank to me to the floor. Then he drops, grabbing papers and desperately sorting them into a pile to repopulate the desk.

"Um! Oh, um. I'm sorry. I'm so sorry, I—"

I wander over to help clean up, replacing the stapler and saying, "You should maybe warn people about the snake."

"Lain!" Sigmund hisses. Everything about him screams, *You're going to get us fired, you asshole!*, especially his thoughts.

Nic just sighs. "Boots has been Mr. Hale's . . . companion for many years. She will not harm you."

I take the papers from Sigmund, reordering them and letting him worry about the pens. While he's busy, I give Nic a grin and a gormless shrug, earning another scowl as she storms out of the room, pulling the door closed behind her.

I don't take it personally. Nic's job is to look after the company, to stop me wrecking it with shitty fucking decisions. Hence her not approving of my current actions.

When she's gone, Sigmund says, "Oh god, we're both *so dead.*"

"It'll be fine, man." I take the cup of pens Sigmund is waving around and put them back on the desk. "See? Good as new!"

"So. Dead," he repeats. "Fired. Axed. Gone."

"I wouldn't worry."

"Utterly unemployable." Sigmund scrambles upright. "That happens, you know. People get blacklisted for things like this."

I laugh. "Not for things like this," I say. Not that I've *never* ruined someone's life over an office fuckup before, but it wasn't exactly spilled pens and ophidiophobia. I thump Sigmund playfully on the arm and add, "I mean, maybe if we don't manage to fix Hale's printer . . ."

He groans, hiding his face behind his hands, and I laugh.

The fix does actually take him longer than I expected, and he resorts to Google more than once. But he gets there in the end.

And, in the meantime, I stand back, eyes closed, and watch him work.

FIVE

YOU'RE A FILTHY traitor and I hate you forever." Then, because lies always burnt on his tongue, "Or at least until lunchtime."

"Sorry, man." Em, apparently, had no such issues with untruths. "But the shrink moved my appointment to Friday. I can't miss it, so . . . gotta pike on camping. Sorry."

Sigmund groaned, slumping down across the table. Nine forty-six a.m. and they were at the café across the road from the office, having coffees and skipping work. Sigmund's favorite pastime.

Em's favorite, meanwhile, was ruining people's days.

"God, I don't wanna *gooooo*! 'Specially not by myself. Em!" The table muffled Sigmund's pleas. When he looked up, Em was taking another bite of muffin, thick, dark eyebrows raised above thick, dark-rimmed glasses.

"Then don't go," she said, "if you hate the idea that much."

"Dad will kill me." Sigmund drew out the relevant verb. "You know how he loves all this corporate team-building stuff."

Next weekend, LB's IT department was holding its annual camping trip. Sigmund could probably think of things he'd less rather be spending a long weekend doing, but it would be a short list. Which is why, three months ago, Em had taken pity on his suffering and agreed to join him. That was before she'd decided to be a dirty piking traitor.

"Dude, you're a grown-ass man," Em said. "Daddy doesn't have to make your decisions for you anymore."

"Piss off," said Sigmund, without much enthusiasm. "I live in his house."

"So move out." This, at least, was an old argument.

"I can't, man. Housing is expensive—"

"Come move in with us. We've got a spare room."

"—and it's not like Dad's got anyone else. I don't want him to be all alone." Because that's how it was, how it'd always been, in Sigmund's memory. Just him and his dad. And maybe if Dad had found someone in the last twenty years, started dating or whatever, then Sigmund would've been long gone. But he hadn't. So neither had Sigmund.

Net result: Sigmund was going camping. Alone. Goddamnit.

Em sighed, picked at her muffin, and said, "Well . . . why don't you ask your new ranga mate?"

Sigmund blinked. "You mean Lain?"

"Yeah. I mean, you're off to the forest, right? So it'll basically be like coming home for him."

"Har, har," said Sigmund. He tried to imagine Lain cavorting, orangutan-style, through the trees. "I don't think he's really the camping type." He seemed more the lattes-and-fixies type. The Noguchi-coffee-table-and-skinny jeans type.

Em shrugged. "Just puttin' it out there. You say he's not an asshole, right? So ask him. What's the worst that could happen?"

Sigmund stared down into his half-empty cup like it held the answer to Em's question, not just the dregs of an entirely mediocre cappuccino. "Yeah," he said finally. "Maybe."

What's the worst that could happen?

—

When Sigmund got back to the cubicle, Lain was staring at something on his monitor, drumming his fingers on the desk. He looked up at Sigmund's approach, and gave a sharp-toothed smile.

"Hey, man," he said. "Do you know anything about this?" He pointed at the screen.

"About what?" Sigmund stepped around until he could see. A page from the company intranet. Advertising—

Oh.

"This 'adventure weekend' thing. Camping. You going?"

Well. Sigmund supposed that solved that problem.

"Uh, yeah," he said. "Yeah, I, uh . . . Dad's kinda into that sort of thing. Company man. He'll be cut if I don't, so . . ."

"You don't sound thrilled about it."

"Yeah, well. I'm not really a camper, y'know? Outdoors . . ." Sigmund demonstrated his distaste with a shudder.

"I was thinking of going," Lain said. "Outdoors stuff . . . I mean, it's been a while, but all those treks with my brother and his mate when we were younger, y'know? They usually ended badly." And here he gave a dark-edged laugh. "But I kinda miss it."

That wasn't a lie, but only just. Sigmund wondered what it was that Lain was really longing for: camping, or his apparently dead, possibly criminal brother.

"Well," Sigmund said, "you should come, then. I've got a tent. It's small, but . . . I don't snore. Too much." Not after a decade of sleepovers with Emily "You-Snore-I-Kick" Ivanovich.

For a moment, Lain just stared. Sigmund thought he was going to say no. Sigmund thought he was going to make some excuse because, *ew*, spending a weekend with Sigmund? No thanks. Except Lain was too smooth to be that cruel straight-up, so he'd have some slick cover story. One Sigmund would *know* was a lie, and then he'd have to go crawl under his desk and die of—

"Really? Cool. Thanks, man. Yeah, that'd be awesome." Lain smiled. Not his usual razor grin, but an actual honest-to-god smile. Like sharing Sigmund's (dad's) shitty two-man tent from circa 1970 was the nicest thing anyone had ever offered him and the coolest way he could imagine spending a weekend.

Sigmund smiled back. It was hard not to, the way Lain's odd-bright eyes seemed to almost glow.

"Cool," said Sigmund, ever the dork.

"Camping," Lain said. He turned back to his screen, still smiling. "It's sure been a while. Let's go sign this bad boy up." He glanced up at Sigmund one last time. "Thanks again, man," he said. "This weekend's gonna be sweet. I can just feel it."

—

After that, camping didn't seem like such a death sentence. Sure, they'd have to do shitty games and outdoors stuff of the kind that Sigmund hated, but Lain sounded like maybe he was more the type. So maybe he'd be able to give instructions, and Sigmund could do his best to follow, and maybe the weekend wouldn't be a total clusterfuck. Maybe.

Lain was looking forward to it, even if Sigmund was still fence sitting, and Lain's enthusiasm was infectious. All his moods were. He was handsome and charming and loved life. Meaning, when he was happy, it was hard not to be the same.

Sigmund didn't think about it much, just sort of rolled with it. At least until the following Tuesday, when Katia from Gateway cornered him in the tearoom.

"So I hear Lain asked you out camping."

Sigmund looked up from where he was washing his coffee mug. The one in grave danger of gaining sentience.

"Huh?" Sentience not shared by Sigmund, apparently.

"Lain," Katia said. "Asking you out. Everyone is *sooooo* jealous."

Sometimes, when he was younger, Sigmund had imagined himself to be an alien. Maybe his mum, too, fleeing on one last trip to escape a dying planet. Or maybe Sigmund had been abandoned on Earth as a baby, and his parents had adopted him, tried their best to raise him as a human. Except, being an alien, there would always be some things Sigmund just didn't get about humanity.

Like this one.

"What are you talking about?"

"Oh. My. God." Katia looked like Sigmund had just confessed to stabbing puppies. "It's true. You have *no* idea."

Sigmund felt his fingers tightening around the handle of his mug. "No idea about what?"

Katia rolled her eyes. "You," she said. "And Lain. And the camping. And him liking you. Like, *like* liking you."

It took Sigmund a moment, but he *got* it.

"Whoa," he said. "Whoa, whoa, whoa. No. No way. It's not like that. Lain isn't . . . He's not—"

"Gay?" Katia said. She was leaning forward across the kitchen island, mischief sparking in her expression. "I hate to break it to you, but that guy makes Stephen Fry look straight."

"Wait. *Stephen Fry* is gay?"

"Ohmigod, how are you *alive?*"

"I thought he was just British!"

Katia rolled her eyes again. Sigmund tried not to break

the handle off his cup. "Stephen Fry is gay," she said, voice pitched at schoolchildren. "Lain is even gayer. *And* he totally has a crush on you."

Sigmund blinked. "No," he said. "No way."

"Look." Katia was scowling now, all teasing gone. "He likes you, okay? Just trust me. People have been trying to ask him out since he got here, but the only person he's ever shown any kind of interest in is you. The rest of us may as well not exist. You make him *laugh*. He *smiles* at you. Whenever anyone else tries to talk to him it's always, 'Oh, Sigmund this . . . ,' or, 'Well, Sig says that . . . '"

"No. Way."

"Way," said Katia, who'd apparently watched the same films as a kid. "If you're not into that sort of thing, that's your business. But let him down gently, okay? Otherwise things are gonna get pretty rough for you 'round here."

There was a chip in the side of Sigmund's mug. His favorite mug. The Aperture Science one. Funny how he'd never noticed that before.

Katia was wrong. She had to be wrong. People didn't get crushes on Sigmund. Sigmund was a loser, he knew that. He was fat and nerdy and had bad hair. All his jokes referenced video games or comic books or shitty cartoons from the '90s. And it was okay. It was. He'd gotten used to it after twenty-odd years.

High school had sucked. But high school was over. And the people like Lain . . . after high school, things had evened out a bit. It wasn't like the Cool Kids blew spitballs at him in class or tried to trip him in the corridor anymore. Because Cool Kids grew up, too. And some of them got MBAs and some of them worked at McDonald's, but it was different, being an adult. There were workplace harassment lawsuits, for one thing.

Still. People like Lain didn't get crushes on people like Sigmund.

"Look," said Katia, and, when Sigmund did, she was giving him a tight and awkward smile. "He likes you. Just . . . be kind, okay?"

Sigmund nodded.

"Yeah," he said. "Okay."

SIX

FRIDAY SAW SIGMUND stepping out of Dad's car onto the grass outside LB, carrying his tent and sleeping bag and flashlight and Swiss Army knife and towel and compass and mosquito repellant and sunscreen and, *Jesus, Dad. I'll be okay. It's only for the weekend.*

Except Dad had been so excited about it all. More excited than Sigmund, even. So Sigmund hadn't had the heart to say anything.

Which was why here he was, standing on the lawn, weighted down with ten million packs like a huge nerd while everyone else was standing around clutching small gym bags.

(FML)

"Sig! Hey, you're here. Whoa. You brought some stuff."

And, suddenly, there was Lain. All freckles and long copper hair, gleaming under the January sun. Cool shirt and skinny jeans and one too-hip duffel

"Uh," said Sigmund, feeling like the world's most influential loser. "Yeah."

But Lain just smiled his bright smile and said, "Here. Let me take some of that." And began helping himself to Sigmund's burdens. Sigmund decided not to stop him and so, when the bus rolled up, the both of them were more or less equal in the shouldering-of-bags stakes.

Sigmund hated bus trips. They threw the luggage in underneath, then found a free seat somewhere near the back. Lain slid in next to Sigmund, grinning and unperturbed, trendy-ugly sunglasses obscuring half his face.

"Free day off work," he said. "Cool, huh?" His thigh was warm where it brushed against Sigmund's.

Sigmund—whose stomach felt like a writhing pit of snakes—still managed part of a smile. "Yeah," he said, trying not to think of kitchens or Katia. "Cool." Did straight guys think about the warmth of each other's thighs?

Lain's grin split open into rows of shark-white teeth. "Still not convinced?"

"No computer, no Internet, no showers," Sigmund said. "For three days." He grimaced, pushing all non-camping-related thoughts away for later. Or never.

"Aw, c'mon," Lain said. "You've got your phone, right? There'll still be reception."

"Yeah, maybe. For the, like, ten minutes until the batteries die."

They weren't going very far. Just out to Woolridge Reserve, about an hour's drive. There was a campground there. A river, some rocks, some bush. Nothing too threatening. Except emus, maybe. Sigmund hated emus. And mosquitoes. And flies. Probably redback spiders too. Maybe funnel-webs. Did they get funnel-webs out this way? Sigmund didn't know. Then there were the snakes. Browns, taipans, red-bellied blacks . . . he didn't know if all those were local, either. He was sort of hoping to keep it that way.

Fuck. They were all gonna die.

The bus lurched to life. Between Lain's warmth and his smile and thoughts of the poisoned fangs of death incarnate, Sigmund already felt like throwing up.

A fist connected with his shoulder. Playful, not violent. "Hey, man," Lain said. "Relax. It'll be fun."

Sigmund exhaled, looking down to where his hands were busy fumbling in his lap. "Sorry. I'm just . . . kinda a buzzkill."

Lain shrugged. "Nah," he said. "You're doing this for your dad. That's cool. Making the old man proud and all."

"Yeah," said Sigmund. "I guess." Then he remembered Lain was, like, an orphan or a runaway or whatever, and the only family member he ever talked about was dead. So maybe Sigmund should try and be less of a spoiled moping brat. Appreciate what he had and all. "I, uh. Dad took it pretty hard when Mum died," he said, surprising himself. "So it's just the two of us, you know?" The two of them, and the company. Dad's only other love.

"I'm sorry, man," Lain said, and meant it. "Did you, ah . . . ?" He trailed off, as if suddenly unsure of the topic of conversation.

Sigmund got the question a lot, though. He knew what it was. Awkward, but better than warping himself into a panic over Lain's romantic intentions, or lack thereof.

"I was pretty young," he said. "And most of that time Mum was in and out of hospital, meaning I don't really remember her." He tried something like a smile, but didn't get one in return. "That makes me sound like such a dick, doesn't it? Like I don't care my mum is dead. But, I mean . . . I never knew her, you know? It was always just Dad. Mum was . . . she was like this sword hanging over Dad's head the whole time. This thing he couldn't get rid of, even after she died, and . . ." Sigmund stopped himself, teeth clicking shut, too loud, even against the rumble of the bus. "Sorry. You didn't need to hear that. I'm . . . I'm just a douche. Ignore me."

Lain was silent for a moment. "My brother was an asshole," he said finally. "Manipulative, selfish motherfucker. And I loved him. More than . . . Enough to give up *everything,* just because he asked. And he did. All the time. And I adored him for it. But I'm glad he's gone. And I wouldn't want him back."

Sigmund nodded, bit his lip. It wasn't the same, because nothing ever was. But . . . it was something.

"Feelings are hard," he said when the silence began to itch.

Lain laughed at that, a sharp little razor to excise the choking angst. "Yeah," he said. "Yeah, they are." Then he shifted, and his thigh was gone. Sigmund's skin felt colder for its absence.

The rest of the trip, they mostly discussed video games.

—

The Friday, Sigmund had to admit, was not terrible.

As far as civilization went, the campground wasn't that far from it: a wide flat space of grass nestled within the trees, buildings and barbecues ringed around the edge. There was a shower block, a squat and ugly relic from the '70s, but walking into it didn't make Sigmund fear for his health.

"See," said Lain, "this isn't too bad. Look, there's even electricity. You can charge your phone."

Sigmund thought he was going to have to fight off the rest of the IT department to do so. But it was still nice to have the option.

The first thing involved gathering in the hall for the Welcome to the Annual LBIT Retreat induction speeches. Some way-too-fit and too-perky-looking course coordinators in bright blue hats smiled at them so much, Sigmund's own teeth started aching. Then they threatened the group with fun and team building, and also workplace safety regulations, and Sigmund leaned over to ask Lain when the Kool-Aid was being distributed. That got him a grin and an elbow in the ribs, but also a choked laugh out of Dean from Storage.

The first "team-building" activity, as it turned out, was to find a buddy or group of buddies with whom to share accommodations, which was easy. The second activity was to swap tents.

"I assume you all know how to put up your own tents," said Perky Hat Lady Lisa. "So what I want everyone to do, if you've got a tent, is to line up here. Two-person tents, three, four, six . . . anyone over six?"

Everyone shuffled into position with the apathetic obedience of office workers. Sigmund ended up tent swapping with Loi from Networking.

"Sorry, man," he said. "I think Dad bought this surplus from World War II. I hope it doesn't fall down on you."

Loi grinned, hefting the enormous canvas bag. "Well, I only bought mine the other day," he said. "If it comes back with stains, I'm sending you the receipt."

Sigmund made it halfway back to Lain before it occurred to him that he'd maybe just been . . . insulted? Or something?

He decided not to think about it, instead rescuing Lain from the attentions of three girls from Service Desk. They all sighed and looked at Sigmund wistfully when he approached, and he tried not to think too much about that, either.

Then he and Lain found a likely patch of grass, and stared at each other.

"So," Sigmund said. "You know how to do this?"

"Not a fucking clue," Lain confessed. "Google?"

"Google."

In the end, it wasn't that difficult, thanks to the magic of instructional videos. The worst part was trying not to giggle every time someone said *erect* because, yes, apparently they both still had a level of emotional maturity below that of schoolchildren on YouTube. When everything was done, they crawled inside to make their beds.

"Wow," Sigmund's mouth said, before his brain could stop it, "it's kinda cozy, hey?" Two-person tents. Not exactly spacious, as it turned out.

Lain shook out his sleeping bag, smoothing big hands across the fabric. "Well," he said, "if it makes you feel better, I don't sleep much. So mostly it'll be all you in here."

It was supposed to be reassuring, but really it just made Sigmund feel like the world's biggest jackass. Because it was a lie, and because what if everyone was right and Lain really was . . . a little bit Stephen Fry? And what if he now thought Sigmund was a homophobic jerk, as opposed to just a dorky loser? Sigmund should probably say something about that, right? Something cool and charming, like the sort of thing Lain would say if it were him, except of course it never would've been him because he was, well, cool and charming. Unlike Sigmund. Except by the time Sigmund looked up to open his big loser mouth, Lain was already shuffling backward out the tent door. Flap. Whatever.

"Shit."

Sigmund hurried to follow, just in case Lain was, like, upset or something. By the time he'd wormed his own way out, Lain was standing, hands on hips, peering down. The sun caught in his hair and turned it into a crown of flame around his shadowed face.

"I think," he said, "that we need a rule."

"Oh?" said Sigmund's traitorous mouth and, Jesus, Lain was kinda tall. He didn't seem like the type—some people didn't, something about personality or posture, maybe—but Sigmund thought the guy had to be over six feet at least.

And Lain said: "No shoes in the tent."

"No . . . shoes?"

"Right. If you're going in the tent, shoes come off. Otherwise we're gonna be sleeping in mud within an hour."

"Oh," said Sigmund. "Okay." That sounded reasonable. Except his own shoes were totally still hanging over the threshold. So he dragged them out quickly, and stood up.

Lain grinned, punching Sigmund gently in the arm. "Cool," he said, and it was.

—

The afternoon was tents, then icebreakers. Between Sigmund's built-in lie detector and Lain's . . . Lainness, they both dominated the latter, earning themselves handfuls of candies. Mostly Fantales, after Lain went around the room doing swaps with all and sundry after Sigmund professed a liking for the chocolate-coated toffees.

After that came dinner. Then sitting around the campfire, nursing a beer, watching Lain tell more outrageous stories to their coworkers.

Maybe it was the day talking—Sigmund was tired from activities and muzzy from the beer—but there was something about Lain in the firelight. Something about the way his hair caught the glow that made it seem to burn all on its own, loose curls dancing around cheekbones that were very high and very, very sharp. Lain's skin was clear and smooth and freckled, and, just for a moment, Sigmund found himself wondering what it would feel like to touch. Warm, probably. And soft.

Lain really was terribly handsome.

Sigmund was staring; he knew he was. Eyes glassy while his mind danced like the flames, a strange and flickering heat, fueled by Lain's easy grins and Katia's office gossip and the width of a too-small tent.

Sigmund had seen *Brokeback Mountain*. He knew how these things went.

Except they didn't.

The campfire burnt down and the crowds began to vanish. Sigmund followed—not the first to go, easily not the last— then spent a good twenty minutes fighting tinea in the shower block.

When he got back to the tent, it looked smaller than he remembered, cut in harsh chiaroscuro from the flashlight on Sigmund's phone. He crawled inside, kicking his shoes off as he went, settling onto his bedroll and inside his sleeping bag.

Lain was still outside, entertaining. Sigmund could hear him, bright voice a muffled crackle, surrounded by the laughter of his audience.

Charming and handsome and popular. Katia had to be wrong. Otherwise Lain would be here, surely? Tucked in beside Sigmund, close enough for his heat to radiate through nylon and through down, eyes bright disks of green within the darkness.

It was easy to tell secrets, in the dark. Sigmund knew that from experience, from a hundred sleepovers with Em as kids, whispering things they'd never daresay under the sun.

He'd ask Lain the Question, voice barely a breath. *Do you, y'know. Like like me?*

In response, Lain would just grin his sharp white grin, shifting a little closer as he'd say, *Why? Do you, y'know. Like like me?*

He wouldn't wait for an answer. Instead, he'd lean closer, until his warmth ghosted across Sigmund's lips, parted but not touching, waiting for Sigmund to close the distance and—

"Fuck!"

Sigmund's eyes shot open, fantasies blown apart as the tent shook around him.

"Lain?" he called.

"Yeah," came the voice. Outside, silhouetted against blue

ripstop, Sigmund could make out Lain's shadow, stumbling across the grass.

"You okay?"

A second later, Lain's head appeared inside the tent, grimacing. "Yeah. Yeah, I just tripped over the ropes. Sorry. Did I wake you?"

Sigmund relaxed, propped up on his elbows. "Nah," he said, since, *I was just fantasizing about kissing you,* was probably the wrong response. "Didn't kick the tent down, that's good."

"Hah, yeah. It's dark out there." Lain crawled inside, just enough to rummage through his pack. "I'm gonna have a shower. I'll try not to wake you up again."

"Don't worry about it," said Sigmund, settling back down.

Lain's light disappeared, taking Lain with it. "Night, man," he said as he went.

"Night," said Sigmund, and tried to banish all thoughts of grins and kisses.

—

"Dude. Are you *sure* it's this way? I think we've been here before."

"*Yes,* I'm sure. Jesus."

"Dude . . ."

"Look, the map says . . . It says . . . Shit. There should be a trail just up here, and we might even be able to find it if the compass would just *fucking work!*" Sigmund shook the object in question. Ungently. The needle spinning and spinning and spinning and refusing to settle.

(*think it's broken. how the fuck does a compass break, anyway?*)

Day two, Saturday. Sometime in the afternoon. Sigmund didn't know when exactly because his fucking phone had run out of fucking batteries and all the other fuckers had been using the power outlets so Sigmund had decided to leave it back in the tent and then they'd gone on this fucking orienteering course and that had been hours ago except it felt like they'd been trekking around the fucking bush for fucking eons and Sigmund had the fucking map except he could've sworn it'd stopped looking like any of their fucking surroundings way back and Lain was right that rock was totally familiar and—

"We're fucking *lost!*"

"Yeah, man. I've been trying to tell you for—"

"Fuck! Fuck fuck *fuck!*"

"Dude. Calm down."

Sigmund spun, and suddenly he was there. Right up in Lain's face. Or, well, underneath it. Because *of course* Lain was a fucking giant skinny motherfucker. "We're lost. In the bush, Lain," he said. "People *die* in the bush!" With the snakes and the spiders and the emus and the fact that it was one hundred fucking million degrees in the shade. People died! Stupid fucking over-perky Hat People and their team-building orienteering death-march bullshit and, Christ. Sigmund had gotten them lost. Because he couldn't read a fucking map. Parading around all proud with his dad's broken fucking compass like a big fucking bush expert. Like they were in press-M-to-display-the-minimap territory instead of in the Really Fucking Real World where loser wannabe video game skills didn't fucking apply.

"Sig, we're not gonna die. We can't be that far from camp."

Except Lain didn't believe that, and the lie taunted Sigmund's already humiliated nerves. "We've been walking for hours. Who knows where we are!" Deeper and deeper into the fucking bush, like fucking idiots. Until the trees had closed in overhead and the ground looked like it hadn't been walked on in a thousand years. "I don't have my phone," Sigmund added. "You don't have your phone. We're going to die."

"You know," Lain said, all stupid little sharp-toothed smirk, "people have been around a lot longer than phones. I think we can probably make it back without."

Fucking smug-ass Lain I'm-So-Good-at-Fucking-Everything Laufeyjarson. "Fine," snapped Sigmund, "*you* get us back, then." And kinda . . . threw the map and compass Lain's way.

"Whoa. Sig. Sigmund! What's gotten *into* you?"

He was hot and tired and his feet ached and they would've been back by now if he wasn't such a fucking failure at life, that's what had gotten into him. Except he couldn't exactly yell that at Lain in the middle of the bush. So Sigmund took the manly option, and stormed off instead. Because that was totally what they needed: Sigmund getting them even more lost because he was a stupid child who couldn't read a fucking map and who'd been tromping them around in circles. Because he'd been too proud to admit to Lain it'd been a thing. Lain, who'd known it was happening, because of fucking course he had. Humoring Sigmund like a fucking—

It was about then that the ground dropped away.

"Sigmund!"

One moment it was there, the next, Sigmund's foot broke through leaves and roots and twigs and onto absolutely nothing underneath.

"*Fuuhhh—!*"

And then gravity. Em didn't look up from where she was busy.

("*no!*")

And then—

"Got you!"

—*agony*, tearing down his arm, lancing through his shoulder, into his ribs.

"Give me your other hand!"

Sigmund blinked. Someone was yelling at him. Someone was yelling at him, his arm ached, and he was swinging. In midair. Nothing below his feet.

He looked down. Then wished he hadn't.

"Sig? Your other hand, c'mon, man!"

He looked up. And there was Lain. Half of Lain, his face and shoulders protruding through the leaves. One hand open and reaching forward, the other gripped tight around Sigmund's wrist.

Lain had caught him. Sigmund had fallen off a *fucking cliff* and Lain had caught him.

"Yeah, I gotcha, man," Lain said. "But I need another hand here, okay?"

Moving felt . . . strange. Painful and thick. Slow. Like his limbs belonged to someone else.

He raised his hand. Lain grabbed it, then he pulled.

Later, it would occur to Sigmund to wonder how, exactly, Lain managed it. Sigmund wasn't light. Lain wasn't holding on to anything. He should've been dragged off the edge too, surely? But he wasn't. He hauled Sigmund up instead.

Later, Sigmund would wonder. Not yet.

—

Not quite later enough yet, he was sitting on the ground, back against some huge wall of weathered rock.

"Jesus. Jesus fuck. Jesus. Fuck. Jesus . . ."

Someone had been saying that for a while. Using Sigmund's voice.

"Fuck. We gotta—we gotta get back, man. The compass. Gotta get Dad's compass. Get—get back to the camp. It'll be dark, man. Gotta get . . ."

He'd stopped trying to stand. Every time he did, huge hands pushed him back down against the rock.

They were very, very strong, those hands. Very strong, and

very big, and very gentle. Where they touched him, Sigmund felt hot enough to burn.

Lain's hands, their owner sitting on his haunches nearby, like some skinny hipster bird. Watching Sigmund with eyes as green and endless as the forest.

A part of Sigmund knew what this was. He'd nearly died. This was shock. He'd felt it once before, when he was younger and had fallen off the monkey bars and snapped his arm. Just shock. It'd pass. Lain was here. Lain was A Good Guy. He'd saved Sigmund's life. He'd make sure Sigmund didn't do anything else mortally stupid.

"J-Jesus. I nearly d-died." Lain was getting kinda blurry. Almost like Sigmund was looking at him from underwater.

"Yeah," said Lain. "Nearly. But I got you."

"My arm h-hurts."

"I bet it does."

"I th-think it's dis-dislocated." He was having trouble moving his shoulder. When he touched the skin, it felt stiff and hot. And not Lain-hot. Lain-hot was nice. This was . . . not that.

"It's not dislocated," Lain said. "I should ice it, but . . ." His expression was strange, hands drumming against each other as if turning some difficult thing over in his mind.

" 'S okay," Sigmund said. "You d-don't have a-any ice." He couldn't seem to make his voice stop shaking. Or his body.

Lain nodded. "Yeah," he said. "Yeah. I don't have any ice." It wasn't a lie, exactly. But it did sound like maybe he was trying to convince himself.

"I'm p-pretty sure it's disloc-dislocated, though."

That got him the thin edge of a grin, then a sigh. Then Lain, turning around to sit beside Sigmund on the ground, back against the rock.

"I'm an id-idiot," Sigmund said.

"Yeah. You are." Sigmund could feel Lain's warmth through his shirt. Even in the middle of summer, sitting next to Lain felt like sitting next to a bonfire.

"I got . . . got us lo-lost. 'C-cause I was too pr-roud to . . . to admit . . ." Except his voice hitched, and the end of the sentence wouldn't come.

Lain heard it anyway. "Yeah," he said. "You did. And obviously you're the first person ever in history to do something like that and should therefore feel hideously ashamed forever until the end of time." Except he was grinning, and elbowed Sigmund gently in the ribs.

When Sigmund laughed, it was a wet and broken sound. "Oh, god. I'm su-such a di-dick. We're g-gonna die out h-here. You shou-should've let me fa-fall."

Lain snorted. "If we're gonna die," he said, "we'll do it sticking together. That way, I can eat you when we run out of Fantales. But I don't think it'll come to that. The Hat People will be searching for us. LB will sue the shit outta them if they lose its staff."

"We'll ru-run outta w-water. And dehydrate. Or get . . . get p-pecked to death by e-emus."

"Mate, emus won't come near me. I'm a redhead. They're superstitious about that sort of thing. And there's a stream not far back. I'll go get us water when you're done with your freak-out."

Sigmund laughed again. A gross explosion of snot and tears. "Je-Jesus. Y-you have a smug-ass answer to ev-everything."

"True," said Lain, all sharp and bright and wild. "It's kinda my thing."

Sigmund bit his lip, then looked down. "And you know how to g-get us ba-back, too? D-don't you?"

"Yeah," Lain admitted. "More or less. We're a bit farther out than we should be, but . . . I've got a good sense of direction. If no one finds us tonight, we can start walking back tomorrow."

Sigmund nodded, trying not to let shame swallow him whole. "I'm su-such a f-fucking idiot."

"Hey." Heat against Sigmund's uninjured shoulder, and when he looked, Lain was very, very close. Hand on Sigmund's biceps, strange gaze stripping Sigmund raw. "We've done that already. Time for something else, okay? Sig's a cool guy. No talking crap about him."

And then, because—despite Lain's protestations to the contrary—Sigmund was and always would be a total loser, he heard himself say: "Are you hitting on me?"

Lain froze.

"It's just people at work say you like me, like, *like* like me, and I just thought we were kinda friends maybe, yeah? But they're pretty convinced you're gay and that you like me and you've been hitting on me, and I thought they were just gossiping, y'know, but I nearly died and you saved me, and I kinda just wanna know . . . Are you?"

Lain's eyebrows had gotten very high, his eyes very wide. When Sigmund fell silent, Lain exhaled. Big and loud, puffed-out cheeks and all. Then he lifted his hand and moved away. Not far. Just not right up in Sigmund's personal space.

"I, uh. Maybe this isn't the best time to be having thi—"

"*Are* you?"

Lain was silent for a moment, then, "Yeah. Yeah, a bit. Does it bother you?"

"Yes!" Then, because that made him sound like a dick: "No! I mean, why would you? No one ever . . . with me." Let alone handsome cool-kid hipster types like Lain.

Lain, who snorted. "Ah, that's not true, man. You've just taught yourself not to see it. But trust me. They do."

"Why? I don't . . . I'm not . . ."

"You're kind," Lain said, "and funny, and smart—"

"When I'm not falling into holes."

"Well, we all have off days." Lain leaned back against the rock, eyes closed and smiling. "Believe me, some of mine have been . . . legendary. But you, you do this . . . thing with your mouth when you concentrate. It's really fucking cute. I guess no one's ever told you."

"What thing?"

Lain chuckled. "And you're honest. Always. Even when it hurts you, makes you vulnerable. There's strength in that, you don't realize it, but there is. It makes the rest of us—makes me—want to be . . . better."

"I don't . . . I don't really think—"

"And you love things, wholly and unashamedly. Video games or comics, and you think it's trivial, that it's silly. But you're wrong. The topics don't matter. What matters is the passion and the joy. You can't see it, but I can, and it burns *so* brightly. Like the fires of— like the sun. It's life. It's beauty."

Somewhere, deep inside his chest, Sigmund's heart began to pound. This time, it wasn't shock. Not that kind, anyway.

"That's what I see when I look at you. Strength and honesty. Joy. Life. So, yeah, man. They're right, I *like* like you. How can anyone not?"

When Sigmund dared look over, Lain was still smiling, eyes closed. Seeing the Sigmund that lived inside his head, maybe. The one he'd just described, that strange and alien thing. The one who didn't sound like Sigmund at all.

But Lain hadn't been lying.

"Oh," Sigmund said. "Oh . . . man."

Lain opened his eyes. Sigmund couldn't meet them.

"Too much?" Lain asked.

"Um. I just . . . No one's really . . . ah."

"Well. That's their loss."

Sigmund's hands turned over in his lap, fingers rubbing against his palms, against each other. "You're a really good guy. A good friend." Then he winced. Because, wow. Great response to the guy who'd basically just declared his love and adoration.

Lain snorted. "Mate," he said, "I'm a hustler and a liar and a thief and you don't even know the half of it. But"—he paused, just for a moment, before confessing—"sometimes, in the past, not very often, I have been accused of using my powers for good."

Like saving Sigmund's life, and sitting with him and talking through the shock. Giving him something to think about that wasn't dying.

Pretty much the opposite thereof, actually.

Sigmund still didn't know what his answer was. Lain was . . . he was really cool. Really, *really* cool. And funny. And fun to be around. And apparently good at everything. And looked like a rock god movie star supermodel, and had saved Sigmund's life and apparently *like* liked him, and . . .

And had huge, warm, gentle hands. And Sigmund hadn't minded when they'd touched him, not at all.

He'd never been in love with a guy before. Never even thought about it. Except . . .

Except, if Sigmund was being honest with himself, maybe he'd have to admit he'd never been in love with a girl, either. Had always just sort of assumed that was the Thing to Do. And he liked girls, in the Ladies of the Internet way, as it were. But . . . so what? That wasn't that unusual, right? Sigmund was pretty sure Em was into both. Heaps of people were. It wasn't like someone was standing in front of him with a contract he had to sign in blood swearing to like only sex A or sex B forever and ever amen. Maybe sometimes it wasn't about that. Maybe sometimes it was just about people.

Maybe. Sigmund wasn't sure.

"Hey?"

He looked up.

"How 'bout I go get us some of this water, you hang here and nurse your arm, and when I get back, we have a badass afternoon tea of Fantales and almost-certainly-potable liquids?"

Sigmund smiled. Because Lain was cool, and fun to be around, and Sigmund's arm hurt like motherfucking hell and he'd think about the rest of it later.

"Yeah," he said. "Yeah, that sounds cool."

—

The Hat People didn't find them, not that night. It might've sucked, but for the fact that Lain didn't just come back with filled-up water bottles. He also brought a rabbit.

"What the hell, man?" Sigmund was laughing, not sure if he should be grossed out or impressed.

The rabbit was dead, and not exactly small. Lain was holding it up with the skill of someone who'd done exactly that on many previous occasions.

"I dunno about you," Lain said, "but I plan on getting hungry in an hour or so."

"Dude, it's got, like, fur. And it's raw. And how did you even kill it? You did kill it, right? I mean, it's not roadkill or something?" Sigmund had been asleep, flat-out exhausted, when Lain had returned. Lain had been gone a while, judging from the way the sun was starting to kiss the edge of the mountains.

"Sig, please," Lain said, pulling something out of the waistband of his jeans. A knife. Not a small one. "I told you, I used to do this stuff with my brother, way back when." He flicked the knife up into the air. It spun, over and over, and Lain caught it again by the blade without even looking. "I have mad survivalist skills."

Sigmund tried not to stare. "Yeah," he said. "Well. You still suck at third-level support."

Lain laughed, and went to gut the rabbit.

He also magicked up a fire out of somewhere to cook it.

Sigmund would figure out the pieces, eventually.

SEVEN

The Hat People did find them on Sunday, stumbling out of the bush. Sigmund was feeling okay about it all, though. They'd eaten rabbit and Fantales and laughed around the fire. Then Sigmund had fallen asleep on the rocks, the day's panic catching up to him. When he woke, he was sore from the ground but less so from his arm. Then Lain had asked if he felt like a badass yet, roughing it in the bush.

Most of the rest of Sunday was spent getting fussed over by doctors and pumped full of ibuprofen for his shoulder. As long as he didn't try lifting anything heavy, or reaching upward, he was okay.

He did have to sign a lot of forms, though. Waivers saying he wouldn't sue the company or speak to the press. Lain scowled at his paperwork for a long time before putting his own name down.

"Do you think there'd be money in it?" Sigmund asked, only half joking. "Suing, I mean."

"No," said Lain. "And I wouldn't try. LB's lawyers are notoriously vicious."

Sigmund sighed.

—

They got driven back in a special car, which Sigmund thought was nicer than the bus, even if he did sleep most of the way. The driver dropped him off outside his house, and he waved good-bye to Lain from the lawn.

By the time Sigmund's keys turned in the lock, the whole trip was starting to feel a long way away.

Apparently he hadn't been missing long enough to be on the news or anything. When he walked into the kitchen, Dad was busy chopping onions and looked up with an "I thought you weren't back until later tonight?"

"Yeah," Sigmund said. "About that." And he told his dad the story.

He wasn't sure what reaction he was expecting, really. What he got was a face full of Dad's oniony apron, and arms crushing him so tight it hurt to breathe.

"Dad," he said. "Dad, I'm okay, really."

But David didn't let go for a very, very long time.

—

Tuesday morning, back at work after the long weekend. Harrison had emailed, offering Sigmund the day off. He'd declined. His arm was mostly fine and he wasn't dead. Besides, he had things to do.

"How was camping?"

Like this.

"I nearly fell off a cliff and died," Sigmund said. "Then we got lost in the bush and slept overnight on rocks eating Fantales."

Em didn't look up from where she was busy fiddling with her tablet, a Pyre Flash. "Mmm. So I heard. A good time was had by all, then."

Sigmund leaned against the edge of the desk, feigning nonchalance. Em's cubicle was at the end of the row, wedged between a wall and a window. Their nearest neighbor was at least two desks away and busy throwing a tiny football to someone across the partition.

(*now or never . . .*)

"Em . . . can I ask you something?"

"Is it work related?"

"No."

"Well good. I'd hate to have to do actual work at work. Shoot." She still wasn't looking up, which made the next part easier.

"How do you know if you're, you know. Bisexual."

Em didn't miss a beat. "You find yourself sexually and/or romantically attracted to both men and women."

"Oh." Sigmund thought for a moment. "What if it's, y'know. Not *all* men and women, just, like. Some."

Em did look up, then, arching one eyebrow above her glasses. "Then maybe you're a two on the Kinsey scale."

The Kinsey scale. Right. Sigmund had seen the film, the one with Liam Neeson. "What if it's, like. Just one. Man or woman." He had Em's full attention now, which was not helping. She was giving him That Look, the one that made him feel five years old and two feet away from the broken vase. Em was good at that look. Sigmund hated it.

"So what, exactly, happened on your so-called adventure weekend again?"

Sigmund's cheeks were getting darker and suddenly his shoes were about the most interesting things on the planet. He needed new ones. And jeans, for that matter. And a life.

"Nothing. I mean . . . nothing, really. It's just, when we were lost, I kinda asked Lain if, like, maybe he'd been. Y'know. Hitting on me."

"Oh?" Em's second brow joined the first. "And what did he say, exactly?"

"He asked me if I minded."

"And do you?"

"I . . . sort of . . . told him I'd get back to him."

For a while, the only sounds were the staccato tap of Em's nails against the Flash's glass, and the distant whooping of the office football game.

"You like him, yeah?"

Another blush. "Yeah. I do. Even though he's just so . . . weird sometimes."

"But?"

"But he's . . . I dunno. Nice to me. Or . . . something."

"That's not really what I asked."

And no, it wasn't. Sigmund took a deep breath. "He's . . . attractive. I mean, he is. Isn't he?" He looked up at her, which, in retrospect, might have been a mistake. Em looked like she didn't want to be having this conversation, at all. And that was weird, because Em *loved* giving advice, loved being the Expert.

"Sigmund . . ." Em sighed, looked down at her fingers for a moment, then said, "I don't think these are questions you need to be asking me, y'know? I think . . . I think if you wanna give things a go with Lain, then do it. But be honest with yourself, and with him. If they don't work out, they don't work out. It happens."

Sigmund nodded, thinking of a too-sharp laugh and big, warm hands. Of brilliant green eyes and the smell of loam and charcoal.

"Does that help?" Em asked after a while.

Sigmund smiled. "Yeah," he said. "It does. A lot. Thanks, man." Honesty. If nothing else, he could do honesty.

"No problem," Em said, and her smile didn't reach her eyes.

—

Lain was slouching in his chair, staring out the window, by the time Sigmund got back to the desk.

"Hey, man." Not the greatest opening line, but Lain looked up and flashed Sigmund a mouth full of sharp white teeth in response. It was nice, even with the fangs.

"I was gonna go grab a coffee, you wanna come?"

"From the place downstairs, or across the street?"

"Across the street?" The place downstairs always burned the milk.

"Sounds fun."

They managed to sneak out without Harrison noticing, which always made Sigmund feel a little bit truant. Even if they were adults now and sneaking off-campus for ten minutes for a coffee was hardly the illicit escapade it might've been in high school. The air was dry as they left the building, the sun a bright and blinding orb. A postcard-perfect summer's day by any measure, and Sigmund couldn't help the smile on his face, even if he suspected it looked a little bit silly.

"You seem happy." Lain's expression was caught somewhere between appraising and cautiously pleased.

"Yeah, I guess so," Sigmund said. "I mean, after Saturday I guess I'm just enjoying being alive and stuff."

"Yeah, well, you should keep that up, you know. Being alive and stuff."

The coffee place was a little hole-in-the-wall at the edge of Osko Park. Across the street from LB, but Sigmund had never been sure whether the company owned the land or the city did. Then again, in Pandemonium, maybe there wasn't much difference.

They ordered—a flat white for Sigmund, a cappuccino for Lain—and stood around in the meager shade while the girl behind the counter fiddled with the espresso machine.

"So . . . I've had a think about it," Sigmund said, after a while. "You know, about what you said on the weekend." He wondered if he'd managed to convey the appropriate amount of detached cool when speaking, despite his lurching heart.

Lain frowned for a second before his memory kicked in. "Oh, yeah. And what did you decide?" But he was smiling, which Sigmund figured meant he knew. That made it easier. A *lot* easier.

"I've decided I don't mind." And then, because he figured part of Not Minding was being able to say it out loud, "If you hit on me, that is. If you want to."

Lain's grin could cut glass. "Cool." He looked like he was going to say something else, except the girl called the order and they went to the counter to collect.

They turned to head back to LB, and before Sigmund could stop himself, he said, "So I was wondering if you wanted to, like, come to *DnD* on Friday night?" Then instantly felt like the biggest loser in the entire universe.

Lain, apparently oblivious to Sigmund's desire for spontaneous death, said, "*DnD*? Which ed?"

"Fourth." The reply was not, Sigmund thought, doing much to win him any cool points.

Not that Lain seemed to mind. "Awesome. I've never actually played. Collected the source books for a while, but . . . I dunno. Never found anyone to run a game with."

"You should totally come on Friday, then. Em is DM and, like, there's been this murder in some town we stopped at and because it's Em, there's probably, like, some huge, evil conspiracy thing going on. It's awesome."

"Sounds awesome," Lain said, not even lying. "Where is it?"

"It's in town, but I'll pick you up. Where do you live?"

And for one single moment, Sigmund almost thought he saw panic on Lain's face. "Uh . . ."

"Or you can pick me up." He decided to let it slide, just throw it into the bucket along with all the rest of the Weird Shit About Lain. There were plenty of totally sane, rational reasons why Lain might not want Sigmund to see his place, and what did it matter, anyway, when Lain was smiling at him like that?

"Sounds like a plan. You should email me your address and the time and stuff. Do I need to bring anything?"

By the time they got back to their desks, Sigmund was deep in explanation about the role of THACo in second ed and why it hadn't survived into the modern era. Lain listened attentively and asked questions whenever Sigmund took a breath. And soon—in between explaining hit dice and level modifiers and why it was always better to shoot the horse and not the rider—Sigmund forgot Lain's weird reaction to the question about his house.

EIGHT

"LEFT! ROLL LEFT!"

"I've got it, I've got it!"

Five seconds later, staring up at the briar-and-circuitry-covered crotch of a Dark Faerunner, Wayne had to admit she did not got it.

It'd been a long, long day.

"I'll res you, just gimmie a sec." Sigmund's voice came through the computer's speakers, accompanied by the sharp clash of swinging axes. On her screen, the Faerunner's gloating over Wayne's lifeless corpse was interrupted by the arrival of Sigmund. Or, well, his avatar, at any rate.

Hack, slash, whirl. Wayne followed the motions, writ large in bright HD. A standard chain, followed by a Cleave on the follow-up. The Faerunner pulled back, lights dancing down its arms and in a whirling arc on the ground, pulling together the beginnings of its Blackstatic attack.

Wayne hated that attack. That attack was why Wayne was currently lying on the ground, yelling, "Dodge! Dodge!" into her mike.

Blackstatic wasn't a one-hit, but it could be close. Getting stuck in it would knock Sigmund on his perky blonde ass, taking off a good third of his health and leaving him with a paralysis effect that would make further dodging almost impossible. That was what had happened to Wayne, one of those, followed by two stacks of the Faerunner's follow-up, Bad Dreams. That one bled health. Together with the static, they were why every *Dark Assiah* player hated traveling the rose-thorn and steel tangle that was Tiferet.

Above her, Sigmund gave one final twirl, leaping upward with a roar and landing straight on the Faerunner's head. The thing screamed, clawing at its face as gouts of thick, black blood began to leak from its limbs, gradually fading into bright blue geometric code that sucked its artificial life right out of the withered husk of its body.

A body that, when it hit the ground, was little more than a badly carved doll of burnt wood and rusting wire.

"I hate those things." Wayne huffed, watching Sigmund crouch over her, hands waving in the air, summoning together the gold-lit code that would jolt Wayne back to life.

"Aw, they're not so bad."

"Well, not to *you*. You've got interrupts. And a shield." Sig was a Protectorate, a tank class. He didn't go down easy, despite his tiny frame.

Wayne would be lying to say that didn't bother her a bit. The fact that Sigmund always made his avatars into the sort of pale, blonde waif-fu girls that would make Joss Whedon cry.

Then again, Wayne was playing a four-foot anthropomorphic cat with pink fur, so maybe she shouldn't judge.

Thirty seconds for the res, and they were off again, Wayne trying to stay behind Sigmund's tiny, ax-wielding frame. They'd been playing DA all night, just the two of them, Em off on a date with some guy she'd met playing *Dota2*. Em was the Cybermage, the healer, and her absence meant no big boss fights for just the two of them. So they were out grinding in the PvE, mining Briarwood and Faestones for their Keep instead. Wayne wanted new crafting tables; Em said they needed to upgrade the ballistas before the next shadowsiege came through. This way, they could gather stuff for both.

Even if it did mean dealing with the Faerunners.

Another pack of two loomed ahead, this time standing right on top of a tangle of thorny wood, just right for mining. Sigmund targeted the guy on the left, then leaped in, ax raised, the gold light of his shield flickering to life. Wayne gave him a second, then followed, vanishing in a cloud of darkness, reappearing behind the Faerunner with a pistol shot to the face and a dagger to the heart.

The second Faerunner shouted as it picked up the aggro, turning on Wayne. Sigmund hit it with a slam of his shield, sending it tumbling in a cascade of golden sparks. Meanwhile, the first one started giving off the telltale crackle of Blackstatic.

This time, both Sigmund and Wayne made the dodge.

Then another dagger to the heart, plus a pullback for the head shot. The first Faerunner went down just as the second raised its arms in front of its face, giving the inhale for Bad Dreams. Wayne teleported back in for Weakspot, a nice euphemism for the kick-'em-in-the-crotch move that would stagger the Faerunner and stop its attack, but she was half a second too slow, and Sigmund got caught in the scream of bile and nightmares.

"Shit!"

Annoying, but not enough to send him down. And a Cleave and a Heartbreaker later, the Faerunner joined its double on the ground.

They weren't carrying anything interesting, just some vendor junk. So Wayne got to mining while Sigmund stood guard, waiting for respawns. She'd cut maybe two feet into the briar when she heard him say:

"So I asked Lain to *DnD* today."

"Like . . . on a date?" Wayne had heard about Lain. Ooh, boy, had she ever, both from Sigmund and from Em. He was pretty much all the former had talked about since New Year's.

"Uh. Yeah." Wayne heard the echoing creak as Sigmund shifted in his chair. "Like on a date."

"To *DnD*?"

"Yeah."

"You are *such* a dork."

That earned her both a chuckle and a /rude. "Yeah. But he said yes, so he can't think I'm that hopeless."

"I guess this means I finally get to meet him, huh?" That'd be something. Meeting the King of the Hipsters. "Did you tell Em?"

"Uh . . ."

"You didn't?" Chop, chop, chop. Another foot of briar down, another stack of supplies for the Keep.

"I got distracted!"

"You are so dead."

"Why? She has premades, right?"

Which, of course, was exactly not the point. Because Sigmund was, quite possibly, the most clueless of all clueless males on the planet. Which is how he'd managed to go nearly a decade without realizing his best friend would totally have jumped his bones, if only Sigmund had ever displayed a single ounce of interest.

Wayne sighed. "I'm sure it'll be fine." She'd been sworn to secrecy on the Sigmund Crush Issue for years. No point starting something now.

Wayne made a note on her phone to buy Em extra wine and ice cream.

"So is Lain, like, your boyfriend?"

"I dunno. Maybe?"

Gods. Sigmund, clueless. So much. Wayne rolled her eyes, glad Sigmund couldn't see it, and asked, "Have you Googled him?"

"What?"

Point proven. "Google. Jeez, dooder. Get with the twenty-first century. You always have to Google someone before dating them in case they're, like, a serial killer or something. He's got a weird last name, right? So he should be easy to find."

"Wayne! That's like, invasion of privacy." Except Wayne could totally hear mouse clicks coming through the speakers. "Besides," Sigmund added. "I think he's been lying about his name." And Sigmund would know. What with his Thing. With the lies and all. The one Wayne believed in, and Em most definitely didn't.

"All the more reason to do it, then."

Down the wire, Wayne heard the clatter of too-loud mechanical keys. Then silence, then:

"Oh . . . wow."

"What?"

A weird crackling down the headset, like . . . lip licking, maybe? "Lain's last name is Laufeyjarson," Sigmund said, then spelled it out. Catching the hint, Wayne alt tabbed to the second monitor, bringing up the browser and typing out letters she wouldn't have guessed from the pronunciation alone.

Google delivered a page of results, and Wayne picked up the theme straight away. "It's the last name of Loki," she said. "Douchebag god of the north. So? I'm sure normal people are called that, too." Probably. Somewhere.

"Google Lokabrenna," Sigmund said. "As in the company, but don't look at those. Find the Wiki page that says where the name's from."

Wayne did as instructed, winding up on the Wiki entry for the star Sirius. Also known, according to the text, as Lokabrenna, literal translation "Loki's torch."

Wayne's phone, a Pyre Flame, was sitting on the desk between her monitor and keyboard. She gave it the side-eye as she read. LB really was keen on giving its products ridiculous fire-themed names. Go figure.

"So?" came Sigmund's voice.

Wayne tabbed back into game, where her character had run out of reachable briar. She inched forward a few steps and resumed the task. "So . . . what?" she said. "You think Lain—or whoever he is—is like some corporate spy?"

"No." The answer came out in a staticky huff that Wayne knew really meant yes. Sigmund added, "It's just . . . it's a bit of a coincidence, right?"

Wayne leaned back in her chair, legs folding up underneath her. "Well . . ." She twirled a candy pink dreadlock around her finger. "You met Hale, right? Mr. Bigshot CEO?"

"Yeah, I guess."

Wayne grinned. "And you said he was kinda cool, so . . . maybe he thinks you're cool, too, and he's sent down some guy to keep tabs on you." Because Sigmund was a dork who'd managed to not recognize the world's third richest man, and now they had teasing fodder until they died.

"Wayne!" Sigmund laughed, self-conscious and forced. "No."

"Oh!" Except Wayne was warming up to her idea. "But the guy fell for you first—"

"Wayne . . ."

"—and now it's going to be the dodgy corporate spy with the heart of gold versus the world's third richest man, vying for the most eligible bachelor in third-level support."

"Wayne, seriously. I'm pretty sure things like that don't happen in the Really Real World."

"Why not?" Wayne asked. "Rich people have to da— Oh! Oh, I've got an even better one."

"Oh, Jesus." Wayne could hear Sigmund shifting in his chair, the creaking echoing down the wire.

"How about," she started, "Lain *is* Travis. It kinda makes sense, what with the whole fiery Norse mythology obsession and all that. Maybe it's easier for him to, like, date if he pretends to be a nobody?"

"Wayne, they don't even *look* the same."

"Don't they?"

"No!" His voice was nearly a squawk, and Wayne couldn't help but grin at his discomfort. Em would be proud. "They are *not* the same person," Sigmund continued. "Lain's a redhead. Hale is like, I dunno. Egyptian or Turkish or something."

"Suuuure." With a name like Travis Cameron Hale. Yeah, right. That was almost as likely as—

(*oh! perfect*)

Wayne grinned a wicked grin and said, "So maybe they're both Loki, asshole god of Pandemonium. He's a shapeshifter, right?"

"No. Just. Stop, now. You're giving me a headache." Sigmund's voice was muffled, mike giving off a bunch of dull thuds as if something kept bumping into it. Something like a hand, rubbing over a brow.

Wayne was laughing, but decided Sig had had enough. He got headaches a lot, that was a serious thing. Like, not *Buffy*-level brain cancer serious. But Wayne didn't want him to be in pain.

"Well," she said. "You know what this means, right?"

"What?"

"Either Lain is, like, a, the hottest guy on the floor; b, a bazillionaire in disguise; or c, a *god* . . . and you invited him on a *Dungeons and Dragons* date."

Silence for a moment, then one long, low groan. "Oh my god. It's true." Then a crack, as if Sigmund's head had just slammed into something solid. The spacebar, judging by the way his avatar jumped. "Biggest. Dork—"

"In the *universe*," Wayne finished, just as the Faerunners respawned.

—

Meanwhile, across the other side of town, hidden in the darkness just beyond a young man's bedroom, something was listening. Not for much longer. Not when, after scouring every Realm and back, it'd finally—*finally*—found what it was looking for. What its boss had sent it to find.

The kid had been the tip-off. The sort of Wyrdtouched brat that could've gone his entire life without anyone noticing what he was. If only he hadn't been in the wrong place at the wrong time, lost in the Járnviðr. Something had happened in the forest; Munin wasn't sure what, only that it'd woken something up. That one brief, bright flash, as cold and endless as a glacier, and they'd all felt it. The boss included, which is why Munin was here, perched in a tree, eavesdropping on mortals.

All it'd taken was a name, the sound of something that should be dead and wasn't. Then everything had fallen into place, connecting the dots between old memories and dead gods. The boss was gonna kick himself when Munin delivered the news, since it wasn't like his killer had kept a low profile in Miðgarðr. But delivering bad news was half the fun, wasn't it? And fun had certainly been thin on the ground lately, especially after what happened to Hugin.

Poor Hugin.

Munin waited until the boy's soft bed sounds had quieted down and he was sound asleep. Then the huge raven shook itself down, opened its wings, and took to the sky.

It had a message to deliver.

NINE

FRIDAY.

Sigmund's dad answered the door, which was about the worst possible way to start the evening. Sigmund could hear murmured introductions as he pulled on his shoes and hopped down the stairs half-in, half-out of his jacket, but by the time he reached the door he was pretty sure words like *boyfriend* and *date* hadn't been uttered and—thank gods—Lain wasn't carrying flowers or something equally humiliating.

(*does that mean this isn't a date?*)

"—st go get, oh here he is."

"Hey, Lain." Lain gave a knowing grin and a nod, and Sigmund turned back to his dad. "I'll see you tomorrow, okay, Dad?"

David nodded. "You take care, boys," he said, because apparently not even twenty-two was old enough for a parent to think of his son as anything other than a boy. It was kinda nice, Sigmund supposed, even if maybe a bit embarrassing in front of Lain. His boyfriend. Or something.

David closed the door behind them with a little wave, and Sigmund noticed Lain was trying hard not to laugh.

"What?"

"'See you tomorrow'? I'm not sure what kind of boy you think I am, Sigmund Sussman."

And, oh jeez. Sigmund was pretty sure his blush could be seen from space. "I, uh. Usually spend the night at Em and Wayne's," he said. Lain's grin and raised eyebrow gave him the impression this wasn't exactly the exonerating statement it'd sounded in his head. "Oh my god! I've known them since I was like . . . Holy shit, is that your car?"

There was . . . a thing in the driveway. It was huge and black and glimmered under the streetlights. The soft top was up against the light evening rain, and through the tinted windows Sigmund could just about make out a flash of red velvet and mirror-finished chrome.

"Uh, yes?" Lain almost sounded embarrassed. "It's totally roadworthy," he added, as if this was Sigmund's main concern.

"I'm not sure I'm badass enough to be allowed to touch this car." The hood ornament was a tiny chrome horse's skull, but other than that it had no obvious maker's badging. "Where on earth did you get this thing?"

Lain just shrugged. "I kinda inherited it," he said and, oddly, this was exactly the truth.

Sigmund popped the door open. The inside was done entirely in bloodred velvet, black leather, and chrome. A skull motif dominated, and a tassel of black feathers hung from the rearview mirror.

It was, Sigmund thought, possibly the gothest car in the entire universe. Em and Wayne would die if they saw it.

Lain climbed into the driver's seat, and the engine rumbled to life. He hadn't used a key. Come to think of it, he hadn't used one to open the doors, either.

The radio started pounding out OK Go as they left Sigmund's driveway. He was just about to comment when Lain started driving like he meant it and talking was no longer Sigmund's highest priority.

There were seven stoplights between Sigmund's house and the mall. Not a single one was red tonight, which Sigmund knew only because he'd cracked his eyes open in terror, checking to make sure they weren't just running them. He didn't even dare to look at Lain. Was it bad manners to leap out of his date's car in mortal fear? If his hands hadn't been clamped around the edge of his seat, Sigmund might even have pulled out his phone and looked it up.

"We're going into town, right?" Lain shouted above the music.

It took effort to answer "Yeah" and not *Drive slower, you maniac,* but somehow Sigmund managed it.

Fortunately, the Torr Mall parking lot slowed Lain down enough for Sigmund to uncurl his fingers and calm his breathing, as they got out of the car.

(*right, okay.* GTA *driving. not a problem. do it all the time . . . in* GTA. *would it be rude to get a lift back with Wayne?*)

Lain was grinning, though, and when he fell in step with Sigmund their hands brushed against each other.

"Do you mind?" Lain asked as he twined their fingers.

Sigmund did not, in fact, mind, but coming right on the tail end of the Car Ride from Hell, didn't quite trust his voice enough to say so. So he just shook his head and hoped it looked coy and flirtatious instead of, like, terrified.

He'd never held hands with anyone before. Not since he'd been a kid, anyway, and he was pretty sure it didn't count when it was your dad. This was nice. Better than nice, actually, ally.

Sigmund took them up the escalators, through the mall, and across the street, all the while desperately trying to think of something to say. Anything. Preferably something witty and charming and, oh, god, he was the biggest loser in the entire universe. Also, holy crap, he was holding hands with another man in public.

No one seemed to notice. Sigmund wasn't an expert or anything, but he got the impression that wasn't exactly normal.

Friday night *DnD* was held upstairs in a store that was called Minotaur but which they all referred to as the Nerd Shop, due to both its stock and its clientele. It was outside the mall proper, fronting onto Diamond Square and located two doors down from Wayne's comic store.

Owner Guy Paul greeted them as they walked in, sizing Lain up in a glance. "New blood, hey?" he said.

Sigmund gave a noncommittal answer as they passed. Lain was dressed more for lattes and Instagram than for *DnD*, but that was just Lain. Sigmund figured embarrassing his date in front of the shop guy for his choice of clothing wasn't a good first-date strategy.

Minotaur wasn't huge, with a ground floor dominated by normal-people stuff like board games and executive puzzles. Sigmund took them past all that to where a narrow set of steps ascended to the second level.

Here was where they hid the nerds; walls lined with RPG books, Magic cards and Warhammer figurines, the center of the room dominated by four rows of tightly packed tables. The whole place smelled like sweat and awkwardness.

Em waved at them from the farthest table. Despite Lain's creative approach to driving, they were late. The rest of the group looked up as they approached.

"Hey, guys," Sigmund said. "This is Lain. Lain, Simon, Ben, Chris, Wayne, and Em."

Lain greeted everyone as they took their seats at the table. The men were noncommittal, and Em was busy with her books and dice, but Wayne's eyes went very, very round. The second Lain's attentions were elsewhere, she mouthed *Wow* in Sigmund's direction, making a little heart shape with her fingers. Sigmund tried not to blush. Or feel inadequate.

"You've got two choices," Em said to Lain. "Dwarf Paladin or Tiefling Warlock."

"Ugh, dwarves." Lain's repulsion seemed oddly authentic. "Give me the tiefthingie."

It was Sigmund's unspoken job to explain the game as they went along, which he did. Not that Lain needed many hints, and, after a while, he confessed to having studied up on the sourcebooks during the week. Sigmund felt warm inside at that, particularly when Lain's knee bumped against his under the table and just sort of stayed there for the rest of the evening.

About an hour in, Paul came around and took money, returning some time later with pizza. Sigmund shared one with Wayne and Em, and they all watched Lain devour a whole three-sixty degrees by himself, followed by everyone else's leftovers. Lain ate like it was going out of style, which Sigmund thought was totally unfair for a guy with not a single ounce of fat on his body. On the other hand, that was not a single ounce of fat on Sigmund's boyfriend's body they were talking about and, oh wow. Boyfriend. There was that word again.

For his part, Sigmund kept shooting glances at Lain throughout the evening. Checking for any signs of boredom, he supposed, but none appeared. As far as Sigmund could tell, Lain was having a great time. He'd taken to his warlock like a man born to wield the chaotic energies of the universe, and even ended up role-playing them all out of a bad situation with a local baron. Chris and Ben wanted to fight it out, Wayne suggested rolling Diplomacy. Lain just started talking, in character, and after ten minutes they'd waltzed out with new gear and a sack of treasure. Em looked a bit shell-shocked for a while afterward, as if not even she was exactly sure what had happened.

Sigmund thought he might just be in love.

"So you had fun, then?" he asked later, as they were making their way back to the car. They'd said their good-byes, and Lain's tiefling had been filed into the characters box rather than returned to the pile of premades. Sigmund took it as a good sign.

"Man, I can't believe I've never played that before." Lain's grin was like honey and razor blades.

"Well, we try and play at least once a month, barring emergencies."

Lain stopped walking, and, thanks to their linked hands, Sigmund did too.

"Can I kiss you?"

Sigmund blinked. Pushed his glasses up his nose. Reran the last sentence over in his head. "Um. Okay." Because, yes. Sigmund. Loser. World's biggest.

Lain didn't seem to mind, though, giving one of his rare, soft smiles. Not toilet-paper-ad soft, but not glass-cutter sharp, either. It was also, Sigmund realized when it started getting closer, slightly scarred.

Scars or not, Lain's lips were gentle and his hand was warm where it came to rest against Sigmund's hip. It occurred to Sigmund he had no idea what he was supposed to be doing here, exactly, so he closed his eyes—that seemed like a good start—and just kinda . . . tried to go with it. To feel. Warmth and longing and a smell like burnt forests and dark caves.

His toes tingled. So did his lips. And . . . other things.

When Lain pulled back, it wasn't far. His face was very close and his eyes were very green, and Sigmund realized he could count the freckles across Lain's nose. Neither of them could seem to stop smiling.

"That was okay?" Lain looked pleased with himself, but Sigmund couldn't really mind. After all, they'd just had their first kiss at the bottom of the Torr Mall escalators. No tongue, no pressure. Just the flutter of Sigmund's heart and the warmth settling somewhere beneath his belly.

Sigmund was grinning, because he couldn't help it. He was grinning, and Lain was grinning, and Lain's grin pulled at the scars that crossed his lips. Sigmund brought his fingers up to trace them before he'd really thought about it. There were eight little marks in total. Two marks on each side of the top lip, and two on each side of the bottom.

"What are these?" Sigmund asked. "I've never noticed them before . . ."

Lain gave a not-quite wince, running his tongue across the ridges. "A dumb bet," he said. "When I was a kid." It wasn't a lie, but Sigmund got the impression it wasn't even close to the truth.

They could've been piercings, Sigmund thought. The scars were kinda ragged, though, so maybe they'd gotten infected or . . . pulled out, or something. That seemed like the safest explanation. It certainly kept Sigmund's mind off the other one, the one he didn't want to think about. Because what the scars actually looked like were stitches, and that was just . . . not a thought he wanted to be having right now.

Lain seemed to read his hesitation. "It was a long time ago," he said. "It's fine." The implication of *now* was quite loud, even to Sigmund.

"I had a really great time tonight," Sigmund said, because it was true, and holding on to that feeling seemed more important than all the mysteries and old pain. He didn't want to go home. He didn't want Lain to go home. He wanted—

"We could go back to my place, if you want," Lain said. Then, brighter, "I have Wii!"

Sigmund pretended to think it over. *"Mario Kart?"* he asked, mock scowling.

"Rainbow Road!" Lain said, gushing such overstated enthusiasm that Sigmund couldn't help but giggle. He was glad for the excuse, even if it was silly. He was pretty sure, if he said yes, that the racetracks of the Mushroom Kingdom would be safe.

He was pretty sure his hands were shaking. He was pretty sure Lain was pretending not to notice.

"Yeah," Sigmund said finally. "Let's go . . . play Wii at your place."

Lain squeezed his hand, before pulling away. Despite the evening heat, Sigmund still felt cold as they made their way through the parking garage. His heart was hammering. First date, first kiss, first . . . game of *Mario Kart* at Lain's house and, wait a second. Lain's house. The one Sigmund had, earlier in the week, been convinced Lain didn't have.

Maybe he'd magicked one up in the days between then and now, just on the off chance that Sigmund might like to come back to it.

It had been a great night.

And then, when they got back to the car, a raven the size of a cat was sitting on the roof, waiting for them, and everything went to hell.

TEN

Y OU HAVE TO understand that, up until about two seconds ago, I'd been having a really fantastic night.

It took five hours of pretending to fight dragons, but Sigmund's finally started to relax. He's sweet and shy and those two friends of his have almost stopped looking at me like ravens circling a carcass. Which fits, given they used to be valkyries, back before Ragnarøkkr. Sigyn's friends. It's nice they decided to stick around.

Right now I'm looking forward to that night of *Mario Kart* and nervous fumbling. Sigmund thinks we're going back to my place—the one I bought on Wednesday and haven't seen since the army of decorators got to it—to fuck, but honestly, where's the fun? Travis could've done that. I didn't invent an entire new identity for a one-night stand.

I'm thinking of my next move as we make our way back to the car. I know Sigmund isn't totally buying Lain's kayfabe, but then he never really did and I can work with that. Particularly the part where he's going along with the ruse in spite of his suspicions. I've been struggling with the Big Reveal for a while, and letting Sigmund work it out on his own might be cheating, but cheating is what I do. Besides, *Hey, so did I ever tell you about the time I used to be a god?* is such an awkward conversation starter.

So I'm busy thinking. Distracted, you could say, which is why I don't notice Munin until we're practically standing on top of it.

Well, strictly speaking, it's standing on top of my car. If it shits on the paint I swear I'm starting a war. If we don't already have one, that is.

Fuck.

"Uh, why is there a huge crow sitting on your car?"

"Raven." Munin hates being called a crow; all ravens do.

It's hard to tell, but I'm pretty sure the fucking thing is grinning. "Found you," it says.

Sigmund twitches at the words. Mortals can't hear Munin talk, but Sigmund isn't quite mortal. He knows he's missing something, even if he has no idea what.

"Long time no see, you carrion-stinking bag of feathers," I say, because I'm pretty sure that by this point I'm fucked no matter what I do. "How's Hugin these days?"

"Lain are you talking to the—"

"Dead," says Munin. "Like you should be."

"How 'bout that," I say. "Guess that *völva* wasn't all she was cracked up to be." Prophecy. Fuck me, but do I hate prophecy.

And then a voice behind me says, "Isn't it strange how these things turn out." And any hope I'd been harboring re not being totally fucked goes flying off with Munin in a flurry of black feathers and cawed laughter.

I don't turn, not at first. It's funny, in the way that isn't. I've been waiting for this for nearly seventy years. Of course it would be this night, of all nights.

Sigmund is less hesitant, spinning to look at the source of the new voice. His hand is clammy where it's still clasped in mine, the sweet cloud of self-conscious lust he's been extruding all night replaced now by sharply spiking anxiety. He knows this is wrong, even if he doesn't yet know why or how.

"Uh, Lain? Why is there an angry Viking guy with a spear talking in, um, Norwegian?"

That's . . . unexpected. It's not Norwegian, it's Godstongue. Theoretically, everyone hears Godstongue as their native language. Everyone, it seems, except for Sigmund. That bears further investigation. Later. When we're not about to die.

"Hello, Baldr." I switch to Godstongue, too. It's sort of rude, what with Sigmund standing right there, but I get the impression this conversation isn't going to be something he really wants to hear. That I really want him to hear.

Now I turn. Sigmund's description is accurate, and Baldr hasn't bothered to make any concessions to modernity beneath the tunic and the furs. He'd look funny, standing in the middle of a mall parking garage, except for the fact that I'm about ten seconds from shitting myself. He was a kid the last time I saw him, staring down an arrow as I guided his brother's hand to murder. Baldr then had been pale and scrawny and a bit of a mummy's boy. Sometime in the last thousand years he grew up. And out. And angry. I guess an age trapped in Hel will do that to a guy.

I should know, after all.

Baldr is holding a spear. It's not Gungnir—his father's favorite phallic symbol—but it'd fool most people into thinking that it was. I gather from the fact that he's holding it at all that this meeting is booked in to be short and violent.

"Liesmith." My least-favorite kenning, wonderful. Except annoyance is replaced by terror when Baldr's one golden eye flicks to Sigmund. "And your usurping whore, too. How convenient, when it was her who lead us to you."

Shit. Sig's near-death experience in the Járnviðr. I'd felt Sigyn then—bright as a pulsar and as frozen as space—and apparently I hadn't been the only one. Fuck.

I push Sigmund behind me a bit. "Get in the car," I say in English. "As soon as he's distracted, get the fuck out of here. Don't worry about me."

"Lain?"

"Just trust me, man."

There's something about my voice. Something about the fact that the Weird Shit is officially going down that makes Sigmund nod and start backing off.

"She won't get far," Baldr promises, voice flat and certain.

Baldr had a wife once. I didn't technically kill her, but, then again, I didn't technically kill him, either.

Still, that's no excuse for threatening my boyfriend on our first date. "Fuck off, you glass-backed jackass. What are you doing here?"

"I'm here to kill you, slanderer," Baldr says, picking another nickname I could do without. "Normally, this is a task I would not relish." He'd almost look regretful, to someone with a strictly theoretical understanding of the term.

"Then there's no need to start now," I try. "Turn around, go home. I'm done. I got out, got a new life. That's what I wanted." This, perhaps, is true only in retrospect. I hope Baldr doesn't realize that. Mostly I hope that the fact that he's still talking might mean I can get out of this without a fight. Maybe.

"Even should I believe them, your lies are meaningless." Baldr sounds tired, a little bit impatient. Actually, he sounds like his dad. That's probably not a good sign. "Ásgarðr is suffering. Languishing in twilight while the prophecy of Ragnarøkkr goes unfulfilled. For decades I have searched for the reason this is so. Now that I have my answer, I cannot allow such treachery to go unpunished."

So. I'm pretty much screwed, then. Fuck.

I give it a shot, anyway. "Kid, prophecy doesn't work that way. If the golden age hasn't come, then . . ." It occurs to me, as I say this, that it's probably about the worst fucking tack I could've taken.

"Enough." Baldr hefts his spear, and I know talking time is done. "If you will not submit quietly then so be it."

He lunges, but I'm ready for it and feint left. I come up from a roll to see Baldr pulling not-Gungnir out of the concrete a hair shy of the rear bumper of my car. If the sun-kissed little bastard scratches it, I swear I'm going to kill him.

I might have to kill him, anyway. Somehow.

Baldr is big and strong, and his spear is very pointy. He was never much of a warrior, back in the day, but he stands now with confidence and swings his weapon like he means it. I guess he's learned.

It's been a good thousand years since I've been in melee combat. I hope it's one of those things you don't forget, like riding your first great bike, in either the literal or metaphorical sense of the phrase. I guess I'm about to find out.

There's a place, a sort of nothingspace between the edges of what's real and what isn't, and I reach into it. I left two *langseax* here once, just in case, and I feel for the shape of them in my mind. The bone-carved hilts, the cold kiss of iron. Preserved for a thousand years, ready for my call. I call now, and the blades materialize in my hands. Mostly like I remember, except that they now appear to be on fire. The nothingspace does that. Nothing ever comes back the way it went in.

Flaming daggers I can work with and, when Baldr thrusts forward again, I catch the haft between the backs of the blades and pull downward.

He stumbles, and I leap back in a crouch. It doesn't buy me much. Baldr's on the offensive again almost immediately, and I end up doing a weaving dance backward through the parking garage, trying to keep out of range of the spearhead.

Spears have reach, and in the hands of a skilled fighter, they're fast weapons. But they're designed for keeping people back, not fighting them up close. If I can get behind the point, I can win.

Plan forming, I feint backward again and wait for Baldr to follow. He does, and halfway through his thrust I pull a wall of fire up between us. It's been a while since I've done something like that and, honestly, I'm glad it works at all. While I'm busy congratulating myself, I leap up onto the roof of one of the cars on Baldr's right, then use the momentum to bring myself down against his flank.

It works. Just. Baldr's distracted by the fire, but notices at the last minute and turns, catching me in the side with the haft of not-Gungnir. I hear an awful crack at chest level as the wood connects. The force sends me flying back into the opposite row of cars, but not before my *langseax* bites flesh.

Baldr gives a roar, and when I look up, he's clutching his right shoulder.

He's left-handed, and the cut isn't deep, so it's not as good as it could be. Honestly, it's amazing that I could wound him at all, and even now I feel the Wyrd of my bloodied knife scream from its broken oath. Still. "First blood," I say, grinning.

Baldr doesn't take the gloating well, roaring and lunging again. I almost don't roll out of the way fast enough, not-Gungnir slamming through the hood of the car I've already wrecked with the weight of my own impact.

First blood might be mine, but Baldr is starting to fight like he intends to finish. Losing some finesse and making up for it in strength and brutality, and it's all I can do to keep out of the way of his thrusts. Not to mention that I can see the paint bubble and peel off cars as the guy passes, and I'm pretty sure he's started to radiate sunlight.

My ribs are definitely cracked. I haven't breathed since the cave, which is useful, but pain lances into my chest every time I move. Baldr's had me on the defensive ever since we started, and it occurs to me to wonder why I ever thought I could beat him in a straight-up fight. I'm used to press conferences and board meetings. Not this.

Emboldened by previous successes with calling up walls of fire, I run one along a row of cars. I'm rewarded a moment later with three rather nice explosions. Not movie-huge, but enough to catch Baldr in the backdraft.

It's about now that two things start to happen. One is that my skin starts itching, all along my back and biceps. I have a tattoo there—hidden under suits and hipster jackets—and it will become important in just a second. First, however, I'm distracted by a flash of bright-sharp terror coming from my left. It's not Baldr; it's Sigmund, still hiding amid the cars. He's wild eyed, breathing heavily, and slightly singed. Shit.

"I told you to get the fuck outta here!"

"Lain!" He panics, looking at something behind me. Shit. I roll, but not fast enough, feeling the tip of not-Gungnir as it slices a thick gash right down my back. Right through the pattern of the ink.

"Guh!"

There's a trail of purple-black blood leading from where I'm crouched to where Baldr is pulling his spear out of the concrete. The blood sizzles, oxidizing green as it eats holes in the ground. I'm not worried about that, though, or even about the burning pain lancing down my spine. Because now it's time to pay attention to the itching. The itching that feels like a thousand beetles crawling just beneath my skin. That feels like a promise, like something forgotten. But most of all, that feels like home.

The ground around me starts to crack, and when my hands clench, they feel more like claws.

Baldr notices. His eyes widen as he takes a step backward, muttering a single word.

When I stand up, I'm taller than I was before. When I laugh, I can feel four leather stitches pulling at the corners of my mouth.

"Surprise!" I hear myself say. I'm pretty sure it's me, though the voice is deeper and rougher than I'm used to. "I made a deal with your father, boy, long before you were ever born. But he's dead, and his wards no longer hold." It's definitely me talking, but the words feel like they're coming from a very, very long time ago.

Baldr banishes the fear from his eyes and sets his jaw. "Monster!" he says. "My father was a fool. I will not repeat his mistakes."

He lunges again. This time I don't bother to dodge, taking the point of his spear straight through the shoulder. It hurts, but it's nothing compared to the fire burning beneath my skin, and I grab Baldr by the throat before he can pull back.

My lips part, my tongue lolls. Suddenly, I'm very, very hungry . . .

And then Baldr calls down the sun, and the world is filled with light and pain.

I roar, ripping my hand away from molten skin and throwing my arm up against the glare. Except it's not an arm that comes up; it's a wing. I have another one, too, and a tail.

(. . . *jötunn* . . .)

I was about two seconds away from biting Baldr's throat out. About five from eating his still-beating heart.

Now I remember the reason Odin used to like me.

Baldr is still glowing, clutching at his burnt and blistering throat, staring at me. Kid looks shell-shocked, and for a moment I sympathize. It's only a moment, though, because I remember Sigmund is still here somewhere and I really doubt the calm is going to last more than the second it takes Baldr to get his breath back. So I do the only sensible thing I can think of, given the situation. I turn tail, literally, and run.

Sigmund is cowering behind a support pillar, trying not to pass out, and I grab him before he can scream.

"Time to go!" I say, because when you're a seven-foot-tall monster abducting people it's probably a good idea to explain what you're doing. I'm surprised when, after one startled instant, Sigmund's limbs wrap around my neck and waist and he hangs on like a bush tick. He probably needs to. I can run fast like this. Much faster than I'm used to, in a kind of three-limbed loping gait, one arm still holding Sigmund in case he decides to let go.

I don't bother to check whether Baldr follows. I don't think he does, and I can see the exit to the parking lot looming up ahead. I jump right over the boom gate, and as soon as I can see the sky I do something I haven't done in . . . well, honestly, I can't remember ever having done it quite like this.

I fly.

Getting airborne is easy. It's just a jump. Staying airborne, on the other hand, is harder. I'm already about four stories up when I realize I have absolutely no fucking idea how any of this works, but my wings apparently do and we continue our arc upward rather than down. Sigmund is screaming in my ear. I think I'm screaming in his, too.

Fortunately, it's not raining. Unfortunately, it's windy, especially when we start getting above the buildings, and I drop and rise on the currents, wings flapping like mad and catching the air in ways I don't understand and can't predict. I hope Sigmund doesn't hurl. I hope I don't hurl. Honestly, I'm not even sure if I can anymore, and right now is absolutely not the time to find out.

It takes me a block or so, but I do get confident in the concept of up, the city sprawling out underneath us like a glittering Hubble photograph. Pandemonium is a planned city—no prizes for guessing whose idea that was—and from here the ley lines built into the avenues and town centers are obvious. They all spiral back to a single building, burning powerful and bright, right in the center of the sprawl.

Lokabrenna HQ. Home. It also happens to be where we're going. Or will be. Once I can work out *down*.

My first attempt drops us a good three stories, and Sigmund screams.

"Sorry!" I'm not sure he hears me. The wind up here is ferocious. It's also freezing, and I'm pretty sure that at least part of Sigmund's trembling is from the cold rather than from fear. I have to get him somewhere warm and solid. Hell, I have to get me somewhere warm and solid.

My next attempts at descent are smoother, and I peel into the air above LB in a wide spiral. There's a small garden on the roof, attached to the penthouse, which is where I'm aiming. I'm so busy congratulating myself on my even approach that it doesn't occur to me that I have no idea how to land until I'm a few hundred feet away. We're traveling fast and Sigmund has that whole problem of being a squishy, breakable mortal to consider, so I do the best with what I've got.

What I've got entails leveling off, mostly parallel, a few feet higher than the balcony. As soon as we're over solid ground, I drop Sigmund. Well, *pull him off* might be more accurate. High school physics is against me, so I call up some wind—wind is my other thing, after fire, the one everyone forgets about—and have it break his fall. He gives an ungracious yelp and lands awkwardly on his ass, but he doesn't sound hurt.

I don't have much time to think about it, though, because suddenly I'm about two seconds away from a date with five feet of concrete.

That hurts.

I hit the ground with a sound like snapping branches and pounded liver, the momentum rolling me head over tail for a good couple of feet. A wall puts a stop to it before the nausea hits, then there's silence, and the world is a hazy blur of orange and gray and brown.

The first thing I'm really aware of, other than *ouch,* is something tickling my nose. It takes me a moment to collect myself enough to realize it's a tail. My tail. Or, more specifically, the fringe of feathers running along the edge of it.

I can't believe I have a fucking tail.

I've come to rest on my back, with my shoulders on the ground and my ass up against the wall. I don't see anything below the waist I recognize, just skin the color of burnt earth, feathers like fire and ash, and far too many scars. Beneath the feathers, my feet look more like talons, and it occurs to me that this is what I actually, really truly look like. I wasn't kidding when I told Baldr that I once made a promise to his father. Apparently it's been so long that I've forgotten what it means not to pass as human. To be myself.

To be *jötunn.*

Right now, being *jötunn* feels like a world of pain. My left arm is trapped under my shoulders the wrong way in its socket, and even though I don't remember ever seeing it before, I'm pretty sure my tail isn't supposed to have that right angle. I can feel the smashed bones and minced internal organs already trying to pull themselves together. Here, of all places, I am powerful. Just . . . not very elegant right now.

Unsteady footsteps begin to make their way toward me across the concrete, and I roll my head down—or up or whichever way it is—in response, some new shape on my skull jarring against the concrete and cutting the motion off halfway. Sigmund, meanwhile, is looking at the crater in the ground and the trail of hissing and spitting blood, eyes and mouth wide, dark circles. He's also limping. Shit.

He looks up, startled when he sees me looking back at him. "L-Lain?" he tries.

"In a minute, I think," I manage. It feels like talking through a sponge soaked in blood. Still, Sigmund is limping, so I ask, "Sorry about the landing. Are you okay?"

His eyes get even wider behind thick glasses, eyebrows lifting into a clashing furrow. "Am I . . . ? Are *you* okay? Should I, uh, call someone?" As soon as he says it, he winces.

"No," I say. "It looks worse than it is." This is true. I heal up the big stuff pretty fast, but the bruises and lacerations will be pissing me off for weeks. "Uh. I'm gonna stand up now. You might wanna . . ."

I'm not quite sure how to politely say *Turn around in case you hurl,* but Sigmund bites his lip and pushes his glasses up his nose, and I know he gets the gist when he squeezes his eyes shut.

Standing up turns out not to be as awful as I'd thought. It's only really the arm that's out of place, and I put that right with a loud snap by throwing myself against the wall.

"Okay, done," I say, flexing my newly mobile hand. Well, claw, really. It's huge, dark skin turning the color of splotched blood along the fingers. It's not actually blood, but it is actually a metaphor, and not a very subtle one at that. I sigh.

"Um . . ."

I look up at Sigmund's voice, and he taps his left collarbone. Frowning, I mimic the gesture and, oh. Right. A good portion of Baldr's spear is still buried there, though most of the haft has been burnt off. I grab what's left and pull.

It doesn't come free without a fight—the skin already starting to heal around it—and, it's funny. Because it hurts, I know it does, except . . . it doesn't. Like hitting the ground traveling at a hundred miles hurt but didn't.

I spent a thousand years in agony, once. I guess all pain since then is just a shadow.

When the spear comes out, the wound begins to ooze again. Sigmund makes a motion to reach for it, then remembers the way the blood eats through metal and concrete and thinks better of it.

"What . . . what are you?" he asks, and I try not to grimace.

"I was sort of hoping we could start with 'who' first."

But Sigmund shakes his head. I'm not sure whether his next words are wondrous or terrifying. Maybe both. "I know who you are," he says. "I figured that one out when you started fighting the blond guy."

"Oh." And, because there's not really any other answer. "*Jötunn*. I'm a *jötunn*."

"Yo— What now?"

I almost laugh, and Sigmund startles at the aborted sound. "*Jötunn*. It, uh, it usually gets translated as 'giant' "—Sigmund looks me up and up, I'm taller like this, almost ridiculously so—"but the word means something closer to 'eater.' "

"Oh," he says. "Okay." He huddles down into his jacket, trying to hide shivers that are half from shock, half from the wind that blows cold and endless, this high up above the city. The burn holes in Sig's clothes probably don't help with the latter. I hope he wasn't too attached to his outfit, because he's not going to be wearing it anywhere else.

"Um, we should go inside," I say, gesturing to the door.

Sigmund nods, sour uncertainty clouding around a frozen core, determined and brave. "This is the LB building, isn't it?" he says, but doesn't wait for an answer. "You're him too, aren't you?"

I don't have to ask who he means. "Yeah," I say. "Sorry."

"It's . . . okay, I guess. We kinda figured that out, too."

I don't think to ask what he means by "we," because by now

I've turned around. There's a large set of French doors a few feet away that connect the balcony to the penthouse suite on the top floor of the building. The doors, being French, are glass.

And there, right in front of me, is my reflection.

"Holy shit . . ."

I step closer to the doppelgänger, raising my fingers against the image. I have horns. Horns! And, honestly, they're the least of my problems. Corpse bloat, stitched-shut lips, and dark-ringed, milk-blind eyes, glowing in the night. A crest of long, flame orange feathers in place of hair. More feathers on the outside of my forearms and down the back and inside of my thighs. And those wings. I look like the bastard child of a vulture and a bonfire.

This is what I look like. Minus some recent additions—the stitches, the ruined eyes, the scars—this is what I've always looked like. And somehow I'd just . . . forgotten.

"Are . . . are you okay?"

Sigmund's voice makes me jerk my hand back and half turn, not quite laughing. "Yeah. Yeah it's just . . . It's the tattoo," I say. I can feel it itching, burning bright against dark skin. "It's a promise I made, ages ago, to . . . to my brother. Blood brother." This is not quite the right word, but it's the word the sagas remember, so . . . "It keeps me human. Human-ish." More than this, at any rate. "But all the scars . . . the wards are breaking. Hence . . ." I make a kind of abortive gesture at myself, and Sigmund nods.

The tattoo really is itching or burning or something, so I reach inside and try and find the end of it. It's ragged, but there, and I pull. The pain flares up my back and down my arms, and there's a strange sensation of tightness, but when it's over I'm just me again. Or Lain. Or . . . someone.

And it's funny, because I'd thought that being the seven-foot flaming monster felt wrong. But Lain's skin, now that I'm back inside it, is . . . too tight, somehow. Fragile and soft and alien.

Huh.

I'll think about it later. Right now, I key in the entry code for the doors, and gesture Sigmund inside. "After you, sir." I try a grin. Sigmund almost returns it.

Inside, the lights flick on when they see us. The place is sterile like a hotel room but modern and comfortable. The decor is beige and white and tan, trendy and expensive and impersonal. We may as well have just walked into a display at IKEA. Well, millionaire IKEA.

"Is this . . . your house?" Sigmund asks, lost in the alien space. He's tracking ash over the plush white rug, but I decide not to mention it.

"Nah," I say. Travis has a mansion in Aldershot, and Lain has an apartment in Torr (or so they tell me). That's already pretty excessive for a guy who doesn't sleep, but a house is one of those things people are supposed to have. Actually, I guess I technically have a place back in Ásgarðr, too—I have vague memories of something made from stone and nestled next to water—assuming Baldr hasn't burned it to the ground by now.

"Nic mostly uses this place," I say, just to fill the silence. "She works too hard."

"Oh," says Sigmund, lost inside the awkward void. He looks around, pushes his glasses up his nose, and finally asks, "So that guy, in the parking garage . . . ?"

"Baldr," I say.

"Oh," says Sigmund again. Then, frowning, "Didn't you, like, kill him?"

So, apparently Sigmund wasn't being cute or romantic or metaphorical when he said he knew who I was. I'm not used to that. Normal humans don't notice the Wyrdborn—gods and the like—and I remind myself once more about Sigmund's tenuous association with normality.

"Um, sort of. Technically, I tricked his brother into doing it." Poor, blind Höðr. Funny how the whole thing doesn't seem like such an awesome plan, a thousand-odd years after the fact. Honestly, I'm still a bit confused as to why I ever thought it was going to be an awesome plan.

"Actually," Sigmund says, as if just remembering something. "Weren't you supposed to be, like, imprisoned until Armageddon or something? With the snake and the poison and whatever?"

"Ragnarøkkr," I say. "And yes, I was."

There are two obvious implications from this, and Sigmund picks them both up. "So, like, the end of the world already happened?" At my nod, he continues, "Weren't you, like, supposed to die?"

"And now you're starting to see what Baldr's problem with me is," I say, wincing a little. "I've sort of been in hiding. In Miðgarðr. For nearly seventy years."

Sigmund does the backward math. "World War Two," he says. "The end of the world was World War Two?"

" 'Brothers will fight and kill each other, sisters' children will defile kinship. It is harsh in the world, no man will have mercy on another.' From the *'Völuspá,'* " I add. "I'm paraphrasing a bit, but that was the prophecy. When northern Europe went to war . . ." I shrug. "Apparently it looked good enough for rock and roll. So we went to war too."

"How come no one noticed?"

I laugh, but it's not kind. " 'No one noticed'? It was the Second World War! Something like sixty million people died in Miðgarðr alone." Sigmund looks suitably horrified and ashamed—quite likely remembering that his last name is, in fact, Sussman, and his family did move here for a reason—so I let it drop. "Life went on afterward, but it was always supposed to. The Ragnarøkkr was only ever going to be the end of an era, not the end of the world forever and ever amen." I pause for a minute, then add, "I think that's why Odin hated it so much. Everything going on without him, and better. This is supposed to be the golden age."

"So how come you didn't die?"

I knew it was coming, but I'm still hesitant. "I remember the cave," I say, voice slow and deliberate. "I remember being chained.

"I remember the chains . . . dissolving. Iron turning back to offal and blood. I remember standing up. I probably laughed . . . And the next thing I remember is waking up on the floor of the cave with a raging headache, the battle already over." I turn to Sigmund and give him a not-quite smile. "Sigyn, my wife, knocked me out. I found her dead on the battlefield, impaled on Heimdallr's sword."

"She took your place?" Sigmund looks surprised. I don't blame him. Seventy years later and I'm still pretty fucking surprised, too.

I shrug. "I don't know why. She was dressed as me." Sigyn hadn't been beautiful, but she'd looked it, lying there on the battlefield, face smudged with blood and dirt.

Life is cruel.

"Do you miss her?" Sigmund asks. It's relevant to his current situation, I guess, even if he isn't yet aware of exactly how much.

It's a good question, and I don't have an honest answer to it. I was a pretty lousy husband. "She died for me," I say finally. "I owe her a blood debt I can't repay." I sigh. "I burnt her body, hoping anyone who'd figured out the deception was dead. Then I ran. Ended up in Miðgarðr wandering around a mortal battlefield. Some Allied soldiers found me, sent me to a military hospital." I'd been pretty out of it. Babbling in a thousand-year-dead tongue, dirty and ragged and thin. I guess they'd figured shell shock, or a camp escapee. "The guy in the bed next to me was an Australian pilot. Burn victim, of all things. He died in the night, but he had a name and an identity, something I didn't."

"So you took them." It sounds so tawdry when Sigmund says it, but I nod. His eyes go wide suddenly, and he falls down onto the neat white leather sofa. It's been that sort of a day. "Hale. Cameron Hale."

I nod again. Australia had seemed so far away to me, then. So perfect. So I'd cowered in this dark corner of the world, carving out my own niche, surrounding myself in the wards and leys I'd need to keep hidden from Ásgarðr's roaming eyes.

"I had to do something with myself when I got here," I say. "Turns out, I'm excellent at capitalism. Go figure."

Now it's Sigmund's turn to nod, looking down at his ash-smudged hands as if he's never seen them before. "What I don't understand," he says, "is why me? Why choose me? Why even tell me all of this? Surely you don't have to, right? I mean, you could just, like, wipe my mind or something with magic god powers or whatever?" He looks up, wild eyed, as if the thought only just occurred to him and he's still digesting its implications.

"Because you're her," I tell him. It seems as good an opening as any. "I don't know how or why, but I can feel it. You're Sigyn."

Sigmund goes still at that. I'm not sure what response I was hoping for, but it occurs to me that this probably isn't going to be it. Too fucking late now, I guess.

"You've been hanging out with me because you think I'm your dead wife?" he says, and I take an ill-advised step forward at the tone.

"Sig—"

"No!" he says, standing up. "No, come on man. Give me a— *Fuck!* Of all the . . . I thought it was about *me!*" He laughs, but it's a broken sort of sound. "How fucking stupid was that? I thought . . . Fuck, what does it even matter what I fucking thought!"

He's angry, bright-dark and flaring. I have no idea why, and, after everything else that's happened, for some reason this is the thing that scares me. This isn't supposed to happen. Sigyn is supposed to help when the bad shit goes down, not get angry.

"Sig," I say. I reach out to touch him, but he jerks away.

"Don't! Just . . . just don't. Fuck. I can't fucking believe—" There are tears in his eyes, and he blinks them away. "Fuck you," he finally declares.

Then he runs.

"Sigmund!" I'm halfway across the room and halfway through the word when the bathroom door slams. The stark and trendy chrome clock on the wall reads 1:37 a.m.

This was not, in retrospect, how I was planning on spending my Saturday. My fingers itch for a cigarette, but Nic will kill me if I set the detectors off. So I sigh, curse Baldr and the universe, and walk over to the closed bathroom door. I could open it, I suppose, except I don't. I'm a coward at heart, and I never was very good at this sort of thing.

Instead, I stand in the sterile gulf of a display home I call my penthouse, lean my head against the bathroom door, and listen to Sigmund cry himself to sleep.

BALDR

[A]xe-age, sword-age,
shields cloven,
wind-age, wolf-age,
ere the world falls;
no man will
spare another.

—"Völuspá," stanza 45

ELEVEN

Considering Sigmund spent the night sleeping in a bathtub, Saturday morning wasn't as horrible as it could have been.

Someone had brought him blankets.

Blankets and pillows, in fact. They looked stripped straight off the bed outside and were cocooned around him. It was comfortable, despite the porcelain beneath, and Sigmund didn't want to get up.

He had a killer headache.

It felt like a hangover, but at least that would've been kinda manly. Not like crying himself to sleep in his

(*husband's*)

boyfriend's bathtub. That was just embarrassing. Sigmund wondered, if he concentrated hard enough, if he could manage to sink through the tiles and die.

Five minutes later he had to admit that plan just wasn't working. So he poked his head out from under the covers, blinking at the blur beyond. The bathroom was still a bathroom. All expensive stone and meticulous gleaming fixtures. Frosted-glass windows ran around the tops of the walls, and by the light it looked to be fast approaching lunchtime on a blinding summer's day.

Sigmund's glasses were waiting within arm's reach on the counter. He didn't remember taking them off. He certainly didn't remember leaving them on top of a pile of clean clothes from his drawer at home. It must've been a miracle.

There seemed to be a lot of those going around, lately.

In the mirror, the same mud brown eyes blinked at him from underneath the same tousled, nothing-colored hair. He had stubble, and acne, and the beginnings of what was going to grow into a prodigious double chin, given a decade or so. He didn't look like a boy who'd spent last night watching gods fight in the parking lot of Torr Mall.

He certainly didn't look like a goddess. Not even the one he'd dreamed about. The one with hair like matted straw and the dark, nearly mono brow. The one who'd glared at him like ice. The one he'd failed.

"Fuck you," he said, but the only thing in the bathroom to hear him was his reflection.

His clothes were wrecked. Covered in ash and holes from where that . . . stuff had leaked out of the thing he'd once thought was Lain. His ankle ached from where he'd twisted it coming down onto the roof . . .

(*we were flying!*)

. . . and the grazes on his palms and knees stung. Plus, his shoulder hurt again. He wondered if this was what his life was going to be like from now on. He wondered if he was okay with that or not.

He was dating a god. A god who was apparently convinced that Sigmund was the reincarnation of his dead wife. Or . . . something. He'd been a bit vague on the details.

A god that Sigmund had yelled at. A god who'd brought him blankets and a fresh change of clothes in the night, because (*a-har*) gods forbid Sigmund to be uncomfortable sleeping in a bathtub.

Jesus.

Bereft of a coherent plan of action, Sigmund decided to have a shower.

It was a bloody awesome shower. Showerheads everywhere, and Sigmund turned the water up hot and hard and just stood there, trying not to think. There was an alcove of expensive-looking soaps and lotions at eye level, so Sigmund used them, and then he finally dragged himself from the shower's comforting spray, smelling like one of the New Age crystal shops Em used to drag him to before ditching paganism for skeptical atheism.

He wondered what she'd make of last night.

Fancy wifi scales in the corner of the room informed him he was still fat. A search through the medicine cabinet revealed a toothbrush, toothpaste, and a razor, all neatly packaged up and waiting to be used. By the time Sigmund had cleaned his teeth, shaved, dressed, and spent a minute trying to tame down his hair, he had to admit he was running out of reasons to procrastinate.

He could hear someone moving around outside. Not close or impatient, just normal walking around this-is-my-house-thank-you-very-much sort of sounds. He wondered who he'd open the door to.

It turned out to be Lain. He was standing in the kitchen, dressed in a black tank top and loose lounge pants, all broad shoulders and slim waist. Movie-star beautiful, effortless in that five-hours-with-the-stylist sort of way. Sigmund tried not to notice, failed, then wondered whether Lain was doing it on purpose or he really just always looked like that. Maybe it was a god thing.

The whole penthouse smelled of hotcakes.

Lain looked up when Sigmund walked over and gave a brilliant, if slightly hesitant, smile. He really did have very sharp teeth. Inhumanly sharp.

"I made hotcakes," he announced when Sigmund sat down on the other side of the breakfast island. Sigmund thought the claim was probably an understatement. The counter was covered with containers of honey, whipped butter, caramel glaze, and a variety of fruits. Lain was assembling everything into café-style stacks, finished off with a dusting of powdered sugar because of course he'd be a Michelin-star chef as well as a CEO, outdoorsman, filthy rich, ridiculously attractive, a god, and whatever the hell else he was.

Still. He'd made hotcakes.

"I love hotcakes," Sigmund said, trying not to wince at the flatness in his voice.

"I know."

Sigmund didn't bother asking how, instead just watching Lain arrange their breakfast. Or, well, brunch, if the clock on the wall was anything to go by.

It occurred to Sigmund that he'd never actually seen Lain's arms before; they'd always been hidden under long sleeves and jackets. The mass of scars crisscrossing freckled skin probably explained why, not to mention the tattoos or . . . whatever they were that wrapped around Lain's biceps. The ink was black today, not the near-iridescent white of last night, the pattern made of scrolling knot work and runes. Looking at it too long made Sigmund's eyes hurt, so he looked at Lain's hands instead. There were bandages across the knuckles.

"How are you feeling?"

Lain looked up at him, confused, and Sigmund gestured to the bandages. The ones complementing Lain's split lip, abrasions, and masses of purple-green bruises. Lain looked,

Sigmund thought, like Bruce Willis at the end of a *Die Hard* film. All he needed to complete the cosplay was less hair and a Band-Aid somewhere on his face.

Lain glanced down and did something Sigmund almost thought could be a blush. "Oh. Um, the blood is, um, poisonous. As well as, uh, caustic. So I didn't want to, like, bleed in the food?" It was part question, part apology. "I was really careful!"

"I trust you," Sigmund said. For a second, Lain blinked, as if the notion was novel and foreign, and maybe it was. "I'm not angry at you anymore," Sigmund continued, because it seemed like an appropriate time. Lain almost looked relieved, so Sigmund added, "Because there's no point, is there? I mean, getting angry at you—of all people—for thinking up some shitty romcom con is like getting angry at fire for being hot."

Lain winced. "Ouch. Touché."

So maybe Sigmund was still a bit angry. He'd get over it, probably right after he figured out why, exactly, he'd been so mad in the first place.

Lain finished dusting on the sugar and presented the plate to Sigmund with a flourish and a "Ta-dah!" Sigmund gave him a smile for his efforts, and Lain returned it. He was still watching Sigmund, keeping his movements small and non-threatening, like he wasn't sure he was allowed to be there. For a god in his own temple, it was sort of sad.

Sigmund ate a bite of hotcake. Then, "These are . . . really good."

Lain gave one of his toothy grins at the praise, then started eating from his own plate.

As it turned out, Sigmund was ravenous. He tore through the stack, making himself slow down only on the last hotcake out of embarrassment. Then again, with the way Lain ate, he wasn't in a position to judge.

"So, how much trouble are you in, exactly?" Sigmund asked, if only to slow down his eating. Besides, he should probably know the answer. He had the feeling that Lain's kind of trouble was contagious.

Lain gave a look, as if in agreement with this unspoken assessment. "Exactly? On a scale of one to ten? Eleven or twelvish, I think."

"Awesome." The irony there was practically rusting. "And me?"

Lain opened his mouth, then closed it again and seemed to reconsider.

"Incidentally, I can tell when you lie."

"Ah." Lain seemed relieved at that. Like an alcoholic nursing a soda, watching with bitter satisfaction as the last of his friends' glasses emptied. "Yeah. I suppose you can." A long pause, then, "You have to understand, Baldr is the Good Guy. He wants me dead, because I'm the villain, and killing the villain is what the Good Guys do. Ásgarðr"—Lain said it with all the umlauts, his real accent coming through—"will never be restored so long as I'm alive."

Sigmund tried to convey his incredulity in his expression. "Do you believe that?"

"It doesn't matter what I believe. What matters is the Wyrd. Fate. It's off-kilter, it's been off-kilter since everything went wrong at Ragnarøkkr—"

"Since your wife screwed it up by saving you, you mean?"

"Yeah. And you'll have to forgive me if I fail to get too cut up about that fact."

"I take it Captain Aryan Nation doesn't share your sentiments?"

"Something like that." Lain gave the edge of a fang-tipped smirk.

"So I'm back to my original question," Sigmund said. "Am

I in danger?" A horrifying thought struck him. "Ohmigod, Dad."

"Your dad is fine." Lain's brows furrowed, his hands raised as if in warding. "You're maybe fair game, because of Sigyn's involvement in the war. But going after your dad would be *nið*. Shameful. Something the Bad Guys would do."

" 'Bad Guys' like you?"

"Now you're catching on." Lain's grin split open. It was sharp and unpleasant, and his eyes burned poison green, even against the bright light of the penthouse.

It was hard to meet that gaze, so Sigmund didn't, pushing the last of the crumbs around his plate instead. "What are you going to do?" he asked.

He half expected some convoluted plan, some twisting mess of cons and traps and blinds. Break-ins and montages and at least one set of big red numbers, ticking down the time. But, in the end, all Lain said was, "I'm going to kill Baldr." He sounded resolved, though it lasted only a moment. "Admittedly, that might be easier said than done." When Sigmund looked up, Lain was frowning.

"I sense this is a long story."

"You sense correctly. The short of it is that things don't injure the coddled bastard. Wood, metals, stone, diseases: They gave a promise, years ago."

Sigmund was dubious. "How does wood give a promise?" He got the feeling the answer was going to be something inane, like, *MAGIC!!!*, so he added, "Besides, you seemed to be doing a pretty good job of it last night." Or, well, earlier this morning.

"Well, obviously I never promised anyone anything. Jesus, I couldn't stand the snot-nosed little kid. Fucking golden-haired wunderkind."

Sigmund didn't doubt it. He knew the type. Most of them

worked in Sales. "So can't you just, like, I dunno, rip out his heart with your claws or something?" Which, okay, was totally not a cool thing to say, but the whole day was just so surreal. Heart ripping was totally fine. It would be, like, self-defense and everything.

Sigmund wondered when he'd started running on video game logic. He figured this was the sort of thing lobbyists warned about.

Lain didn't look particularly impressed either. "It's a bit uncivilized," he said, as if this was some major deciding factor. Hell, maybe it was.

"So, what happens now?"

The question earned him a huff of breath and a scowl, not quite directed his way. "Now I figure out what the alternative to hiding is when running's out of the question. Pandemonium is my city. I'm strong here, and Baldr knows it. That limits his options. But luring me out somehow, getting me onto *his* turf instead . . ." Lain ran his hand across his lips, across the scars. "That's what I'd do, in his place."

"Great. That's doing a lot to bolster my confidence in my safety, just FYI." Sigmund's enthusiasm for ending up In Another Castle was at an all-time low. If that was the price of dating a god, he wasn't sure he'd be prepared to pay it.

But Lain just waved his hand. "That's *nið* again." Then, after a moment, "Er. I think."

"You think?" Sigmund was still a bit unclear on what that word was, exactly. It sounded a bit like *neath,* but he could practically hear the italics.

"Look, it's been a while since I've done this sort of thing, and I never was very good at it to start with." Lain was agitated, gesticulating with his fork in one hand and drumming his fingernails on the countertop with the other. Although, *fingernails* might not have been a strong enough word. They were a dark, reddish brown today and almost looked like claws. It occurred to Sigmund that maybe Lain was less human that he had been previously. Maybe more of the shape from last night was bleeding through. Maybe Sigmund was only noticing it now.

He must have been quiet for a while, because when Lain spoke again his voice was softer.

"I know this is a lot to dump on you all at once. Believe me when I say I didn't plan things being quite this . . . full on."

Suddenly, the countertop was the most fascinating thing in the room; expensive reconstituted stone, thickly cut and tastefully off-white. No chips, no marks. Perfect. The Kitchen Counter of the Gods. "When were you planning on telling me, then? Before you'd fucked me, or after?" *Full on* was an understatement.

But Lain laughed. "Is that what you're worried about? Sig, if I'd just wanted to fuck you, I would've done it as Travis."

Sigmund looked up, Lain's expression hovering somewhere between fond and perplexed. It was terrifying, that expression. It promised things.

"Then what do you want?"

Lain shrugged. "At first? Satisfy my curiosity." He was doing honesty again. Sigmund wasn't sure he liked it. "Then, attempt to repay a blood debt. Now, I want to play *Dungeons and Dragons* and cook hotcakes."

That was almost saccharine, but it was true and probably one of the nicest things anyone had ever said to Sigmund. One of the nicest things anyone had bothered to try saying to him.

"I think I'm just, like, in shock or something," he said, eyes dropping to the countertop again. "I'm sure in a few days I'll think this is just about the coolest thing ever." He tried a smile, then stood and collected up their empty plates. "What should I do with . . . ?"

Lain's eyebrows hiked, then furrowed, as if cleaning up his own dishes was something unusual. Maybe it was. Maybe he was rich enough to have people who came in and did that stuff for him. Maybe being a god meant never having to do housework.

"Uh, dishwasher under the sink?"

There was, indeed, a dishwasher under the sink, laminated in the same glossy white as the rest of the cupboards. It looked lonely with two plates and four pieces of cutlery, so Sigmund started stacking the mixing bowls and other hotcake preparation tools as well. Lain watched him in amusement for a while, then started to help. It was all very domestic.

The kitchen wasn't what anyone would be calling large—just a few feet of wall and an island—and they kept brushing against each other as they stacked and scrubbed and put things back into cupboards. It was . . . sort of sexy, actually. Lain wasn't intruding into his space, but he wasn't avoiding it either. A calculated dance of light touches and near misses, and Sigmund's heart began to keep time as he was caught up in the rhythm. He didn't mind. It was nice. No one had ever bothered trying to seduce him before.

Maybe if more chores were like this, people wouldn't complain about having to do them so much.

When he touched Lain's arm, the skin beneath his fingers felt like linen, fresh from the drier: warm and soft, dusted in hair and freckles and textured by a latticework of scars.

"I had a really nice time, last night," Sigmund said. "Right up until the part where we almost died." Even that had been sort of fun, in a holy-shit-what-the-fuck sort of way. "And I don't care if you're really, like, some giant flaming monster thing. It's kinda cool, actually." Except for the wings, but Sigmund had always been a little scared of birds. The way they *stared* and all. He decided not to mention it.

Lain's expression got weird, anyway, almost like he was about to cry. But what he actually did was bend down and part his lips. Sigmund wasn't a bastion of knowledge on the subject, but he watched movies and knew the start of a kiss when he saw one. So he tilted his head, too, and closed his eyes, and hoped like hell he was doing it right.

A moment later, Lain's lips, hot and smooth and scarred, closed the gap, one of his hands coming to rest against the curve of Sigmund's spine. Sigmund was getting used to the lip part of kissing—and the feel of Lain's tongue, brushing against them—but his hands were kind of flailing and there was just so much to keep track of and, Jesus, Lain was like a zillion years old and a god, and he probably thought Sigmund was such a loser and—

And one of Lain's hands found one of Sigmund's and placed it on his waist. "You can touch," he said, breath ghosting across Sigmund's cheek. "I like it when you touch."

(*oh*)

Oh.

Lain's waist was slender and firm under Sigmund's fingers, and when his hands "accidentally" slid under the hem of Lain's tank top, he got a breathy moan for his efforts. That seemed like a good sound, so Sigmund explored farther, Lain's skin just as warm and just as scarred here as on his arms. Sigmund traced some of the jagged lines with his fingers, and about halfway up Lain's waist encountered something odd. A sort of buzzing, electrical sensation. Like brushing the metal case of a running laptop. It was there in some places and not in others, and—somewhere in between the heat in Sigmund's belly and the hand curling through his hair—he realized his fingers had found Lain's tattoo.

He pulled back from the kiss just enough to ask, "Does it hurt?" His voice sounded deep and husky, sexy almost.

Lain's eyes were very bright, his kiss-swollen lips emphasizing those scars, too. "Not exactly," he said. "But I can feel it, like background noise. Never noticed it before." He moved his hand to brush the side of Sigmund's face. "I should probably take you home." He didn't sound happy about it.

Sigmund moved closer, head resting against Lain's broad shoulder and enjoying the way Lain curled around him. Being together like that made Sigmund feel short—Lain had a good six inches on him, easy—but it was nice, too. Standing here in Travis Hale's hotel room kitchen, holding and being held, feeling the small shifts of Lain's muscles beneath his skin.

"Yeah," Sigmund said eventually. "Dad might start wondering where I am." Probably not, really, but it was possible. Maybe.

They pulled apart a few moments later, spurred by some kind of simultaneous reluctance. Sigmund almost wanted to ask to stay, but it had been a pretty weird night. He needed to go home and process for a bit. Work out what he was going to tell Em and Wayne. Or Dad.

That was a pretty good question, actually. "What should I tell people?" he asked as they waited for the elevator down to the parking garage "About you, I mean."

Lain shrugged. "Whatever you want." He sounded a bit guarded, despite the words, and Sigmund frowned.

"What, that you're a seven-foot godmonster?"

That got him a startled bark of laughter. "Oh!" Lain said. The elevator pinged and they stepped in. "You mean about that. It doesn't matter. It's not a secret, people just don't notice."

"I noticed. So did Wayne." Sort of.

This information didn't seem to faze Lain. "Well, yeah," he said. "But you're . . . you know. And your friends used to be *valkyrjur*. Valkyries."

That was just getting silly. Sigmund's face must have shown it, because Lain continued, "It's true! Hrist and Hlökk, the Shaker and the Screamer. You all have a little bit of Wyrd in you, hence with the noticing and stuff."

"That all seems a bit coincidental . . ."

"That's what the Wyrd is, Sig. Coincidence, fate. I'm not here accidentally. Mannheim is thin here, and the Wyrd is heavy. Fate, uh . . . It rolls down hills." He was gesticulating again, obviously struggling for an explanation. "You know that thing with the rubber sheet and the lead ball that's supposed to explain gravity?"

"Yeah . . ."

"Well, the Wyrd is like that. Pandemonium is the rubber sheet—thin and stretchy—and I'm the lead ball. One of them. Other places in Mannheim aren't so elastic, so the Wyrd isn't as"—another big hand motion—"sucky. Not so good for gods."

The doors pinged again, and they stepped out into a part of the garage that Sigmund had never been to before. There weren't many cars here, but the ones that were looked like their total worth was greater than the sum of all the cars in the other garages combined. Sigmund wondered why they were all here on a Saturday. Maybe they all belonged to Travis.

"So, what," he said. "You're saying Pandemonium is like some huge black hole for drunk Viking stories?"

"Short version? Yes."

They were standing in front of Lain's car, not looking any worse for wear despite last night's violence. Sigmund wondered how it got back here, considering they'd left it at the mall. Then again, Lain had obviously been running errands in the night. Maybe he'd picked it up.

The top was down, and Lain leaped into the driver's side, literally vaulting over the door. Sigmund had never seen anyone do that outside of movies.

"What's wrong?" Lain asked when Sigmund didn't join him.

"I've just remembered you drive like a maniac."

"Oh." Lain looked surprised at that, then thoughtful. He glanced at the steering wheel, then back at Sigmund. "You could drive," he said. "Or I could try driving slower?"

Sigmund approached the passenger side and climbed in. Through the door, like a normal person. He was pretty sure trying to vault over the edge would just end in pain and humiliation. "I'll take my chances with you trying out human driving," he said. "I'm not convinced your 'car' runs on enough Really Real World logic for me to handle it." As if to prove his point, the car rumbled to life as soon as he sat down. Today, the stereo was playing Electric Six. Out of curiosity, Sigmund pressed some of the buttons as Lain pulled (carefully!) out of the parking garage.

He spent most of the drive staring out the window, watching the city fly (carefully!) by. He'd never actually been in a convertible before. Well, last night, obviously, but then the top had been up and it hadn't counted. Sigmund had never really been a car person, but he had to admit there was an appeal, sitting in the pocket of stillness formed by the windscreen. Warm summer air roaring over the top, tousling his hair, but quiet and calm just below. He wanted to throw his arms up, into the wind, laughing and feeling the pressure of movement on his skin.

He didn't. Safety first, and all that.

They'd been driving (carefully!) for about five minutes when it occurred to Sigmund they hadn't had to stop in traffic. Not once. Not at stoplights, which were always green, and not at intersections, which were always clear. It was as if the city knew where Lain wanted to go and was pushing aside the traffic to help him get there. And when Sigmund thought about it like that, the maniac driving started to make sense. It was the sort of way anyone would drive if there was no one else in the entire world. No other cars, no pedestrians, no cops. Just the wheels and the road.

There was something important in that. Probably more than one thing, in fact, but it'd been a long few days and thinking wasn't high up on Sigmund's priority list.

The one thing it did mean, of course, was that they were pulling up outside his house in pretty short order. He tried not to feel disappointed.

Lain let out a heavy breath as soon as they'd stopped. It sounded like he'd just finished diffusing a bomb, not like he'd been driving a few suburbs across town. "There," he said. "How was that?" He looked like a puppy who'd peed on the paper, not on the carpet.

Sigmund gave him a smile. "I didn't feel like screaming once." He ducked his head almost as soon as he'd said it, pushing his glasses up his nose. "Thanks, though. For, y'know. Taking me seriously."

Something in Lain's expression turned at the words, ancient and inscrutable and alien. "I'm a bit out of practice with mortals," he said. "So you can tell me if I'm being . . ." He trailed off, waving his hand. It left sparks of flame in its wake.

"I don't have a lot of practice with gods," Sigmund said. "So you can tell me the same."

That seemed to be the right thing to say, and when Sigmund blinked, Lain was just Lain again. All red haired and freckled, and, because he could, Sigmund leaned across the seat and gave Lain a brief, chaste kiss.

"I'll see you Monday?" he said.

Lain's grin was back. It really was quite sexy, with the protruding canines and faint scars. "I wouldn't miss it for the end of the world," he said, and Sigmund climbed out of the car hoping that wouldn't prove to be prophetic. He waved as Lain pulled away (carefully!), still practicing his human driving, and Sigmund had to laugh.

It faded before he reached the door.

It took Sigmund three tries to get his key in the lock, then another two to turn it. The house was still and quiet, and his dad seemed to be out, so Sigmund retreated upstairs to his room. With Lain gone, the past twelve-odd hours were feeling further and further away, vanishing at some rate accelerated beyond one second per second. A strange memory from a stranger, something that had happened to someone else, and when Sigmund tried to push his mind back to those frantic minutes in the parking garage, they felt faded and third-hand.

He figured it was some kind of coping thing, then wondered if he was in shock. Again. That probably wasn't good. Maybe he should ask Google.

He got as far as shaking his computer awake with the mouse. The desktop wallpaper was a picture of a mage. She was a woman, and dressed slightly inappropriately, but she had a fireball in one hand and . . .

(heat and smoke and the stink of burning plastic and holy shit what the fuck is happening that thing is that thing Lain what the hell is going on oh fuck oh fuck they're fighting Lain Lain or whatever you are be careful please oh fuck fire again and blood and . . .)

Dad found him like that, just staring at the screen, mouse clenched in one hand, breath coming in short, sharp gasps.

"—gmund? Sigmund, son?"

His dad's hand on his shoulder felt heavy and real, and Sigmund jerked when it descended.

"Hey, Dad," he said, blinking too fast in the glow of his monitor. "You're back." His voice sounded strange, weak and thready and hollow. Maybe Dad wouldn't notice.

"Sigmund. Are you all right?"

Guess not. His father was looking at him with wide eyes and a furrowed brow. He was holding a bag of groceries that he seemed to have forgotten about. Sigmund could see upstairs things, like toothpaste and tissues, poking out the top.

"Did something happen?"

Answers ranging from *No, nothing* to *I nearly died, again* flashed through Sigmund's head. The first one was a lie and the second one might put his dad in the hospital, so he tried to come up with something in the middle.

And then someone, somewhere, said, "I'm dating Lain." Which was funny, because that someone sounded an awful lot like it was using Sigmund's voice.

Oh, shit.

David didn't even blink. "He seems like a nice boy." It was, Sigmund thought, almost a question. Almost a question with a teeny, tiny hint of violence behind it.

Sigmund had thought of his father as a lot of things—particularly during his brooding teenage years—but violent had never been one of them.

"Yeah," Sigmund said, making his breath slow and his voice steady. Slower. Steadier. Maybe. "Yeah, Lain's pretty cool." That wasn't even the half of it, but something in his expression must've been right, because, after a moment, his dad seemed to unwind.

"You took him on a date to *DnD* night, huh? How'd that work out for you?" David's smile said things that Sigmund thought he had no business knowing about his dad. Nice things, though. Things that pulled against the edges of Sigmund's lips as well.

"Good. I just . . . Yeah. Really, really good." Sigmund pushed his glasses up his nose and tried hard not to blush.

His dad laughed and clapped him on the shoulder, then

turned serious. "You know I love you, right, Sig? After your mum died . . ." He trailed off, tried again, "I know I haven't always been the best father—"

"Dad, no—"

But David held up his hand, and Sigmund cut off what he'd been about to say. Whatever it had been.

"I just want you to know how proud I am of you, of what a smart, capable young man you've grown up to be. All I want for you—all any father should want for his son—is for you to be happy."

"Dad . . . Thanks. I am. Happy. Things are kinda intense right now—"

"New relationships almost always are, in my experience."

"Dad!" More things he didn't want to know, and Sigmund found himself laughing. "So. Kinda intense. But . . . I think it's gonna be cool."

David nodded, lips thin and expression serious. "That's good to hear. You should invite Lain around for dinner sometime. That's usually how it's done, right?"

"So says the TV."

"Well, can't argue with that." David shifted the shopping bag against his hip, then glanced down as if he'd forgotten he'd been holding it. "Now how about you help your old man out with this stuff, huh? Some of us aren't as young as we used to be."

"Dad!" But he was grinning, and by the time the car was unloaded and the groceries put away, Friday night had started to feel like another country. One with closed borders and expired visas. And by Sunday, Sigmund had even almost stopped seeing milky green eyes and stitched-shut lips every time he closed his eyes.

Almost.

TWELVE

THE WORLD STILL hadn't ended by Monday, which Sigmund decided to take as a good sign, even if it did mean that he had to get up for work. Sunday had been uneventful, minus a bit of ribbing from Em and Wayne about his date and the fact that their progression raid kept wiping on the last boss. But that was all regular, Really Real World stuff. No gods, no monsters—well, the ones on the computer, but pixels didn't count—and, most important, no apocalypse. Sigmund had considered messaging Lain on Sunday evening, but had decided against it, and Lain, for his part, seemed to be respecting Sigmund's tacit suggestion to leave him alone for the weekend. He did that a lot, Sigmund realized. Respected boundaries, at least when Sigmund set them. It was nice.

Sigmund spent the rest of the weekend sorting out his thoughts via the medium of mind mapping. By Sunday evening, he had a huge chart full of colorful bubbles and lines that seemed to boil the situation down to a few salient points.

Point the First: Lain was probably right about Sigmund's

connection to Sigyn. It just *felt* true, for starters, and the fact that he could even sense that to begin with counted for something, even if only begging the question. Plus, he knew what Sigyn looked like and always had. He dreamed about her. He dreamed things that, in retrospect, must have been fragments of her memory. War and blood. Black feathers, and a taste of apples that lingered long into the day.

So, yeah. Probably Sigyn.

Point the Second: He really was okay with Lain being some kind of giant, feathered, anthropomorphic vulture thing. It was sexy, even, once he'd gotten over the weird. And it wasn't that far removed from the folder of Twi'lek porn Sigmund totally didn't have buried on his computer. Or that . . . other one with the—

Anyway. Giant monster, pretty sexy, what with the cut abs and smooth, burnt-dark skin. The stitches in the lips were a bit off-putting at first—the way they stretched when Lain spoke and stuff—but no scarier than an average lip ring, and Sigmund had seen way worse on 4chan (another one of those places he never went to ever and had absolutely no knowledge of).

Point the Third: He was mostly okay with Lain being Loki. Mostly. And, okay, he'd done some research, and Loki was apparently a bit of a jerk, but to be fair to the guy, that had seemed to be the Style at the Time. Also, he'd fucked a horse. Sigmund was kinda hoping that part of the story was allegorical, though he had a sinking feeling it totally wasn't. He wondered whether it would be considered rude to ask.

Point the Fourth: Sigmund had definitely picked the Red Team. The sources were unambiguous: Baldr was the God of Lawful Good, while Loki was well into Chaotic Evil territory, having slipped down a few notches from Chaotic Neutral back in the old days. Meaning Lain's assessment of the plot seemed to be the historically correct one.

And that? That left Sigmund with a moral dilemma. Because Lain being the Designated Villain, despite seeming sort of an okay guy most of the time in person, implied the existence of a kind of predestined, absolutist morality that Sigmund wasn't totally down with. Not to mention that Sigmund didn't see himself as being a card-carrying member of Team Evil. Would he still be okay with joining up just because that seemed to be where his friends were hanging out? And did that make him, like, the Misguided Love Interest in this story? Was Baldr going to come swooping through his window one night and try to have him join the Forces of Good through the power of persuasive argument and/or seduction? 'Cause Sigmund? Totally wasn't into Baldr *in that way*. He was just too . . . blond. He looked like he should be carrying a surfboard and saying *dude* a lot.

Did relating a cosmic battle of good and evil to his love life make Sigmund shallow?

There were an awful lot of rhetorical questions there.

And finally, Point the Fifth: Sigmund didn't want to die. Gods were cool in theory (or video games), but in actuality they seemed to be accompanied by a lot of screaming and violence. Sigmund had read the account of Loki and Sigyn's imprisonment and had just sort of stared at the wall for a while afterward. He wasn't sure if time worked the same way for gods as it did for mortals, but Lain had said he'd escaped during World War II. The actual age of the Vikings had been around 800 to 1100 CE. So that made, what? A thousand years imprisoned in writhing agony, chained by the entrails of his son, held beneath the dripping poison of a snake's fangs? Sigmund couldn't imagine a thousand years of *anything*, let alone unspeakable suffering. It was astounding Lain was, well . . . Lain, and not some seething mass of hate and resentment, raging violently against the universe.

Maybe that's why Sigyn had done it. Or was that too trite?

Point being, Sigmund was gaining a newfound appreciation for his boring, normal life. With his boring, normal (if extremely nerdy) hobbies and his boring, normal job and his . . . okay, Em and Wayne were neither boring nor normal but they weren't marauding gods of supposed evil, either.

Just, apparently, former valkyries. Sigmund tried to imagine Em in a horned helmet and bustier, serving mead to dead Vikings, and not only failed miserably but received an extensive mental lecture on the objectification of women for his efforts. Even imagination-Wayne drew the line at serving mead, though she'd been okay with the bustier so long as it had been adequately goth.

That was all an awful lot to think about and, by the time Monday morning rolled around, Sigmund still wasn't sure what he'd decided the answer to it all was. At least he understood the question better. Maybe.

—

At work, Sigmund caught up with Em in the parking lot. The first thing she asked him was, "What happened to your hands?" For someone with only a passing interest in other people, Em could be alarmingly observant.

"Oh, uh. I fell," Sigmund said, trying not to rub at the wounds. It was true, in a sense, though the edge of obfuscation still itched. It occurred to him that having a god for a boyfriend might get complicated.

Em seemed to accept his explanation, however, and ribbed him for a while on his clumsiness. They exchanged some small talk and then, as they crossed the wide-open expanse of the LB foyer, Sigmund asked, "What do you know about Sigyn?"

"As in, the god Loki's wife?" Norse mythology was one of those things Em did. Had done, ever since Sigmund had known her. *Saga* (née *Gangleri*) wasn't based on it for nothing.

Sigmund nodded. Google hadn't brought up much, but Em read all kinds of tediously dry books on the subject, so . . .

Except she just shrugged. "That's about all there is to know," she said. "She's an *ásynja*, a goddess. Her name means something like, 'victorious girlfriend.' Some of the main kennings for Loki are along the lines of, 'Sigyn's burden.' They had two kids. She stuck with Loki through his imprisonment. That's about it, really. She might've been more important at some point, but any other stories about her have been lost."

All of which Sigmund already knew, care of the magic of Wikipedia.

Em took his silence as permission to continue. "There've been a few modern incarnations of her, but not many. Some paintings. A few comics. Mostly she's misguided, long-suffering, and ignored."

"What about Loki?" Sigmund asked. "I mean, he's supposed to be, like, evil or something, right?"

Em rocked her hand back and forth in a *maybe* motion. "The thing you have to understand about Loki," she said, "is that the stories we tell about him today have probably changed a lot over the centuries. Like, you know why Loki got imprisoned?"

"He killed Baldr." Sigmund tried not to think of pale skin and an eye that burnt like the sun.

"Hah!" said Em. "No. Everyone thinks that, but no. Loki didn't kill Baldr, not technically: He tricked Baldr's brother into doing the deed. And it's that poor schlub who got topped for the murder. *Loki's* problem was that he crashed the wake uninvited, then went on a mad insult spree. Questioned everyone's sexual morals and so on. That's why they imprisoned him."

"That seems . . . harsh," Sigmund said, hitting the floor button on the elevator panel.

"Insults were serious business back in those days," Em said. "There's this word. It's like . . . *neath*, except—"

"*Nið.*"

"Right." Em's eyes narrowed for a moment, and Sigmund did his best not to look like a guy who'd learned the term from the source. It must've worked, because Em continued, "Well, it was serious stuff. If someone accused you of it, you were legally obliged to kill them to prove them wrong." She stepped into the elevator as the doors opened, Sigmund following behind in face-twisting incredulity.

"That's ridiculous!"

"That's what it was like," she said. "And remember, Loki insulted *everyone,* even Odin, his blood brother and ruler and grieving father. Getting bound was a light punishment, really, and only because the gods wouldn't kill one of their own. Even a shitty one like Loki."

Sigmund thought of Sigyn and of Loki's sons, cursed and murdered to chain their father. He thought maybe his definition of *light punishment* may have been different from Em's.

When they got to the seventh floor, Sigmund waved to Em as he went left at the lift and she went right. When she'd disappeared around the corner, he turned and almost ran straight into Harrison.

"Sussman! Lain won't be in today"—Harrison had never quite gotten the hang of pronouncing Laufeyjarson—"he's been in a car accident."

"Is he okay?" Sigmund's mouth blurted before his brain managed to catch up to common sense.

Harrison's expression was soft for once. "He says he's banged up and a bit sore, but he'll be okay. No major damage."

Sigmund had a sudden flash to a wind-scoured rooftop and a sound like wet liver and broken branches. "Th-that's good," he said, pushing his glasses up his nose and wiping his palms against his jeans.

"You should call him later," Harrison suggested. "I'm sure he'd like to hear a friendly voice. Kid doesn't have any other family in the country, right?"

"Not that I know of" was about as truthful an answer as Sigmund could manage, and only because Harrison had accidentally thrown the word *other* in there. He tried not to shake.

Harrison either didn't notice or assumed Sigmund was upset over the "car accident" and was pretending not to notice out of kindness.

Sigmund managed to escape back to his desk with a muttered, "I'd better go check the thing and stuff." He was so ready for some kind of quiet freaking out—under the desk, maybe—he almost missed the envelope sitting on his keyboard. It was just a regular, tan-colored internal-mail envelope, his name written underneath a list of crossed-out previous recipients. The handwriting was thick and sharp, as if the writer never quite got used to the idea of curved letterforms.

When Sigmund touched the paper, his fingers left damp marks around the edges.

Inside, was a pass card. Unlike the standard-issue staff cards, this one had no photo and no writing other than the LB logo printed in one corner. A mauve Post-it note was stuck to the back, written in the same angular handwriting as the front of the envelope. It said:

S.

For the top floors. Don't let Nic take this one, k?

—L

The words were hard to read. They kept jerking around weirdly and it took Sigmund a moment to realize it was because his hands were shaking.

(*car accident, for fuck's sake*)

Then he was moving. Up and away from his desk, through the cubicles and past the potted plants, until he was standing between the rows of shiny chrome elevator doors, swiping the card against the reader. He was almost hoping it didn't work.

It did.

It was still a long way up, all dull humming and the dim sounds from the other floors. No one else got on.

When the doors opened, Sigmund hadn't thought of what he was doing there, exactly. Other than striding across to where the LB logo gleamed against polished wood, warding the entry to Hale's office. The doors weren't locked when Sigmund threw them back, and it occurred to him that maybe Hale was up there doing something important only when he'd already stepped into the room.

Hale wasn't, as it turned out, doing anything important and neither was Lain. He was just leaning against Hale's—

(*his*)

—desk, legs crossed, one hand tucked in his armpit and the other watching his cell phone. When Sigmund entered, Lain touched the screen and turned the device around. The room was huge and Sigmund's eyesight was awful, but he was pretty sure it was the stopwatch app.

"Seven minutes?" Lain almost sounded offended, though he was grinning. "What took you so long?"

That was enough to derail Sigmund's purposeful stride but not his anger. "You were waiting for me?"

Lain shrugged, then put his phone in his pocket and leaned back against the desk, arms straight and hands gripping the edge. He looked like something out of a hipster fashion ad, and somehow that just made Sigmund angrier.

"I can't lie," he said, striding into the room just enough to let the doors fall shut. "Not about this, not about you. Not about . . . about *traffic accidents* and swipe cards and . . . and *everything*." He took a step forward, then another, and another, Lain watching, head tilted and expression guarded.

Sigmund continued: "Em asked me about my hands this morning. She's my best friend. It's not just that I can't lie to her, it's that I don't wan . . ." A motion in the corner of his eye caught Sigmund's attention, but it was only Hale's pet—

"Holy *shit*, you kept the snake?"

Sigmund was staring at it, rant forgotten, mouth slack, and something awful clawing at his heart. The last time he'd been up here, a pet snake in an open herpetarium was the foible of an eccentric billionaire. And it still might have been, except it wasn't just *a* snake, Sigmund was sure of it. It was *the* snake, the one that had tormented Loki for an eternity underground.

Jesus, its name was Boots. That couldn't be a coincidence.

Lain was quiet for a moment. Then: "In the end, I realized she was just as much a prisoner as we'd been."

Sigmund wondered whether Team Evil got compassion. It hadn't been in any of the brochures.

Boots regarded him with inscrutable red eyes as Sigmund approached its tank. He'd been too scared to get close before, and even now his heart was pounding, but by the time he was within touching distance he had to admit it wasn't a python. Not that he was a big snake expert or anything, but pythons had that distinctive head shape, right? And this one didn't. It was huge though, and the more Sigmund looked at the patterns on its back, the more they looked like knot work.

It was definitely watching him.

"Hey, Boots," he said, and despite the fact that it was probably about the worst idea in the entire world, he put his hand out to touch it.

Boots felt cool and muscular and scaly, pretty much what Sigmund remembered from the only other time he'd touched a snake, back in primary school when the man had come around to talk at assembly. This snake didn't shy away from Sigmund's hand or try to bite him—which, considering, was probably a good thing—but it did curl its head around to flick a dark, forked tongue against his fingers.

"You can feed her if you want." Lain's voice was very close, and though Sigmund hadn't heard him move, he could feel Lain's body heat over his left shoulder. "Except she eats dead rats and it's kinda gross."

Boots had started coiling her way up Sigmund's arm, and he watched her hypnotic undulations. "Urgh. Pass," he said. "I don't think we're at that stage in our relationship just yet."

Lain gave a chuckle, though it almost sounded sad. "I know you can't lie, Sig," he said.

"Then why—?"

"An excuse. For you. I need to be Hale for a little while. I've been putting some things off"—*to spend time with you,* was the implication, though Lain didn't say so—"that I can't put off any longer. I do actually have a company to run, you know."

Sigmund couldn't see Lain's expression, but his voice sounded more amused than accusatory.

"But when people ask me about the 'accident,' I can't—"

"Omigod, Sig, you'll never guess what happened on the weekend, right?" Lain's voice was abruptly casual, a little bit disbelieving. "I was driving out past the hospital, you know on the road that goes between Torr and Aldershot, and, like, how there's that set of lights there? Well, they went red, right? So I stopped, but the lady behind me? Totally didn't. She must've been going, like, ninety. Knocked my car right out into the middle of the intersection, and I get T-boned by this guy coming the other way. Man. The car is wrecked. I'm okay, though. Bit banged up, so I probably won't be in for a while. Totally sucks."

Sigmund understood. And he understood why Lain had been waiting for him, too. Lain and not Travis. Because now he didn't have to lie, exactly, so long as he prefixed everything with, *Lain told me* . . . He could manage that. Just.

"Okay," he said, closing his eyes. "Okay, I get it." He opened his eyes again, turning slightly. Lain was standing very close, warm and tall, waiting for Sigmund's reaction. He was sweet, Sigmund thought. Not Team Evil at all.

Sigmund shifted, just enough for his shoulder to rest against Lain's chest. In response, a big, warm hand settled against his hip.

This wasn't too hard. World's biggest virgin or not, being with Lain wasn't difficult, even if Sigmund's heart hammered and his palms were sweaty against Boots's scales. And it was nice, standing here, feeling the ends of coppery hair ghost across his cheek and hearing the soft, wet sounds of Lain parting his lips and shifting his tongue. Not for talking, Sigmund knew. He also knew what would happen, should he happen to turn his face upward. Just a fraction.

Instead, Sigmund looked at Boots, who'd made her way across his shoulders and was working on traversing Lain's. Sigmund's right hand was still wrapped around her body, feeling smooth, dry scales, shifting through his palm.

It was hard to stay angry, he thought, wrapped up in a snake. Hard to stay angry with Lain not-quite nuzzling against his scalp, for that matter.

So yeah. It was nice, just standing there, not thinking about anything except warmth and the smell of cinders and the huge and quite possibly deadly reptile that was slowly tying them together. Nothing to really do, nothing to say, and no pressure to say it. Except, oh.

"Dad invited you to dinner."

Lain chuckled, the huff of his breath ruffling through Sigmund's hair. "What did you tell him?"

"Just that we're, y'know. Dating." A horrible thought occurred, and Sigmund pulled back, just enough to meet Lain's big green eyes. "We are, right? I mean, dating? That's what this is?"

Lain made a strange sound, not quite a laugh, not quite a sigh. "Yeah," he said. "Yeah, this is dating."

"Oh. Good." Sigmund felt himself relaxing, enjoying the feel of Lain's broad chest under his fingers. The skin beneath the T-shirt was ridged. More scars, clumped in a long slash across Lain's chest. He had a similar set across his hips, a third across his ankles; Sigmund had seen them when Lain had been the godmonster. Three horizontal bands, like something had once rubbed those places raw, over and over and over. For a thousand years.

So much pain, and Sigmund pulled himself closer to Lain at the thought. It was useless wishing he'd been there to stop it. He probably had been. It hadn't helped.

"Oh, it helped. I can't even begin to tell you how fucking much."

Sigmund's eyes snapped open, body pulled taut and heart skipping. He hadn't said that out loud. He knew he hadn't.

Lain tensed too, and pulled back. Boots hissed her displeasure at his departure.

(*my, what big teeth you have . . .*)

Lain winced and ran a hand back through his hair, sending coppery curls bouncing around his face. "Ah, no. You did not say that out loud." He looked as if the words were being pulled from him by force.

"I didn't say that out loud either!"

"No."

"You can read my mind!" Sigmund took a step backward, almost tripping over a side table while he was at it. Boots hissed at him for the jolt, and he muffled a scream at the closeness of the faceful of fangs. She turned away, and Sigmund got the impression she'd be blushing if she could.

Boots didn't complain when Lain unwound her from Sigmund's shoulders and laid her back on the branch in her tank. She went obediently, dragging herself off to some foliage-covered corner to sulk. Sigmund felt bad for her. She was just a snake, after all.

Lain, on the other hand, was apparently a traitorous mind-reading asshole!

"Sigmund, I—"

"You can, can't you?"

"Yes! No. Sort of, look, it's complicated . . ."

Lain looked miserable. Sigmund decided to be lenient. For now. "Then you'd better explain," he said.

Lain nodded. *We come from the minds of mortals. It's not that we read them, exactly, it's just that we feel your thoughts. Because that's what we are. That's where we start.*

"Holy. Shit." Lain wasn't speaking. At least, his mouth wasn't moving. And it wasn't that the words that appeared in Sigmund's head had a voice, exactly. They were just . . . words in his head. If he didn't know—if he hadn't been expecting it—he might even have thought they were his own.

But there was a presence behind the words. Sigmund could feel it now, pressed up against his mind. A vast and terrifying inferno, the unembodied essence of the thing standing before him. He tried to shy away, to get closer, but his mind was paralyzed, and the realization sent a stab of fear deep inside his gut, cold and atavistic.

The raging maelstrom retreated. "Sorry." Lain was speaking

with his Really Real World words again. "Mortal minds . . . They're all about the meat in your head. Gods, not so much."

Sigmund could *feel* Lain's compassion, like the taste of purple or the color sweet. He closed his eyes and sought the presence again, though it had retreated frustratingly far, the only traces of it lingering in the smell of burning pines and the taste of deep, dark earth.

"That's you, isn't it?" Sigmund said. "That . . . feeling. That's what you really are."

Lain shrugged. "It's part of me. I can't turn it off any more than you can stop hearing or feeling."

He could close his eyes, Sigmund thought. Except it occurred to him that, even then, he was still technically seeing the inside of his eyelids.

"Okay," he said. There was a chair nearby and he fell backward into it. "So you're an ancient, huge, feathered, pyrokinetic, psychic, flying godmonster. Is there anything else I should know, before I go freak out in the toilet for a while?"

Lain appeared to give this question serious consideration. "I can cause earthquakes by screaming," he said finally. "And I'm not too bad at magic."

"'Magic' as distinct from psychic powers and pyrokinesis because of . . . ?"

Lain frowned, gesturing as he struggled for an explanation. "Because of because," he finally said. "Like, magic is all runes and chanting and blood. Setting things on fire is just setting them on fire."

"Great."

Sigmund closed his eyes again and threw his head back, groaning. He wondered if new relationships were always this fraught, or if it was a side effect of his boyfriend being an ancient deity. Dating certainly seemed to be very dramatic, on TV and so forth, so maybe this was all normal. Except maybe normal people relationships were more like, *I once slept with your brother,* and less like, *I'm a personified force of nature.* Maybe the latter being so outlandish made it easier to handle. Maybe.

There was a squeak of leather as Lain sat down in the adjacent seat. When Sigmund looked up, Lain was regarding him, sharp and bright. He was leaning forward, elbows on his knees, hands clasped in front. "All a bit much?" he asked.

Sigmund huffed out a breath and rolled his eyes upward. "I can't decided whether this is all completely cool or totally freaking me out." Hale had a proper ceiling up here, no crappy cheap tiles for him. Sigmund wondered if Lain could hear his observation.

"That's understandable," Lain said. "And yes, I feel your derision of the ceiling." Close enough, and when Sigmund looked back down again, Lain was smiling his scarred smile.

"Can you do it to anyone?" It still freaked him out—a fair bit, in fact—but he was trying to be tolerant. It wasn't Lain's fault he wasn't human. "Like, can you tell me what Em is thinking right now?"

Lain shook his head, not fast enough to disguise the roll of his eyes. "I'm meta, not omniscient," he said. It wasn't quite a lie.

They sat in silence for a while, things heavy and awkward in a way that Sigmund didn't like and wasn't used to. He wished he'd chosen to freak out on the couch across the other side of the room. At least then they could've watched TV. And maybe, like, snuggled or something.

He winced. "You did not just hear that, incidentally," he said, pointing a finger at Lain.

Lain leaned back in his chair, hands held up, placating. "Hear what?" he said, though he was laughing. Then, "It'd be nice though, that thing I didn't hear."

Sigmund was trying not to blush and failing miserably. "Don't you have, like, work to be doing or something?"

"Strictly speaking? Travis should've been in a board meeting about ten minutes ago." He didn't sound too urgent about it.

"What? You should go! Why are you here?" *Babysitting me,* Sigmund didn't say, but he figured Lain heard it, anyway.

"I want to make sure you're okay." That was the truth, and Lain was leaning forward again, watching for Sigmund's response.

It was . . . weird, having someone so unfathomably ancient look at him like that. Have them care about his silly freak-out enough to ignore a whole room of some of the most important people in the country. Weird in a sort of warm, squirmy, pit-of-the-stomach way. Sigmund pushed his glasses up his nose and stared at his sneakers. The holes were still there.

Lain stood, and Sigmund heard him moving around the room, collecting things off his desk. Soon, shoes appeared next to Sigmund's on the carpet, shiny and black and hole free, and when Sigmund looked up it was at Travis, not Lain.

The eyes were the same, Sigmund realized, even if the rest of the details were different. And something about the shape of the face; a strong-but-androgynous Tilda Swinton sort of vibe.

"You can stay here as long as you want," said Travis. It was Lain's voice, too. Though deeper, with a slightly different accent, more Sydney private school. "I'll log the time so Harrison thinks you're fixing something."

Sigmund tried a grin. Travis was still terrifying in that *Time*'s-most-influential-*Forbes*-100 sort of way, even if he technically was the same guy who—

(grew giant wings and burned down half a parking garage)

—had played *Dungeons and Dragons* with them just a few days ago.

"You're kind of bad at computers for the head of the world's biggest technology company," Sigmund said.

This earned him a wink and a gun finger. "I just sell 'em, mate. Don't ask me to use the damn things."

Travis turned to go and, before he'd really had time to think about it, Sigmund stood up. "Wait."

Travis stopped, shooting a look over his shoulder. He didn't have the eyebrow ring like Lain did, but the expression was familiar, all the same.

Sigmund crossed the distance and kissed him. Just quickly, on the lips, hands crushing the sleeves of Travis's outrageous bespoke suit as he did so. When he pulled back, he received another slightly crooked grin.

"Have fun, or whatever it is you do," Sigmund said, pushing his glasses back up his nose and trying not to run his fingers across his mouth. He'd just kissed the third richest man in the world. Technically he'd done it before, but he hadn't known he'd been doing it then. This time it was, like, legit or something.

Travis didn't say anything, just gave Sigmund another promising wink and threw open the doors to his office. Both of them, at once. The flair for the cinematic apparently didn't change between personas, either.

Arin was waiting on the other side. She gave Sigmund only the briefest of glances, before saying, "The board has been waiting for—"

"Fifty years. To die. I know, I know." This response got him the sigh and the rolled eyes of a long-suffering majordomo. Sigmund watched them both disappear into the elevator—Travis blew him one last kiss as the doors closed—and wondered how much Nicole Arin knew about her boss.

Then they were gone, and Sigmund was alone in Hale's office. It was, perhaps, not as exciting as it might have been.

Mostly, it was just a very, very large, very, very executive office. Couch, chairs, desk, fireplace. Enormous set of doors.

There was a large glass case above the doors, something hanging inside like a museum exhibit. It looked suspiciously similar to Lain's tattoo, spread out onto what Sigmund was hoping was tattered cow or sheep leather.

And now that he'd noticed that, there were other things around the room that started looking suspicious, too. Like a painting next to the TV of a woman in a wafty silk gown, gazing in Rubenesque soft focus at something that might have been an artist's impression of a falcon. Yellow apples spilled out around her feet, and Sigmund thought it was a phenomenally ugly painting, particularly considering the sleek, modern decor of the rest of the room.

Also, Sigyn didn't look like that *at all.*

The bowl sitting on the fireplace's mantel was more worrisome. It was heavy and stone—more like the bottom half of a mortar and pestle than an actual bowl—and the inside was polished to a glassy smoothness. It had grooves on the outside that looked suspiciously like handprints, and a huge crack down one side. Sigmund didn't want to touch it, didn't want to . . .

(*the snake, the bowl . . .*)

"Jesus . . ."

He ran to the window and looked down, nose pressed against the glass, heedless of the drop. Seventy stories below, little more than white dots in a field of black and green, Sigmund could see the weird LB statue. The one outside the main doors that everyone thought was modern art. The one that, from the right angle, looked like the LB company logo. Three upright stone slabs, a hole through the middle of each, strange groove worn into the top.

Sigmund felt sick. Staggered backward until his knees hit

the edge of Hale's huge leather chair, then he fell into that, too.

The snake. The bowl. The stones.

(*it's still exile. still a prison. the scenery is a bit better, but . . .*)

One thousand years, or thereabouts. Bound to three stone slabs by the enchanted guts of his own son, snake dripping poison into his eyes until the end of time.

Christ. No wonder Lain's blood ate through concrete.

Sigmund sat there, staring out at the sky, for . . . a while. Trying not to think, to focus on the scenery instead: bright blue sky and the mottled brown of the land below. It was a nice view, nicer than the one from Sigmund's desk, because of course it was, and he had a sudden flash of Travis, sitting up here, fingers steepled and ankle on one knee, surveying his city. Lokabrenna might be a prison, but Travis was its god king.

Sigmund wondered if that made him its queen. Some kind of mistress or concubine at the very least.

He took a photo of the view. It wasn't a great photo, the light catching Sigmund's own reflection in the glass, superimposing a ghostly portrait in the sky, right above the shimmer of the lake and the barren gray rise of Golgotha Hill.

He sent the photo to Wayne, along with the message:

You were right about Lain. All of it. <

The reply took less than a minute:

> All of it? :0

ALL of it, even Option C. I saw horns. And
feathers. <

That earned him a selfie in reply, Wayne's eyes bright and pink and wide and shocked against dark skin.

Sigmund texted:

He has enemies. Serious ones. <

Like with magic powers and stuff. <

I'm kinda in the shit. ‹

› I guess that's expected :(

› What are you going to do?

Sigmund didn't know, and said as much.

› Well if you need anyone beaten up give us a
yell.

› Remember I know kung fu! ♥

Sigmund had to smile at the offer. Wayne was a, well, she was a valkyrie of a woman: nearly as tall as Lain and built out of curves and boobs and muscle. As a girl, men had noticed. So had Wayne's dad, hence the martial arts lessons. Em called it "victim-blaming rape culture"—putting the onus on a kid to avoid sexual attention, not on the adult men who groped and pursued her—but, on the other hand, Wayne also just really enjoyed beating the shit out of people, and her theory was that doing it in an official tournament setting was better than getting charged with assault.

It was a debate Sigmund stayed out of, particularly since that one time he'd begged Wayne for a demonstration and she'd karate-chopped him in the solar plexus. It hadn't even been hard, but it'd knocked the breath out of him for an hour.

No one messed around with Wayne. Sigmund didn't know how she'd fare against a god like Baldr, but he wouldn't be entirely sure who to bet on as the victor, either.

His phone buzzed again, and when he looked down he saw:

› Does em know?

He thought for a moment, then:

No. Don't tell her. She'll flip. ‹

Then silence for a long time, until:

› K. Up to you

Wayne didn't like it. She didn't like keeping secrets, and neither did Sigmund. Not from his friends, his only friends, and especially not from Em, who'd been there forever. Ever since their lonely, awkward school days, playing *Magic: the Gathering* on the grass under the oak trees.

At one point, Sigmund had been convinced he was going to marry Em. Not for any actual reason, just because neither of them had anyone else. That hadn't turned out to be the case. Em had started dating at uni, taking her pick of the gamers and nerds who'd flocked around, trying to impress her with their APM and finesse with head shots. Sigmund hadn't minded, had felt relief even. Em was Em and Sigmund loved her, but . . .

But he had to tell her about Lain. And he would. Soon.

First, he had to figure out how.

THIRTEEN

B Y Tuesday morning, Sigmund still hadn't figured out what to tell Em. Mostly because if he was being honest, he'd been too busy daydreaming about Lain.

They hadn't seen each other again that Monday. Lain sent an apologetic text around lunchtime mentioning he'd been waylaid by VPs wanting to discuss advertising campaigns for the next major PyreOS release. So Sigmund had played video games on the Inferno in Travis's office for a while, until guilt had started to gnaw and he'd dragged himself back downstairs to do work.

It hadn't been easy, and Sigmund was gaining a newfound appreciation for the Basement's nickname when compared to the light and vistas of the CEO's suite. He'd picked at the job queues, but it'd seemed so petty all of a sudden. Who the hell cared about a few lost emails when the gods themselves were sharpening knives and heading for war?

Later, at home, Sigmund's thoughts had been a whirl of fire and feather. Of bright tattoos and dark, scarred skin.

Dappled. Lain's true skin was dappled, little splotches of charcoal markings clustered across his shoulders and down his back, tracing the dips and grooves between the bulges of his muscle.

He had a lot of that. Muscle. Not bulky, but smooth and sleek and strong. Like a dancer or an acrobat or Nightwing and, wow, that train of thought was both incredibly nerdy and really, really gay. Sigmund was okay with it, though. He thought Lain probably would be as well. Lain seemed like the type to be all over the stage, gyrating to LMFAO, reveling in his own allure. Or standing and grinning while hands ran all over tattooed flesh to have a one-on-one examination of the same.

Sigmund had a sudden image of Lain, all wings and horns and tail, dancing around like a bird of paradise. Rippling his muscle and fanning his feathers, rolling blank eyes and grinning his stitched-through grin. All for Sigmund's amusement and . . .

And, after that, Sigmund had to have a little quiet time alone. Then he'd come to the conclusion that he was, maybe, just a little bit of a weirdo.

A lucky weirdo, though. Very, very lucky.

Point being that, by Tuesday, he was itching to see Lain again. Or Travis. Or whoever he felt like being today. Anyone would be okay, really, so long as they grinned that too-sharp grin and looked at Sigmund with those too-bright eyes. It was an intense feeling, that desire. Sort of frightening, and Sigmund wondered if it was normal. He wondered who he could ask.

Today, Lain turned out to be Travis. He was sitting on the floor in the middle of his office, in front of a map of the city—the old-fashioned folding kind that Sigmund had been half convinced no longer existed in the brave new world of GPS and Google. Travis seemed to be inscribing runes onto the paper in his own blood. Sigmund tried not to look.

"Heya," he said, going for nonchalance as he walked into the office.

Travis grinned—

(*score!*)

—as he looked up from . . . whatever it was he was doing. "Morning." He was definitely using his own blood. Sigmund could see it pooling like green-black oil in his left hand. He was also using the fingernail of the index finger on his right hand like a pen.

"Do I want to know what you're doing?" Sigmund was still trying not to look too hard at the blood-scrawled map. Or to smell the faint stink of melting plastic.

"Reading the leys," Travis said, looking back down. "Figure out what Baldr's planning."

"Like divination or something?" Wayne had a bag of cow-bone runes at home. She used to cast them sometimes, until Em had given one too many lectures on how divination was sixty percent confirmation bias, thirty percent hindsight bias, ten percent magical thinking, and one hundred percent bullshit.

Travis winced, shedding doubt on Em's conclusions. "Pretty much exactly not like divination, no," he said. "That's . . . dangerous magic. This is just reading what is, not what will be."

Sigmund wasn't sure he understood the distinction, but decided to let it slide. Travis drew one final line, then flicked the remaining blood onto the map with a muttered . . . something. The map released a puff of dramatic purple-green smoke, then the runes on it started to glow. It almost looked as if they were lifting above the paper, that streets and suburbs themselves were spiraling in front of Sigmund's eyes, turning into a whirling vortex all centered on—

He blinked. By the time his eyes were open again, the effect had faded, and the map was just a map. No blood, no runes, no glowing lines, no inexorable spiral. Travis sighed, settling back on his haunches and tapping his goatee with one long finger.

"No good?"

"I don't know." Travis sounded distracted. "There's something going on, but it's not happening here. It almost feels like . . . bah!" He lashed out a hand and the map burst into sharp white-blue flames. When they cleared, there was nothing left, not even ash. Wiping his hands on his pants, Travis stood. "What's up?"

Sigmund tried not to stare too hard at the decidedly unburnt spot on the floor. "Uh. Dad wants to know if you want to come to dinner tonight? At sevenish?"

"Who wants to come?" Travis had a sly sort of look, and Sigmund felt his face burning at the innuendo, even if that wasn't actually what Travis was asking. Especially because that wasn't actually what he was asking.

"Lain. I haven't told Dad about . . ." Sigmund made a gesture in Travis's direction. "He's such a salaryman, he'd freak out."

That earned him the edge of white fangs and a wiggle of dark eyebrows. "All right, I'll be there."

"Cool," said Sigmund, just as Travis's computer, phone, and tablet all simultaneously made chiming noises. "What . . . ?"

Travis rolled his eyes

(*toward Ásgarðr*)

heavenward. "Con call to our Chinese manufacturer," he said.

"Oh." Because, duh. Travis was like a super-important billionaire CEO, standing there in a three-piece suit and tie probably worth more than Sigmund's salary. And here was

Sigmund, just barging into his office and inviting him to dinner and, Jesus, he was such a dork. "I should go then. Let you . . . do that."

Except, moving was apparently not high on the agenda. Sigmund's feet shuffled a few inches but didn't manage to get any closer to the door. Waiting for . . . something. For—

For Travis to close the few steps between them, to cup his hand on Sigmund's cheek, to exhale against Sigmund's lips as he said, "That wasn't a hint, you know. I don't want you to go, either."

"Oh." The fabric of Travis's suit was soft and warm under Sigmund's fingers. "Good." When his mouth parted, one long finger stroked his bottom lip.

"Yeah," said Travis, eyes bright enough to glow. "Good."

Like this, Travis didn't feel much different from Lain. Same too-warm, solid body, same loam-and-charcoal smell, same huge, vaguely terrifying presence just behind Sigmund's eyelids. He was still an amazing kisser, too. Hot hands cupping Sigmund's face, holding him still while Travis's mouth and tongue went to work in ways they hadn't the last few times they'd done this.

Travis had a beard. That was new. Sort of . . . ticklish.

"Hnngh!" said Sigmund. One of his own hands had slipped underneath Travis's jacket, the other was threading through long, soft, dark hair.

When Travis pulled back, it was with one last sharp-toothed bite. Not hard enough to hurt, just hard enough to send strange little cinders burning somewhere beneath Sigmund's heart.

He felt . . . light. Blown apart and wrecked. But not nearly as wrecked as Travis looked, eyes closed and tongue still dancing over his bottom lip, forehead pressed to Sigmund's.

"Oh, the things I'd do to you." Travis's words were barely

audible, just gusts of breath ghosting across Sigmund's skin. "And I'm trying to be *so good* . . ."

"Why?" It was much easier to ask Travis's tie than his face. Cowardly, maybe, and Sigmund could feel the not-quite-fear churning in his gut.

Travis gave a dark sort of chuckle. "I don't really know." He sounded a bit perplexed himself. "The fun of it, perhaps. Maybe I'm worried I'll screw it up if it's too easy."

"I have no idea what I'm doing." It was true. Sigmund's last girlfriend had been a fling in high school that had lasted all of a month. They'd spent a couple of bleary afternoons locked in his room, fumbling and kissing, but nothing beyond that. He'd certainly never . . . *done the ellipsis* with anyone. Certainly not another man and *really* certainly not a god. He didn't know if he was ready for that. He didn't know if anyone could be ready.

He was pretty keen on finding out.

"I know," said Travis. Whether in response to Sigmund's words or his thoughts, Sigmund wasn't sure. "But it isn't rock-et surgery. Just a dance."

"I'm a terrible dancer."

Lips caressed Sigmund's again, just briefly, just enough for Sigmund to miss them when they left. "Keep a pocketful of dollars and jump in time to the scrolling arrows," Travis said. "As long as you're having fun, you're doing it right."

"And you?"

Travis pulled closer, hand sliding down Sigmund's back, *below* his back, onto the soft curve of his ass. "Oh," Travis said, all wicked grin. "I'm *always* having fun." He winked.

It wasn't the truth, not quite. But it was true enough here, now, in this moment, and it would do.

The third kiss was easier. Not as many teeth as the first, not as chaste as the second. Just a kiss, lips and tongues and

maybe a few teeth, too.
    Only a few. Not enough to bleed.

FOURTEEN

The con call is long and difficult and not at all like the feel of Sigmund's lips or the taste of his self-conscious lust, meaning that my mind's not so much on the work as it is on him. On the coarse feel of his hair and sharp scent of his soap, on the softness of his flesh and the hesitance of his embrace.

He's not a great kisser. Unpracticed. But that can be fixed, with time, and I'd be lying if I said the thought of plucking open his awkward virginity wasn't something I was looking forward to, the very best kind of *déjà vu*.

By modern standards, Sigyn had been young when we'd married. Young and mortal, caught in the firestorm of the most capricious of the gods. But she'd devoured the apple and taken to her place in Ásgarðr with a ferocity unmatched across the heavens, and the whole Nine Realms had been the rubes and patsies for our mayhem.

Funny how none of those stories made it down the ages. Wicked Loki and loyal Sigyn, victorious and terrible, filled with such rage and compassion as to unmake the Wyrd itself.

Sigmund isn't Sigyn, but he could've been, in a different time and different skin. Now his seed cracks open in the wake of a new inferno, and I revel in the opportunity to watch his leaves unfurl and his branches reach up to grasp the heavens. A new consort for a new era, a new god for a new land. And a new me, standing by his side.

It will be glorious.

So will sucking Sigmund until he screams, which is another thing I'm looking forward to doing at some point in the future. On top of Travis's desk, perhaps, looking out over the city—our city—driving Sigmund's ecstasy down into the very bones of Pandemonium. Imprinting it into concrete and steel and glass.

I make a note on my To-Do list, scheduling it somewhere down the line. Not today, though. We're not quite at the mind-blowing-city-altering sex phase of our relationship just yet. More like the awkward-hand-holding lunch-date phase, and so I arrange to meet Sigmund in the bookstore in the mall at one o'clock for exactly that. There's a pho place just downstairs that I think he'd like, or, failing that, we can have our pick of one of the million other cafés that have sprung up along Torr Row like hipster cancer. It's lunchtime, but reservations are things that happen to other people.

When I get there, the mall is covered in yellow tape and security barricades, and it takes me a moment to realize all the blocked-off entrances lead down to the parking garage. The one I set on fire the other week. Oops.

People don't seem too perturbed, though. Whatever spin story the mall's owners put out for the fire evidently didn't contain the word *terrorism*, and thus does commerce march blithely on.

The bookstore, an Angus & Robertson, is wedged at the end of one of Torr Mall's newer wings, in between a Pyre

Computers store and a movie theater. The shop's not small—two floors sprawling back into the building—and I can feel Sigmund upstairs, trying to calm his nerves by browsing the hyperbolic covers of the sci-fi/fantasy section. I lope my way past the front of the store, past the magazines and the stationery, and up to the escalators at the back.

I'm halfway between floors when the shift happens.

I don't feel it, at first, though I certainly feel the way the escalators shudder to a halt and the overhead lights flicker off.

"What the . . . ?"

In the space between breaths, the store is plunged into blackness. And I'm not talking like, oh-the-lights-are-off blackness. I'm talking really, serious, cannot-see-a-fucking-thing blackness. And, y'know, technically I've been blind since the cave—I don't use my eyes to see, that is, all the working parts having long since burnt away—but this blackness gets even me. A total void of senses for a second, maybe less, and when the world reboots . . .

Oh. Oh, this is bad. This is what the map meant this morning. Fuck.

We've been hit by a Helbleed.

Bleeds aren't all that uncommon. There are two around Pandemonium alone, which is the reason I moved here in the first place. It's the rubber sheet analogy again: A Bleed is when that sheet gets stretched a bit *too* thin, and tiny holes start appearing. Tiny holes that let parts of the Outyards, the Útgarðar, bleed through into Mannheim.

And like I said, Pandemonium has two. One at Woolridge Reserve, leading to Jötunheimr, and a second on Golgotha Hill, leading to Niflhel.

When the lights come back—sickly, pale, and flickering—it becomes apparent that the latter is my current problem.

The mall is dead silent. Literally. And that's worrying, because malls are never silent. But mortals walk right over the top of Bleeds, and the things that are native to Niflhel don't, as a general rule, make a lot of noise.

At first.

And all this would be fine—annoying, but fine—if it weren't for the fact that I'm not currently the only Wyrdborn thing in the store.

I'm vaulting up the broken escalators before I've even finished the narration. The metal ridges have turned sharp and rusted, and they rip through Lain's thin-soled hipster shoes like talons. That's okay, though, because my wards are burning and it's becoming very difficult to hold on to Lain's human form.

So I don't. I let it go, feeling the horns erupt from my skull and the claws from the tips of my fingers. By the time I've hit the top of the escalators, my legs have changed, and my only concessions to modesty are my own feathers and a single leather wrist-cuff that, for some reason, survived the transformation.

The top floor is deeper into the Bleed, and the nihilism of the void carpets everything in ash and mold. Books are stacked haphazardly all over the floor, and when my tail brushes against a pile, it disintegrates into pulp and scurrying things it's probably best to think of as cockroaches.

There's something here. I can hear it, shuffling and gurgling, and I leap up onto the tops of the tall shelves in the reference section to get a better view.

Perched like a garish, fiery (and book-loving) gargoyle, I can see Sigmund, nose deep in a paperback and oblivious to the change in the world around him. That doesn't make the *draugr* in the next row over any less threatening.

I vault across the tops of the shelves and drop down in the space between Naomi Novik and Terry Pratchett. Sigmund stifles a scream when he sees me, then another when he sees the Bleed, then a third when he sees the shambling, unformed mass behind me.

"Lain, behin—"

But I've already turned, and by the time he's finished his sentence my claw is sticking through the back of the *draugr*'s skull. Or what probably used to be a skull, at some point.

The *draugr*—dead now twice over—gives a gurgling moan and falls to the floor. Then begins oozing into an amorphous pile on the carpet. I feel Sigmund's fingers close around my biceps, and he chokes back bile as he peers around my side. "Oh . . . oh, *Jesus*." He covers his mouth with his free hand, eyes closed as he wills himself not to hurl.

Not that it would make much of a difference to the decor, and what's a little upchuck on the feathers when I've already got mushed *draugr* brain up to my elbow. I set fire to my filth-covered arm, the flames green and putrid as they burn the gunk from my skin. It's unpleasant, but over quickly, and when it clears I'm clean once more.

Handy.

Sigmund is pressed up against me, looking around the ruins of the bookstore, oozing his own oil slick of terror. "Wh-what the hell was that?" he stammers. "What the h-hell happened to the sh-shop?" His heart and breath race, his emotions an unpleasant metallic tang in the back of my throat.

"That," I say, "was a *draugr*."

He knows the word, sort of. "A z-zombie?"

I shrug, shifting my arms to pull Sigmund closer. His comparison is not completely inaccurate. *Draugar* are memories who've lost themselves. Who haven't managed to form enough of an identity to wind up as *einherjar* or one of the denizens of Helheimr. They're shambling piles of neuroses and fears, hatreds and obsessions. The vermin scurrying between the roots of the Tree.

I sum this up for Sigmund, more or less, then say, "We're stuck in a Helbleed. A thin spot between Miðgarðr and Niflhel."

"The mall was full of people!"

"Who are fine." Probably. "Bleeds are only dangerous to things touched by the Wyrd. Or born in it."

Sigmund blinks behind his glasses, looking around the tattered shelves, atavistic revulsion sending a tremble through his limbs.

"Try not to read the titles of the books," I suggest, and he shudders. "It looks worse than it really is."

"Except for the horrible monsters trying to kill me!"

"It probably wasn't trying to kill you, exactly. *Draugar* are more like rats than tigers." Honestly, it's hard to say what your average *draugr* wants, other than to follow some loathsome instinct to seek out the living. When they find one, usually all they do is stand around and moan. Problem is, like rats, *draugar* carry disease. Not physical diseases, but a kind of seeping malaise of the soul. And they do bite. Sometimes.

"J-Jesus," Sigmund says. It occurs to me, as I feel him force stillness back into his breath, that Sigmund is mortal, and for a second I see flashes behind my milky eyes. Of teeth and blades and spikes and chains. Of soft dark flesh, pulped and split beneath the onslaught.

The stitches pull as my lips curl back, exposing a bright and jagged maw to any who would *dare*.

"We need to get out of here," I say, snarl lurking beneath the words. I scan around the shop lest any other *draugar* wander near. If they do, we'll see just how well they burn.

"Y-yes, please."

"C'mon, we need to find a path." I press my hand against the small of Sigmund's back, urging him forward.

"Oh." He stumbles when he tries to move, legs stiff and

shaking. His disappointment is a cloying yellow fog, thick and reeking in the unreality of the Outyards. He was hoping I'd just be able to magic us out of here at will.

I start walking toward the shop entrance. Sigmund follows me, hand sliding down to grasp my own.

"So," he says, "d-does this sort of thing h-happen to you often?" The humor is thin, but, in this place, even thin armor is better than going naked.

"Surprisingly no," I say. I avoid the Bleeds. Avoid the eyes that might be watching, away from the safety of my self-made prison. "It's been pretty dull since I got out." And for the thousand-odd years before that, too. Even the screaming agony became routine, eventually.

"This . . . this is Baldr, then?"

"Bingo." Bleeds are natural, and Sigmund's been in one before, even if he didn't realize at the time. We didn't get lost in the forest the other week because the map was wrong; it just wasn't the map of where we were.

The Helbleed touches Pandemonium on Golgotha Hill, the huge, barren monstrosity everyone in town assumes is a slag heap left over from the town's mining days. They're not wrong, but that's not the reason nothing grows up in the shale, not the reason the suburb around it is the poster child for urban decay. Golgotha Hill is the natural Bleed. Its single feature, a lone, dead ash tree, is an extension of the roots of the world tree, Yggdrasill.

But that Bleed doesn't extend much farther than the Hill itself, and it's not this deep or this unstable.

This, what we're in right now? This is a Wound, a forced Bleed, and it's spread out over the entire city in the space of roughly half a day. That's not good. There's only one thing I can think of that would cause such a chronic breakdown of the boundaries between realms, and the next time I see Baldr?

He's a dead man. Again.

When we get to the broken escalators, I stop. "I'll need to carry you down," I tell Sigmund. My feet still hurt from running up in the first place.

Sigmund doesn't protest, but makes a squeaking noise as I pick him up in a bridal carry.

"This is not very manly," he says, pushing his glasses up his nose and trying on a laugh.

"Sigmund," I say, "you are looking at the queen of unmanly. Believe me, this doesn't even register." The word is *ergi*, and it's a kind of *Níð*. A kind I specialized in.

Sigmund worries about his own masculinity, or supposed lack thereof. About his soft belly and lack of interest in manly things, like cars and protein shakes. About his friends, the feminist and the misandrist, who see him as One of the Girls.

About the fact that he used to be a goddess.

Goddess or not, I don't want Sigmund's feet ripped to shreds on the rusted stairs, and I'm not enthused about it happening to mine, either. So I run us down the handrails in the middle. The rubber has liquefied, and it oozes between my toes in thick and sticky strands.

I put Sigmund down when we reach the bottom, and he goes back to lacing his fingers through my claws. He stands close against my side, eyes darting from shadow to shadow, afraid of every monster in this place but one.

The *draugar* don't share Sigmund's comfort. A few more shamble around the bookstore's bottom floor, but they're wary of me and don't approach. Sig's second hand comes up to grasp my arm as we walk, his white-knuckled grip tearing small feathers from the skin. When I touch him, he startles, turning to look at me with white-ringed eyes as I say, "Relax. I'm the scariest thing here. They won't get closer."

He swallows. "It's just . . . They're so . . ." But his fingers loosen, just a little.

"I know," I say. Sigmund hates himself for being cowardly, so I add, "You know Pandemonium used to be called Eden, back in the twenties?"

"Y-yeah," he says. "They changed the name after some miners went nuts and k-killed most of the rest of the town."

Killed is certainly the family-viewing explanation. "Right," I say. "Because those guys? Dug into the Helbleed. Ten minutes in this place and they were ready to slaughter the entire town. You're doing fine."

Sigmund gives a morbid chuckle, more an exhalation than a laugh. "Thanks," he says. "But I've got you. I bet those miners didn't have a god to hide behind." He thinks for a moment, then, "Well, maybe in an allegoric . . . Ah, bugger."

This last because the entrance to the store is now visible through the haze. The extremely *closed* entrance to the store.

We walk closer, and I study the doors. They're stock-standard mall roller doors, except with more rust and razor wire. I give one an experimental kick. The metal screams.

"Um!" Sigmund utters what is possibly the most startled polite interjection ever. "I don't think it liked that."

"There should be some kind of staff entrance around here somewhere." I peer around, trying not to look at the fleshy, writhing sacks chained behind the counter; the sloughed-off anxiety and hopelessness of a thousand different clerks.

"Oh!" says Sigmund. "This way." He tugs me back into the shelves. "I worked here once in high school for, like, two minutes."

"Not a fan, then?"

"Let's just say there's a reason I have a degree and a desk job, and it's not because I was dying to follow in Dad's footsteps."

We have to avoid the YA section due to impenetrable emotional trauma, but we route back via audiobooks and eventually I catch sight of Sigmund's exit. It, too, is blocked, but this time with a pallid membrane that splits easily beneath my claws.

Behind the now-open door lurks not some horrific back room from Hel, but rather the actual Really Real World store, as if we were looking out rather than in.

"That's promising?" Sigmund suggests.

"Yes," I say, ushering him forward. "After you." No way am I leaving Sigmund alone in this place, even if only for a moment. In Niflhel, the line between death and isolation is really very thin.

Heart pounding but trying to appear brave, he steps through the doorway. I follow him. On the other side we do, indeed, find ourselves back in the Really Real World. People bustle all around us, more intent on procuring books and related products than paying attention to two Gen-Y hipsters who may as well be off-duty staff.

"There you go." I punch Sigmund in the shoulder, light and playful. "You survived your first Helbleed." I'm not sure if it's more my relief or his. Fucking Baldr.

Sigmund blinks, expecting to see his giant feathered god-monster, and is a bit thrown when I turn out to be just Lain again. "It's the 'first' part of that sentence that worries me," he says as we start making our way to the (open, unobstructed) exit. "So what do we do now?"

"Now, we have that lunch."

Sigmund gives me an incredulous look. "Don't you, like, have to do something about the thingie?" He means the Wound.

"I am doing something," I say. "I'm grieving. Right now, that's all I can do." Fixing a Wound this large is not trivial, and I don't have the power to just snap my fingers and do it. At the moment I'm not even sure *how* to do it. What I am sure of, however, is the shake Sigmund can't quite force from his fingers, or the way he not quite jumps at every noise. Taking care of my city—taking care of my enemies—is one thing.

Taking care of my lover is something else again.

—

We end up going for pho, as planned. Sigmund is anxious and jumpy the whole time, but I manage to distract him by flirting with the waitress. She gives me her number. I give her a tip, left beneath an upside-down glass still filled with water, and her outraged shriek echoes all the way across Torr Row.

"That was cruel," Sigmund says, but he's laughing.

"No," I say, "flirting with me when I'm obviously there with you is cruel."

"Maybe she didn't realize that?" That's the thing about Sigmund: He's good-hearted. Sigyn was too, at first. Look where it got her.

We're crossing Diamond Square on our way back to LB when we hear a voice behind us call, "Sigmund!"

It's Wayne Murphy, an explosion of pink and black, of leather and lace, among the beige of hipsters and office drones. Murphy's sitting on one of the square's metal bean-bag sculptures, eating sushi out of a plastic *bento* and waving at us with her chopsticks.

Sigmund wanders over to say hi, I follow behind. It's stinking hot and sweat-drenchingly humid, dark clouds rolling overhead and the square filled with people determined to brave lunch outside before the storm breaks.

Murphy gives us a huge grin when we walk up, bright against dark skin and darker lipstick. "Hey, dooder," she says to Sigmund. "Who let you out of the office?"

"Him," says Sigmund, pointing over his shoulder at me. "Then we got sucked into a hell dimension and nearly died."

I've apparently missed a conversation, because Murphy's

reaction to this is to turn to me and say, "You'd better be keeping him safe, you hear me?" It's definitely a threat, accompanied by the tugging sense of *déjà vu*.

" 'Nearly died' is a decided overstatement."

Murphy's suspicion tastes like rotten feathers as she sizes me up against what she thinks she knows of who I am.

"I can kind of see it," she tells Sigmund. "I mean, you'd never guess, but . . . I thought he'd be shorter."

"I'm a giant!" I snap. "We're not called giants because we're short!" This is not entirely true. I used to be short, back in Ásgarðr. It's an affectation I feel under no obligation to continue in the modern world.

The pair make small talk in the space around me. Something about Ivanovich, something about *DnD*, something about Murphy's mum, something about this thing Sigmund totally saw on the Internet the other day and ohmigawd it was just the funniest thing ever.

I'm not really there. Instead, I'm feeling out over the city—between the pavement and the pipes, across the minds of students and of salarymen—looking for the Bleed. It's all over the place, scattered like blood drops, an oozing red stain of wartime propaganda. Golgotha is bad, of course—much deeper than usual, nearly dangerous to mortals—but there are other patches, too, in places that shouldn't Bleed. Whitebread middle-class suburbia, like Aldershot and North Eden, plus the one that's currently crawling through Torr Mall.

That's not good.

Like I said, Bleeds usually occupy a space beneath the one mortals live in. They're a part of Miðgarðr, not Mannheimr. But they're called "Bleeds" for a reason, and humans can feel them, even if they don't know what it is they're feeling. A low-grade miasma of ennui and apathy might not make much of an impact on the hipsters and store clerks of the local Angus

& Robertson, but the size of the Bleed exacerbates its effects. And to have one growing so close to Lokabrenna . . .

"Lain?"

"Huh?" I snap back to Diamond Square in a cacophony of the sounds and stink of the lunchtime rush. I blink. My tattoo itches.

Sigmund radiates curious concern, cool and smooth and green. "You all right? You looked kinda zoned out."

It occurs to me that Murphy has gone. I wonder how long I've been staring off into space.

"Yeah, sorry," I say. "I was miles away."

"Oh, well . . . We should probably get back." Sigmund doesn't sound happy about the idea, and I squeeze his hand.

"Hey, I got the new *Savage Turbine* alpha up in my office. Reckon it needs some play testing if you're up for it. I haven't had the time, and the dev team is getting antsy."

That does the trick. "*Turbine 3?*" Sigmund asks, a new gleam of hope and wonder scratching through the tarnish of the Bleed. "That's not due out for like six months."

I grin, deciding to take that as a yes. The perks of being a CEO: distracting your boyfriend with prerelease AAA megatitles. It's good to be me.

The walk back to LB is amiable, if humid. By the time we're on campus, it's started to rain, and I dash up the stairs and into the foyer, watching Sigmund follow me at his own pace.

"I can practically see your tail flicking from here," he says when he catches up. His glasses are covered in water drops and I've got no idea how he's seeing through all of that.

"Hey, water's not my fucking thing, okay?" I say as we cross the foyer and head toward the elevators.

"Evidently not." Sigmund laughs, but it's fraying.

His affected calm lasts all the way back into the office. Nic ambushes me outside with a folio of papers, but I give her a meaningful look of *Not now*, as I usher Sigmund through the doors. Instead, I sit him down on the couch, hand him a controller for the Inferno, then turn to boot it and the TV up. By the time I've looked back, Sigmund is shaking, staring down at the controller in his hand as if he's never seen one before. When he blinks, tears hit the plastic.

I take the controller from his fingers and put it back on the coffee table. Then I pull him against my chest, surrounding him in the feeling of warmth and safety and home.

He doesn't say anything. I know he wants to. This close, I can feel his internal narration seethe across the surface of his mind, heavy-handed with themes of shame and self-loathing. He hates that he's not better at this, that he's not braver, stronger. Hates that this is the second time now I've seen him cry, because even though he pretends to reject them, the rules for Be a Man and Stop Crying You Pussy are so ingrained that they're practically bursting him at the seams.

So I say, "You're doing fine, Sig. Helbleeds are rough. I don't like them either." I try not to think of the glistening masses of unformed resentment, slumped behind the counter in the Bleedside Angus & Robertson.

Sigmund's voice is weak and thready, coming from somewhere underneath the edge of my jacket. "You-you're not . . . you're not—"

"I know," I say, "but I've have a long time to get used to it. A *really* long time. And getting used to something like that? Isn't necessarily that great a thing, you know? I've certainly done my share of fetal crying on the floor." Fuck, have I ever. Sigyn was there to get me through a lot of it, all soft hands and clean bandages. The least I can do is return the favor.

Sigmund nods. Still shaky, but his fingers unwind from my T-shirt, just a fraction. "Is i-it all like that? A-all so . . . so . . . ?"

"No," I say. "Just Niflhel. I mean, it's not called the misty hell because it's full of campfires and kumbaya, you know? It's not even the first Bleed you've been to. Remember the other week when we got lost at Woolridge? That's because you wandered into the Járnviðr Bleed. You were about a day's hike away from the edge of Jötunheimr. That wasn't so bad, right? You didn't even notice." I decide not to mention the giant spiders.

Sigmund nods, putting two and two together to come up with the realization that it really wasn't his map-reading skills that got us lost.

"Most of the realms are more like Járnvidr," I say, just filling the space up with words. "There's Jötunheimr, where I'm from. No human has ever been there"—well, voluntarily, and they don't stay human for long—"but it's a massive city, cut out of the top of a mountain rising from the center of the Járnvidr. It's all glistening spires and Better Living Through Magic, and the *drekar*—the dragons—circle endlessly overhead." Sigmund starts imagining it, and I touch up his mental image a little. It's been nearly an eternity since I've been back there, but I still remember it. You don't forget a place like that.

"Then there's Niflheimr and Múspellsheimr, the primordial realms of ice and fire, void and chaos. Where they meet, in Ginnungagap, the world is formed. Grown upon a great ash tree, the Yggdrasill, with three mighty roots and branches big enough to hold the sky. Beneath one root lies Mímisbrunnr, a well, where one can drink and learn great wisdom . . . for a great price. And there are rivers, Sig. Greater than you can imagine. And all spring from the same source, Hvergelmir, which bubbles beneath . . ." And so on, and so forth.

I spend the next half hour or so filling in the cosmology. Sigmund listens, rapt, for as long as he can, but eventually the day catches up with him and he falls asleep in my arms.

FIFTEEN

SIGMUND SPENDS MOST of the afternoon asleep in my office, his dreams dark and restless.

He wakes up a little after five, tousled and confused, and blinks at his surroundings for a few moments before his brain catches up to where he is. Stuttering and apologetic, he's more interesting than emails and spreadsheets, and so I join him on the couch, pressing him back against the leather and devouring his awkwardness with all the want of a nerd at Comic-Con.

Much better than spreadsheets, particularly when my hands slip underneath Sigmund's too-worn, once-black T-shirt, caressing soft, dark skin. Despite the pounding of his blood he feels cool beneath my hands and mouth. Mortals always do.

Outside, the city Bleeds.

—

We get back to Sigmund's place a fraction after six.

"Hey, Dad, we're here!" Sigmund calls from the entryway.

He kicks his shoes off and throws his keys into a tray next to the front door. I do the same. With the shoes, not the keys.

"Hey, boys." David appears at the other end of the hall. He's wearing a humorous novelty apron that looks like someone's well-intentioned Father's Day gift, and is vaguely familiar in the way of all of LB's middle-management. He doesn't look much like Sigmund, who bears greater resemblance to the smiling woman in the photo near the door.

We meet David halfway down the hall, and he holds out his hand. "You must be Lain," he says. "We weren't properly introduced the other day"—the teeniest, tiniest glance at Sigmund as he says this—"I'm David Sussman, Sigmund's father."

I give David my best CEO handshake. "Nice to meet you," I say, remembering that I'm supposed to be in my early twenties and not, in fact, the man's employer. "Thanks for inviting me over."

David nods and looks serious. "It's the least I can do. Sigmund tells me you saved his life." He means during the camping trip. I decide not to mention the other occasions.

"So Sig tells it," I say. "But I saw him slip, and . . ." I shrug, letting David fill in the gaps with whatever he needs to believe the tale. "I couldn't let him fall."

"Well, thank you for it," David says. Then he smiles, and turns to Sigmund. "Dinner will be about twenty minutes. Why don't you take Lain upstairs for a while? I'll call you when it's done."

"Okay, Dad."

David disappears back into the kitchen, and Sigmund tilts his head toward the stairs. "Best to keep out of Dad's way when he's cooking." Sigmund is nervous, but now it's just totally normal, meet-the-parents nerves rather than oh-shit-we're-going-to-die visceral horror nerves.

"He likes me," I assure him as we walk up the stairs. "He's not sure about the nose ring, though."

"But the one in your eyebrow is fine?"

"I don't think he noticed that one."

Sigmund takes the last few steps in a bound, then stops as soon as he gets to the landing. "Man," he says, turning around to look at me. "I just remembered I have, like, the most embarrassing room in the entire universe." He pushes his glasses up his nose forcing himself to laugh.

"I'm pretty sure I'm not going to think less of you because you have posters of dragons on your walls," I say.

Sigmund's eyes go round. "How did you . . . Never mind, I don't care." Apparently he's forgotten the somewhat awkward night after our *DnD* date. I decide not to remind him, and he looks down to where he's been picking at the hem of his jumper. "It's just, I'm twenty-two, you know? It's not like I left home at sixteen and Dad kept my room preserved as it was."

"Sigmund," I say, stepping closer. Into his personal space, fingers twining in his belt loops. "This is me conveying to you how much I really, really don't care. I know you're a huge dork. It's cool, really."

"Gee, thanks." He gives me half a grin, then a whole kiss, hands threading through my hair as we press against the unfashionably '90s maroon wall. "How does it work?" he says when he pulls back.

"Huh?"

He's staring at my hair, running one hand through loose curls and the other over the bridge of my nose.

"Your hair. It's different from"—he whispers the next two words, eyes flicking downstairs—"from Travis's. And he doesn't have freckles. How does it work?"

The shape-shifting, right. "Magic," I say, because it is. More or less.

"Can you be anyone?"

"Who do you want me to be?"

"You," he says, voice fast. "I didn't mean— I'm just curious, is all."

"Mm." I'm curious too, for different things. I satisfy myself by running nipped kisses up Sigmund's neck as I say, "I suppose so. If I have to be." Sigmund has a sensitive spot just beneath his jawline. I rub at it with my tongue, gaining a sigh and a shudder for my efforts.

When he closes his eyes, it's claws and horns and feathers that dance behind his lids.

"God . . ." he breathes. Most appropriately in my opinion, so:

"Yes?"

He gasps laughter and tells me I'm awful, then he's pushing me away. Not far, just enough to grab my hand and drag me down the short hallway to a door. It has a poster tacked to the outside. It's a picture of a dragon.

He turns to make a joke about the poster, but I'm not hungry for self-depreciation anymore. I want lust, and heat, and desire. A roaring inferno looking for new wood to burn and burn I will, until all that's left is coal and ash.

Sigmund fumbles for the door handle as we kiss, his mind swirling with every filthy thing we could be doing and all the time we don't have in which to do them.

The door opens.

I freeze.

Ultimately, it's not the video game posters or the *Star Wars* curtains or the entire wall of fantasy paperbacks that get me. It's the bed.

It has ribs protruding through the mattress.

"Um . . ." Sigmund has turned as well, spurred on by my sudden change in mood. When he catches sight of his bedroom, he becomes a slicing whirl of ice and fear in my arms.

In the middle of the bones is a box. Just a brown, slightly battered cardboard box, except the bottom of it is stained a horrid reddish purple.

I know what's in that box. I haven't opened it, and I still know.

He's still here, in the house. I can feel the edge of him, moving downstairs, and I don't know whether he meant me to feel it or if he's just careless, thinking that the box will keep me distracted. Except I'm not distracted, far from it. I'm furious.

I'm also out the door and down the stairs before Sigmund can call my name. My tattoos burn but I tear through them, not thinking of David or of dinner or of being good and making nice. Right now I'm thinking of blood and fire and *that fucker killed my fucking daughter* and I am going to *rip his fucking head off, too.*

Baldr is in the kitchen. Remember that thing about the *nið* and assuming Baldr wouldn't go after David? Well, turns out I was wrong. Fortunately, I'm just-in-time wrong, and the tip of Baldr's (new) spear only grazes David's throat as I throw myself against the homicidal bastard.

We crash through the sliding doors and into the dining room table, which cracks a bit but doesn't break.

I'm saying something like, "Fucking die you fucking motherfucker!" while I try and slam Baldr's head through the wood. I can hear two voices scream behind me, but I'm not interested in that.

I'm interested in *pain.*

In between beatings, Baldr lets out a broken gurgle and starts laughing. The sound is wet and wheezing—his nose is currently smashed across his face—but the incongruity of it throws me. Just a bit.

This pause, as it turns out, is enough for Baldr to throw me in turn, and he does. Back through the smashed doors and skidding along the kitchen floor on my tail, Sigmund and David lunging sideways out of my path.

When the momentum goes, I roll up into a crouch. Baldr is stalking toward me, not in any hurry, the point of his spear digging a long groove in the Sussmans' hardwood floors.

"How does it feel, boy?" he says in Godstongue. "To watch your family suffer? To die?"

My stitches pull as my teeth show, my next words a rough and tangled snarl. "Fuck you. I didn't kill your father. He killed us. He doomed us all, chasing power, chasing prophecies." Only the proud and foolish mess with the Wyrd. The Wyrd messes back.

And, the thing is, Baldr surprises me by saying: "I know." He sneers, coming to a stop a few feet away. "I speak of others. My children."

His what? I have no idea what the hell he's talking about: Baldr has one son but the guy's fine, far as I know.

I don't get to say as much, instead having to roll sideways to avoid another downward thrust of his spear. It looks like talking time is over. So we fight.

It's easier this time. Much easier. My claws and my skin and my strength feel like my own, so I use them, throwing myself at Baldr with bloodlust and with violence. I can tell he feels it. His eyes go wide and he stumbles, retreating into the shattered dining room, trying to retake the offensive, looking for an opening.

I don't give him one, all teeth and fire and fury, and the world burns in my rage. Rage at this *child*, this *boy*, who would dare come into the realm I've built, this sanctuary I've made, and defile my home and murder my family.

I leap, and Baldr calls down the sun, an inferno of light that blinds even the Wyrdsight. I howl but, midair, there's little I can do and, when I land, it's not Baldr's flesh beneath my claws but the leather and stuffing of the Sussmans' couch. A moment later, pain lances my gut as Baldr's spear pierces through, pinning me to the furniture. Something in my spine snaps as a knee drives into the small of my back, Baldr's weight pressing down as he leans over me and says, "You spoiled, coal-biting brat! I will relish your destruction, taking you apart piece by piece for every life you've ruined."

His breath ruffles my feathers, his face very close, and the crunch is satisfying when I whip my skull backward and my occipital bone makes friends with his broken nose. He grunts, stumbling back, and I feel the metal of the spear slide out of my flesh. I fall to the carpet, which is about as much as I can manage, and am busy trying to get my legs to work when a heavy boot makes itself acquainted with my injured stomach.

When I cough, I cough up blood, the purple-green globs hissing as they burn holes into the carpet.

"*Tssch,*" I hear. "Even your insides are filth."

Then fingers are winding through the feathers on my head, wrenching me upright, Baldr's free hand hovering near the wound in my gut with a heat even I can feel.

Baldr's not a sun god. Not exactly. But the associations—death and rebirth, the cycle of days and seasons—is close enough from him to draw it down, and I bite back a howl as agony lances through my skin.

I lash out the only way I can think of, by setting my entire self ablaze. I feel Baldr's hand free itself from my hair, and I roll forward, across the carpet, desperate for distance. I end up behind the recliner, and a quick glance down at my abdomen reveals not a charred and bleeding mess but clean unblemished skin.

Baldr *healed* me.

The blood. It has to be the blood. He can't get it on him, and the wound was dangerous. I can use that. I have to use it.

First, I have to get in close. This doesn't prove difficult when, in the next instant, Baldr is upon me once again. I'm ready for it, sort of, standing on unsteady legs, claws catching the haft of the spear he's using more like a quarterstaff, now the point has corroded away.

I push back with the staff-come-spear even as Baldr tries to crush the length of it against my throat. I'm strong, but he's stronger—feral, somehow, and desperate in a way he wasn't, last we fought—and step by agonizing step he drives me backward. Until my shoulders are up against the wall, the impact knocking free a picture of Sigmund dressed up for some childhood play.

Baldr's loathing is a living thing, a roiling supernova of pain and loss. I don't understand it, I don't understand *him*, this twisted black hole so unlike the shining star he used to be.

The haft of the spear presses against my throat, the muscles in my own arms screaming as I try to hold it back. If I let go, I wonder if the force will take my head.

Voice rough and rasping, I manage to bite out, "If you cut me, my blood will melt the flesh right off your bones." Behind me, flames begin to lick the walls. I'm not sure if they're mine or Baldr's.

"Not if I burn you first," Baldr snarls.

"Burn fire? I don't think so." It's hard to speak around the spear.

"You may have the flame, boy," Baldr says. "But I am the *sun*. Now *burn!*" Around me, the heat begins to rise. This time, I don't think it's going to heal.

And so, Baldr's breath wet against my cheek, I let go of the spear.

The next part isn't fun; the wood crushes down against my neck, and I feel it. Feel as my throat collapses, esophagus and larynx. Feel cartilage crumble, feel flesh rupture.

Feel the blood, filling up my mouth, over my tongue and held behind my teeth.

Then I lunge forward. And *bite.*

Bite down hard against Baldr's eye, the same I once shot through a thousand lifetimes ago. A death scar, a mark, re-grown now but it's still mine and I take it back. Poison-coated teeth sinking into soft flesh and scraping bone, then the barest of resistance before a sound like the dawn and my mouth is filled with the taste of—

(watch him, strange and alien, across the fields of Ásgarðr and wonder, wonder what father saw in something so different, one who plays at being one of you he does and he is oh so very good but still you know you feel he is so different he can only be—)

(the others laugh they play their games throwing rocks and stones and other things and you laugh too though not so hard, not so carefree as once before because mother made them promise made them all but the dreams still come though you tell no one, dreams and nightmares and behind every end and every death you see—)

(oh, oh brother, oh poor blind brother you were so alone wanting something getting nothing, nothing from your brother beloved by all and so you make a deal, just a game, just an afternoon, but his deal is death the price too high and as you see the arrow you see your brother and behind him the twisted smile of—)

(it's cold, cold and dark for so long oh so long and you can't do this you need the sun you are the sun but down here there's nothing nothing but mist and misery and her and even she belongs to—)

(it is done the end of all things has come and gone and you are free, free but something's wrong, reborn yet still so dead inside, something you can't see can't find so you send out your

eye only one now but it is sharp and oh it takes an age but finally you find—)

(father oh father you brought the viper to our breast this monster and even now we pay the price and that price has the name—)

"Lain?"

Pain. Pain and memories, so many memories. Flashes of color, of light. Of hate. They fade, and there's a sound outside so I open my eyes and see—

"*Hórkona!*"

My fingers close around her neck before she can open her traitorous mouth. Her eyes go wide and she tries to plead, tries to call a name but it is not my name, it is his and she has betrayed me to him and so she will *pay*.

"L-Lain? Lain! *Loki!*"

Ah. That does it.

My hand jerks open and Sigmund crumples to the floor, clutching his neck and breathing hard. Loki. Right. Fuck. That's me, that's my name, I bit out Baldr's eye and, fuck, that's old magic, deep magic and I nearly lost myself but I'm back, I think, almost back and all it took was nearly killing my wife to get him to finally, finally, say my name.

About now—just a fraction of a moment of a second, really—the world explodes in pain, and everything goes black.

I can hear Sigmund screaming out, *No, Dad, stop, it's okay please don't!* I can smell blood and ash and fear. And I can feel, even though I wish I couldn't. Bone-deep pain ringing through my skull and behind my eyeballs and down into my teeth. But I can't see, not with my eyes, and not with the Wyrd.

It's the horns. I've been hit over the back of the head and it's clipped my horns. *Jötunn* horns. They're not for fighting. They are, as they say, for Display Purposes Only. Display and sensing, the heart of a *jötunn*'s Wyrdsight, and without them? Without them I really am blind.

I feel cool hands against my shoulders and, unseeing, I jerk back. But the hands are gentle and familiar and so is the voice that says, "Ohmigod, are you okay?"

I blink, the ringing in my horns is fading and I can start to make out the blurry outlines of Sigmund's narrative, of David's.

David is clutching an iron poker he took from the fireplace, having just hit me over the head with it. He's been dissuaded from further actions along this line by his son, though he's currently reserving judgment on the issue. I did, after all, nearly just strangle his only child.

Sigmund is still trying to get some kind of response, so I groan and half uncurl from where I've rolled into a ball on the floor.

" 'M okay," I manage to slur, throat already healing but still raw and shattered. Cool, soft hands help me sit up and the world comes back into focus. Or whatever passes for focus with the Wyrdsight. Mostly. I run a hand across my horns, checking for damage and wincing when my fingers encounter a rough edge.

"The left one's missing a chunk off the end," Sigmund says, meaning his left. "Dad whacked you one good."

"Fuck. You're not wrong." Hence the fuzziness in the Sight. Damn. "Where's Baldr?" I look around, directing sightless eyes mostly out of habit. I know he's not here, and all moving my head does is exacerbate the pain.

Sigmund looks, too, as if expecting Baldr to leap out from behind the sofa. Well, what's left of it beneath the ash. "After you, uh"—he makes an awkward sort of hand gesture indicating *bit out his eye like a fucking monster*, and I duck my head and wipe my lips and try not to taste vitreous humor in my throat—"he kinda just vanished and actually why was he here in the first place you said he wouldn't attack my dad and now my dining room is trashed and my house is on fire and my dad nearly died and fucking what the fuck man!" His voice has had some serious turning up of the volume controls by the end of this, not to mention that he starts getting a bit punchy. He's not hitting hard, but he is angry and scared and I do deserve it.

"Sigmund!" I've almost forgotten David is there. He takes a half step forward, still clutching the fire poker, eyeing me in horror.

Me, I just hold up my arms and fall onto my back, making sure to take the fires still burning in the living and dining rooms down with me. The house is a mess. Fuck. What a fucking lousy way to meet your in-laws. "Sorry. Man, I just . . . Sorry. Fuck." I don't know what else to say, but Sigmund stops hitting me so I can't be doing too badly. He's still angry, though, and it's a sharp and jagged taste. Scared and pissed off, wild eyed and breath racing. He's beautiful.

I say, "I'll pay for the damage to the house."

"It's not about the fucking house, Lain." Sigmund gives me one more whack on the arm for good measure. I thwack my tail against the floor in response. I know it's not about the house.

We just sit there for a while. Me staring sightlessly up at the roof, drumming my tail against the carpet, Sigmund kneeling next to me and rubbing his eyes underneath his glasses. I'm halfway through thinking about what the fuck I'm going to do next, when a voice from the corner says, "Would one of you boys mind explaining to your old man what the bloody hell is going on here?"

Ah. Right.

—

An exchange of meaningful looks later, I retreat upstairs to let Sigmund deal with his father. I try not to listen to their harsh murmuring or the burnt-edged emotions that swirl around them, instead feeling out into the house itself. It's the center of a Bleed that takes up at least an entire block, but it's not deep in the house itself. For all their problems, the Sussmans are a pretty normal family, and their house is a place of sanctuary and calm for both of them. That makes it hard for the Bleed to get a foothold, which is why about the worst it's managed to do so far is spread a bit of rising damp up the walls.

There are some exceptions. There's something under the stairs I don't want to think about, as well as in David's study, and the portrait of Mum on the wall in the corridor has started to get a bit difficult to look at. The portrait and the study are linked—Lynne Sussman's death being one of the turning points in the lives of her son and husband—but the thing under the stairs is just an accident. I don't think either of them are dangerous, exactly, but they're both traumas I assume Sigmund and David would rather avoid.

The stairs creak a little when I walk up them, but there's nothing too horrific waiting for me on the landing. The door to Sigmund's room is open, and I peer inside. The bed still has its ossified accoutrements, and now the ceiling has started to grow what look like fleshy stalactites. This kind of sucks. What with my teensy little fear of caves and all, and the fact that the box is still sitting in the middle of the bed.

I manage to grab it via a sequence of artful barrel rolls, and make it back into the hallway just in time to watch the door slam shut with enough force to shake a photo of David and a very young Sigmund off the wall. There's a pause in the conversation downstairs, and Sigmund's voice calls, "Lain? You okay?"

If my hearts still worked, they'd be racing. As it is, I just peel myself off the plaster and hope my voice doesn't shake when I say, "Yeah. All good."

The downstairs murmuring resumes, and I walk to sit on the edge of the landing, huge hind claws scratching up the stairs, box sitting on my knees.

I open it.

Two minutes later, I close the lid and set fire to the entire thing, then watch the severed head of my daughter burn purple and green in my lap. It takes concentration to keep the fireball contained. That's good. I need concentration right now. Need focus.

Baldr murdered my daughter to turn my city against me. Without Hel to keep them in check, the mists of Niflhel will creep into the world with the inevitability of the heat death of the universe. Hel's head is a catalyst for the Bleed, the shrapnel keeping the Wound open. I can burn it to ash but I doubt it's the only piece, and even if I track down every last one, the damage is already done. Pandemonium is dying, and its convalescence will be long and agonizing.

Baldr can't beat me in a one-on-one fight in my own city so he's torn my sanctuary down around me. It's a move worthy of his father. Of me. Not like the kid at all.

A thousand years in Hel. I wonder what happened to him. I wonder if I care. I wonder if my daughter greeted him with open arms and a skeleton smile before he took her life. Mostly, I wonder how I'm going to end this. My current best plan is still *kill Baldr*, but, honestly, aside from the sense of vicious satisfaction, I'm not exactly sure how that's going to help me. Help my city, help my lover and his father and his friends.

I've seen cities die. Seen their industry move offshore, seen their people drift away and their houses empty and their stores close. Seen the rotting husks they leave behind.

Killing Hel was one thing. She's the goddess of death, and I doubt it'll slow her down for long. But killing Pandemonium? You're talking about destroying the lives of over a quarter of million humans. And LB won't recover—after all this time, it *is* the city—which is going to totally throw out the entire technology sector for a good decade or so.

This, incidentally, is why gods aren't supposed to meddle around in the mortal world. It's considered *déclassé* when it goes wrong. And it always, always goes wrong. Badly.

Shit.

I hate this. I have no fucking clue what the fuck I'm supposed to do, and there are two people downstairs—and a whole crap-ton more outside—waiting for me to be the Big Damn Hero and save the fucking day.

If my brother were here, he'd know what to do.

Fuck, who am I kidding? His plan would probably involve beating me into fixing it for him.

Fuck my brother. Fuck him in his dead-rotting eye socket.

The last of Hel's ashes slip between my claws and I stand up, put on my game face, and head back into the den.

Sigmund and David are still whisper fighting, but they shut up when I storm into the room.

"Pack your shit up, kids," I say before either can speak. "I've gotta take you somewhere safe."

"Now wait just one second—"

"Shut it, Sussman." I point at David as I say it, but the thing that makes him take a step back is when I put Travis into the words. He sees it, just for an eye blink, and he *knows*. "You don't get a say. This isn't a democracy, this is the fucking end of the fucking world we're talking about, and you are going to shut the fuck up and do what I fucking say, understood?"

David's response is Pavlovian. "Yes, sir!" he says, straightening up and trying to look professional, even if he's still barefoot and wearing a slightly singed novelty apron.

"Dad—"

"No. We should listen. This . . . this is beyond us. The only thing I want now is to keep you safe." David turns to his son, lays a fatherly hand on his shoulder. The gesture shouldn't make me wince, but it does. Fuck you, brother. Fuck you right in your fucking hat.

Sigmund glances at me, then back at his father. He's not happy, and I am *so* sleeping on the couch tonight. Or would be. If I slept. And assuming we don't all die horribly in the next few hours.

After a moment, Sigmund nods. "Okay, Dad."

"That's my boy." David slaps his son on the back, then turns to me. He manages to meet my eyes. Just. "Keep my son safe and I'll do whatever you say." His fingers tighten around the fire poker, though, and there's a threat there.

I nod. "Get whatever you need from upstairs. We leave in five."

"Where?" Sigmund asks, though he already knows the answer.

"LB. If you're going to be safe anywhere, it's there."

He nods, and David lays a hand on his back. "Come on, Sig."

They file past me, David first—making sure not to get too close—then Sigmund. As he passes, I say, "I'm sorry it turned out like this."

He stops, but doesn't look up. "Yeah," he says. "Yeah, me too." Then he vanishes up the stairs after his father.

The *thump* that follows is me slamming my fist into the too-damp hallway wall. The impact leaves a hole in the plaster, revealing a fleshy, pulsing mass beneath. The Bleed is getting deeper. We need to get out of here.

When I walk up the stairs, I can hear something shuffling underneath. I still don't think it's dangerous, but I don't want to stick around here any longer than I have to on the off chance that I end up finding out.

David is the first to emerge from his room. He's got shoes and a jacket, and is clutching a photo of his wife and son. Before I can compliment him on his minimalist choice of travel attire he says, "I have a gun. In the study. I'll just . . ." He makes an abortive gesture, and when I don't complain he half jogs the few feet over to the study door. The closed study door.

The closed study door with the thing behind it.

"No!" I move fast. One second I'm leaning against the wall in the landing, the next I've grabbed David's hand, a hairbreadth from the door handle. He jerks back, startled, and when he rips his hand out of mine, my claws catch on his flesh, not quite hard enough to draw blood. It surprises him, though, and he cries out and stumbles backward into the wall, clutching his hand, heart hammering, radiating enough fear to send the paint peeling.

That's not good. So I take a step back, hands up, trying to look as nonthreatening as a seven-foot feathered guy with horns ever can. "Sorry," I say, just as Sigmund pokes his head out of his room.

"Dad?" he asks, giving me his best Glare of Death. I shrink farther back against the wall and try and look innocent. I'm pretty sure I fail.

"I-it's okay, son." David almost manages to keep his voice steady as he straightens up, still rubbing his injured hand, even as he tries not to. "I was just about to get the gun out of the study."

Sigmund looks at his dad, then me, then the closed study door. Then he says, "What's behind the door?" He's very pointedly looking at me when he says it.

"I don't know," I admit.

"But there is something?"

"Yeah."

"Can it hurt you?"

I have to think a second before answering. *Hurt* is such a subjective word. "Probably not," I say.

Sigmund nods, expression hard and tight. "Dad keeps the gun in a safe in the bottom drawer—"

"Sigmund!" David is horrified that his son knows this, but Sigmund ignores him.

"—and a box of ammo in the filing cabinet. They're both locked, but I'm sure that won't stop you." His expression dares me to refuse, to challenge him. And I want to, oh how I do, but I don't. Because he's Sigmund, and I owe him.

"Yeah," I say instead. "Yeah, okay. Give me a minute."

I gesture for David to stand back and he does so, retreating down the hallway to be near his son. When they're safe—for whatever arbitrary value of "safe" we're working on—I open the door.

Inside, the room is black. And by that I don't mean dark; it's like there's a wall of solid nothing just beyond the jamb. I exhale slowly, mostly out of habit, and step forward.

As I do, I hear Sigmund's voice, stripped of the confidence it held just moments ago, say, "Lain, wait!" But I'm already gone, plunged into the silent void inside the study. And after that, there's nothing, no sound, no light. Just a cloying, damp warmth, and the air feels thick somehow. Thick and close and before I can scream, before I can turn and run because *tooclosetoodarkohfuckimtrappedcantmovei—*

Before any of that, the door slams shut behind me and I'm alone.

Well, almost alone.

It takes me a while before I can make myself move again, swallowing down the panic and remembering that it's okay.

I'm not trapped, not held down, not helpless. It's just dark. Dark and gross, but that's par for the Helbleed, and Sigmund and David are outside waiting, my brother and his ilk are long dead, I'm still alive, and there's nothing in here that can hurt me. Much.

I still can't see a fucking thing. And honestly, I'm not sure if this is because it's actually dark, or because of some failure in the Wyrdsight. It's good at compensating, but it needs a narrative in the first place and this room is coming up blank. Except for that thing, of course, but its input isn't helpful. So I'm blind. More or less.

Great.

I take a step forward, then another. The floor feels wet and tacky under my claws and I'm glad I can't tell what it actually is. I'm just going to pretend carpet. Wet, squelchy carpet.

I find the desk mostly by running into it. It's in the center of the room, facing the door. A real old-fashioned oak Hemingway contraption. Lynne bought it for David shortly before Sigmund was born, back when David had dreams of reaching the LB executive. It has some good memories—and one really good memory, about nine months before Sigmund was born, that I could absolutely have died without ever knowing, fuck you very much Wyrdsight, you useless fucking piece of meta—but they're very far away, buried deep under twenty years of loneliness and doubt and misery and failure.

There's a lot of pain in this desk. No wonder it's a magnet for the Bleed.

I inch my way around it, keeping my hands on the edge and trying not to brush up against the room's other occupant. I don't think it moves toward me, but it does writhe occasionally, and the sound it makes when it does is wet and breathy and really, really not something I want to think about. I'm not sure where it is, exactly. Sometimes the noise comes from the back of the room, sometimes from the ceiling. But it's not at the desk, so I stick close.

The desk has one shallow central drawer and three larger drawers down each side. Sigmund neglected to mention which side I should be investigating, so I try the left. It's always the left. It's also always locked, but barely, and I wrench the aluminum latch out of its socket without difficulty.

Damnit. It's not the left, and by the time I've realized that, my hand is gooey and the room stinks like rotting dreams.

The lock on the right-hand side is no more secure, though the safe inside is. It's an electronic lock, and I punch numbers on the keypad at random, then try the handle.

Here's the thing about being a god: There's no middle ground. When you open the cupboard, either everything falls (humorously) onto your head, or the thing you're looking for is right there in front of you. Either the door is open and the room is empty, or there's a dozen guys with guns standing behind, waiting for you to pick the lock. There's no such thing as mild inconvenience. Either the narrative flows or it doesn't.

The safe opens.

Inside, my fingers close around the handle of a small-caliber pistol, as promised. Guns are something that happened in that time I wasn't paying attention and are honestly kind of petty when you have the ability to throw fireballs with your mind, so I have to admit to a kind of broad-spectrum ignorance as to their function. Sigmund mentioned bullets being in the filing cabinet, but I've got no idea where that might be, and fumbling around in the dark trying not to run into the Thing I Can't See isn't exactly my idea of fun.

Besides, now that I'm thinking about it, I'm not really sure I want the humans carrying firearms in the first place. David's excuse for the weapon was taking up target shooting as a kind of therapy after Lynne's death.

The real reason? Well. It didn't happen. Because Sigmund.

And why am I in here again? Oh, right. Because I'm a sucker, that's why.

Well, fuck that shit. I've done Sigmund's dare and it's not my fault I can't get to the filing cabinet. He'll just have to deal. This is good enough.

Getting out of the room is much easier than getting in. I vault over the desk—the tips of my horns brush up against something soft on the ceiling but I try to ignore it—and take the two strides back to the door. The handle turns easily, and the Wyrdsight explodes back into something useful as I step out into the corridor saying, "Got the gun, but no-go on the amm—"

Then cut myself off. Because there's no one here.

No one at all.

Fuck.

LOKI

*Unsown then
the fields will grow,
evil be amended;
Baldr is coming.*

—"Völuspá," stanza 62

SIXTEEN

The night started out awesome: ice cream, video games, nail polish, and Em. A real girls' night in, doing girly things, to make up for all the time Em had been spending recently with that guy she'd met online. LambChop, or whatever his real name was.

It was just at the pinkest part of dusk, and Wayne was in the kitchen, fetching food while Em lounged around on the couch, newly painted toenails up in a foam thingie. They were a good hour into their main activity for the night, replaying *Remnant World 2: Red August* without saving (or dying) in order to unlock the final costume. It was about three hours of gameplay, if they took the short route (which they would). Em was working through the "normal day" intro scenes, up until the opening of the August Room, after which she would hand the controller over to Wayne and spend most of the rest of the evening hiding behind a pillow.

It was that sort of game.

Wayne was adding choc chips to their ice cream when she heard, "Wayne! Cutscene!"

She hurried back into the lounge room with the bowls, just in time to watch Carol rip the red tape off the August Room door. Wayne had played *RW2* at least five times already, and the scene was still creepy as hell. Watching Carol walk into the featureless corridor, Wayne silently chanting *Go back go back Carol go back* as the latter vanished farther and farther into the blackness, knowing what she'd find on the other side, the room full of—

The lights flickered.

Distracted from the screen, Wayne looked up at the ceiling before sharing a glance with Em. They weren't that far along, but . . .

"Is it still raining outside?"

"Nah, I think it's cleared," Wayne said. On the screen, Carol came to the end of the Black Hall and opened the First Door.

Em opened her mouth to reply, but it was about then that every single light in the house went dark.

"Uh . . ."

The click-whirr of the Inferno and the TV restarting happened first, then all the lights flickering back to life.

"Aurgh!"

They both curled up, covering their ears against the roar of static coming from the TV. Em lunged for the controller and started dialing down the volume. The little bar on the screen was filled all the way to the right, which was totally not how they'd left it.

Also, why was their digital TV playing static? And why wasn't the Inferno coming back online?

"What the fucking Christ was that?" Em said as soon as they could hear themselves think above the white-noise roar.

Wayne had scooted in front of the TV and was poking at the console. The lights were all on, but it didn't seem to be spinning the disc.

The TV flickered as Em tried cycling through the channels: a flash of blackness followed by another burst of static, over and over again.

"What the hell . . . ?"

"Is it fried?" Wayne peered at the TV screen.

"Something like that." Em sounded thoughtful. "I can't see how, though. Every channel is dead."

"Yeah. Inferno's gone too . . ." Wayne stood up. Whatever was wrong with the thing, poking at it wasn't going to help.

"Hell of a thing to happen, tonight of all nights."

"Creepy," Wayne agreed, just as the lights flickered again. Em flinched, but Wayne pretended not to notice.

"We should check the other TV." Em tapped her toenails, checking whether the polish had set. Then she pulled out the separators. "See whether it's just the one in here that's screwed."

The second TV was in Em's room. A tiny, ancient CRT she'd been lugging around since high school and kept in memory of the epic battle she'd waged with her parents over being allowed to have it in the first place. Wayne thought that probably made it the most cost-to-viewing-hours effective TV in the history of time, even if the picture was crap and the tiny mono speaker made everyone sound like they were Skyping on 3G in a thunderstorm. Still, it worked. Usually.

Not tonight.

"Damn." Em was flicking through channels, using the buttons on the front, scowling as channel after channel of static appeared. "Maybe something's taken out the broadcast towers?"

"Why would that break the Inferno?" A thought occurred, and Wayne shook Em's computer to life with the mouse. Or tried to, anyway. "Computer's dead, too."

"What! No way!" Em's computer meant more to her than

all the TVs and consoles in the house combined, and Wayne found herself shouldered aside as Em went through the motions of flicking switches on and off and trying to reboot. She got the disks whirring up, but the pained beeping from the motherboard made her pull the plug.

"That's no good . . ."

"Sounds like the RAM," Wayne said. Of all the things that could be wrong, it'd be the least worst.

"This is seriously weird, man." Wayne could all but see the churning gears reflected in Em's glasses. "It's like some massive EMP pulse fried everything."

Wayne decided not to point out the redundancy. "I don't think that sort of thing really happens."

"Me either, but do you have a better theory?"

Wayne did, sort of, but she wasn't about to tell Em about it. Not just yet. Instead, she said, "Better go see if my stuff is dead, too."

Wayne's room was next down the hall, not far at all, and her door was closed. She put her hand on the handle and—

Thump.

Em jumped. "What the hell was that?"

It'd come from Wayne's room. "Something falling off the shelf, maybe?" She had a bunch of action figures that were a bit unstable, and the slightest jiggle in the floor could send them tumbling. Except . . .

Except it hadn't sounded like action figures. Too heavy. And almost . . . wet.

But Em was wide eyed and skittish, because the creepy stuff got to her. Em knew it was irrational, but that didn't help much, when it was dark and things went bump. So Wayne said, "It's probably nothing."

She opened the door.

And it was true, what she'd said. It was probably nothing.

It almost always was, after all: every bump in the night, every unidentified noise. Just nothing. Just normal sounds, taken out of context.

Wayne's room was set in shadow, the only light spilling in from the hallway, their silhouettes casting long streaks across the carpet. There was something on the floor, a *Final Fantasy* statue Wayne had bought years ago. It must've been what had made the noise. Just nothing, except . . .

Except there was something in the room. Hiding in the far corner, between the foot of her bed and the closet. Wayne couldn't see it in the gloom, couldn't make out anything except the sheen of the hall light against slick, wet skin and the overpowering stench of rot and filth and misery and *holy crap*!

Wayne slammed the door shut.

"There's something in your room!" Em's eyes were wide, her face ashen. She was a skeptic. One who didn't believe in monsters or demons or ghosts. But she did believe in fear, and Wayne could see it in her now.

Which is probably why, heart racing, she said, "Possum?"

Em's eyes said, *No it fucking wasn't, you liar,* but her mouth said, "Yeah. Yeah maybe." She gave a forced laugh, and Wayne returned it. Silly girls, jumping at shadows, scared of nothing.

Except it hadn't been a possum, or a stray dog, or a bloody dropbear. None of those things had flesh that glistened like an oil slick. None of them stank of fear and loathing and, gods, Wayne could *still* smell it, even through the door. Thick and meaty and then, in the space between breaths, Wayne was fifteen again. Sleeping in the spare room in her grandparents' house in Blacktown, the place where her grandfather had decayed during his last, painful months. And Mardi had changed the sheets and Dad had flipped the mattress, but cancer was a brutal master and it hadn't taken Pardi easy.

This was that smell, the rot of sickness and of pain. Of inevitability, of despair.

Of things denied a decent death.

And Em said, "I'll go get a broom. You know . . ." She trailed off, miming chasing something in a halfhearted sort of way.

"Yeah. I'll . . . I'll come with." To carry the other end of the broom. Or something.

The broom was in the cupboard next to the front door. It was maybe a thirty-second walk. It felt like an hour. The lights kept flickering, and something about the walls just didn't look right. They seemed damp. Soft somehow. Bulging.

(*"we fell into a hell dimension and nearly died"*)

A weird, offhanded comment. And this was the part Wayne was trying not to think about. About what that meant, exactly. About . . . about the thing Sigmund had told her about Lain and how that had seemed so much cooler in the middle of the day in Diamond Square and so much less so now in the brooding rot of their not-quite house.

They got the broom and returned to the closed bedroom door. Wayne felt her fingers tighten around the handle and her feet start to slide outward. Into the beginnings of *ma bu,* the first fighting stance she'd ever learned. The one that always came back when she felt violence itch against her mind.

Em noticed. "It . . . it wasn't a possum, hey."

Wayne swallowed. "No," she said. "It wasn't a possum. But it was in my room. Knocking over my stuff." And it was funny, really, how calm she felt, care of a life spent in and out of dojos.

(*thanks for the lessons, Dad. bet you never had this in mind*)

The first thump against the door made Em scream. Just a bit. More of a startled gasp, really. The second had her backing off down the hall. Wayne stood resolute.

(*this is it, this is where it matters*)

One.

"Better get back, dooder."

Em nodded, retreating into the doorway of her own room.

Two.

Another wet thud, this one almost enough to splinter wood. The door opened inward. Wayne figured the whatever it was probably didn't care.

Three.

It was remarkably easy to kick the door in. Much easier than Wayne would've thought, even if now she'd have to get a new door and, ha, if it really was a possum Em would never let her forget it.

It wasn't a possum.

As far as Wayne could tell, it wasn't anything. She got the briefest glimpse of glistening meat and quivering limbs, then the thing moved. Fast.

It lunged toward Wayne and she brought the broom down, the end of the wood sinking into the creature's flesh with a gelatinous sucking noise that Wayne was pretty sure she'd remember until she died.

It didn't stop coming, and Wayne leaped backward against the far wall, readying her—

(*staff*)

—broom for another strike. The lights flickered as the thing finally emerged, and Wayne got one impression of writhing and fear and *hate* before the mass feinted left and was gone, vanishing down the corridor and into the living room. Em's scream as the mass passed was punctuated by the sound of the front windows smashing as it, presumably, escaped.

For a moment, nothing. Just the sound of their breathing and the death rattle of failing light globes.

Then: "What the fucking hell Christ was that fucking thing?"

Wayne turned to look at Em, her entire body so tense she was surprised it wasn't creaking.

Em was wide eyed and breathing hard. "That thing—that thing was no fucking possum Wayne what the fucking fuck is happening I don't fucking believe any of this shit we were supposed to be fucking having fun and now *fucking what the fuck man!*"

("*fell into a hell dimension and nearly died*")

"Sigmund!"

"What?"

The thing had left a trail of . . . best not to finish that sentence, actually. Just a trail as it had passed, and Wayne almost slipped on it in her haste. She'd left her phone on the desk next to her computer, within easy reach of the door. There was nothing in the room now, but she still retreated back into the sick yellow light of the corridor once her fingers closed around smooth black glass and chrome.

Sigmund's number was two finger taps away, and Wayne put it on speaker as she dialed.

When the call connected, the static scream that echoed out of the phone's speaker made her wish she hadn't. She slapped disconnect.

"What the *fuck?*"

Em was freaking out. She probably would be for a while yet, which left Wayne as designated driver.

Something was very, very obviously not right. The monster in her bedroom—well, the monster out in the street now, she supposed—was a pretty strong hint, and Wayne kept flashing back to Sigmund and Lain in the square earlier that day. Sigmund didn't lie, and he'd looked pretty frayed. And Lain . . . was a god. Apparently. At least, Sigmund seemed to think so, and Lain seemed on board with the idea. Sigmund couldn't lie, but he wasn't an idiot either. He wouldn't be saying ridiculous things unless he had some pretty concrete proof of them being true. Like, say, falling into some horrific alternate universe.

Wayne didn't know whether they were in danger or not, but there was something about the house that was starting to feel wrong. The fact that the lights were screwed up, but also the place just looked . . . worse than Wayne remembered. Shabbier, more destitute. As if the only things that had share-housed here for years were rising damp, mold, and cockroaches.

Lain, as far as Wayne knew, was at Sigmund's place, having dinner. Whether he was a god or not, he seemed to be familiar with whatever was happening. And if he was a god, then surely he could fix it. Or at least, if he was feeling noninterventionist today, point them in the direction of what they needed to do.

So. Sigmund's house, then Lain.

It wasn't a great plan, as far as plans went, but it was what she had. Now all she had to do was figure out how to get Em along for the ride.

"Wayne? Wayne, man, what—?"

"There's something going on." Wayne decided to just come right out and say it. There really was no way to make things sound any less unbelievable than they were, and Em was going to flip no matter what. "We, me and Sig, we didn't tell you about it 'cause, like, we knew you wouldn't believe it."

"Believe what?" Em's expression, Wayne thought, could cut glass. She wasn't angry, exactly, but . . .

It all came out in a rush. "Lain is a god, or at least, like, Sigmund thinks so. I saw them in town and Sig was looking pretty freaked out. He said something about falling into a hell dimension and nearly dying but I guess he was okay since Lain was there and all except Lain's not here now and I think we're in the same place and I'm so sorry we didn't say anything but we know you wouldn't have believed us and it all sounds so crazy I know but Sigmund swears it's true and you know what he's like and I really, *really* think we need to go find him, him and Lain, because I've no idea what's going on but something is and it sucks and that was like some kind of freaking *monster* in my room just now and I don't want to die and we need help so please please please don't argue just come, okay? Come to Sigmund's place with me so maybe we can try and get out of this hellhole." Wayne was out of breath by the end of it, and she'd squeezed her eyes shut to avoid seeing Em's expression and, oh crap, she'd stopped talking and that meant Em was going to say something and what Em said, ultimately, was:

"Okay."

Wayne's eyes flew open so fast she was surprised the lids didn't snap. "Oka—what?"

"Okay," Em said. She looked pale, sort of shaky. "I just . . . okay. If you say this—this is real. We can do that." She swallowed, hand shaking as she rubbed it across her lips. "Just . . . let me grab my meds first, okay?"

Wayne exhaled, breath coming loud and fast. Em's medication. Crap. "Of course," she said. "You gonna be okay?" The lights flickered again, and when they came back, it was dimmer than before. Sicker.

Em nodded. "Yeah. I just . . ." She squeezed her eyes shut, then opened them again. "I'll be okay," she said, voice stronger. "It's real. I'll be okay. We should go now, though. Before whatever this is gets worse."

Wayne had expected an argument. Not getting one had thrown her, and it took a moment for her brain to scramble upright. "Yeah. We can take my car." Assuming it worked.

Em nodded, and from her expression, Wayne could tell she was thinking the same thing.

"We should . . . we should get some things," Em said, looking around. "Flashlights." She almost said *radios*, Wayne could practically see the word hanging in the air between them. She was glad when it stayed there. There was such a thing as being too genre savvy.

As it turned out, they didn't actually own a flashlight, but the LEDs on the backs of their phones worked almost as well. While Em rattled around with pill bottles in the bathroom, Wayne got busy with the broom. When Em saw it, her eyeballs nearly bulged against her glasses.

"Wayne!"

"Just in case, man."

"You can't go walking around the streets carrying a *spear*."

Wayne had pulled the head off the broom, then duct-taped a chef's knife in its place. Wayne was good with spears, they'd always been the weapon she'd liked the most at training. The one that'd always felt natural.

"It's just in case," Wayne said. She didn't add, *In case we meet another thing like in the bedroom,* but Em's expression indicated she heard it anyway. In the end, she pulled a rolling pin out of the drawer.

"Just in case," she said.

Which was pretty much how they found themselves in Wayne's car, phone-flashlights and DIY armory and all.

It did start. Wayne thanked whomever for small favors.

—

Give me a minute, Lain had said. Sigmund gave him five, then another three after that.

It hadn't helped.

"Sigmund." His dad's voice was soft, careful. "Maybe we'd better—"

"No. Lain said he'd be back." He was just going into the study, into that terrifying wall of nothing. Going because Sigmund had been angry, furious even. At Lain, at Baldr, at life, the universe, and everything. For screwing him around, again, just when he thought he'd found something fun. Something secret, something cool.

Something deadly.

So he'd been a jerk, thinking Lain would be okay, even though he'd looked kinda nervous and, Jesus. Sigmund didn't want to know what could make a god nervous.

"Sig, it'll be okay." David looked like he was going to continue, to try out that horrible lie,

(*it's not your fault*)

except Sigmund didn't let him. Instead, he spun on his heel, took the few paces down the hall, and threw open the door to the study.

"Fuck!"

Nothing. Nothing at all, but not the same as the nothing from before, which had been something-nothing. This nothing was just . . . nothing. Just the inside of his dad's study, slightly damp and shabby like everything else, but no monsters, no impenetrable blackness.

And no Lain.

"Lain?" Sigmund lunged into the room, whipping his head around to look into the corners not visible from the corridor, in case Lain was hiding. For some reason.

He wasn't. He wasn't hiding under the desk, either. The desk whose bottom drawers had been wrenched open, the safe unlocked.

The gun was gone.

Sigmund stared into the empty drawer. He couldn't seem to stop blinking and, Christ. It wasn't because he was about to cry, damnit, it was just . . . It was just . . .

Lain had been here. He'd been here, and he'd taken the gun, and then he'd vanished. Sigmund and David had been standing outside the door the entire time. Sigmund supposed it was possible that Lain could have crept past them, out the study window or just used some kind of magic, secret god-escape route. Except . . . why? Because Sigmund had been kind of a dick? Leaving them alone here, unprotected, seemed like an overly harsh retribution for that. Maybe gods were into that sort of thing.

Either way, now they were alone. Alone in the Bleed and oh fuck what the fuck were they supposed to do, their god was gone and now they had to fend for themselves. Sigmund had to fend for both of them, keep them safe, except he had no idea, no fucking clue what to do and he wasn't any good at this sort of shit and what the—

(*"stop sniveling, girl"*)

The words hit his mind like shattering ice, and Sigmund's eyes snapped open.

(*"you don't have time for this"*)

They were his thoughts, except not, coming from somewhere deeper and darker and older than he remembered. A place of endless blue and rolling green. Of dank, dripping darkness and the agonized roars of monsters. Places he knew, yet didn't.

(*"you know what to do"*)

Did he? Lain had vanished into thin air and the entire city was sliding into Hel, but they'd had a plan, hadn't they? Wherever Lain was, he could probably look after himself. The scariest thing here, he'd said, and Sigmund didn't totally buy it—if nothing else, he'd never found Lain particularly scary—but at least he seemed to know what he was doing. Unlike Sigmund.

(*"not knowing and being afraid are not the same thing"*)

And that was it, really. Not being afraid, and maybe Sigmund had been afraid all his life. Afraid of failure, afraid of success, afraid of fitting in, of standing out, of being someone, of being no one. Except it looked like that last one was very definitively out. The rest, well they were just choices, weren't they?

So. What would he choose?

The roar snap of the drawer closing was like a gunshot, and Sigmund almost slammed into his father as he stood up. "We have to go," he said, as steady and as ancient as a glacier. "We can't help Lain now, except by staying safe." It *felt* true. Sigmund hoped that was enough.

Dad didn't argue, just followed Sigmund back into the hall, still clutching the fire poker. Sigmund picked up his backpack from the hallway and lead them downstairs, into the smell of smoke and ozone and blood.

He'd seen gods fight, twice now, and survived. That meant something, even if it was just a destroyed living room and ruined dining table.

"What was that?"

"Ignore it, Dad." Sigmund was. A pitiful, broken sound coming from the darkness beneath the stairs. He knew what it was, knew it couldn't hurt them and knew there wasn't anything more they could do for it. They'd tried, once. Peeled the kangaroo's broken, shattered body off the asphalt and put it in the dark and the quiet while they tried to find someone to help. By the time they had, it'd been too late. Just another lost soul, dying terrified and alone, abandoned in the dark.

(*that won't be me*)

When the front door opened, Sigmund was almost surprised. It threatened to stick in the jamb, and the wood was . . . swollen, somehow, but it came free after a few hard pulls. Outside, ash was piling on the ground like snow

("*the fires of Múspell burn eternal*")

but the area around and inside of Lain's car was clear.

Lain's car, top down and looming in the driveway where he'd left it.

Sigmund approached the car, Dad hanging back. Sigmund didn't blame him. Without Lain here, the vehicle radiated a kind of untamed menace that Sigmund hadn't been expecting. All gleaming chrome and darkness and something *wrong* between it and the road. Too thick, too many shadows. But it was Lain's car, and it was the best chance they had.

Sigmund put his hand on the hood—gently, slowly, like touching a half-wild animal—and tried not to flinch when the engine roared to life. Headlights flicking on, lancing clarity through ash and fog.

"Sigmund!"

He flicked the briefest glance back over his shoulder at his dad, before turning to the car again.

"I need you to get us to Lokabrenna," he said, watching his own distorted reflection in the duco. "Can you do that? Please?"

The engine's hum changed tone, just slightly. Maybe.

It'd have to do.

Sigmund tried the driver's door and it popped open. He looked at his dad. "Get in."

David looked at Sigmund, then at the car. "This is L-Lain's car?" he asked, approaching it slowly. Like a man walking toward a tamed tiger, or toward the edge of a well-marked cliff.

"Yeah," Sigmund said, getting in. The driver's seat smelled of Lain. Sigmund was expecting the stab of melancholy, but it still hurt when it came.

"You have keys?" David opened the passenger door and sat down.

"No."

"Oh." A moment, then, "This sure is some car."

"Heh, yeah."

Sigmund watched his dad buckle himself in, then glanced upward. The sky wasn't dark. Instead, it faded out into a kind of nothing-gray just above the streetlights. The light was similarly nondescript, despite the fact that night should've been approaching. Sigmund supposed it was the Bleed. He raised one arm, above where the car's roof would go, if it'd been up. He felt ash fall on his fingers, and when he pulled his hand down again, the flakes smeared onto his skin like oily snow.

"What is it?" his dad asked, watching him from the passenger seat.

"Ash," Sigmund found himself answering. "From the fires of Múspellsheimr, the Eternal Chaos." His voice felt like an echo, transmitted down the ages.

David had an expression that Sigmund had never seen before. "Where are we now?" he asked. "You said something before about a 'bleed' between worlds?"

Sigmund nodded, or rather the thing inside him did. "This is Niflhel," he heard himself say. "Land of mists. Home of the forgotten dead, between the glorious city of Helheimr and the wasteland of the Eternal Void." The ash left long, oily white streaks on his hands.

Then David said, "Who are you? What have you done to my son?"

"An ally." When Sigmund looked over at his father, David gasped at what he saw. "I have no wish to see your child harmed."

"Then let him go." David's fingers clenched around the poker, though Sigmund knew he wouldn't use it. Not on his own blood.

"I cannot do this. Nor would I, if I could. Your son and I share a soul."

Everything seemed far away. Filtered though fog and ash and time. But Sigmund wasn't afraid, not of this. His dad should know that. "It's okay, Dad," he said, and David startled at the change in his voice, blinking and pressing himself against the car door.

"Sigmund?"

"Yeah. It's cool, see?" He smiled. David didn't return it.

Movement caught his attention, and Sigmund turned. He could see shapes out there in the fog, lumbering toward them. The car's idling engine had taken on a different tone. Lower, more threatening.

Sigmund turned back to his father. "We have to go," he said. "It's not safe here, but we're okay so long as we stay in the car."

He put one hand on the steering wheel, used the other to push the car into reverse.

"Giddyup," he said, because it seemed appropriate.

The car did.

SEVENTEEN

IT'S A DIFFERENT hallway.

"Sig? Sigmund?"

He's not here. Even with blurred Wyrdsight I can tell that much, the door to the study having opened back out into a much deeper part of the Bleed than it opened in from. Very deep, in fact, down past the mist and isolation, into the blood and bile.

"David?" I try, just on the off chance. He's not here either, but that doesn't mean I'm alone. The hallway carpet squelches under my feet, and my outstretched claws leave wet, glistening grooves in the walls as I walk toward the staircase. The house doesn't like that much; I can hear the wheeze in its breath at the wounds but fuck it. I'm well past the mood of being nice.

There's light coming from the staircase, red and flickering, accompanied by the greasy smell of rancid flesh, slowly roasting. Peering over the landing, I can see huge swathes of downstairs are on fire, and they don't look like they plan on being in any other state any time soon. I try to calm it, but it doesn't listen. Fire at all in Niflhel is unusual, but when it does take root it's Múspell all the way down. And the fires of Múspell burn eternal.

They're also hot, one of the few fires that can burn me, and the memory of the one other—of Baldr's hands searing on my skin—sends me back a step.

The last thing I told Sigmund was to head to the LB building. It's both the literal and figurative heart of town and the bastion of my temporal power. The Great Church of Me. Even deep in the Bleed it should still provide sanctuary for my allies, at least while I'm still alive. I hope. I also hope Sigmund has remembered this was the plan and has decided to execute it with or without my involvement. Traversing the Bleed will be tough for him alone, but he's a smart boy and Sigyn always was a warrior, back when she thought no one was watching. No one's watching now, so the most I can do is pray to whatever it is gods pray to that they make it, and hope like Hel I can meet them there. This part of Niflhel is dangerous, even for me, doubly so with Baldr on the loose. He was stuck in this place for a thousand years. Somehow, I get the sneaking suspicion he didn't spend all that time pining in his room.

I still need to think of a way to kill him. I can rip out his heart with my claws if I have to, but I doubt Baldr is just going to open his shirt and present me with the opportunity.

I've got another problem. It's more of a niggling suspicion, really. A half-formed notion I'm forgetting something, or maybe never knew it in the first place. And it's not like I was all friendly like with Baldr Back in the Day or anything like that—I was Dad's Bad Brother from Before He Settled Down and, ergo, not considered Healthy for the Children—but something about the version I've seen recently has just felt . . .

wrong. Off. Baldr was a good kid. I remember, because it used to make me retch how sweet the coddled little shit used to be. I didn't think he had a mean bone in his entire body. This new Baldr, though . . .

Or maybe not. Maybe a thousand years in Hel really does change a man.

Maybe I have a way of finding out. Maybe I need to get down this fucking flight of stairs first.

The noise starts up when I'm about halfway down: a wet, fleshy smacking coming from underneath the boards. The door rattles with each impact, as if something on the other side is throwing itself against the wood, over and over again. Before, higher up in the Bleed, it'd felt pitiful, abandoned, alone. Here, it feels like rage. Like hate. It's not coherent enough to use the door handle, and not strong enough to break the door by force. Yet. I'm fairly certain I don't want to be around when it is.

Keeping close to the far side of the hallway and away from the roaring fire in the living room, it soon becomes obvious that I won't be getting out the front door. That picture of Mum? Yeah, well, apparently she's not keen on things leaving her roost. The door blinks at me with one huge, pus-filled eye, and wet, ropey tongues flail in my direction, but thankfully it doesn't have much reach. Gun still in hand, I shoot at it. The first shot—not bullets, just will that burns like magma—goes wide and buries itself in pale flesh the approximate color of the house's walls. Something black and oily squirts from the hole, and I have to jump back to avoid the splash. The motion, ironically, corrects my second shot. I really have pretty piss-poor aim, meaning doormum gets hit right in its hideous giant pupil. The eye pops with a wet sound, more black gunk spraying out in all directions, and for a moment the entire house shakes as it screams. I scream, too, mostly because I'm now covered in horrible goo. Horrible, flammable goo, if the reaction of the fire in the lounge room is anything to go by.

Well, that was unsuccessful. Doormum is pissed and I need a shower, and I'm still not any closer to leaving the house.

I'm going to have to go out via the back door. This is not a fantastic option on the narrative metaphor scale, but it's either that or jump out a window. And I hate picking shards of glass from my skin. They're so *itchy*.

The Sussmans' back door is located in the kitchen. Since the dining room is also on fire, I'll need to route past the staircase door to get there, which means braving the *thump-thump*-whine monster beneath.

I do this, jumping between patches of light like a child afraid of shadows, eventually making it into the kitchen in a gore-slicked three-point glide across the floor.

Awesome. Go me.

The back door to the house is a wall of sliding glass just behind the breakfast bar. It's maybe three meters away. The light is weak and sickly but, contrasted against the midnight outside, it's turned the entire rear of the kitchen into one huge, dingy mirror, broken only by the prison-bar slats of the Sussmans' hideous vertical blinds. I skirt my way toward the exit, a sense of unease shivering across my horns, causing the feathers on my head and arms to stand on end.

There's something I'm missing.

I have one claw on the door handle when I realize what it is: The Noise from Under the Stairs has stopped. Has been stopped, in fact, since I passed it in the hallway. Only a few seconds, but . . .

I look up, into the dim mirror of the sliding glass door. My own ruined face is there, my faintly glowing eyes wide in animal terror, and behind that, inches above my feathers, inches behind my head, so quiet but so close now that I can *feel* it, hangs a single, glowing eye.

(*draugadróttinn*)

I drop, rolling to the side and around one-eighty degrees as I do so. When I come back up in a crouch, the lights flicker twice, then snap off with the sound of blowing bulbs. Silhouetted in front of me, between the dark of the kitchen and the fire in the dining room is . . . a shape. Or shapes, maybe. That red eye and what might be the outline of a broad-brimmed hat and a ragged cloak. The rest is filler. Shifting. And I have half a second to leap sideways again before something long and sharp and rusted streaks out of the shadow with the sound of screaming metal. It hits into the back door like an ice pick—the glass crazes, but doesn't smash—before pulling back just as fast. It doesn't occur to me that the shadow might have two of the things until I see a second one headed toward my chest. I dodge again, diving and rolling forward, this time, back into the kitchen. But I'm too slow, and when the spike slashes across my biceps, it *burns*.

The pain makes me stumble, and I fall to the tiles, clutching my bleeding arm. I don't have time to recover. The kitchen island is between me and the shadow-thing, and I can hear it chittering and whirring as it moves across the floor. I slide myself backward on my ass, kicking out with my feet to propel myself along, and, as my back hits the far wall, one long, metallic spike drives right through the feathers of my trailing tail.

The thing rounds the island, rearing above me for one horrible moment. It's a *draugr*, I guess. At least, I hope it is. Because what it really looks like,

(**brother**)

is something I'm trying desperately not to think about.

I don't know why it's here. I don't know *how* it's here. It's not something from the Sussmans. It's not even from Miðgarðr.

It's getting closer. Me cowering on the floor, wedged in the corner of wall between the hall and the dining room, isn't helping.

The thing takes a few jerking steps forward, then rears back for another strike. I can't let it wound me a second time. I'm tough and I heal, but *draugar* are diseased and my arm feels . . . wrong somehow. Numb. So I do the only thing I can think of on short notice: I slap at the thing's legs with my tail.

It's not a small tail, more dinosaur than cat, and the *draugr*'s legs are just more of those thin, rusted spikes. They're great weapons, but they don't give it great balance, and the tail swipe is enough to send it teetering like a drunk teen in stilettos. Its shriek is awful—the tortured sound of collapsing buildings—but I manage to scramble upright, bracing myself against the wall, and a well-placed kick sends the thing into the counter in a crash of pots and dinner plates.

It smells like lasagna. Rotten by the Bleed, but David's not a bad cook, and there's still something homey and appealing beneath the stench. I remember to lament the dinner that never was as I dash around the edge of the island and to the back door. I don't bother wasting time with the handle, instead taking a flying leap into the already-weakened glass.

It probably shouldn't work, even with momentum and weight and the cracked pane. It does, and I crash through and skid across the deck in a shower of razor-bright shards.

I lurch upright, and for a moment everything is the chime of falling glass, the hiss of bubbling blood, and the endless *click-click-click* as the *draugr* emerges from the kitchen.

It isn't going to stop. Facing down its single eye and suddenly I'm more certain of this than I am of any other thing. Because this is no lost and whimpering *draugr*. This is the Dead God itself, free of living flesh, cheated of a soul, and come to collect, to finish what Ragnarøkkr started.

No one can outrun death. Not even gods.

That doesn't mean I'm not going to try, leaping over the patio table and down onto grass that crumples like aluminum beneath my claws.

Behind me, I hear a guillotine scream, then the rattle as rusted crab legs make their way across the deck. Meanwhile, I'm already over the back fence, pain burning down my arm and itching in my skin.

In the next yard, I trip over a tricycle, landing hard enough on the ground that my teeth drive up like knives through my tongue. I howl in agony, claws scrabbling at my bloodied mouth, and the moment is enough for death to catch up once again, its shadow looming over me as, all around, a flock of raven-feathered *valkyrjur* begin to caw.

Hel is dead, and now her throne sits empty, ready for any with the will to take it. Perhaps, if Ásgarðr's gates are closed to Odin, he has another Realm in mind to rule. And, if so, what then of Loki? Blood-bound red right hand of the Allfather, and it was good, once. Back when we were young, back before crowns and titles, queens and heirs. It could be like that again, in blood and dark and cunning, the two of us against the Realms.

No breath, no heartbeat. I'm already half dead. Why not let the bastard finish the job? At least then we'd be together.

Above me, the Dead God rears. Behind it, through the endless darkness of the Bleed, a set of *Star Wars* curtains slowly rots.

"Fuck!"

My arm *aches*, the slow misery of a grave. A malaise of the soul made flesh.

And then David's gun is in my hand again, the stillness of the Bleed torn open as I pull the trigger. Once, twice, three times.

The first two shots miss, the second hits the Dead God in the "shoulder." It screams, and I finish up by throwing the whole fucking gun at the rotting thing's shadowed face.

That misses, too, but meanwhile I've scrambled onto all

fours, over the rusting tricycle and past a decaying chicken coop. The Dead God's limbs skewer the ground again and again, trying to pin me like a huge and tattooed moth, but I'm fast in this form, and all they manage is to clip a few more feathers.

Once upon a time, Odin made his choice. Tonight, I make mine.

I jump over one fence, then another, then a third, Dead God and his corpse eaters screaming in my wake, my very own Wild Hunt.

No one can outrun death. But some of us can cheat it, if only for a little while.

It takes me five backyards to find what I'm looking for: a huge, gaping pit of a swimming pool, oily black water lapping at the sides. I stop at the edge, hind claws curling around pavers, anchoring in the gaps between.

"Come at me, you rusted motherfucker!"

The Dead God does, lunging forward with a *draugr*'s mindless certainty. Odin's dead memory, it seems, lacks the cunning of his living self, and, as it hurtles toward me, I leap. Up and over the back of it, kicking as I go.

When my foot connects, I feel gears, grinding under leather. Then I'm on the ground again, rolling across another brittle lawn as, behind me, I hear the sound of something heavy falling into water.

Spikes and metal. Not very good for swimming, as it turns out.

Not very good, but not impossible, and by the time I turn, the Dead God has already found purchase on the pavers around the pool's edge. Snarling, I snap my fingers, and the entire roiling pit erupts in flames.

Fire is difficult to call in Niflhel. Difficult, but not impossible, and, when it comes, it's Múspell all the way.

The Dead God gives another girder-tearing shriek as flames lick along the wide brim of its "hat." In the next instant, it's vanished beneath the water.

I don't stay around to watch it drown. The flames won't keep it contained for long, particularly not when it finds the pool's shallow end. The *valkyrjur* still circle overhead, watching, and I don't have a lot of time. Just enough for a head start.

A head start means running, back through the yards and out into the street. No skittering *click-click* follows, and after a while even the sound of ragged wings is swallowed by the void.

When I finally get there, I see my car is gone from the Sussmans' driveway. I decide this is a good sign, and that it means that Sigmund and David are driving to LB right this moment. Unfortunately, it also means I'm going to have to walk there in order to meet up with them. Or fly, except my wings have vanished and I'm not sure how to get them back (jumping up and down while flapping my arms is not effective). I'm almost confident the Sussmans will be safe by themselves—or with Nic, perhaps—in the LB building, but not quite confident enough to leave them there for longer than I have to. Besides, it's the center of the city, the center of my power. When the final showdown comes, it's going to be there. That's the way these things work, that's the way I'll *make* them work, whatever the cost.

It's while I'm staring at the Sussmans' empty driveway that I hear the car.

I have just enough time to turn, feathers flattened and eyes wide, when a blinding flash of green bumper smashes into my calves, and everything explodes in pain.

Again.

EIGHTEEN

SIGMUND GAVE UP trying to drive the car by the time they got to Von Neumann Avenue.

"Sigmund!" his dad said when Sigmund took his hands off the wheel. "What are you doing?"

"It doesn't need me, I guess." Sigmund gestured as the wheel turned itself to round them onto Briers Way.

David watched in existential horror for a moment, before swallowing and closing his eyes. Sigmund didn't blame him. They could barely see through the ash and smoke, and the air was heavy and scratchy and smelled like sulphur and rendered fat. The car wasn't driving fast and, as they crawled through the streets, he could see vague, malformed shadows writhing along sidewalks and in abandoned front yards. There were a lot of them. Lain claimed they weren't aggressive, but Sigmund was thankful he was in the car. He felt even better when he found the button on the dash that put the convertible's top up.

His father opened his eyes at the sound, and afterward had taken to staring out at the streets.

"What are they?" David finally asked. His voice sounded flat, dead. Sigmund hadn't heard that tone in a very, very long time.

(. . . *monster* . . .)

When he turned, Sigmund found his father looking at him. "Lain calls them *draugar*. I guess they're . . . ghosts?"

Dad seemed waxy, pale, and old somehow. Sigmund didn't like it.

("—*monster strangling my son.*"

"*Dad, don't call him that.*")

"Ghosts? They're dead people?"

"I guess. I don't know really." Sigmund thought about the things he'd seen shuffling through the mall, chained behind the cash registers. Were they ghosts? He'd never heard of anyone dying tending the tills at Angus & Robertson. Maybe it didn't work that way.

("*Then what the hell should I call him?*")

"Are they . . . dangerous? Will they attack us?" Dad didn't sound afraid. He didn't sound much of anything.

"Maybe. Lain says they're like vermin."

That did provoke a reaction. "The ghosts of dead people are vermin?" Great, now his dad was pissed off for some reason. What the hell, man!

"Jeez, Dad, I don't know! I don't even know if they're people or just . . . just ghosts! It's not like I've done this before either, okay?"

("*Just . . . just call him Lain, Dad. I don't know.*")

The car's steering wheel was trimmed in chrome and black leather. Sigmund picked at red stitching and tried not to fume. Or pout. Out of the corner of his eye, he could see David looking at him.

His dad was quiet and still for what seemed like forever, then, "I though . . . I thought I was doing all right. As a father."

"Dad."

"My son comes home and tells me he's gay—"

"I'm not—"

"And I think, Okay, David. You can handle that. No problem. I looked it up online, how to meet your adult son's first boyfriend. I thought I was going to do fine." Dad paused, face gaunt and pale, lines etched around his mouth and on his brow. Then, "But this? I can't deal with this, Sigmund. I don't even know what *this* is. And I just . . . I just wish . . ."

He didn't finish the sentence. He didn't have to, Sigmund heard the end of it anyway: *I wish your mother was here.* And it hurt, because Dad never, ever said that. Never spoke about Mum, really, even though he'd never remarried and even though he visited her grave constantly when he thought Sigmund wasn't looking and even though he kept her photo on the bedside table and all of her things still in the closet, like she'd just gone away for business and would be back at any moment.

Sigmund had been three when she'd died. He didn't even remember her. Would probably walk past her on the street without recognizing her, even after seeing her photo just about every day for his entire life. Mum was an abstract concept, as distant and foreign as the surface of the moon or 1964. Other people had been there, had seen it, but not Sigmund. Its importance filtered down through their experiences, not because it mattered to Sigmund directly.

So his mum had died. Technically, Sigmund didn't even really know how she'd died. Dad, and the doctors, had said it was postpartum depression, but three years after Sigmund had been born? PPD wasn't fatal by itself, and it wasn't like Mum had hung herself in the basement or taken a pill cocktail or gone down-the-highway-not-across-the-street. Sigmund had thought so, all through his teens. Had gotten into a huge fight with his dad about it, even though he *knew* his dad wasn't lying. It was how he'd gotten to see the death certificate.

No suicide. She'd just died, PPD being listed as a contributing complication. Dad had said it was the best explanation they had. Lynne's physical and mental health had deteriorated after Sigmund had been born, for no discernible reason. They'd seen a litany of specialists, all of whom had said there was nothing physically wrong. They'd tried psychiatrists, but the drugs were all side effects, and therapy didn't help. They'd hid it all from their son, even after Lynne's death, because his parents never wanted Sigmund to come to what David had described as "the wrong conclusion."

"S-stop the car!"

Sigmund jerked at the abruptness of his father's voice. "What?"

"Stop the bloody car!"

David was staring out the window with one hand on the door handle, as if he was ready to leap out at any moment.

There was just one problem: "I don't know how!"

"The brake, damnit! Hit the break!"

Sigmund did.

Surprisingly, the car responded, screaming into a one-eighty that threw up a wall of greasy ash in its wake. It'd barely finished moving when Sigmund—heart hammering and back pressed into his seat in terror—heard the passenger door pop and his dad leap out.

"Dad!"

David shot the briefest of glances back. "Stay there! I saw . . . I'll be right back!"

"Dad!"

But his dad wasn't listening, instead lurching off in an awkward run through the fog. Toward a side street, between two low, squat apartment blocks.

"Dad!" Sigmund threw himself out of the car, nearly forgetting to pop his seat belt in his panic. What the hell was Dad thinking?

"Dad! Dad, come back! It's dangerous!"

But David had vanished into the fog. Sigmund was about to give chase, when the sound of the car's horn made him turn.

"My dad, I have to—" he managed, before wondering why he was justifying himself to a car. A car that was lowering its roof and windows and, Sigmund noticed, had opened its glove box.

Giving one last glance back where he'd seen his dad vanish, Sigmund jogged back to the car and leaned over the passenger's side to peer into the glove box. It was full of weird detritus: half a chewed sneaker, a Collingwood Magpies belt buckle, and a key. It was big and black and had one huge button as well as the actual metal key shaft. The chain was a silver horse's skull. Sigmund took the offering, stuffing it into his pocket.

"Um, thanks," he said, feeling only vaguely dorky for talking to an inanimate object that obviously wasn't.

The car turned off its lights and its engine, which Sigmund took to mean that it would wait for them. He gave it a hesitant wave, before jogging toward the gap between the buildings. The one he'd seen Dad enter.

Away from the car, the fog got very thick, very fast. Sigmund was kicking up clouds of ash with every step, his jeans soon coated with oily, pale gray filth from the knees down. It wasn't cold, which was something, but it wasn't hot either. Almost as if temperature was something that happened elsewhere, not here. Temperature and everything else, maybe: Sigmund's footsteps seemed muffled in the silence, his fingers numb. It occurred to him that maybe the fog wasn't fog. Maybe his eyes just weren't working right.

He blinked. "Dad!" The sound of his own voice echoing off the buildings was reassuring in its clarity, and Sigmund steeled himself and entered the alleyway. It wasn't wide—he could touch both walls if he held out his arms—but it was strewn with trash bags and mounds of rotting somethings. Some of it looked like it'd been knocked over recently, skittering things Sigmund decided to think of as cockroaches scurrying in between the piles. He hoped it'd been his dad who'd stumbled.

He thought he could maybe hear something up ahead, so kept walking. This always happened, didn't it? They'd been doing fine in the car, but Dad just had to leap out and run off on his own, so of course Sigmund just had to follow. Alone. He vowed to make Dad watch more horror films with him

(*if*)

when they got out of this mess. Obviously Dad was suffering from a lashing of potentially fatal Genre Blindness.

Then again, so was Sigmund.

Maybe that was the secret. It was easy to yell at the screen from the sofa at home, but maybe when they got out there, among the blood and bile, people fell into the story whether they wanted to or not. Sucked in by some terrible, inexorable gyre.

A shuffling noise behind Sigmund made him turn. Through the haze, he could just about make out the grotesque shape of a *draugr*, watching him from the entrance to the alley. He stood frozen for a long moment, heart hammering and unsure. The thing didn't make any attempt to follow.

"Vermin," he murmured to himself, forcing his muscles to unwind. "They're just like . . . like huge rats, man." Huge, glistening, almost-but-not-human-shaped rats. Fantastic.

He turned, forcing himself to continue down the alley, ears straining to hear even the slightest whisper of noise from the watching *draugr*. A few more feet and he emerged into a courtyard between the buildings. In the Really Real World, Sigmund could imagine it would be a nice place to sit and read. In Niflhel it was . . . less like that.

"Dad?" He couldn't see the other side of the courtyard through the fog, but he thought he could hear noise. He hoped it was his father.

"—nne! Stop! Wait, please!"

"Dad!" Sigmund turned. That had been his father's voice, though the way it echoed between the buildings made it impossible to tell where it had come from. It'd sounded close, but in the bleak and vast silence of the dead city, it occurred to Sigmund that he really had no way of telling. Sound traveled pretty far in silence, didn't it? Like, people in the outback reckoned they could hear the sound of birds flapping their wings, miles and miles away.

"Dad?" He inched forward, farther into the courtyard. A cracked fountain came into view, still half full of oil-dark water, as well as the skeletons of trees and a few rotting benches. And then, just beyond that, a weirdly dark patch of ground that Sigmund couldn't identify.

He was almost standing on top of it when he realized it was a hole. An impossibly huge, impossibly round sinkhole plummeting straight into the earth. Unobscured by the fog, yet all Sigmund could see within was blackness. It wasn't better.

There were noises coming from the hole. The sound of shuffling movement, clinking metal, and a murmuring that Sigmund couldn't quite make out.

"Dad?" But the only thing he got in response was the sound of his own voice, echoing back at him.

He inched around the hole, being careful not to get too close to the drop. Eventually, he came up against the wall of one of the apartments ringing the courtyard, and the sight of it made him stop. The hole bisected the building, as if some giant had taken a clean, semicircular bite out of the whole thing. Sigmund could see inside the floors like it was some kind of perverse dollhouse. A TV, half of someone's couch, a room that looked like it belonged to a little girl.

"Holy shit."

This, he thought, was getting into real impossible geometry territory. And Sigmund watched TV, he played games and read books. He knew what it meant when the impossible geometry in the hell dimension started ramping up.

It meant he was fucked, is what it meant.

There was nowhere else to go. He'd seen his dad run into the alleyway, though, which meant he had to have passed through this courtyard. So he must've seen the hole, but then what?

Sigmund turned, and started pacing back around the circumference. Sure enough, he was soon stopped at the point where the second apartment block had also been sliced clean through. There was no other exit to the courtyard, unless his dad had climbed into one of the ground-floor windows—Sigmund repaced the boundary of the space to be sure, but none were broken or opened—or slipped quietly back through the alley when Sigmund's back was turned. But why would he do that?

Sigmund peered down the alley just in case, but the only thing he could see was the *draugr*, flopping itself back and forth in the narrow space

(*narrower? it was wider before, wasn't it?*)

like a wet, sagging pendulum. The idea of squeezing himself past it was abhorrent, and Sigmund backed away.

That just left the hole.

Sigmund returned to the edge and stared down. The blackness made it impossible to tell how deep it was. He dropped to his belly and wriggled right up to the hole's rim, then used the flash from his phone's camera to try to see the bottom, but this darkness was unmoved in the face of technology. It started up about three feet from the top and that was apparently where it was staying. Sigmund tried tossing a stone into the maw and listening for the bottom, but got nothing. Nothing except the sound of distant movement and that voice, speaking words he couldn't hear.

"Hello?" he finally tried. "Dad, is that you?" And then, somewhat optimistically, "Lain?"

And then, for one terrible moment, the noise from the hole stopped.

(okay, that's . . . that's just great)

Sigmund was still staring over the edge, fingers gripping against bisected pavement and the entire front of his body damp from the wet-ash ground, when he noticed the stairs. They were easy to miss: a narrow, awkward line cut into the edge and just barely peeking out above the blackness. They would've been completely invisible from even a foot or so back. As it was, they didn't look encouraging. The walls of the hole were made from slippery, mud-covered rock, and the stairs were barely wide enough for a person, let alone in possession of something as gauche as a safety rail.

It occurred to Sigmund that he was going to have to walk down the stairs. Which was crazy, because there was no way in hell Sigmund would ever even attempt something so ridiculous in the Really Real World: Dad or no Dad, he'd break his neck. But they weren't in Panda anymore, Toto. This was the Bleed. And things in the Bleed, Sigmund was beginning to realize, ran less on logic and more on narrative. So he went down the giant scary sinkhole, even though doing so was a suicidally Bad Idea, because going down the giant scary sinkhole was what he was supposed to do. The only reason the thing existed in the first place was to make him go down it. It was probably a Campbellian metaphor of some kind.

"Okay, Sussman. We can do this." And then, because lying made him sweat and itch, "Maybe."

The initial logistics turned out to be not terribly complex, albeit still terrifying. Sigmund ended up sitting himself on the edge of the hole, tips of his sneakers barely brushing the first step as he did so. Then it was just a matter of lowering himself down and . . .

He was in. Standing on the first step, head and torso still above ground level. Terrified, but determined in the face of that one, tiny, success.

Getting down the next steps proved more difficult. They were narrow, slippery, and tilted at irregular angles. Sigmund ended up sitting and sliding himself down on his ass. It was wet and muddy and cold and totally gross, but at least he wasn't in (as much) danger of breaking his neck. The stairs were sturdy, though, which was both relieving and surprising, and as long as he took things slow and kept his left shoulder pressed hard against the wall, Sigmund figured he should be able to make it down to the bottom.

Wherever that turned out to be.

He'd been shuffling downward for about a minute when two things occurred to him. The first was that, despite the blackness, it wasn't actually dark. He could see about three feet in front of him and three feet behind, and that was it. That was always it. The light on his phone didn't help, even if he extended it out at arm's length. The walls of nothing were intractable, almost as if someone had turned the world's draw distance right down in the video settings. Sigmund couldn't even see the glow from the opening anymore, even though it couldn't have been much more than twelve feet above his head, if that. Sigmund wondered, if he turned around and started climbing upward, whether he really would emerge back out into the courtyard within a minute or so, or whether the hole had swallowed him completely. Was, even now, extending upward, the exit getting farther and farther out of reach with every passing moment.

The second thing that occurred to Sigmund on his descent was the fact that the walls of the hole were solid. Sigmund wasn't a civil engineering expert, but he figured that, right now, he was supposedly underneath an apartment block in a major city. Cities had things underneath them, like sewers and cables. A sinkhole should bisect those; he should be seeing the severed ends of water pipes and arcing wires jutting from the walls. He wasn't. What he was seeing was solid rock, or something close enough, and surely that was unusual, too. There should be dirt or clay or something, right? At least for the first few meters down.

But all there was, was rock.

Sigmund's phone said he'd been traveling downward for around ten minutes when he realized that the circumference of the hole was getting smaller. It felt like it'd been longer. Maybe it had been. Maybe time was as distorted here as space was.

Either way, Sigmund was certain the stairs had been spiraling around the wall, and that the spiral was getting tighter. He wondered how he would check. If he reached his arm out, would he find his fingers brushing stone? If he kept going, would the hole grow tighter and tighter until he was wriggling through it, feet first, like a worm? Would he keep going if it did, or would he turn back?

Could he turn back?

And then, quite suddenly, there were no more steps.

The realization was jolting, unexpected, Sigmund finding himself sitting on the floor at the bottom of the pit, feeling around with his hands before the truth of it set in.

He'd made it.

He stood, carefully. His limbs felt both stiff and like jelly, all at the same time, and he had to steady himself against the wall in order to make it upright. Once he did, he just leaned there for a while, trying to still the heart that he hadn't, until that point, realized was racing. He glanced upward, and saw a small circle of silvery light hung against the blackness. It might have been the entrance to the hole, but what it really looked like was the moon.

Sigmund's phone said he'd been traveling downward for about twenty minutes. It felt more like a thousand years.

On the other hand, at least the phone's light worked like it was supposed to, away from whatever intrinsic claustrophobia clung to the stairs. In the harsh glare of the LED, Sigmund saw that he'd arrived at the mouth of some great underground cavern. The walls here were still the same slimy, muddy rock but now laced through with a network of massive roots. Sigmund touched one, expecting flesh or something equally horrific, and was surprised when he encountered simple wood.

He ventured farther into the damp, dark space, footsteps quiet and slow. The roots got thicker and denser as he progressed, until the rock walls almost completely disappeared. Unlike the stairs, this place was warm. Like the stairs, it smelled of cave—that dark, earthy sort of smell—but there was something else, too. An edge of something unpleasant, something rotten.

Sigmund moved deeper into the cavern, into what must have been a truly enormous space. The light from his phone was effective, but it illuminated only one wall, the rest being lost in darkness. It would have been sort of cool, almost—exploring some unseen world like a supernatural David Attenborough—if it weren't for the fact that Sigmund knew he wasn't alone.

The murmuring and shuffling sounds he'd heard in the courtyard hadn't gone away. They'd grown clearer, in fact. Clear enough that Sigmund could tell the words weren't being said in English. They didn't sound like happy words, and down here they were accompanied by what sounded an awful lot like the clinking of chains.

The smell got worse as the sounds got louder. A deep body stench: sweat and piss and shit and vomit and blood and death. By the time the stairs had vanished beyond the reach of Sigmund's light, the smell was a tangible thing, pressing itself against Sigmund's throat, sending him retching and choking on his own bile.

Still, he kept walking. It wasn't that he was afraid, exactly. Sure, he was shaking and his grip was damp enough to make holding on to his phone difficult, but the terror lived somewhere deeper than physical fear. He knew where he was. Or, rather, a part of him did. The part that had been here before.

The edge of something caught on the light, and Sigmund veered toward it. Away from the wall, into the blackness, stumbling over slippery roots.

The new shape was large, rectangular, pale, and awfully familiar. It should've been. Sigmund had been walking past it nearly every day of his adult life and many times before. Three huge stone slabs, a hole piercing the center of each and a strange depression in the top. In front of the LB headquarters it was an eccentric and slightly ugly piece of modern art. Here it was . . .

Here, it *was*.

The stone blocks were taller than Sigmund, but a large, arching root rose up beside them. Sigmund crawled up it, fingers digging between whorls in the bark, trying not to slip on the surface and wishing he didn't feel like he'd done this all before.

The noises were coming from the top of the slabs. Incoherent whimpering, punctuated by the clinking of metal and, this close, a hissing sound.

Slowly, Sigmund stood up, already knowing what he'd see when he peered over the stone. And there, chained in place by heavy irons wrapped around his chest and his hips and his ankles, was a man.

An apt description, really. The thing certainly *had* been a man at some point, though now only the barest of evidence survived. A gaunt, bloodstained outline of something that had once lived, and now only waited.

Sigmund could see the thing's scarred lips moving in time with its cracked voice, milky green eyes staring sightlessly into the void, not responding to Sigmund's light or his presence. The clinking sound came regularly, every few seconds, caused by the violent jerks that ran through the thing's limbs. Jerks caused by a poison drip, falling in its face from somewhere in the darkness up above. Each drop burning into flesh with tiny, hissing bubbles, turning lips and sockets a rotten, necrotic black.

Sigmund wondered how long the thing had been here, alone, that it didn't even scream.

Next to the figure's head, sitting on the slab, was a stone bowl. Sigmund had seen that before, too, though only more recently and that version had been cracked. This one wasn't.

Which made it a small thing, really, to pick the bowl up—it was surprisingly light, though Sigmund doubted that would last—and hold it out, over the man's face, and catch the drops.

NINETEEN

EVEN KNOWING THEY were going to hit, the impact was still shocking.

"Hold on!" Wayne yelled. She floored the accelerator, pointing the Beetle straight at the thing standing outside Sigmund's house. She didn't know what it was, but it hadn't noticed them and she wasn't about to take the risk that it might.

"Wayne what are—?" was all Em managed before they hit the monster. Wayne got a flash of milky green eyes, wide in shock, set in a face that almost looked familiar. Then, in the next instant, the car shuddered and the windshield shattered as the thing's huge, charcoal dark body rolled up the hood.

Wayne lost control of the car for one heart-stopping moment after that. Careening across the street in a squeal of tires, before managing to pull to a halt about three houses down. They'd spun completely around in the chaos, and in the fluttering glow from the headlights, Wayne could just make out the shape of the thing they'd hit. It was lying on the ground, unmoving.

"What the fucking fuck was that!" Em, unsurprisingly, didn't sound amused. Wayne wasn't sure if she was inquiring about the thing on the ground or the fact that Wayne had just run it over.

"It was looking at Sig's house, man!"

"It's a public street!"

Wayne turned to look at Em, who returned her incredulous stare with interest paid in sheer, unadulterated terror.

Still, Wayne wasn't going to be made to feel guilty. " 'Public street'? That thing wasn't human!"

"That doesn't mean you can just run it down!"

Wayne opened her mouth to argue, then closed it again. Em might have had a point. Maybe. But if the thing was hostile, then what? They were trapped in some crazy hell dimension. Wayne hardly thought that stopping to ask for directions was going to be a good opening gambit.

"Fuck! Oh fuck it's moving!" Em had flicked her eyes back to the street. "Wayne! Fuck! It's moving, Wayne, you've pissed it off oh fuck oh fuck!" Her hand shot out, wrapping itself in a painful, white-knuckled grip around Wayne's bicep. Em wasn't cut out for this sort of thing, not really. She liked video games as much as the next girl, but in her heart of hearts she was an office worker. Strictly white collar. Wayne was sympathetic, even if it was a sentiment she didn't share.

She'd left her makeshift spear lying in the back of the car, and she unbuckled her belt and jumped out in order to retrieve it. Em's fingernails scratched when Wayne's arm pulled out of reach, and Wayne's back twanged a bit from the accident, but she ignored both sensations. Instead, she threw open the Beetle's rear door, retrieving the spear with only a minimum of awkwardness.

Em was right, and the thing they'd hit was moving. Groaning, too, from the sound of it. Wayne didn't care. Blood and adrenaline, fight or flight. She was armed and she was coming, crossing the distance between the car and the monster, spear raised and ready.

And then, when she was almost within striking distance, the thing looked up. Its face—monstrous and ruined and suspiciously familiar—flicking between all-too-human expressions of rage and shock as it said, "Murphy?"

When Wayne's foot next fell, the jolt from the disrupted momentum rattled up her entire leg. Wayne ignored it, spear tip clattering to the road in one horrific moment of realization, of recognition. Because that voice, that face. They were wrong somehow, grotesque and distorted but still recognizable as—

"Lain?"

The Lain-thing's shoulders sagged in relief as the expected blow was diverted. It opened its mouth as if to answer, but something about the way leather stitches pulled against its black, too-wide lips snapped Wayne out of her confusion.

"What the bloody hell are you?" she demanded, bringing the spear back up again, the tip a fraction of an inch from the thing's neck. It was still mostly prone on the ground, and Wayne was determined to keep it that way. "Where's Sigmund?"

It was at about this point that Em arrived, jogging up beside Wayne, calling her name in terror. Em was brandishing her rolling pin, but she didn't look convincing. Breathing hard, her face contorted into a double take when she caught sight of not-Lain. "Wh-what the fu—?"

"I asked you a question! Where is Sigmund?" Wayne pushed the tip of the spear into not-Lain's throat, hard enough to draw a line of dark blood. It sizzled against the surface of Em's best chef's knife. Wayne decided she'd apologize later.

Not-Lain's eyes were a weird, uniform milky green that almost seemed to glow in the darkness, but Wayne could still tell when it flicked them between her and Em. It pulled its head back to extract its throat from the tip of Wayne's spear and said, "I don't know. We got separated. I hope he's taken my car back to LB like I told him to." Its voice was cracked and rough, the register jumping all over the place, but still identifiably Lain's.

Em noticed it, too. "Wayne! Wayne, Jesus fuck that's—"

"No," Wayne could hear the threat in her voice as she said it, low and quiet. "It's not Lain. Lain doesn't exist, does he?"

The thing on the ground returned her stare. "I wasn't aware we were here for semantics," it said finally. Then, "You already know what I am, Ms. Murphy."

It had a point. "Yeah," she said, lowering the spear. "Yeah. I just didn't expect . . ." Sigmund had said something about horns, though, hadn't he? He'd apparently neglected to mention the tail and the talons and the almost-glowing tattoos and, gods, the scars. So many scars.

"Well, this is all fantastic," Em said. "Would someone like to explain what the fuck is going on?"

"Em, meet Loki. The god. Loki, you already know Em."

Grinning a grin that was all fangs and stitches, Loki stood up. And up. Lain was tall but Loki was huge, easily seven feet. Huge and broad and charcoal skinned and topped off with a swept-back pair of horns and a shaggy mane of flame-colored feathers that seemed to flicker in the dim light.

Em's mouth snapped shut with a click when the god held out his claw. She shook it, dazed, eyes still glued to the thing in front of her.

"You're a . . . god?" Em's voice cracked when she spoke.

"Yes." Loki's expression was patient and, for the moment, faintly amused.

"You're dating Sigmund!" Then, as if to emphasize the point, "Sigmund!"

"Yes," Loki said.

"And you're a god. Like, actually, *literally* a god?" Em's voice had turned skeptical, which Wayne took to be a good sign.

"Yes."

"Prove it!"

Loki laughed. It sounded like a wildfire, like an earthquake, and Wayne winced. He was amused. She wouldn't like to hear his laugh when he wasn't. "Maybe later," he said. "I think there are more important things right now."

"Like *what* is going on around here," Wayne prompted.

The god nodded, then started walking toward where Wayne's smashed VW had skidded to a halt a few meters down the street. When no explanation was forthcoming, Wayne shot Em a look. Or tried to. Em was still staring sort of blankly into the middle distance, lips muttering something inaudible. She looked like someone who'd just watched her entire worldview tilt ninety degrees and was still struggling with the vertigo. Wayne decided to leave her to it, taking her arm and leading her over to where Loki was peering into the driver's side of the car. As they approached, the engine gunned to life. Wayne didn't remember turning it off.

"Success!" the god declared, turning toward them with a grin like an open wound.

Wayne indicated the shattered windshield. "Visibility might be a problem."

Loki inspected the damage, elbow in one hand and claw picking at the stitches in his lip. It was more than just a little uncomfortable to watch, so Wayne didn't.

The car's windscreen was screwed. The impact of the god's body had turned the entire surface into a mass of opaque crazing. It glittered sort of prettily, but didn't do much for visibility.

The laminating had held the glass together in a single sheet, but one of the corners was lifted slightly out of its frame. Wayne watched as Loki pushed his fingers into the gap and pulled. The glass screamed as he tore it free, but when he was done, Wayne's car was minus one visibility problem.

"I hope you're gonna pay for that."

"Sure," Loki said, a bit too cheerfully. "As soon as you apologize for running me over."

"Uh . . ."

Wayne got an elbow in the ribs at the words, and when she looked down, Em was giving her best I-told-you-so glare.

"It hurt, you know," Loki was saying, voice still laced with faux cheer and teeth. "Shattered my collarbone, hip, broke three ribs, spinal fracture . . . not to mention what the road did to my skin. I heal fast but th—"

"Okay, I get it," Wayne blurted, popping between the squeeze of Loki's narrative and Em's glare. "I'm sorry. I just— I thought you were—"

"A monster?" Loki gave her a look, the ridge of one brow cocked. When he put it like that, it did sound sort of . . . not like the greatest excuse in the world.

"I told her it was a public street," Em said, the urge to be right temporarily overriding her existential horror. "You can't just go running people down because they look different."

Wayne was certain her face was fast approaching the color of her dreads. Loki studied her for a while longer, and she found herself fidgeting under the unfocused, milk green gaze. When he turned away, it felt like something physical. The release of a pressure that Wayne hadn't noticed until it was gone. Her breath started again in a gasp, heart racing.

(he's a god, he acts like he's just some guy but he isn't he's deeper and older and dangerous and be careful, be very careful)

Apparently done with Wayne, Loki returned his attention to the car. "Someone's going to have to drive," he said finally. "This thing isn't made for my feet."

That was probably an understatement. Loki's "feet" looked like something out of a museum. Wayne loved dinosaurs, real-life dragons that they were. She'd put Loki as coming from somewhere in the late Jurassic.

A thought occurred. "Um, hey. You realize you're, like, naked, right?" It was true, more or less. It wasn't like she could *see* anything—Loki had ash gray feathers running down from his navel and across the backs of his thighs and down his lower legs—but Wayne felt it was the principle of the thing.

Loki apparently didn't agree and gave her another raised-brow look. He was good at those, she thought, trying to ignore her cheeks heating up yet again.

"Dude, he's totally not." That was Em. "He's wearing a wrist cuff." She was smirking when Wayne glanced down at her.

Loki gave a dark bark of laughter in return, holding up his left arm: He did, indeed, have a black leather wrist cuff. Wayne remembered seeing it on Lain.

"If we're done, we need to go." The tip of the god's tail flicked like a cat's, huge fringe exaggerating the otherwise subtle gesture.

"I'll drive," Wayne said. She didn't ask why Loki didn't just assume Lain's form again. Maybe he couldn't, not here. It seemed as good a reason as any.

"Shotgun backseat," Em said. Then, when they both looked at her, "Front's fucking dangerous, man. No windscreen."

She had a point. "I'll go slow," Wayne said as they climbed into the battered-but-still-functioning vehicle. She half expected Loki to contradict her, but the god kept quiet.

"You said you think Sig headed to LB?" Wayne asked as

she started to pull down the Sussmans' street. With no glass protecting them, the wind picked up quickly. She really was going to have to take it slow.

Loki nodded. He definitely wasn't designed for the car. He'd pushed the seat all the way back and was still an awkward-looking curl of limbs and tail, too big, too tall, and too inhuman.

"Take a right down the bottom here," he said.

"But that—" Would take them in totally the opposite direction to town.

"I know. There's somewhere else we have to go first."

TWENTY

DRIP. *D*RIP. *D*RIP.

One drop, one second. Almost like clockwork.

Drip. Drip.

Sixty seconds in a minute, three thousand six hundred in an hour. Eighty-six thousand four hundred in a day.

Drip.

Impossible to be sure without measuring, but assuming one drop equaled a minim, that meant five milliliters a minute or three hundred in an hour. A thousand in a liter: three and a half hours, give or take.

Drip. Drip. Drip.

Six hours: one point eight liters. Twelve hours: three point six.

Seven point two liters per day.

Drip. Drip.

About two thousand six hundred and twenty eight liters per year. For one thousand years. So two point six megaliters, give or take.

Or, to put it another way, about one Olympic-sized swimming pool.

Drip.

The bowl was maybe fifteen centimeters wide inside the rim and slightly less than half a sphere. So maybe it could hold two liters. Meaning it would have to be emptied about four times a day.

Or, six hundred and fifty thousand times in total. Plus change.

Drip. Drip.

The bowl was stone, thick rimmed and heavy. Say about one kilo. Plus about another two when full. So a varying weight of one to three kilograms, held up at right angles from the body, all day every day.

For one thousand years.

Drip. Drip.

There was no way of measuring time, other than by the filling of the bowl. Sigmund's phone was in his pocket, but he didn't trust his shaking arms enough to reach for it. He should have thought about that earlier.

But he hadn't.

His arms were trembling and his feet ached, legs and lower back threatening to go next. Even a chair would've been an improvement. Or some kind of really huge retort stand.

Anything.

He'd been working out the volume of the drips when the . . . thing had noticed his presence. Thin, bony claws reaching out and snatching at the hem of Sigmund's hoodie, fast enough to make him shriek and jerk backward.

He hadn't spilled anything, but it'd been close.

"Sigyn?" The thing's voice was raspy and thin, a cold wind punctuated by a crackling bonfire.

"Um . . ."

The thing had gone still at the sound of Sigmund's voice, blind eyes blinking up at the roof, withered claw desperately trying to grasp him again. But Sigmund had moved, and the chains strung across the thing's chest and hips didn't give much in the way of mobility.

"*Hvar ert þú? Hverr ert þú?*"

"Um, man, I'm sorry I don't speak, like, Viking." Sigmund wondered about the sense of trying to talk to a hallucination. Because that's what this was, right? It had to be, didn't it? Because this wasn't Lain. Sigmund didn't know where Lain was, but this thing didn't look like him, didn't feel like him. Plus, Lain, like, spoke English with a pretty strong Australian accent.

Except . . .

Except if it was a hallucination, why was it speaking Viking? Sigmund didn't know Viking, didn't even really know what language Viking would have been. Ancient Icelandic, maybe?

The next words the maybe-hallucination spoke were different again. That strange tongue that Lain had used once or twice that felt like a broken speaker and left an itch at the back of Sigmund's throat.

"Uh, I don't . . . I can't do that one either. Um. Sorry."

Sigmund thought the thing looked thoughtful at that, though it was a little hard to tell, and, besides, Sigmund was trying really, really hard not to look at it too much.

That hadn't stopped it talking, though, and it'd been going nonstop ever since. A crackling, sibilant hiss, and Sigmund didn't have to be a linguist to know the words weren't nice.

He'd pushed the words and, worse, the occasional bouts of unhinged giggling to the back of his awareness. Behind the ache in his limbs and the maths in his brain and the stench and despair and the niggling feeling that he was forgetting something.

How had he gotten here, exactly?

More important: Why was he staying?

Drip. Drip.

Loki stayed because he had to. Sigyn had stayed . . .

(*out of guilt*)

. . . to be with her husband. Sigmund was staying because . . . ?

And actually, maybe that was the entire point. Lok—the thing was chained up, and suffering, and Sigmund couldn't just leave it. That wasn't how it worked, wasn't how the story progressed. He'd picked up the bowl and now he was stuck here, watching it slowly fill up, trying to figure out the right combination of items to solve the puzzle so they could make it to the next cutscene.

So. Step one: take stock of his inventory.

Sigmund figured he had one set of house keys, one key to Lain's car, one wallet, one phone-cum-flashlight-cum-calculator-cum-whatever-other-apps-he-had-loaded, his clothes, a pair of glasses, and one stone bowl of poison.

The puzzle involved freeing Loki from three sets of iron chains, preferably while not causing him any more undue facial burning.

"Oh," Sigmund said. "Oh!"

"*Hvat?*" Loki was looking at him speculatively, or at least looking at the place where he thought Sigmund was. He was off by about two feet.

This was going to be tricky. It was obvious, really, but tricky. Was going to require some mad twitch and an über micro. Fortunately, Sigmund had both.

Loki's jaw felt fragile under Sigmund's fingers. Sharp beneath skin like damp cellophane.

"*Hvat ert þú—?*"

"Turn your head and don't move." Loki tried to move back,

maybe just to be contrary, but Sigmund turned his face away again. "Face the wall or . . . the darkness or whatever." Loki looked like he was going to argue again, so, "Just trust me, okay? Please?"

The jaw underneath his fingers was tense for one eternal moment, before relaxing. *"Eins og þú vilt."*

That sounded affirmative, so Sigmund pulled his hand back—his fingers were slightly . . . damp, but he tried not to notice—and said, "Awesome." He put the bowl down on Loki's sunken cheek.

"Hvat?"

"Sorry, man, just gimmie a sec . . ." The bowl wobbled a little when Sigmund took his hands away, but it didn't tip and it didn't spill. He didn't dare take his eyes off it, even as he unzipped his hoodie and pulled it off. It was an old favorite and had seen the inside of a few too many washing machines. Sigmund folded it over a few times, ending up with a somewhat flat lump roughly half a foot thick. It'd have to do.

Holding it in his right hand, he picked the bowl back up with his left. It was heavy, hard to get a grip on one handed, and Sigmund ended up lifting it by the rim, one finger pinched dangerously close to the liquid inside. Loki had just enough time to turn his head before Sigmund covered it with the folded hoodie.

"Sorry, sorry!" he said in answer to Loki's muffled protest.

There was no really good way to time the next part. The drips were coming too fast. Sigmund counted them anyway, getting a feel for the rhythm. Then two deep breaths, then go.

Drip.

One hand braced against Loki's arm in case he got any ideas about moving.

Drip.

Empty the contents of the bowl onto the chains. They were

iron, and for one heart-stopping moment they did nothing, then—

Drip.

—that horrible sizzling sound, cut with the metallic tang of rust and the acrid smoke of burning cotton as the still-dripping poison soaked into the fabric.

Drip.

It wasn't going to be enough. The poison was caustic but the iron was thick and it wasn't enough. A roar of frustration and a harsh clang as Sigmund brought the stone bowl down against the chains, once—

Drip.

—twice—

Drip.

—three times and *there*! One final ringing snap and Sigmund was jerking Loki toward him, even as the god was scrabbling twisted fingers against his eyes, burnt by the first fumes of poison-soaked fabric.

Sigmund dropped the bowl and helped pull the ruined hoodie from Loki's face, tossing it aside into the dark. For a moment after, nothing moved. Then Loki threw back his head and began to howl. Laughing. It wasn't a pleasant sound, but perhaps if any time was a time for mania, this was. Sigmund took a stumbling step back as the god stood, steady and lithe despite his withered form, the remaining chains sliding from his hips and ankles. When they hit the ground, they were no longer iron, and the pile of gore glistened in the gloom.

It was about now that it occurred to Sigmund he hadn't planned for this part. He'd figured solving the bowl puzzle would be enough, but real life—even this current weird, warped version of it—wasn't much like a game. Here, even the FMVs required his player input.

"Dude, we should like, go or something. Before . . ." He trailed off with an abortive gesture, unsure.

Then not-Loki looked at him, and Sigmund's stomach turned to ice.

Loki—real Loki, not this parody of a thing—was huge and monstrous and weird but, despite all that, Sigmund had never actually found him frightening. All glowing dead eyes and stitch-swollen lips and jagged fangs and still he had nothing, *nothing*, on the monstrosity standing in front of Sigmund in this moment.

The one that said, "You got this far, boy. What will you do now?"

"What the fuck?" Sigmund stumbled backward as the definitely-not-Loki advanced toward him, steps sure and precise on the slippery roots of the World Tree.

"What will you do when cunning is not enough? When loyalty becomes a vice? When they come for you as well as him? And come they will. They always come."

The thing wasn't speaking English, not exactly. Actually, Sigmund wasn't convinced it was speaking at all.

"Who the hell are you?" Another step backward. Into air this time, and Sigmund was falling, tumbling to the cave floor, roots slimy and warm against the skin of his arms.

The fall was short, but it *hurt*. Curled in terror on the ground and, oh Christ, those footsteps were still coming, were stopping in front of his head.

"Get up, boy, and stop sniveling." Fingers like iron clamped around his wrist and Sigmund found himself jerked to his knees. He looked up.

"Oh, no. No. No. No."

The thing was changing, its shriveled skin filling. Like water into a balloon, revealing a proud, handsome face; broad, strong shoulders; round, full breasts—

"Oh fuck no, not you!"

—and hips, and thighs, and a cascade of hair like rotting straw, and eyes as ancient and cold as glaciers.

Sigyn, the Victorious.

"Get up, boy." She shook his arm, not gently, from where she still held his wrist. He tried to pull back but her grip was as inescapable as time, and his skin burned where she touched.

"You're hurting me!" he cried, ashamed by his own weakness. Ashamed that Sigyn could see it.

"Of course," she said, raising one dark eyebrow. "And you will hurt a thousand times worse before this is over."

"Before what is over? What do you *want*?"

"For you to be ready, boy. Nothing more. You walk a road between a sun and an inferno. You must be ready for it. If you are not, they will destroy you."

And that was the thing, really. Sigyn's grip was iron, the bones in Sigmund's wrist grinding together from the pressure of her fingers. The skin on his arm burned like he'd plunged it into liquid nitrogen, and the agony forced him to his knees.

Sigyn stood above him, cold and merciless. She was a goddess, he was just some mouth-breather from the IT department. Not even one of the cool ones, the ones that did the R & D. The biggest, hippest technology company in the world and all Sigmund had ever managed was to ask people with multiple PhDs in computer science whether they'd tried turning it off and on.

He was nothing. A Joe Nobody, one of the faceless white-collar masses, gristle in the mill of the corporate world. He wasn't brave, he wasn't strong, and he was so unfit zombies could've outrun him. Not to mention that he applied video games and comic books to real life as if they meant something, then got surprised when they didn't.

He wasn't a hero and he wasn't a goddess and most important—

"I. Am not. *You!*"

"Really?" said Sigyn. "Then prove it."
So Sigmund did.
He stood up.

TWENTY-ONE

WAYNE TRIED NOT to stare. She really, really did. Not in the rearview mirror and not directly, either. And it totally wasn't her fault if she had to take a lot of left turns, and that meant a head check via the passenger side. Just because they were stuck in some grotesque, depopulated hellscape didn't mean she was free to forego all the rules of the road. And if, during said head checks, she just happened to linger over the . . . being in the passenger seat, just a little. Well. Who could blame her?

Holy crap, she was driving in a car with a god.

Like, an actualfax, (dis)honest-to-himself, blood and fire *god*.

As a little girl, Wayne's father had told her the stories of the land, of the Dreaming and the spirits and the ancestors. Of mighty Wollumbin and wise Dirawong. Her mother, meanwhile, taught her yoga and meditation, chakras and karma, yin and yang and the Horned God and Triple Goddess.

Growing up in Nimbin, New Age neopagan religious syncretism was in Wayne's blood, and she believed it. All of it. But there was a difference, she was learning, between believing in the abstract and having a seven-foot-tall personified force of nature sitting within arm's reach.

Wayne wasn't too down with the Norse mythology—that was more Em's area of expertise—but she did know enough to know that Loki was kind of an asshole. And dangerous. Flame and earthquakes all the way down, and he *felt* it, in some indescribable way. The faint scent of smoke and earth, and the way his feathers (feathers!) seemed to flicker in the gloom.

Also, he was dating Sigmund. What was up with that? Not that Wayne was ragging on Sig or anything. He was a nice guy, and cuter than he gave himself credit for in a chubby, adorkable sort of way. But still. A god? *Really?*

The next time Wayne didn't quite look at Loki, he was grinning, leather stitches pulled tight against dark lips, sharp white canines peeking through the gaps.

"Next left," he said, his voice somewhere between the rumble of a cave-in and the roar of a bushfire.

Wayne obliged, watching the car's headlights slice through darkness that seemed almost like a living thing. The streets were hard to recognize, some mad artist's dream of bleeding signs and dead trees carved from obsidian, hung with bones and feathers. When Wayne caught sight of houses, they were squat and ugly things, too close and too identical, a copy-paste nightmare of windows like black sockets and doorways shattered open in silent screaming.

Wayne had given up asking where Loki was taking them. There were only so many times she could deal with his smug grin and cryptic bullshit answers.

The thought that this may have been a terrible idea had occurred to her, multiple times.

Following Loki's directions, Wayne took two more left

turns, then a right. Out onto a two-way four-lane highway that she almost recognized, bar the garlands of rotting viscera hanging from the streetlights.

From the backseat, Wayne heard, "Why Sigmund?"

Em, who did not believe in gods or monsters or spirits or magic, and had been looking sick and pale and hollow for a while. This was the first thing she'd said since getting in the car.

Loki replied: "He's my wife."

"Bullshit. Sigyn's your wife."

Which earned Em something that wasn't quite a laugh. "She died. Sigmund has her soul."

(*wait, what*)

"No," Em replied. Her voice was still thready, but Wayne could hear the strength creeping back into it. "No, that's not how this works. Sigmund is Sigmund. Don't try to tell me this is all some predestined star-crossed-lovers crap. What's the real reason?"

Loki was silent for a moment, claws drumming on the car door. Wayne could see the end of his tail, flicking where it was curled awkwardly over the dash. Finally, he said, "He makes me honest."

(*did he just say that Sig is a*)

Wayne heard Em shift in her seat. "If you hurt him," Em said, "it won't be just a goat you'll find your balls tied to this time."

"Duly noted." Loki gestured for Wayne to turn right.

"And all of this?" The sharp staccato of Em's rings, tapping against the window, echoed the sound of the car's indicator.

"Bad timing," Loki said. "Ásgarðr wants me dead, and their king is prepared to break reality to do it."

"Odin?"

"No. The next one."

The conversation seemed to make sense to Em, and she said, "You fucked the Ragnarok?"

"Sigyn did."

"Go her."

From the corner of her eye, Wayne saw Loki smile.

Then Em asked, "Who is she? Sigyn, I mean. None of her stories survived."

Loki closed his eyes, their faint glow vanishing behind dark lids. "No, they didn't. She was a girl, a mortal. That's all," he said, in a voice that meant anything but. "The motherless daughter of a shipbuilder, who grew up doing the chores of ten men and dreaming of the lands along the trade routes. Places she knew she'd never get to travel as wife and mother. One day she found a falcon in the forest, broken and fallen from the sky. She nursed him back to health, and in turn he made her a goddess."

"Did he take her traveling, too?"

"At first," Loki said. Wayne heard him shift in his seat. "Not as much as he should have."

"And this time?"

When Wayne flicked her eyes to the mirror, she saw Em's face lit from below by the pale light of her phone. Taking notes, and maybe Sigyn's story wouldn't stay so lost, after all.

Assuming they survived this. Whatever it was.

"This time," Loki started. "This time . . . we'll see. Turn left, pull up beside the fence."

The latter to Wayne, and she obeyed. "We here?"

"We're here," Loki said. As soon as the car stopped, he opened the door and spilled himself out onto the street, groaning and stumbling as he unwound, cursing in a language that wasn't English.

Wayne shared one last look with Em before following, stepping out onto asphalt that felt like taffy under her boots.

Loki was standing a short distance away, lacing his claws through a rusted, chain-link fence. It ran parallel to the road, indecipherable signs decorating it at regular intervals.

Wayne knew what those signs said. The roads had been hard to follow, but, now they'd arrived, the destination was unmistakable.

Golgotha Hill: the huge barren heap of gray shale, rising from the city, its only feature a lone dead tree.

It was a slag heap, or so the story went. Back from the town's old mining days and stubbornly resistant to any form of rehabilitation. The city tried every decade or so; the last push in the late 1990s, spurred on by paranoia over toxic metals in the soil.

But the land wasn't toxic. It was just . . . dead.

And creepy. Major creepy. Wayne had come up here in first year, jumping the fence and getting reference photos for a project. She'd felt the vibe in the air then, a hum beyond hearing and the taste of tin on her tongue. It'd been bad enough back in the real world, here it was—

"You . . . you feel that too, right?"

—bad enough to affect Em, even.

"Yeah," Wayne said. "I feel it."

They walked over to where Loki was threading his claws through the mesh. Wayne could feel the heat radiating from him, see the way the metal was glowing, white-hot in the darkness.

Wayne felt Em's hand close around her elbow. "Look!" she hissed.

Wayne saw. And heard, a moment later when Loki pulled, wrenching a huge chunk of the fence free. He looked from the piece in his hands to the hole and back again, then grinned.

"Cool." The still-glowing section clattered as he threw it aside. Then he turned and said, "Ladies. After you."

The edges of the hole were also glowing, and Wayne could feel the heat as she dashed through, hoping nothing molten dripped on her skin.

Em was next, nearly crawling. When she made it she said, "I thought the fire thing was a mistranslation."

Loki didn't bother with the ducking routine, the tips of his feathers brushing hot metal. "It's what people believe," he said. "Where and why is less important."

"Clap your hands if you believe in fairies," Wayne muttered, getting a sharp-toothed grin in response.

They followed Loki up the hill, ground crunching under their respective boots and claws. There was a trail, of a sort, and they kept to it, weaving in and out as the ground got slowly steeper and more treacherous. It wasn't quite like Wayne remembered, less rocks and dust and more fragments of something, pale and broken. And breaking further still beneath their feet.

Wayne figured out what it was after a good five minutes of silent trekking, when she saw her first skull. Crushed under Loki's claw as he ascended.

"Dooder," she hissed to Em, "we're walking on *bones*." Shattered and scattered in the darkness it wasn't so obvious what they were. Until Wayne's eye caught against the edge of a jawbone or a pelvis.

So many bones. An entire mountain of them.

"Very astute," came Loki's voice, too sharp and too loud. "The bones of the dishonored dead, to be precise."

"We shouldn't be walking on other people's bones." Wayne skipped her way around another skull, or part thereof. "It's, like. Rude." Desecrating the dead. That was bad business everywhere.

Loki waved a claw, a shrug flickering across his feathers. "If you know an alternate route to reach our destination, by all means, point it out."

"Where is 'our destination,' exactly?" Wayne was climbing a hill made of bones and her patience for bullshit was wearing thin. They were supposed to be finding Sigmund. Not . . . doing whatever this was. Wasting time. "What are we doing here?"

"The man chasing me is very, *very* hard to kill," Loki said. "We're here to retrieve something that may help us do it."

"Mistletoe?" Em suggested.

Loki huffed. "No. But close."

"I thought mistletoe was the only thing." Then, to Wayne, "The guy Firecrotch here is worried about, Baldr, mistletoe is, like, his kryptonite."

Hero with one weakness, right. Except Wayne worked in a comic shop, so, "Superman's vulnerable to magic, too."

"Exactly," said Loki. "Mistletoe doesn't exactly grow on trees around here. But I stole something else, after Ragnarøkkr, and hid it up this way. If we're lucky, it'll still there."

"What is it?" Em asked. "The sagas don't mention it."

Loki's grin was bright and vicious against dark lips. "They do," he said. "If you know where to look."

—

Wayne wasn't sure how long they walked. She tried checking her phone once or twice, but the screen kept showing things like 89:29 and 00:00 and he:lp. She gave up after the third or fourth time.

The hill got steeper as they ascended, the bones more treacherous. Em slipped a few times, once ending up with skinned palms and a bruised knee. After that, she steadied herself against Wayne's elbow, breath coming hard and steps uncertain.

"I'm not cut out for this adventure game bullshit," she said.

"Not long now," Loki replied, featureless eyes peering into the darkness, his flicking tail sending little rockfalls of bones cascading down the hill.

Wayne was fairly sure he was getting more and more anxious the farther up they got. Down at the bottom, he'd been standing upright, striding forward. Here, he was hunched over almost, head scanning around, looking for something. After she'd noticed that, Wayne had tried to find it too, eyes straining out beyond the darkness. Light here was about as nonfunctional as time, a dull glow that seemed to come from nowhere and extend only a few feet out in all directions, centered on their party alone. It didn't make sense, but at least that was consistent.

Things didn't improve when Wayne started hearing shuffling in the darkness or seeing bonefalls not started by any of their feet. "I think we're being followed," she said eventually, voice barely a whisper.

Loki didn't bother with the same in his reply. "*Draugar*," he said. "They're all around us, but they're afraid. They won't come close."

"Afraid of what?" Wayne played video games, she knew what the word meant, even if she'd never heard it pronounced out loud quite like that before.

"Us," Loki said. Then, "Look up."

Wayne did.

At first, all she could see was darkness; just a featureless swathe of black. Then, when she blinked, when her eyes adjusted to the not-light . . .

"Are they . . . branches?"

Either branches or cracks, a different sort of shadow, crazing between the abyss that hung above.

Em said, "The World Tree." Her voice was hushed, reverent. Wayne had never heard Em speak like that before. "It is, isn't it?"

Loki nodded. "We're close to one of its roots," he said.

"Hel," Em muttered. Then, louder, "This is Hel, isn't it? That's why it looks like this."

Golgotha Hill, barren but for one dead ash tree, and the suburb around it that seemed cursed with some sort of malignant *genius loci*. A place where the veil between the worlds was thin, and not all realms were Narnia.

"Niflhel," Loki corrected. "Where dead things too broken and forgotten even for my daughter's hall come to rot."

Above her, Wayne could hear the branches shift, hear the creak of ropes as a million hanged men swung for all eternity. Hear the flutter of feathers and cawing of ravens as they picked the bodies clean.

"Join us, sisters. Feast with us once more!"

A sharp tugging at her elbow. Em, stumbling on the bones, and Wayne caught her, pulled her upright again.

"Th-thanks, man." Em's eyes were wide, a thin sheen of clammy sweat covering her skin.

"Just hold tight. We'll get there."

Fear, that's all it'd been. Too many gods and monsters, and Wayne was hearing things, was imagining things. She had to be. She couldn't see the Tree, not that well. Not well enough to make out birds or bodies and . . .

And it'd been a long day, that's all. Maybe it still was. Maybe Wayne'd fallen asleep in front of the Inferno, bowl of ice cream balanced on her stomach and Em sitting with the controller not two feet away. In a little while she'd wake up, maybe make a few sketches of Loki (he'd be great for her character-design class), then suggest they play *Mario Kart*. Wayne could really go for some Mushroom Kingdom right now. Fewer dead things.

This time, it was Wayne who tripped, the toe of her boot catching something solid. Em kept her from landing face-first into someone else's skull, and when Wayne looked behind her she saw a dark shape, rising from the bone.

It took her a moment to recognize it as a tree root.

"We're getting closer," Loki said. "Be careful."

The roots made the ground less even, but they also made it less prone to bonefalls. As they picked their way along the wood, Wayne realized she could make out a shape looming up ahead. A tree. The Tree, no bigger than the one Wayne had taken photos of, the last time she'd been up here in the real world. No bigger, and yet big enough to hold every Realm, cradled in its branches.

"Damn," said Em, peering upward.

A moment later, they were beneath it, within touching distance of the trunk: no wider than a person, with the circumference of the solar system.

There *were* bodies hanging from the branches. And birds, silent and watching. Ravens, big and black and looming. Maybe a dozen of them.

Behind her, Wayne heard the sound of feet, crunching over bone.

"Uh," she said. "Guys?"

Loki called them *draugar*, and said they were afraid. Wayne could see them, now, just outside the circle of visibility. A horde of not-quite-human shapes, shuffling toward them.

They didn't look afraid. They looked like they were waiting.

"The Dead God comes! Our Lord returns, and all the living shall cower in his shadow!"

"What the fuck!" Em's head whipped around. "Wayne. Wayne did you—"

"I heard it. It's real." When Wayne looked up, a dozen dead white eyes peered back down.

No, not a dozen. Eleven. Thirteen minus two . . .

"Em, what—?"

But it wasn't Em who answered. Instead, Loki said, "*Valkyrjur*, choosers of the slain, bound to Odin."

Wayne looked up again. The things that stared back down were, she thought, looking less and less like ravens as she watched. The only thing they looked *less* less like were busty opera singers in horned helmets.

"He wants what I'm here for," Loki continued. "His weapon, Gungnir."

Em said: "I thought Odin was dead."

"He is." Loki wasn't looking at them. He had one hand against the trunk of the Tree, the other picking at his biceps. Reopening a wound there, then using the blood to draw runes into the bark.

Around them, bones shifted as malformed shapes drew closer.

Wayne felt her stance opening, her fists raising. "Odin's weapon," she said. "It's a spear, right?"

"Yeah." Em was very close. Wayne could feel her friend's heat against her back.

"I'm pretty good with spears." And she'd always loved King of the Hill matches.

She expected Loki to argue, to make some excuse about magic artifacts not being suited for mortal hands. Instead, he said: "Yes. Be ready." Then he plunged his claws into the Tree, as if it were no more solid than a hologram, sickly light gushing from the wound as, all around them, the *draugar* howled.

Then pushed forward.

This was when it mattered, when the ten thousand hours counted. When Wayne's fist sank into slimy flesh that popped like a pimple from the strike, reeking black filth exploding up her arm.

She didn't have time to recoil in revulsion, because a second *draugr* was lurching toward Em. A boot against its chest sent it backward, but then the first was on its feet again, closing in despite the ruined mess that had once been its head. That had probably been its head. At least, the lump at the top of its body.

The *draugar* were like that. Misshapen men formed by a child's hands, crafted out of rotted flesh. No two were alike, with some parts that could be limbs and some parts that could be heads and, worst of all, some holes that looked like screaming mouths or ruined eyes.

Some of them had bones, too, but protruding, shattered things. Spikes and claws and teeth. Nothing internal, and Wayne's fists and feet tore off limbs and split open torsos with all the resistance of wet clay.

Still the *draugar* came.

At one point, Wayne heard a roar beside her and, when she looked, saw Em standing there, brandishing a black-gored femur like a club.

"There are too many of them!" Em took another swing, sending another *draugr* stumbling backward, head split open like a flower.

"Keep fighting," Wayne replied. "Just a little longer." She hoped.

Loki was behind them, chanting, still elbow-deep in light. Whatever he was doing, Wayne hoped he did it quickly. Her knuckles were stiff and her limbs ached, and she wasn't sure how long she could fight. This wasn't like training. Training was hard and it was brutal but it was structured. Safe. It wasn't standing on a pile of bones, tearing apart monsters lest they do the same to her. Training was air-conditioning and water bottles and laughing with her friends. Not the stink of rotting flesh and the sound of a god slicing reality open like a surgeon.

Five *draugar* down. Seven. Ten. Dislocated parts squirming on the ground around Wayne's feet, reaching for her even as Em darted in and out to kick them back. Still more came, a dozen at least that Wayne could see, and who knew how many behind that. An endless tide of black decay, as inescapable as the thing that made them.

And, somewhere out past the shadows, a single mad red eye. Watching.

On the twelfth *draugr*, Wayne stumbled. Catching her foot against a root and going down in a spray of teeth and flanges. She heard Em scream her name, then howled herself as an ill-formed limb slammed against her side. The world spun, jagged bone tearing her clothes and skin, and when Wayne skidded to a halt it was by slamming into a pile of severed, grasping flesh.

From somewhere else, Wayne heard Em cry: "No! Help her!"

She tried to struggle upright, but her ribs ached and her arm and leg were pinned beneath damp and stinking deadweight.

"If she's your sister then fight for her! Odin's dead, your oaths mean nothing."

A *draugr* loomed above her, arms like clubs raising, ready to strike. Wayne kicked out with her free leg, and the thing stumbled—

"*This* means something! Your sisters mean something! Help us, please!"

—but didn't fall.

Then its arms came down, and Wayne closed her eyes, bracing for the blow.

The blow that didn't come. Instead, Wayne heard the shriek of war and drum of wings, felt feathers and wind against her skin. When she opened her eyes, all she could see was black. A writhing, flapping, living mass of black as the beasts from the branches of the Tree descended on the *draugar*.

Close up, they really didn't look very much like ravens.

Helped by beaks and claws, Wayne pulled herself free from the flesh pile and stood up. Her side still ached and each breath was a lance, but cracked ribs were nothing new. She kept her breathing shallow, controlled, darting back around to where Em was standing, clutching her femur and watching the carnage.

"What did you do?"

Em blinked, pushing her glasses up her nose as if she hadn't realized Wayne was there. She was staring at something else, something just behind Wayne's head. "I think . . . I think I pissed off Daddy," Em said.

Wayne turned, just as a sound like collapsing metal tore across the hill.

"Jesus what the fuck!"

The red eye, the watcher.

(*the Dead God rises*)

It wasn't watching anymore. It was coming toward them, screaming its rusted scream, just the impression of tattered cloth and a broad-brimmed hat. And, somewhere underneath, the clicking whirr of a dozen metal legs, scrambling through the bone.

"Jesus Christ," said Wayne.

"Nope," said Em. "Guess again."

The thing screamed a second time, then lunged, and when it did the raven beasts scattered, taking to the air and vanishing like smoke, leaving fleshy ruins in their wake.

In the distance, beyond the carnage, more *draugar* gathered.

For a moment, one single eye turned toward her, and Wayne felt herself freeze beneath its light.

"*Return, daughters of death. Your flock awaits yo—*"

It never finished, that awful, gallows call cut off midsentence by a cry of: "Mother*fucker!*" And a flaming ball of feathers, leaping overhead.

When Loki landed, fire exploded in his wake, sending flesh and gore blazing. His leap sent the Dead God flying too, and it scrambled to right itself amid the flames.

Loki was holding a spear. A huge pole, carved with runes and hung with feathers, the point made from what Wayne would have sworn looked like an enormous, sharpened tooth. A dinosaur tooth.

"Take it!" he said, eyes and tattoo burning in the darkness. "Take it and *go*. To LB, to Sigmund!"

Wayne's fingers had just closed around the wood, words forming on her lips, when suddenly Loki was gone; thrown backward as the Dead God hit him, the scythes of its limbs raised and thrashing, the "fabric" of its robe burning with a stink that would see Wayne boycott bacon for a year.

Loki howled as one of the limb scythes punctured him through the side, and his voice became a firestorm, throwing the Dead God back.

Beneath them, Wayne thought she felt the ground begin to shake, bones cascading down on every side.

"C'mon! You heard him. Move!" Fingers closed around Wayne's elbow, Em tugging them away from the Tree and the struggling gods. Out into the darkness, with the *draugar*, but Wayne had Gungnir now, and she could feel its power. Feel the song of war, coursing through the wood. She could feel the bloodlust rising.

"C'mon!"

"Right." Wayne shook herself, head feeling hot and strange. Magic artifacts. There was always a price.

Dragged along in Em's wake, Wayne fled. A mad half run, half slide down the shifting heap of Golgotha, lit now by the red glow of the corpse fire. A *draugr* lurched in front of them but Wayne was ready, striking it with the haft of the spear, popping its wet and fleshy sac. Behind her, she heard a howl of pain, and the ground shook once more. When Wayne turned, she saw Loki, pinned to the trunk of the World Tree by the Dead God's blades.

"Move!" Em said again, but Wayne had hefted Gungnir and turned back toward the Tree.

"We can't just leave him!"

"But—"

Then Loki raised his head, turned their way, and said: "Fly, you fools!"

"See!" Em was still clutching the femur, slamming it into the head of another *draugr*. "He said the Gandalf words! Time to go!" Her hand was still on Wayne's arm, still pulling toward the bottom of the hill.

Pinned to the World Tree, quoting The *Lord of the Rings*. Wayne sure as Hel hoped Loki knew what he was doing. She hoped as she slid down the tumbling bones, ribs burning, *draugar* flying, Gungnir clutched between her fingers and Loki's curses echoing in her ears.

Curses against the Dead God, not Gandalf things to say at all. Things more like, "Fuck you, you oath-breaking mother-fucker! Fuck your oaths and your order and your golden fuck-ing age. You're nothing. A ghost, a memory. A half-forgotten legend. But not me. I won. I'm motherfucking Loki and I motherfucking *won*. I survived. You didn't. So just. Fucking. *Die*."

And then the last thing Wayne heard as she tumbled down the hillside. That awful, hollow corpse voice saying:

"*No. You did not. You are deceived.*"

Then nothing but the fall of bone.

TWENTY-TWO

OPENING HIS EYES was a bad idea. So was breathing; greasy ash filling his mouth and nose instead of air.

Sigmund lurched upright, onto his hands and knees, coughing and retching and rubbing his ash-filled eyes. The stuff was everywhere—he was *buried* in it—clinging to his clothes and skin and hair, covering him with its gray and oily film.

"Jesus. Gross."

He scrambled to his feet to escape the awful stuff, or at least escape choking to death. His glasses were ash smeared, leaving the world an indistinct, colorless blur. Sigmund tried to clean them on his shirt, which did more to spread the film than to clean it off.

Where was he? This wasn't the cave. From the drifts of ash and the featureless fog around him, Sigmund thought he was outside again. Somewhere. Not the apartment block, not trapped in that hellish place beneath, with only the echo of his own mind to drive him onward. And Sigyn, proud and relentless, who'd stood over Sigmund and—

His wrist still ached. When Sigmund looked down, he saw ugly purple bruises forming around the circumference, left by a hand that gripped like ice and iron. Sigmund wondered if his own fingers would line up against the shape.

Somewhere, through the silence, came the sound of lapping water.

"Dad?"

The cry of his own voice made Sigmund wince, sharp cry swallowed by the endless, hungry fog. He couldn't see anything in any direction, just the ash beneath his feet, piled up as high as his knees, leaving his jeans feeling stiff and damp.

"Lain?"

Still no reply but the water, and maybe something else. A wooden sound? Like knocking, maybe.

"Baldr?" Sigmund figured he was already yelling. If Baldr was around, he'd have heard. And at least he'd be *someone*.

Either Baldr was not around, or he was lurking in the mists like a huge creeper. Sigmund hoped for the former and started walking toward the sound of water.

Moving through the drifts of ash wasn't as easy as it looked in video games. Like walking through snow, maybe. Except the only time Sigmund had ever seen the stuff for real had been when he was eight, and Dad had taken them for a weekend up at Perisher. Sigmund mostly remembered the experience as being cold and wet and humiliating.

Today was numb and greasy and horrifying, which was similar. The ground beneath Sigmund's feet echoed, like he was walking on something hollow. When he kicked the ash away enough to look, Sigmund saw what looked like thick, dark slats. A boardwalk, maybe? Some sort of modern plastic, not wood, which at least boded well for him still being in Panda.

Through the mist, Sigmund saw a shadow. A rectangle a

few feet high, standing on its narrow end. It didn't seem to be moving, so Sigmund approached it, and the shadow slowly formed into a squat, iron post. A pillar, dark paint worn away in a ring toward the bottom, where a mooring rope would rub. There was another one a little way to the left, a third on the right, and a drop just beyond.

Where Sigmund peered over, he saw water lap black rocks.

This was the lake. The Pier, to be precise. Not a really real pier, just a sort of park area where families came to walk their dogs and buy coffee and gelato. Or fish for carp in the shallow, muddy water. On the plus side, the lake was in the city, and LB wasn't far. On the minus side, where the hell was Dad? And how the hell had Sigmund wound up here?

The knocking sounds were coming from his left, along the waterfront. Sigmund walked toward them, watching as another shape began to emerge from fog. This one was a boat, or half a boat. The front half, in fact, jutting up out of the lake at a nonfunctional angle. The rest of the boat was spread out in a shattered mess against the shore, floating on the gentle tide. When the fragments hit against the rocks, they made a knocking sound.

The boat was made of wood and had a carved dragon on the prow. It wasn't a modern boat. What it looked like, in fact, was a longboat. A Viking longboat.

When Sigmund looked around, he saw more shadows of similar shapes, jutting up like rows and rows of giant shark teeth.

A longboat graveyard, scattered out along the edge of the lake, and this definitely wasn't here in the real world. Sigmund counted maybe a dozen ships in all, some in the water, some beached up on the land, all in various stages of disrepair and looking like they'd been that way for a while. A *long* while, and the wood was soft and rotten under Sigmund's hand, peeling away in paint-flecked chunks. Some of the ships had barnacles, some looked like they'd never been to sea. Like someone had started crafting and carving, only to abandon the exercise halfway through.

Some of the boats looked . . . familiar. Something about the dragons' heads, maybe, the way they curved and snarled. Locked forever in decaying anger, collars of runes carved around their necks.

Sigmund kept walking. Through the shark-tooth shadows, until the outline of a different shape emerged, this one low and long. A tongue, not a tooth, and when Sigmund got close enough he realized it was a house.

The house looked to be a similar vintage as the boats—all stone and wood and mud—and was almost completely buried under the ash. It felt familiar, too.

"Hello?"

A house, surrounded by ships, looking out onto the—

("*sea*")

—lake. Sigmund knew this place. He'd never been here, but he knew it. He'd dreamed it. Inside the house, he knew, was warm and clean and homey. A man lived here, a widower, building ships with the help of his young daughter. Or had done, anyway. Once upon a time.

("*people are not the only things that die. stories do, also*")

The area around the door was cleared, tracks leading away and to the shore. Not Sigmund's tracks, and he wondered if whoever made them had been coming from the house or going.

No one answered when he knocked. "Hello?"

Opening the door and going inside was an awful idea. Sigmund did it anyway. At least it wasn't the hole.

"Um. Is anyone here?"

No one was, but someone had been.

Inside, the house was mostly one big room, walls decorated with hide and shields and axes, floor covered in rushes that looked fresh. Or at least fresh compared to the rot outside. Carved wooden benches ran around the edge of the space, softened here and there by woven blankets. The center of the room was mostly taken up by a huge stone fire pit, cauldrons and skillets hanging above. The cauldrons were empty, but the fire beneath was blazing, sending red-gold light flicking and dancing across the walls.

Woodsmoke and earth, and for a moment Sigmund's heart ached with thoughts of bright eyes and sharper teeth.

A pile of furs and blankets sat on the bench against the far wall, arranged in a sort of doughnut shape. A nest, Sigmund knew, and not just from the scattering of feathers lining the bottom.

Someone had lived here, once. Not for very long. Just long enough to fall in love and make a deal.

On the ground next to the blankets was a wooden chest, carved with wolves and serpents. The lid wasn't locked, and when Sigmund pushed it open, he saw enough gold and jewels to restock Tiffany's for a decade. Arm rings featured heavily in the treasure, all strangely identical, but no less valuable for their out-of-place mass-produced appearance.

("*this was the bride price. trinkets and baubles to a god, yet more riches than a king*")

Sigyn wasn't crushing Sigmund's wrist bones anymore, but she was still there. Watching, not quite buried.

And this? This was her story, or the start of it; Sigmund understood that much. She'd found a bird, broken in the forest, and had spent months carefully nursing it back to health.

Always a dangerous business in fairy tales, nursing strange animals back to health.

There was nothing here. Just a memory, a forgotten legend, comforting and familiar. And Sigmund wasn't stupid, he could see the parallels: a mortal, courted by a god. Lain had called it the Wyrd, called it fate and coincidence and stories. The same stories, told over and over and over again. Two cups *Cinderella,* one tablespoon *Beauty and the Beast,* mixed together in a Hero's Journey, served up on a bed of unhappy endings.

Well fuck that shit. Sigmund would write his own ending if he had to. And Sigmund's ending did *not* involve anyone being trapped in a cave for a thousand years.

The first thing he had to do was finding Dad, the second was meeting up with Lain, and third was escapeing from this ash-choked wasteland. But zeroth was leaving this dead memory of a house.

Sigmund turned.

Then he stopped.

Because there, leaning against the stone wall of the fire pit, was Dad's poker. The one he'd used to send a chunk of Lain's horn flying across the living room. And if it was here, then that meant—

"Dad? Dad!"

Sigmund was out the door, back into the fog and ash. He took the poker as he went. Just in case.

"Daaaad!"

Outside was quiet and still, just the gentle lap of wood and water and the soft flurry, falling from the sky.

And the tracks, the ones heading from the house and to the water.

The shore here was muddy sand, not the neat wall and black rocks from the Pier. The tracks changed from a straight line to a chaos in the dirt, scattered in hops and leaps all around a shallow hole. Some of the marks around the edge looked like handprints, as if someone had spent time digging something from the ground.

The tracks continued toward the water, this time accompanied by one long, single groove.

Sigmund didn't have to be Jimmy James to figure out what had left it. Not standing in the middle of a goddamn ship cemetery.

With the water lapping at his sneakers, Sigmund thought he could see something, out in the lake.

"Shit."

Sigmund didn't have a boat, but the lake wasn't very deep. Supposedly.

It was still decidedly unpleasant walking through it. It wasn't cold, exactly, but the consistency was wrong. Like baby oil, oozing into Sigmund's shoes and up the inside of his jeans, mixing with caked-on ash to leave a pale, oil-slick trail behind him as he walked. The lake was opaque brown, the bottom was rocks and mud, and Sigmund had to shuffle his waterlogged sneakers to avoid slipping.

It was a slow and awful trip. But the shape ahead was clearer, now, and it was definitely a boat. A small one, no more than a dinghy, and there was someone in it. Someone moving.

"Dad?"

The moving stopped. Then:

"Sigmund?"

"Dad!"

Sigmund ran the last few meters, or tried to, feet dragging and sloshing through the mud. He stumbled twice, but didn't fall, and soon the fog parted enough that he could see his father.

David was, indeed, sitting in a small boat. It looked similar to the others on the shore, except for its size, and that the figurehead didn't seem to be a dragon. Sigmund couldn't see what it was, exactly, from where he was standing. A woman, maybe?

"Sigmund." Dad looked . . . okay. Well enough, considering where they were. Wet and covered in ash and streaked with mud across his brow and all up his arms, but Sigmund figured he probably looked about the same. "What are you doing in the lake?"

Sigmund had to laugh at that, something strained and half hysterical. "Looking for you!" he said. "C'mon. This is not the time to go boating. We've gotta get back to the car. Lain said he'd meet us at—"

But Dad held out his hands and said: "Forget all that now. Just get in the boat. We have to hurry. I found her, Sigmund. I found your mother."

"What . . ."

Because Dad looked okay, mostly. A little muddy, perhaps. And pale. And sort of . . . waxy. Like he was covered in some kind of oily film.

"She's here," Dad was saying. "But she needs us, needs our help. We have to go to her. Then we can be together. We can be a family again."

(*no . . .*)

"What are you saying?"

(*no. no no no nonononono Dad no*)

"Won't that be great?" Dad said, grin fixed and eyes glassy. "Think about it, a real family. You, me, and Mum. Finally."

Sigmund took a step backward, away from his father's outstretched hand. "No. What are you talking about? We *are* a family. You and me."

David's expression cracked. Just a little. Just enough for the slightest line of a frown to appear etched into his brow. "Get in the boat, Sigmund," he said. "This isn't up for discussion."

Sigmund was not going to get into the boat. Getting into the boat was a Very Bad Idea. Sigmund was going to get Dad out of the boat, and then they were going to head back to shore, then they were going to leave. No boats involved.

"Listen to me," Sigmund said. "Listen to yourself! It's this place talking. It gets to you. It got to me. But just think about what you're saying. Mum is dead, she—"

"Sigmund Gregor Sussman you stop making excuses and get in this boat right now. Your mother is waiting for us."

Dad definitely wasn't smiling now, and Sigmund knew this expression. This was the one Dad had worn when, at age twelve, Sigmund had announced he was going to be a video game designer.

Parental disapproval, and Sigmund knew it well. But Sigmund wasn't a kid. Not anymore.

"No," he said. "We don't have time for this. I'm taking you back to shore." He grabbed hold of pale, weathered wood, and began to pull.

"Stop that," David said. "Stop that right now." He lunged forward, the motion sending the little boat rocking dangerously in the water. "Sigmund! We have to get your mother. You *will* come with me. We *will* be a family again."

"We're a goddamn family now!"

"Not like your mother would've wanted!" Dad's fingers closed around Sigmund's wrist, crushing the already-bruised skin. Sigmund gasped as the pain lanced up his arm, his fingers uncurling from the boat.

"Mum's *dead*, Dad," he snapped. "She's been dead for twenty years! You have no bloody clue what she would've wanted!"

"I've heard quite enou—"

But Sigmund wasn't done. "Stop co-opting her death for things *you* want, or things *you're* too scared to do yourself. She's gone. Let her go. You have me. Just let that be enough. For once. Please."

Dad shut his eyes, looking away as if the words had cut. "And how long will I have you for?" he said. "You're already a grown man. You have a partner now. You can't live at home forever, and when you move out and I'm alone . . . then what? Who will I have then?"

It felt like a knife through the heart and a fire poker to the horns, all at once. Because Dad's anguish, his loneliness, was finally there. All the awful, broken little things he'd never dared to say, spilling out into the mist.

"Dad," Sigmund tried. "Dad, no. Lain wouldn't . . . even if . . . if things got like that . . . you're my *father*. He wouldn't take me from you."

And David said: "He did before! I sold my girl—my strong and beautiful daughter—to that *monster* for trinkets and I never saw her again. I waited. Every day I waited *bumppfh!*" Then David's eyes went very, very round, his hand slapping across his mouth with a muffled, "Oh my god."

Those weren't the words of Sigmund's father.

("*they are the words of mine*")

The same stories, told over and over and over again.

Sigmund closed his eyes against the ache beneath his heart; not his ache, but close enough. When he opened them, Dad was still looking at him, eyes white rings and face as ashen as the sky.

"What . . . what am I *saying*?"

"It's this place," Sigmund said. "It . . . . Things happened. Now they're happening again. But they don't have to happen the same way. That's the point of it, that's always been the point of it. To change things, to make them better." To make different mistakes, if nothing else.

"Sigmund, I . . ." Dad slumped, head in his hands. "I miss her, every day. I thought it would get better with time but I . . . I still love her *so much*."

Sigmund's vision blurred, then spilled over with a blink. "I know," he said. "I'm sorry. But she's not here. Whatever you saw . . . it wasn't her." No hoodie and no tissue, so Sigmund wiped the tears and snot off with the back of his hand.

(*sorry, Mum . . . wherever you are*)

Dad was still for a while. Then, slowly, he began to nod. "Okay," he said. "I . . . Okay. Let's . . . let's get out of here. Wherever you think is best." His head still buried in his hands, his voice thick and blurry in a way that Sigmund hadn't heard since he was a boy.

This time, when Sigmund pulled the boat toward the shore, Dad didn't try to stop him. After a moment, David even retrieved an oar from beneath his feet and began to row.

They left the boat on the muddy shore, Sigmund spending a little while trying to shake the water out of his shoes before giving the exercise up as futile. He wondered if his old clothes were still in the penthouse at LB. Sure they were a little burnt from blood and fire, but at least they weren't soaking wet.

The wrecked ships and low-slung house were still there, but Sigmund took his dad past them without stopping. Back into the ash drifts and up the slope to where he thought the road should be, if he was remembering the lake right. The world was still blur and shadow, jagged branches catching on their clothes and in their hair as they walked through stands of dying trees, but eventually Sigmund saw the little log fence that marked the partition between grass and road.

And, just beyond that, a figure, standing in the blur. Watching.

The snakes in Sigmund's gut began to churn.

"Wha—?"

Sigmund held up his hand, and Dad fell silent.

The figure got closer, walking across the road and toward them. A man. Not a *draugr*, not by the silhouette. Tall and broad, confident.

Familiar.

(*oh. fuck*)

"Run, Dad."

"I would not. There are far worse things out there than me."

Baldr's voice, clear and vicious through the silence. Sigmund could see him now, brand-new eye patch but otherwise the same. And yeah, they were fucked. They couldn't fight a god. Not alone.

Clenching the fire poker in one hand, Sigmund put his other into his pocket. And prayed.

And said, "Baldr." Because damned if he was gonna let some blond asshole make all the speeches. "Is this what honor is in Asgard, now? Killing civilians?" Lain had mentioned honor, right? It seemed a good place to start taunting.

Baldr made a *tsch* sound, raising his arms to show his empty hands. "Peace, boy. I bring no weapons, only words."

Sigmund shifted his grip on the poker. "Not very convincing from a guy who can shoot sunbeams out his ass." He wondered if iron worked on gods the same way it (allegedly) did on fairies. Probably not.

One single golden eye flicked down to Sigmund's hands, then back up to his face. "Truly has your cuckolding skin thief poisoned you against me. There was a time you did not look on me with such revulsion."

Oh Jesus, *what*? Christ. He couldn't possibly mean . . .

"That was probably a time before you tried to *kill my dad*, dickball."

"Sigmund!" David's voice was a hiss from somewhere behind and to the left. "I really don't think insults are going to get us—"

But Baldr was bowing, just slightly, hand held over his heart. "A shameful act for which I will make repatriations. You must understand my mind was . . . not clear at that time."

"Yeah. Sure." Sigmund felt his brow drawn down into a

scowl. Baldr was being . . . nice? Why was Baldr being nice? There had to be some plot, or con, or game. Because no way was this the part when Sigmund found out that his past self had done the nasty with Baldr behind her husband's back.

Then, as if reading Sigmund's mind—which, shit, he probably could—Baldr said: "Tell me. How much do you know about your . . . *beast*. Has it told you its name? Its true name?"

"Loki." There didn't seem to be any point in obfuscation, what with the mind reading and all.

Except Baldr's reaction was odd. Closing his eyes and looking down, sighing. Sigmund didn't get it. From past behavior he would've expected anger or contempt at a minimum. Not quixotic longing.

"It deceives you, boy," Baldr said, voice soft and raw and, worst of all, utterly honest. "Loki is gone, and this shadow you give his name . . . It has claimed you for its wife, yes?"

"Dude," said Sigmund, trying to ignore both the choking from behind him and the churning in his gut. "Not cool. My dad's like *right there*. Jesus." Somewhere, in the distance, Sigmund thought he heard a rumble.

Baldr huffed and rolled his eye in an expression that could only be read as, *Urgh, mortals*, before saying, "You are tangled in fates you do not understand. Hate me if you must but know I loved you once and could do so again. All I ask is that—"

"Whoa! Whoa whoa whoa *whoa*. Dude. No." Sigmund took a step back, enough to nearly trip over David. "Timeout. Stop."

Baldr seemed to crumple at the words, eye squeezing shut and shoulders hunching. Face contorting as if in pain. "Sigyn—"

"No!" And then the tip of the fire poker was under Baldr's chin. Shaking, but there. "No," Sigmund repeated. "Not that name and not whatever this love-triangle bullshit is. You hear me? One creepy, obsessive god is enough. More than enough. And I like him. You're a violent psycho. So there is no asking, no love, and. No. Sigyn. Got it?"

Baldr still hadn't opened his eye, head hanging and lips curled back in agony. He muttered something in the scratching language. Then, in English, added, "Enough. If you will not listen to reas—"

He never got to finish. Instead, the roar of an engine and the howl of a car horn echoed from the fog. Baldr had just enough time to turn his head in the direction of the sound before he was caught between the high beams.

In the next instant, with the sound of snapping bone, he was gone. Rolling up over a shiny black hood with a series of loud thumps, launching a good few feet in the air from the impact.

"Bloody hell!"

Sigmund didn't wait for Baldr to land. Just grabbed his dad's arm and ran forward onto the road, to where the car was turning around. Heading their way.

Dad was pulling back, trying to get out of the car's path. "Look out! It's coming!"

"It's okay, Dad. Trust me."

Because it was Lain's car, all black and chrome and smears of creepy asshole god blood streaking up the windshield. Summoned by the key the car had given Sigmund, back before the sinkhole. The one he'd kept in his pocket, the one he'd pressed when Baldr had been distracted.

The car screamed to a halt at Sigmund's feet, popping open both doors on their side. Sigmund managed to push his dad into the front, before throwing himself into the back, feeling only slightly bad for squelching his gross wet jeans all over the upholstery. Before he could think to apologize, the doors slammed shut all by themselves, and the car was already moving.

Ahead of them, Sigmund saw Baldr stumble to his feet.

"Hold on!" yelled Dad, ducking down in the front seat. Sigmund did as instructed, grabbing on to the headrests from the back.

Baldr saw them coming, eyes wide and anguished. Just before they hit him, again, Sigmund thought he heard Baldr scream a single word.

Then he was just another set of loud thumps, rolling up the hood and over the roof. When Sigmund checked the back window, all he could see on the road was a body. It didn't move.

"Is . . . is he . . . ?"

Sigmund turned to his dad. "Nah. Gods are harder to kill than that." He glanced back again, though the fog had swallowed Baldr's shape.

Sigmund tried not to think of the expression on the bastard's face, right before the car hit him that second time. Because he'd looked an awful lot like someone betrayed, and that piece didn't fit.

A lot of what Baldr had said didn't fit, in fact. About Sigyn, about Lain. About Loki.

Loki, who wasn't Lain, at least according to Baldr. Baldr, who hadn't been lying.

Except, neither had Lain.

"We have to get somewhere safe," Dad was saying. Sigmund blinked, tearing his eyes away from the retreating road.

"Yeah," he said. "Yeah, we've gotta . . . gotta get to the LB building. Can you, um. Can you take us there? Please?" This last addressed to the car. Sigmund thought it was a testament to their weird-ass day that his dad didn't even comment.

The car, meanwhile, revved its engine. Sigmund figured it was as good a yes as any.

—

Munin watched the boss get taken out by the kid and his old man, trying not to wince too hard from the impact. That had to hurt, god or no god. Which is why Munin waited until the scary "car" was well out of range, before flapping down from its hiding place.

"Boss," it said, hopping forward across the tar. "You want me to follow the kid?"

The boss was moving. Except he wasn't getting up. Just sort of dragging himself to his knees, arms wrapped around his waist, shoulders shaking.

"Boss?"

The boss threw back his head, and roared. Something deep, and dark, and twisted. Pain and anguish. A sound that Munin hadn't known the boss'd had, maybe. That wasn't hurt from the impact. That was soul hurt, heartbreak. Despair.

"Boss?"

"Leave me!" The boss gestured for emphasis and—

Odin's rotting eye! He was not kidding around, and Munin squawked and flapped backward as the ground in front of it exploded in a ball of molten sunlight. For a moment, Munin made eye contact. Just it and the boss's single, golden orb. Just for a moment, just long enough to see the tears tracking down the boss's cheek.

Then he turned away. When the boss spoke again, his voice was barely a whisper.

"Leave me. I am betrayed. By my heart, by my flesh. By myself. Why not by my memory also?"

Munin hopped forward, just once. "Boss?" it said. "What're you talking about?" The boss'd been acting weird for a while. Since he'd come back, maybe. Except they'd all put that down to being stuck in Helheimr for a thousand years. That was enough to mess anyone up, in Munin's opinion.

Even still, what the boss'd done to Hel, to the Lady of the

Dishonored Dead herself . . . that was bad business, no two ways about it. And since then, the boss'd just been getting worse and worse. Really obsessed with killing He Who Must Not Be Named (in the Boss's Presence), even though maybe a couple of them had suggested he just leave it. Loki was a shifty, traitorous asshole who'd weaseled out of his own funeral by convincing his wife to go in his place, but he'd been pretty quiet on Miðgarðr since then. Just laying low, a different sort of exile. Maybe they should've been happy with how things were.

The boss wouldn't have it, though. First it'd been about executing the guy, about finishing what'd been started at the Ragnarøkkr. But then something had changed. Munin didn't know what it was.

And now the boss was curled up in the middle of a Helbled street, crying.

Munin hopped forward again. "Boss," it tried. "Tell me what I can do, boss. That's what I'm for."

"I told you," the boss said. "Leave me. You will not wish to stand by my side when this is over. Save yourself the anguish now, and join the others as they seek my end. When it comes, I will relish it. There is nothing left for me here. I had thought . . ." The boss's hand came up to cover his face. He was silent for a while, shoulders shaking. Then, "It does not matter. Just go."

Except Munin couldn't, could it? It belonged to the boss, just like it'd belonged to his dad before him. "You know I can't do that. We swore to your father—"

The boss hissed, spitting some word Munin didn't catch. Then he straightened, and stared right at Munin with an eye that burned like the twilight sun. "I release you," he said. "Whatever oaths you gave unto Odin are no more. His blood no longer holds you; you are freed. Do as you will across the Realms."

"Boss?"

"No," the bo— *Baldr* said. "I am this no longer. Now go."
He flung out his arm again in demonstration. This time with
no explosions, thankfully.

Munin would've grinned, if it'd had the lips to do so. Instead, all it said was, "Hah! 'Cept you ain't the boss of me no
more. Said so yourself. That means you don't tell me what to
do, whose side to pick. I do what I want. And what I want is
we stick around and finish what you started. Deal?"

It took Baldr a moment, staring at Munin as if he'd never
seen a talking raven before in his whole freakin' life. But, in
the end, he dropped his eye. Then smiled, and gave a half
bow.

"Deal," he said. "Now let's finish this."

TWENTY-THREE

I**T'S THE SOUND** that wakes me. Something like an angle grinder crossed with a dying pig. A hideous cacophony, intruding on the warm and silent darkness in my head.

I want it gone. Now. I'm going to open my eyes, and get out of bed, and I'm going to hunt down whoever approved roadworks outside my fucking bedroom window and I am going to sue them down to the bone and salt the ground with their children's bankrupt tears.

Opening my eyes isn't as easy as it should be. The noise is roaring and my eyelids *stick,* and when I manage to prize them apart—

"Hurngh!"

Light.

Real light. From eyes. Not the strange narrative inference of the Wyrdsight, but actual photons, searing across functioning retinas with all the agony of cut onions, followed by a chili chaser.

I sit up. The world tilts. I have a brief impression of wood and candles, then everything goes one-eighty and the next thing I hear is the crack of a skull (mine) against stone.

It does nothing for the headache. Even less for the nausea.

I manage not to hurl, but only just. Biting back pain and bile and the searing in my (working!) eyes and the stink of sweat and rotting rushes and spilt mead and, oh gods. I am gonna hurl.

I do, beneath a table. Tasting the wrong side of meat and honey. It isn't fun.

I feel better when it's over. Maybe just because it is.

The noise continues, unabated. I stumble backward, getting to my feet by sliding up a wall. Carved wood, by the feel.

Wood. Rushes. Mead. Suddenly, it's not just nausea churning in my gut.

I open my eyes.

Light, again. Dim and weak, but after a thousand years of blindness it may as well be the heart of the fucking sun. I put my hand up to my face, groaning, blinking back agony and tears and another rising tide of bile.

I want to die. I haven't had a hangover since . . . for a very, very long time. The piss on Miðgarðr doesn't do it for me. Not like this.

Through my fingers, I see the shape of a table. Long, made of wood. There's an empty, me-shaped space on top of it, in between the plates of bones and empty goblets. I guess that's where I passed out. Where I just fell off.

Next to the space is the source of the sound. It's a guy. He's asleep, snoring. There are quite a few like him scattered around the room, plus some women. It looks like the morning after a party, except every night is a party, here. Every night's a party, and every day's a battle. Because, yeah. I know where I am. I haven't been here for a thousand fucking years, but I remember it. Remember it by the carvings in the walls and the decorative ax-and-shield motif and the fact that everyone's clothing is giving off one hell of an SCA vibe. Except this isn't Lochac, and the only anachronism here is me.

This is Ásgarðr. Valhöll, to be precise: the great Hall of the Slain. The passed-out guys are *einherjar*, the virtuous dead, taken from battlefields by the *valkyrjur* and brought here, trapped in Odin's gilded cage.

Actually, scratch that. *Most* of the passed-out guys are *einherjar*. Most, but not all. Because that guy, over there? With his face half inside a boar carcass? Yeah, that's Víðarr, one of Odin's multitude of useless brats. He's one of the gods, the *æsir*.

And I am so, *so* fucked.

—

First things first, I do what I'm good at: I turn tail and fucking *run*.

It's been a while, and I get lost twice in Valhöll's corridors, eventually making it out via a kitchen. Servants shriek in my wake, but out of surprise rather than in a holy-shit-kill-him sort of way. I think.

When I burst through the door, the sunlight does nothing for my hangover. Does nothing, and my head is pounding and my eyes are burning and—

Warm sun upon my skin, warm breeze carding though my hair. The smell of grass and pine. Of woodsmoke. The sound of ravens, of laughter. The taste of eternal spring upon my tongue. Endless blue and rolling green. A deer watches me across the grass, then leaps off into a copse. In the distance, men ready themselves for war.

Fuck. It's beautiful. I'd forgotten. Made myself forget, maybe. Because exiled, trapped in the endless gray of Miðgarðr . . . how else could I endure it? What can the dull, small world of mortals offer someone used to breathing the pure air of the home of gods themselves? Of drinking from its streams, eating of its fruits? Of resting upon its fragrant grasses, beneath its perfect sun?

Fuck. Fuck I am so, *so* fucked and—

"Uncle?"

Oh. Fuck. No.

I know that voice. The last time I heard it, it was deeper. Older. Angrier. This voice, today, this is the voice of someone innocent. Pure.

Alive. Very, very definitely alive.

I look . . . well, I look up. Because holy fuck am I short now or what? Baldr is barely out of childhood and the bastard still looms over me. Except less with the looming, maybe. Looming is aggressive, threatening, and there's nothing of either of those things in Baldr. Not yet.

His hair is neat and his beard is trimmed and his eyes are so, *so* achingly kind it's like a knife. Right through the heart, the big one, and I slam my eyes shut against the anguish.

"Uncle!"

Hands against my shoulders, and I have to force myself not to react. Not to lash out, to strike in fear and pain and rage.

"Uncle, are you . . . are you well?"

"Yeah, I—" I start in English, because I'm a fucking idiot, before remembering to switch to the old language. "I will be."

I straighten and make myself stare right into the heart of Baldr's gentle, golden eyes. When I smile, it feels like a bitter, gaping wound.

Baldr returns the expression with a wry smirk like the first light of dawn. "Overindulging with the *einherjar*? Really, Uncle. At this time? I would think you would be at home, tending to your wife."

Oh holy shitfuck. Oh shit. Oh fuck.

"Yes!" I can do this. Shit. I can. I have no fucking clue what's going on, or what Prince Goody Soon-Dead is fucking talking about re my wife . . . but I can bluff it. It's what I'm good at.

I clap my hands, take a few stumbling steps away from Baldr. "She expects me home," I say. "So, um. I should . . . do that. Go make sure everything is, y'know. All good. With the time, and whatever." Smoooooth. I can see why the mortals made me the god of this!

Baldr smiles, bright and beautiful, and gives a little bow. "Send her my regards," he says. "And wishes for a safe delivery. Our thoughts are with you both."

"Cool." *No, you idiot! That's modern idiom!* "Good. Thank you!" I turn to go. As I do, I catch the faint edge of a frown form on Baldr's face.

"Uncle?"

I freeze. Half turn, and try to smile.

Baldr is frowning, but there's a smirk somewhere behind it. "Before you go, you, ah. You may wish to locate your trousers."

"Wha—" I look down.

Oh.

FML.

—

I find my pants. Some guy was using them as a pillow, and they're covered in drool and other things I don't want to think about, but I'm pretty sure they're mine.

So, the good news: Baldr is alive, and people don't want to kill me. As much. The bad news, however, is that I've got no idea why I'm here.

Also, I'm really, really fucking short.

Also also, I'm pretty sure there was something else I was supposed to be doing.

Gods have terrible memories. It's sort of our Thing. Because mortals are bad at sticking to their canon, and when your entire life consists of a few hundred years of self-contradicting fanfic? Yeah. You get over being hung up on the details. It's more about sticking to your archetype, living in the moment. Leaves adrift upon the Wyrd.

In this moment, I'm trying to remember where my fucking house is. I do have one. Not a big fancy hall like the big fancy gods, just a house. For the wife, mostly. Yours truly when I'm home (which is never). And the boys, when they were younger.

I'm pretty sure it's next to a waterfall? Or a pool? Some body of liquid, anyway. Surrounded by trees, past the humorously phallic set of rune stones. So I find a stream that looks familiar, and start walking.

Ásgarðr isn't a huge place, not by New World standards; the population being a couple of thousand on a good day. Mostly *einherjar* and servants of various descriptions, plus a scattering of minor mythological entities that don't quite make the Æ-list (like yours truly, depending on who's writing). A few heckle me with greetings as I pass. A few more scurry away, refusing to meet my eyes.

Just another sunny morning in the Godshome.

Ah. The rune stones. See? Some things you never forget.

The path takes a turn at right angles by the stones, and so do I. Then nearly run smack-bang into—

(*wayne and em*)

—Hrist and Hlökk.

"You!"

Did I mention they don't like me much?

"Ladies." I bow, grin, and try to inch around them. Because they're sort of blocking the path and, being *valkyrjur*, are both armed to the teeth and utterly scornful of anyone answering to the pronoun *he*.

Also, they're Sigyn's besties and did I mention they fucking *loathe* me? Because, hey. They do.

Hlökk spits. "Why are you here, Lie-smith?"

"Uh. Because I live here?"

Smart-ass answers earn me growling and looming—Hlökk is about my height, but Hrist *towers*—and I shrink backward, hands held up in supplication.

"Run back to your whores and drink," Hlökk says. "And spare your wife the suffering of your woe-begotten presence."

Wow. Harsh.

I wince, take a step back, and think for a second. Reach deep inside, and *twist*.

"Fuck off, you self-righteous carrion pickers" is what comes out. "We've all got fucking jobs to do in this fucking place. And, hey. My shift just fucking ended, and I'm tired, and hung over, and all I want to fucking do is go the fuck home and spend some quiet fucking time with my fucking wife. So if you don't fucking mind, get the fuck outta my fucking way." And I stare.

The birds stare back. All glossy eyes and blood-smeared lips.

It's Hrist who stands down first. "Cause her suffering and we will *gut* you, Roarer."

"Yeah yeah yeah," I say. "Join the fucking queue." And I shoulder past.

I feel their ax-sharp regard against my back as I go.

—

Past the standing stones, down along the river. Through the trees and into a clearing. By a pond, beneath a waterfall.

There's a house here. Not large, nothing different from any of the hundreds of others once scattered across the realms. Simple wooden walls, simple carved door. Sloped roof more covered with grass and herbs than thatch. A column of smoke, wafting from a high window.

This is my home.

There's a woman, kneeling by the pool, gathering water.

She's dressed in simple clothes. A rough-spun cotton underdress, plain wool *hangaroc*. Beads and brooches and a scarf to hold back hair the color of matted straw, and before I can think, I'm running across the grass, laughing.

This is my wife.

Sigyn turns at my approach. There's a sadness in her, exhausted shadows around her eyes, but when she sees me her smile is good and true and perfect. The only treasure I ever stole and kept. The only one that mattered.

I want to grab her. To lift her and spin her and laugh and rub noses, but I don't. I can't. Because, beneath her breasts, bulging from the front of her tunic, is an enormous, pregnant belly.

Ah. This was what Baldr meant. This thing that I'd forgotten, poor husband that I am.

Despite that, Sigyn reaches for me as I approach, and I fall into her arms. Pepper her face with kisses that must smell of bile and old mead, because she laughs and pushes me away. Not far. Holding my cheeks between her hands and running her thumbs across my scar-cut lips.

"Loki," she says, eyes soft and mouth parted. "You stink of mead and worse things. Is this the way you greet your pining wife after so long an absence?"

"Ah, light of my heart. Forgive me, I am an unworthy wretch." I grin. "And would be made worse to think so beautiful a woman were ever left pining in my wake."

Sigyn's smile says she does not believe it, even as she would hear more such honeyed words. "Go to our house," she says, "and clean yourself. Then you may greet your wife as she deserves."

I steal a single kiss, heart light and head spinning in a way that has nothing to do with mead, neither on its way up nor down. "As my heart desires," I say, for always was its mad rhythm the only dance that Loki follows.

Even if there is more than one that beats within his chest.

—

I wash, as instructed, replacing stained and gaudy clothes with something clean and simple. There is work to do around the house. Things that need repair, wood to chop, water to fetch. Sigyn is strong and true, yet she is also mere days from birthing our third child. This is, perhaps, the time her errant husband earn his keep.

He does, or tries to. Contentment settling in my gut as fingers fumble unfamiliar tasks. Fire brewing lower still when I steal time away from work to lay kisses upon pale skin and hands upon a swollen belly, feeling the tiny feet that kick within.

Seduction is a simple art, to one whose tongue is made of silver. Yet there is no finer target for the practice than one's own well-married spouse.

The day passes. In the evening, over a simple meal of meat and bread, Sigyn takes my hand in hers and asks, "Husband? Today . . ." She stops, looks away, then starts anew, "Are things well, my love?"

I smile. "With you," I say, "always is this so."

And we kiss. And it is perfection.

—

The next day sees me hunting in the woods behind the house. Ásgarðr is flush with game, and food is not hard to find. Nor hard to kill, and I take the shapes of great predators—the wolf, the hawk, the serpent—to do so. I am in the first of these shapes, stalking a deer, when I come across another doing the same. He startles when he sees me, and I him, before he lowers his bow with something like a smile.

"Uncle," Baldr says. "Forgive me. I did not wish to intrude."

I resume my man shape, even as the deer bounds off into the woods, alive for one more day.

"Baldr," I say, moving closer to where he stands. "This is far from your hall, boy. Surely you have your own deer to hunt. And servants to do it for you."

Baldr laughs, but it is a stained thing and he looks away. There is a shadow writ across his features, hollows beneath his eyes, and a sagging in his once-proud shoulders.

"Ah," he says, "this is true enough. But . . . sometimes, lately, I find it tiring to be with the others. Their games . . ." He trails off, tries a smile. It does not lift his eyes. "They mean well."

Some months past, Baldr had grown vexed by dire dreams. Ill portents of his demise. His mother, Frigg, in her love for her bright son, sought promises from all the things in all the Realms. That they would not cause him harm. Wood and metal, stone and illness, all agreed to swear this oath, so enamored is the world with Baldr the White, Baldr the Good.

The other *æsir*, being *æsir*, have turned this dire thing into a game. And so they throw sticks and stones at Baldr whenever he walks by. Strike him with axes and with swords, marvel as none of these actions cause him harm. And Baldr laughs, and takes their foolishness in his own good-humored way.

Yet inside he withers, just a little.

And so I say, "Well, then. You have chosen the right corner of this place to be alone. Deep within this cursed home of monsters and of *jötnar*. Here, we have no such wicked games."

Baldr smiles, bows his head just slightly. "Thank you, Uncle," he says. "I . . . thank you."

I regard him, just for a moment. He is young among the *æsir*. Has a wife and son to call his own, yet the burden of his father's name hangs heavy.

"Hunt with me, boy," I say. "We both seem to have disturbed each other's prey, and will do better with two than each would alone."

This time, when Baldr smiles, there is brightness and truth about its edges.

"That we shall," he says. "And I would be honored."

—

As it turns out, the boy is terrible with a bow. Laughably so and, in the end, we give up hunting and turn to the practice of archery.

We make little progress but, in the evening, when Baldr leaves, his joy is truer than any seen in months.

—

More days pass. Sigyn's body stubbornly refuses labor, and she laughs at me when I fret for it.

"I have done this before," she reminds me, and I scoff.

"As have I, and more times besides." A whole brood of beasts and monsters, birthed from my loins and no less loved for their wicked shapes.

I feel work-rough fingers thread through my unkempt hair. Somewhere beneath my hands and ears, a second heartbeat stirs within my wife.

"Our child will come when he is ready. As we will be ready for him in turn."

"Her," I say.

"Oh? A daughter, you think?"

I look up, grinning. "Why not? I have had too many sons. I am done with them, and would have more of daughters in their wake. Wild and wicked things, to sow strife and discord between the tepid men of our spoiled Realm."

Sigyn laughs. "And where will you find husbands for these girls?" she asks. "What boys here be brave enough to bed one of Loki's vicious daughters?"

I close my eyes, imagine a host of red-haired witches. As fine and cunning as their father. As bold and loyal as their mother. "Our daughters need no husbands," I say. "Let them scourge the Tree without such petty burdens."

Sigyn laughs, and I feel her bend to press her lips against my hair.

"Oh, husband," she says. "You will see us ruined yet."

—

Another day, and we are woken by an awful pounding on the door. Sigyn groans, rolls closer against my side, and I am about to do the same when I hear the voice call:

"Brother! I know that you are here. Rouse yourself from out your bed, I would have words with you."

Odin. And even here, curled against my warm and loving wife, I cannot help the ice that plunges through my hearts.

"Urgh," Sigyn huffs, eyes still closed and half asleep. "Send him away. Tell him we have been eaten and are not here for his amusement."

Thump, thump, thump!

"Brother!"

I groan, pulling myself from Sigyn's grasp and rising from the bed. She looks up at me, expression cold and warning, "Loki, no. He is a beast, and will not have you. You are mine. Leave him."

This argument is old, and I turn from it. Find my pants and pull them on. "He is Allfather, and my brother by blood," I say. "I must answer when he calls. Else we will both find ourselves unwelcome in this land."

Sigyn's lips thin, and I know her thoughts. She has voiced them many times before, saying that we should flee this bitter Realm. Make home on Miðgarðr, or with the *þursar* of Þrymheimr. She thinks the price to be far less than we pay for our place in Ásgarðr. I would lie to say I had not considered it, at times.

But not this time.

"Husband, you are a fool," she says as I walk through our small house and to the entry. I cannot deny that it is so.

Odin's hand is raised to knock again when I open the door and slip outside.

"Brother," I say. "Why do you disturb us so early when you kn—"

I do not get to finish. Instead, Odin's hands have wrapped about my shoulders and I am thrown back against the wood.

"Enough games." Odin's voice is the cry of battle, his single eye burns with the forbidden secrets of the dead. Trapped beneath both, and I cannot move. Can barely breathe. "The time is not for you to dally here, playing nursemaid to your woman. We have a bargain, blood of my blood. Or do you forget it?" His fingers tighten on my shoulders, hard enough to grind the bone.

I hiss, slipping free from Odin's grasp, stalking away from my small and tender home.

These are not things to sully its herb-laded eaves.

"I have not forgotten." The words are ashes in my mouth. Ashes and blood. "It is simply . . . not yet time."

Odin scowls, cloak billowing as he follows me across the grass. "It is well past time," he says. "My heir is in danger. Our entire Realm. You know what you must do, yet you delay. Know that my patience for this foolishness is ended. You will do as you have promised."

"One more day," I say. "A week. Baldr comes here, spends time around my home. I—"

But Odin is not fooled by honeyed words. "I asked you, brother, when we made this plot, whether you would attempt to worm from underneath its weight. You swore to me that you would not. Do not make liar of yourself now. Not for some squalling unborn brat, yet another of your endless, awful brood."

In that moment, I must look away. Must squeeze shut my hands and eyes against the tide of blood and violence. So many children. So many taken by Odin's hand. Made slaves and exiles, all because—

"I told you I will do your bitter deed."

—because their father, their mother, is a fool.

Odin is silent for a while, and I cannot meet his eye. Finally, I hear him move. "See that you do. By sundown. Do not make me return unto this place."

He leaves. It is longer still until I can bring myself to do the same.

When I return into my home, Sigyn sits upon a bench before the fire. Tears cut tracks across her cheeks and there is anger in her eyes. She has listened at the door, I think.

"What did you *do*?" she demands.

"What I had to." I have no patience for this fight, not today. Instead, I head to the back of the home to find my clothes.

"Loki!" I hear her dress rustle as she stands. "Do not walk away. What did you do?" Her fingers close about my wrist.

When I turn, there is fire in my eyes and shame within my hearts. "I bought you freedom," I say. "A future. For our children."

I pull myself from Sigyn's grasp, cast my eyes about for shirts and belt. She follows, and when she speaks her voice is ice and steel. "At what price?" she asks. "What new humiliation would that beast subject you to? What new suffering must I endure?"

The last makes me pause, but only for a moment. "For you? None. I told you, you will have freedom and a future." The words taste heavy on my tongue. The wool of my tunic itches as I pull it over my head.

"And my husband? What of him?"

The next words have no trace of lie about them, and it

makes them knives and lances both. "You will have your husband," I say. "And he you. He will look at you with love and call you wife. Will hold our children in his arms and think them his."

I cannot look at Sigyn. Not with the horror in her voice as understanding dawns upon her, "But he will not be you."

"Sigga–"

"No!" Her hand grabs my shoulder and she turns me. Still, I cannot meet her eyes. "No, you cannot do this. This wicked, evil thing! I will spurn this beast you send upon me–"

"He will have my shape," I say. "And my mind. And the kind and gentle heart that you deserve."

"But not that which I desire!" She releases me, takes one step backward, then another. "Oh, husband mine. Your foolish ways will yet undo us both." And her voice is agony and loathing.

"It is already done," I say. Reaching to the corner of the room, where a bow is propped against the wall. A bow, and a single arrow, made of mistletoe.

All things swore an oath to do no harm against Frigg's bright and well-loved son. All things but one, too soft and young to be true danger.

Still strong enough to be cut into a point. Still old enough to hold the runes and *galdr* wrought upon it. Such a cruel and bitter spell, a father's gilded cage.

Behind me, as I leave our home for the final time, I hear Sigyn swear revenge over a broken heart.

I keep my bargain with my brother.

Baldr suspects nothing. Not even when the arrow pierces through his eye.

And the spell is cast.

—

And, a thousand years later, broken.

"Hnngh!"

Bones crack beneath my knees as I fall to the ground under the Yggdrasill, the Tree's vision receding from my mind. I'm not alone and, nearby, I hear the clatter as someone throws rusted spikes away into the darkness. My wrists and shoulders bleed from the newly unpinned wounds, the Dead God nowhere to be found.

Someone's pulled me off the Tree.

"Do you see now? There's always a price."

"Fuck!"

I scramble to my feet, but too late. Because Baldr is there, face a twisted sneer.

He's bleeding. I don't get time to wonder why, my head still hazy from the vision. Impaled against the bark by the ghost of Odin. It'd seemed like a good plan at the time. Before this happened.

"Baldr—"

"No," he says. Right before his fist makes friends with my jaw.

Fuck.

TWENTY-FOUR

They broke through the fog on the outskirts of the LB campus. Looking up at the huge, gleaming glass-and-steel monstrosity, Sigmund felt nearly light-headed from relief. They'd made it. Whatever stuff came next, at least they were out of the fucking fog.

He could see stars, in the sky above the tower. Too many for a city, maybe, but at least it was a sky. Not the horrible gray-white nothingness.

The car took them around to a side entrance, a ramp down into the private parking garage. The one Sigmund had been in that time with Lain. A huge set of roller doors greeted their arrival. Sigmund had just enough time to wonder how they were going to get in without a pass card, when the doors began sliding upward all on their own.

He decided not to go staring at horse teeth, and all that.

The car let them out near the elevator, coming to a stop and opening its doors. Sigmund and his dad stepped out onto the concrete, then Sigmund turned and gave the car an awkward hug around its canvas roof.

"Thank you," he told it. "I'll, uh. I owe you a detailing. Or . . . whatever it is that cars like."

The engine rumbled.

When Sigmund let go and turned back to the elevator, he saw his dad was smiling.

"What?"

"I was just remembering," Dad said, "how much you used to love Herbie as a kid."

Sigmund thought of the old white Love Bug and thought of Lain's predatory black monster, and thought they were about as different as two cars could possibly be. "Pretty sure Lain's car would eat Herbie for breakfast," Sigmund said, feeling oddly proud about the statement.

Behind him, he heard an engine roar.

—

The elevators worked, which was a relief; LEDs ticking off the floors as they ascended. Somewhere around the thirtieth, Dad said, "You know, I've never been up this high before."

"It's a nice view," Sigmund said. Then, at his dad's raised eyebrows, "Um. Lain, is . . . uh. Lain is Travis Hale."

Dad's eyebrows didn't lower, though he seemed to turn this over in his mind. Finally, he said, "My son is dating the CEO?"

"Yeah."

"The third richest man in the world?"

"Yeah."

"Who's also . . ." Dad waved his hand. Sigmund got the gist.

"Yeah."

Dad was silent for a moment, then an expression that Sigmund could only think of as a sly grin crept across his face. "That's my boy," he said.

Sigmund smiled, looked at his shoes, and tried not to blush. "Yeah," he said.

—

The doors opened in the penthouse. And onto the scowling shape of Nicole Arin.

"Ms. Arin!" Dad's voice, pitched an octave higher than a squeak. Sigmund tried not to wince. "It's an honor. Um. We, uh—"

"Where's Hale?" Arin ignored Dad, looking straight at Sigmund instead.

Sigmund stepped out of the elevator, which wasn't easy with Arin crowding him down. She was kinda creepy. Really . . . intense. Like Em, except minus twenty kilos and plus two decades and two significant figures (at least) on her paycheck. Still. Sigmund could deal with Em. He could deal with Arin, too. He hoped.

"I don't know," he said. "We got separated at my place. But he told us we should head here."

Arin's lips thinned, but she seemed to accept the explanation, turning to stalk deeper into the penthouse.

"That's the VP of the company!" Dad's hand was wrapped around Sigmund's arm, his voice no louder than a whisper.

"I know," Sigmund said. He tried not to take the exposition personally, mostly on account of his bad track record recognizing the top of the org chart. "It's okay." He extracted himself from Dad's grip, following Arin into the living room. After a moment, he heard Dad do the same.

"This mess is Hale's," Arin was saying. "He's dug up old grudges. Now we all share the cost." Her back was ramrod stiff, hands clasped behind, eyes gazing out over the city. "Negative postings for citizens of the city have risen five hundred eighty-three percent, across all major social media platforms, in the last six hours alone. Sixteen people have been hospitalized for attempted suicide; three have succeeded. There have been two murders. A dozen assaults. This is a black day for our city, Mr. Sussman. For our company."

Sigmund felt something cold and hard ball in the pit of his stomach. "Don't blame Lai— Travis for this," he said. "He's not the one who made the Wound."

Arin half turned. "No," she said. "But he knew he had enemies, knew he was hunted. He's spent so many years being so careful. Not raising the suspicions of his former masters. And yet, do you know what alerted them?"

Sigmund took a half step back. Got a bad feeling he knew where this was heading.

"You, Mr. Sussman." So. Bad feeling confirmed. "You are a relic of his past. A thing he should have done without. Yet here you are. And you bring misery in your wake."

"Now hold on just one minute." Sigmund blinked, turning to where his dad was stepping forward. "Don't you blame my son for this. He's young, and he's in love. He didn't want any of this to happen. Ghosts and monsters and . . . and *gods*. He was dragged into this mess, we both were. And now we both just want it over." Covered in mud and ash, and Sigmund had never seen his father so ferocious.

Arin inclined her head, something mechanical in the movement. "As do I," she said. She turned away, seemed to think for a moment, before adding, "You should be safe in this place. For now. But, perhaps, were I you, I would be praying for—" She stopped midsentence. Gaze lifting and not focused on anything Sigmund could see. Something flickered across her eyes. A moving light, not corresponding to anything in the room. When she blinked, it was gone. "Others are here," she said to Sigmund. "Two women, Wyrdtouched, as yourself. They carry an artifact of great power. One works for this company. A Ms. Ivanovich. I believe you know her."

Sigmund felt his breath catch. "Em and Wayne!" It had to be. Valkyries, Lain had said. "Open the doors and send the elevator," Sigmund said. "You can, can't you? Please."

Arin's lips thinned. "They may be hostile."

"Please, they're my friends." Sigmund bit his lip. Gods, he hoped they were all right. This whole thing was such a mess.

"They call for you," Arin said. Sigmund didn't ask how she knew. Was, in fact, starting to get the distinct impression that the creature known as Nicole Arin wasn't as human as initially advertised. "They say Lain has sent them."

(*Lain . . .*)

"See?" Sigmund said, trying to ignore the roaring of his heart. "They're here to help. Please, let them up."

Arin held out a moment longer, but only a moment. "Very well."

"Thank you," Sigmund said, and meant it. "Thank you so much." Em and Wayne. They were here, and they were safe. So was Dad. Now all they had to do was wait for Lain. Who hopefully had some kind of plan. Some way to fix this whole terrible mess.

Sigmund waited by the elevators, hopping from foot to foot as he watched the numbers on the display drop, then slowly rise. Behind him, he heard Dad trying to make awkward small talk with Arin.

(*never change, Dad*)

Then the doors opened.

"Sigmund!"

The doors opened, and suddenly Sigmund's world was black and pink and full of hugs and laughter.

"Em! Wayne!"

"You're okay. Oh, thank gods."

Em snorted. "Gods nothing," she said. "Your boyfriend is an ass."

Sigmund's heart was thunder and his gut squirmed. "You saw Lain? Is he okay? Where is he?"

"He's a fucking Norse fucking *god!*" Em punched Sigmund in the arm. "What the *fuck*, man!"

Sigmund laughed. There was a tinge of hysteria around the edge, and his arm hurt from Em's fist, but he figured both things were okay. Better than okay. Because his friends were here. And they'd seen Lain. "I know," he said. "I'm sorry I didn't tell you."

"He has horns! And a fucking *tail!*"

"I know, I know."

"Bloody hell . . ." Em was shaking her head, muttering under her breath. Sigmund couldn't stop the laughter bubbling in his throat.

"Sig?" Black-nailed fingers on his arm, and Sigmund turned to look into Wayne's eyes. Missing the contacts, for once, which was weird. Sort of . . . raw. "Your boy told us to give you this." She was holding something. An enormous spear. Or . . . a giant tooth on a stick. Whatever.

"What is it?"

"It's Gungnir," Em said. "Odin's spear."

Wayne was offering, so Sigmund took it. The weapon felt weird in his hand. Heavy and awkward. "What am I supposed to do with it?"

"I don't know," Wayne said. "I think . . . just hold on to it, maybe? Loki said he'd be back for it when he could. I think he's planning on killing someone."

"Baldr," Em supplied.

Sigmund nodded, looking down at the spear. "Okay," he said. "Okay. And La— Loki?" Jesus, they needed to sort out all these names. How many names did one guy need, anyway?

(*how many names does he* own?)

"We left him fighting a . . . a thing," Em said. "On Golgotha Hill, under the Yggdrasill. He told us to take the spear, and run."

"You didn't . . ." Sigmund started, then stopped himself. Because no, that wasn't fair.

His friends heard it anyway. "Sig," Wayne said. "I'm sorry, man. But . . . he told us to run."

"I'm sure he'll be okay," Em said, and Sigmund felt the lie creeping in around the edge. "He seems pretty, y'know. Durable. Wayne ran him over with her car and mostly the only thing that broke was the windscreen."

"Em! You dobber!"

"Wayne!"

"I'm sorry, man. But he looked . . . y'know." Wayne did look sorry, and guilty. Still. Running over Sigmund's boyfriend was totally not okay.

"I told you he had horns."

"*I* told her running people over wasn't cool."

Which, fine. So maybe Sigmund had also run someone over a little bit today. But that had been more the car's fault, and besides, it was Baldr. He totally didn't count on account of being the Bad Guy, right?

Right.

(*he said he loved me once . . .*)

Sigmund looked at Em and he looked at Wayne. His friends, his best friends. Both were a little banged up, a little scuffed and a little wild eyed. But they were safe, and they were here and, despite everything they'd done and seen, they were still Em and Wayne. Sigmund wanted to hug them again. Hug them, and never let go. He didn't. Instead he said, "I'm so glad you guys are here."

He got a smile from Wayne and another punch in the arm from Em. "Us too, dooder," said the former.

"With you to the end, man," said the latter.

Sigmund tried not to take it literally.

—

Sigmund's old clothes were still in the penthouse. Tattered and full of holes, but someone had cleaned them and folded them neatly on the bed. They were better than sopping wet jeans and an ash-streaked shirt, and so Sigmund vanished into the bathroom to get changed. It was still the same as he remembered, back when he'd spent the night there, what felt like an eternity ago.

LB seemed immune to the Bleed, so Sigmund jumped in and out of the shower just long enough to scrub away the greasy film coating his skin. His shoes and socks were gross, so when he emerged—dressed again in his clean-but-ruined clothes—it was without either.

"Shower's free," he said, just in case.

He'd left Gungnir leaning against the couch. Em and Wayne were raiding the kitchen, Dad busy discussing business with Arin. All Sigmund could think about was Lain, and why he wasn't with them.

(*what did Baldr mean about Loki?*)

He was about to suggest they start searching, when Wayne looked up from examining the fridge and said, "What's that noise?"

"What noi—"

Rat-ta-tap-tap.

Oh. That noise: sharp and purposeful, coming from the direction of the balcony doors. Over, and over, and over.

"Probably just nothing," Sigmund suggested. But he was already halfway across the room.

Behind him, he heard Em mutter, "Dude. It is *never* just nothing."

She was right: It was a bird. A huge raven, in fact, pecking at the glass with its beak. Sigmund wasn't a big bird expert or anything, but he was pretty sure he recognized it.

It was standing on top of something. A piece of leather, about four centimeters wide, two silver snap fastners on the ends.

Lain's wrist cuff.

"Where is he you squawking piece of shit I swear if you've hurt him I'm going to pull out your feathers one by one!" Because, suddenly, Sigmund had thrown the door open. Was out on the balcony, lunging for the *fucking* bird, rage a cold ball of ice sitting in his stomach.

The raven cawed, hopping backward out of Sigmund's reach with ease.

"Hey, steady on there, kid. I'm just the messenger. Bringing a message."

The bird wasn't talking. When it cawed, Sigmund could see its beak move, see the feathers on its throat ruffle in time to the sound. But when it spoke, its voice was just . . . there.

He hadn't heard it, before. In the parking garage. There'd been something, but it'd been like a whisper from another room, no words he could make out. There were words now. Sigmund would ponder the significance later.

"Where's Lain?" he said, making another lunge. The bird hopped back again, cawing something that might have been a laugh.

"Downstairs," it said, "in the foyer. With the— With Baldr. That's the message. The Bright One wants to do a deal. Seems he might have something you want."

(*shit. shit shit shit*)

Sigmund's hands clenched and unclenched by his side. Behind him, he heard the others crowd around the balcony door.

"And in return?"

The raven clicked its beak. "The spear," it said. "Bring it down, maybe he lets your fuckup boyfriend live."

Sigmund scowled, ice melting to unease within his stomach. The bird wasn't lying, exactly, but there was still something behind the words. Some untruth that itched. "I thought he wanted Lain dead," Sigmund said. "For the Ragnarok." He wasn't as good with the umlauts as Lain was. He figured the raven got the message.

"Yeah, well," it said. "Priorities change. The spear? Now that's a pretty fucking big priority. Bring it down. Just you, rest of the goon squad stays up here. Anything else, Baldr starts chopping bits off your boy. Finger by finger."

"And they call Loki the monster." The name still felt strange on Sigmund's tongue. Too sharp, somehow. Too final. Like a scratching in his throat.

(*cuckolding skin thief*)

It was hard to read the bird's expression, what with it being a bird and all, but Sigmund thought it almost looked unsettled at the comment. "Like I said, priorities change. I'll tell the boss you'll be down in ten." It opened its wings.

"Fifteen," Sigmund said. Then, "It's a long way down." The lie itched. He bit his tongue, focusing on that pain instead.

"Fine," said the bird. Then it was gone.

When Sigmund turned, four pairs of worried eyes stared back at him. Even Arin's, which wasn't instilling Sigmund with any confidence.

"Dooder. You can't," Wayne said. "You know it's a trap."

"I know," Sigmund said, because he did. "So this is what we're going to do."

—

Ten minutes later, they were down in the office, standing in front of the elevators. Sigmund's dad had been put in charge of the time.

"Five to go."

Sigmund nodded, reminding himself to breathe. He was pretty sure he was leaving sweaty handprints all over Gungnir.

The plan, he had to admit, wasn't much of a plan. More of a proto plan, but, to his credit, it wasn't as if he'd had a lot of time to come up with a full-tilt caper film. Just a distraction, really. Just enough to get downstairs, get the spear to Lain, and hopefully survive the encounter.

He didn't know what else he could do. He wasn't a god, not anymore. He didn't know how to fight, wasn't immortal, couldn't shrug off broken bones like they were nothing. This was all he had. It *had* to be enough.

He looked to Arin. "Start sending them down."

Eight elevators in the Lokabrenna offices, but only two that came all the way up here. Sigmund was hoping Baldr didn't know that.

They'd taken the stairs down from the penthouse, just in case.

"Here. I couldn't find a backpack, but I got this." Wayne, jogging up, carrying a too-hip laptop bag. It bulged in the way laptops didn't, and when she helped Sigmund put it on, the thing weighed a ton.

"It'll do," Sigmund said. "Em?"

"Right," Em said. "So tell me, Mr. Sussman. What *are* your thoughts on the *Star Wars* prequel trilogy?"

Because that was the thing, wasn't it? Gods were psychic. Sort of. According to Arin, it was more like a limited narrative prescience. Like being able to read the whole script, not just their own lines. And Lain was better at it than most, what with the whole being-blind thing. He relied on it a hell of a lot more than, say, Baldr would. Hopefully. Because Sigmund's plan needed surprise, and that meant no cheating god hacks.

And that meant thinking about something that wasn't the Plan.

"—no narrative structure. Like, the originals were so great because they were so simple, y'know? Just your standard Hero's Journey stuff. Farm boy discovers he's special, blah blah blah. But the prequels, like. I dunno. They kinda tried to keep that with the whole junkyard-slave thing, except—"

And that, Sigmund knew, meant harnessing the most deadly power on the whole Internet: Nerd Rage.

"—don't even get me *started* on the use of gross racist stereotypes that—"

Dad put a phone in Sigmund's hand; Em was already holding hers. Arin was making them work, some godly power thing. Sigmund had expected her to disapprove of this part. For whatever reason, she'd been all for it.

He stepped into the elevator.

Over the phone, he heard Em's voice say, "But don't you think the attempt to broaden the scope of the narrative into the more political aspects of interplanetary relationships served to enrich the overall story line?"

"If they hadn't cocked it up, maybe. The books managed it. Like, if you read the ones by—"

All the way down in the elevator.

The idea was, all the doors would open on the ground floor at different times. If Baldr didn't know exactly which one Sigmund would be in, hopefully they could avoid any messy ambushed-through-the-choke-point nonsense.

Sigmund had no delusions he could take on Baldr in any kind of one-on-one fight, even with Gungnir on his side. But he did have to get close enough to take the bastard out. Just for a little while. Just long enough to get the spear to Lain. Who would hopefully be in a position to do something with it.

Lain was downstairs. The bird hadn't been lying about that part, at least.

The elevator stopped moving. Sigmund's hands shook and his palms were slick enough to make holding on to the spear and the phone difficult.

He had a bad feeling about this.

Baldr didn't leap in, screaming, when the doors opened, which Sigmund took to be a good sign.

"I'm here," he told Em.

"Good luck, man."

Upstairs, Dad had spent at least three minutes hugging Sigmund and stating how proud he was. Sigmund tried not to think of it as good-bye.

He put the phone back into his pocket, then left the elevator.

"Ah. Alone and with my spear. So you do have some honor left within your heart."

Sigmund turned.

Baldr was there, just beyond the rows of elevator doors, beside the foyer's garden. Standing, feet apart, chin up, hands behind his back. On the ground, beneath him, was a crumpled shape that Sigmund recognized.

"Lain!" No response. Sigmund took a step forward, looking back up at Baldr. "What have you done to him, you asshole?"

"Very little, I assure you," Baldr said. "And far less than he deserves."

"I brought your bloody spear." Sigmund's feet were walking forward. Baldr watched, head tilted. "Now let us go."

"Look at you." Taunting. Sigmund could deal with taunting. Sigmund *had* dealt with taunting, every day of his goddamn life.

Baldr's expression wasn't quite a sneer when he continued, "Such honor, such loyalty. Such *betrayal*. A thousand years I waited. I brought you freedom, a future. And this is how you squandered it? For *that*?" A gesture to Lain, sharp and angry.

Sigmund still had no idea what the hell Baldr was talking about.

Sigmund didn't, but someone did.

"Do not talk to me of betrayal, husband," said Sigmund's voice. Except it wasn't Sigmund who was saying it, and he wasn't even sure he was saying it in English. Nor was it Sigmund who was moving his feet forward, who'd changed his grip on the spear to something strong and sure. "Not when it was you who sold our family, our love, over and over to the beast you called a brother. That jealous, vicious monster. Who took everything of you, right unto the end. You speak to me of waiting. You know *nothing* of waiting. Not the cold and lonely nights I spent alone. Knowing you would not share my bed, my love, devoted as you were to one who never saw you as aught but a wicked tool to work his will."

(*oh. holy. shit*)

Not adultery, then. At least, not Sigyn's.

Sigmund, meanwhile, couldn't stop walking. Not even when quite-possibly-not-Baldr moved forward as well. Until they were within arm's reach of each other, circling.

"I loved you," not-Baldr was saying. "I gave up everything for you! For our family."

"*Liar!* You gave us up because he asked, paid to him his price. And how well that served us in the end." Sigmund's voice sounded strange. Cold, hard. "Our sons, cursed and murdered. Our daughter, lost."

"Daughter?" And there, in Baldr's eye. That was . . . pain? Hope?

Behind Baldr, on the ground, Sigmund caught the twitch of one long, feathered tail.

"Esia," Sigmund heard himself say. "I held her for but a day. A day until the bitter shell you left us was bound and banished for his deeds. I gave our child to your eldest, went into exile with the thing that bore your name—"

"*Why?*" And that was anguish, pure and true.

"Because he did not deserve to suffer for your foolish choices! And because he was my husband. Is that not what you had wanted?"

"He was to care for you! He failed, by his own jealousy and pride. You were not to pay for his mistakes!"

"When his mistakes were yours as well? Tell me, my awful burden, when have I ever not paid thus? What other choice could I have made?"

"You could have— *No!*"

Sigmund was trying not to look, he really was. He couldn't move anything else, but he could move his eye. Just a little, just enough to watch Lain. Not dead, just unconscious. Or he had been. Now, he was slowly levering himself onto his feet, ready to pounce.

But Sigmund did look, did think. And Baldr noticed, face falling into a sneer.

Baldr got halfway through a turn when Sigmund felt his laptop bag lurch, a huge dark shape emerging from beneath the flap, aiming straight for Baldr's face.

In the next instant, the god screamed.

Sigmund didn't stick around. Just broke into a run, praying Boots would be okay. That Baldr—or whoever he was, and Sigmund was starting to get a really sinking suspicion on that one—wouldn't hurt her too badly.

Even if she did just bite him in the face.

"Lain!"

"Sigmund!"

Lain was on his feet, running. Sigmund held out the spear. Felt it wrench out of his grasp as Lain grabbed it.

"Get to safety!"

Except where was safety, really? Especially when Sigmund heard Baldr (whomever) scream again, in outrage this time. Lain roared in response, and when Sigmund turned, hidden behind a potted plant, he saw gods clash.

Baldr and Loki. Sun and fire. Law and chaos. Good and evil.

The fact that the teams seemed a bit confused as to who, exactly, was whom didn't make the fight any less vicious.

"You were supposed to care for her!" Baldr-who-was-possibly-Loki cried. "Then die. We would be free!"

"What the fuck are you talking about?" Okay so Lain—who was, at minimum, definitely Lain—hadn't yet caught up on all the spoilers. Sigmund winced, especially when oh-Hel-let's-just-call-him-Baldr roared, not pleased by this development.

"You spoiled, mindless *fool!*" He was unarmed, but when his fist connected with Lain's face, the latter went flying backward from the force. "Everything you have been given, squandered! I had a deal with your father. To fulfill the prophecy, to keep you safe within his reach." Lain tried to stumble upright, which earned him a boot to the jaw. "All you had to do was *die!* That's all you ever had to do. Die, then die again. Release us from this loathsome fate. Free us all." Another boot, this one slamming onto Lain's hand. It uncurled from Gungnir, and Baldr went to grab the spear.

Lain was faster, driving his horns up into Baldr's gut which, okay. Ouch. For both of them. Then they were rolling over and over, each trying to gouge the other's eyes or bite or kick. Anything. Lain's tail thrashing wildly.

Thrashing right into Gungnir, sending it skidding across the ground. Right toward Sigmund.

(*"now, boy. end this madness. free us, and your love"*)

Over by the elevators, Baldr slammed Lain's head into the floor, hard enough to crack the tiles. Lain cried out, clutching at his horns.

Baldr went to stand.

Sigmund got there first. Grabbing Gungnir as he did.

In the end, it wasn't even very hard. Sigmund thought it should've been. For a lot of reasons, not just the physical. Stabbing a man through the chest, with enough force for the tooth of the spear to come right out the other side. Sigmund wasn't sure he managed to get the heart. He wasn't sure it mattered. Not with the strange, blood-choked gurgle that Baldr gave. The way he staggered, half turned to look at Sigmund with a single, golden eye.

"S-Sigga? No . . ." he said. Venom from Boots's bite turning his skin a familiar shade of charcoal.

Then, with one final roar, he lunged forward, toward Lain.

Lain, who tried to scramble out of the way. Not fast enough for Baldr, though, who grabbed Lain around the shoulders and pulled him into a crushing hug. Right onto where the wicked point of Gungnir protruded from his chest. There was a horrid sound—a soft sort of crunching—and then Lain's eyes went very wide. When he coughed, blood spilled over his lips, burning where it fell onto Baldr's armor.

"Lain!"

Sigmund saw the exact moment when the strength went out of Baldr's limbs, the exact moment when his weight caused Lain to stumble. When gravity took over, and the pair of them crashed down against the tiles.

Sigmund was screaming Lain's name, over and over. Jolts of pain ran up his knees when he fell to the ground, hands scrabbling against Baldr's tunic, trying to push him off. To make sure Lain was okay. Lain had to be okay. Because that was how these things worked. That was how the story ended. Happily ever after, always.

Lain coughed again. Sigmund could hear the hissing of the tiles where poisoned blood was eating them away.

He had to get Baldr off. He had to free Lain. Lain could heal. He'd been speared before, right? He'd been fine, then. Eventually.

"S-Sig. Sig, stop." A huge, red-taloned claw, pushing gently on Sigmund's chest. "Don't. The . . . the blood."

"No!" Sigmund didn't care about the blood. Didn't care if it burned, if it poisoned. He had to save Lain, he had to—

(*"hush, fool boy. all will be well"*)

Except how could it be? Not when Lain was bleeding out and his eyes were dull and flicking closed and he was saying, " 'S over, Sig. This's the w-way the world ends."

Then he was gone.

And it did.

TWENTY-FIVE

("*vituð ér enn, eða hvat?*")

PEOPLE AREN'T THE only things that die. Sometimes stories do as well, when there's no one left to tell them. Here, now, in the space between the turning of the page, everything comes unraveled. And, for one bright moment, I *see*.

This is what it looks like: the high vaults of Éljúðnir, the sleet-soaked hall of the Queen of Death herself. And there she is, standing, sword drawn, before a man. Before Baldr, who carries a spear and someone else's twisted snarl upon his features.

In the language of the gods, Hel says, "Your plan will fail, Bright One. We have made sure of it."

Baldr sneers. "Too late, girl. You cannot protect your father now. He will die."

"Yes," Hel says, her mouth a lipless, rictus grin, eyes obscured by a veil. "And yet your plan will fail."

Baldr hefts his spear. "Pity then," he says, "you will not be here to gloat over my demise."

They fight. It's long, and brutal, and bloody, and a meta-phor. Life and death, struggling for control.

This time, life wins, and Baldr's spear pierces Hel's breast. As Baldr looms above her, eyes mad and lips split into a blood-soaked grin, a hand raises to caress his cheek.

As she dies, Hel says, "I free you, Father. Free your mind from the chains you placed upon it. Forgive us for what we have done. Trust us that all will end as you desire."

With her own blood, Hel traces runes upon her father's cheek, and, from them, truth worms into his mind.

In the end, life is a fleeting, fragile thing, and death rides victorious in its wake.

It takes only a moment until the thing wearing Baldr's skin is screaming his daughter's name.

It is not himself he blames for her demise.

—

This is the memory death gives: another hall, Valaskjálf, and another god of death within.

"My wife is a childish fool."

"Mm. I would not say such things within her earshot. Lest you favor your bed as cold and empty as your heart."

Odin growls, hands clenching about the edge of the balus-trade. He leans forward, looking out over Ásgarðr as the sun sets beneath the Tree. Behind him, Loki lounges in a chair, whittling wood with a small knife.

"The time of Ragnarøkkr is upon us," Odin says. "My son dreams of his own death and the very Fates themselves con-spire against me. Frigg's petty games will not prevent this."

Loki does not lift his eyes from the shape within his hands. A toy for his unborn child. "Prophecy is her domain. Perhaps her 'petty games' mean more than you know."

Odin scoffs, pride burning in his gaze. "I will not entrust my son and my kingdom to the sentiment of a single, fretting woman. The future has been spoken. Baldr will die, it cannot be avoided."

"Then why fret yourself? Let him die. You have other finer sons. What matters the loss of one?" Beneath Loki's knife, a wolf emerges. This one has no fetters.

"If Baldr falls," Odin says, "he will go to Hel. I will not have a son of Odin held prisoner by that fleshless *íviðja* hag."

The knife stops, and eyes as green as poison look up for just one moment. Just one. Then, "So send another in his place."

Odin turns, looks to his blood brother with furrowed brow. "What do you scheme, Loki?"

"The prophecy is as it says." Loki does not meet his brother's gaze. "Baldr will die. But perhaps if your son were not wearing his own skin when it were to happen . . ."

Very slowly, Odin begins to smile. Very soon, Loki will cease to do the same.

—

And then this, the last piece. Not a hall, this time, merely the inside of one small house.

Someone screams. The thing is curled up in a corner, and it wears the skin of Loki. It is not him, and Sigyn, who stands behind it, knows that this is so.

"My *children*," it howls. "What they did to my children. To *me*. Monsters, every one of them!"

The thing that now wears Loki's skin is a soft and coddled soul. It knows nothing of pain, of heartache, of injustice. Knew nothing. Not until it pulled the tunic from its borrowed flesh and saw the scars beneath.

Remembered every wound that made them.

Sigyn watches the beast that is not Loki. The beast that is her husband. Its agony is a tangible thing, bleeding through the small and ill-kept house, sending the fire leaping.

"Husband," Sigyn says. The title seems the most truthful

of any she could use. "You must not dwell upon such things. They happened long ago." The lie burns upon her tongue, and it does not convince.

"Monsters," the thing that is not Loki hisses. "Hypocrites, liars. I will make them *pay*. Reveal their rotten cores." When he stands, madness burns in bright green eyes.

When he leaves, it is with hatred set in his new hearts. Yet, beneath that, he is a soft and coddled soul. And, ultimately, it is not his enemies who pay the price.

Not yet.

—

Between the turning of the page, in the flicker of the frame, it all falls into place: Loki's scheme, Odin's plan, Sigyn's victory. And Baldr, trapped between all three. The perfect patsy, pulled apart and made anew as, stitch by stitch, the Wyrd unravels.

It was supposed to be a simple trade, a soul for a soul. Baldr held safe in Ásgarðr, beneath his father's all-seeing eye; Loki given pride of place within his daughter's grave-cold hall. When things were over, with "Loki" dead, Baldr's soul would be restored to his true self, ready to take his place upon the throne.

That was the plan. Until Sigyn usurped it, in love and revenge. Mixed it up. Extended the Ragnarøkkr out half a century or so, giving Baldr the freedom to get used to Loki's name, away from Odin and from Ásgarðr. Sigyn reforged herself while she was at it, using her soul to weave a different ending from words writ into the first.

Here, between the turning of the page, I have to make a choice. The outcome was supposed to be preordained.

Loki and Baldr. There's so much of both of them trapped inside, too much for a single heart to hold. Around us, the world begins to crumble, and still all we can think about is soft brown skin and nervous laughter. Of eyes like ice and a heart of frozen steel.

In the end, it's not Odin they call Victorious, and only the *æsir* are stuck with a single beat within their chests.

I make my choice, take Loki's fate, and eat his heart.

—

The first thing we do is breathe. Huge, painful, gasping breaths. The gasps of a newborn. A chorus of agony, kept in time by the discordant feel of rib-caught drumming.

We're alive. For the first time in centuries. Properly alive, not the awful half lives we've had since the cave. Since the arrow. Since everything went wrong. Since it started going right.

"Lain!"

Curled up on the ground, coughing, we feel cool hands against our shoulders.

"Lain!" Someone saying our—saying *my* name, over and over. "You're alive!"

"In—hnngh. In a m-minute." Maybe.

Opening my eyes does nothing, so I feel out with the Wyrd-sight. The first thing I hit is Sigmund, a blaze of relief, of joy, of love. And something under it, too. A core of ice-cold certainty. Of victory.

When I try and sit, he helps me up. We're in the foyer at LB, just near the elevators. In the middle of a big, cracked hole of half-melted tiles. Gungnir is lying on the ground, next to Sigmund. Forgotten. For now.

Sigmund is holding me like someone plans to take me away at any moment. Breathing still hurts and the beat of my hearts is still not quite in sync, so I just sit still and let him do his thing. He's happy. I'm alive. All is well.

"We won," Sigmund says. "We did, right? I mean, Baldr, he just sort of . . . burnt up. Vanished. He's . . . he's dead, right?"

"Uh," I say. "Yeah, about that . . ."

Sigmund goes very, very still. "Loki?" He knows when I lie. Right.

"Sort of," I say. Then, "It's, uh. It's complicated. I'll tell you later. But . . . yeah. We won." Everyone did. Everyone who matters, anyway.

Somewhere deep inside, past the flames, something new coils against my mind. Something dark and vicious. Slippery and ancient.

"Hey, Sig?"

"Yeah?"

I kiss him.

It's good. Really good. He thinks so too, if the pepper flare of lust and the way he grabs my head is anything to go by. He's still not a great kisser, but he's getting better, enthusiasm and near-death experiences working wonders.

Deep inside, the dark thing stirs. Bubbles to the surface. Spreads through my hands and lips and tongue. As it does, the cold core in Sigmund soars to greet it.

See? Everyone wins.

When Sigmund pulls back, he's flushed and blinking. "Wow," he says. There's fog on his glasses.

"Yeah," I say.

"What was that?"

I grin. "Do it again and find out."

He bites his lip, leans forward to oblige. Gets halfway before context comes crashing back. "Um. Maybe . . . not here?" he says. "It's nearly dawn. People are going to start coming in for work soon." He blinks, looking around. "And the Bleed—"

"Healing," I say. One little Wound's got nothing on the reboot of the Realms. Somehow, I get the feeling Hel knew that. I get the feeling she knew a lot of things. One day I might even get the courage to ask about it.

Sigmund slumps, relieved that things seem to be over. "Thank god," he says, and I accept the praise. "Let's get you upstairs. Um. Everyone's up there. Dad and Em and Wayne. Your scary VP lady. I guess we should tell them we're not dead. Can you stand?"

I manage, mostly by leaning against Sigmund. He's cool under my skin, and solid, and there. Banged up and stinking of the ash of Múspellsheimr. Changed by the mists of Hel. But still Sigmund.

Me? I'm . . . someone. I'll work out exactly who some other time.

A stray memory, mine but not mine. Of Sigmund stepping out into the foyer, Gungnir in one hand, mind a storm of anger over *Star Wars*. I'll have to ask him about that. Later, once I've explained why I know it.

As we stagger back toward the elevators, one of them opens. Care of Nic, who watches eternal through the building's cameras. She's gonna want one hell of a debrief on all of this. Fuck.

"Urgh. I need a smoke," I say as the doors close behind us.

Sigmund leans me against the mirrored wall, but doesn't try to move away, hands ghosting over the skin of my chest. There's a new scar there—healed and bloodless—from where Gungnir pierced two hearts, both of them mine, held in separate cages.

"I can think of something better than cigarettes," he says.

"Oh?" I manage, right before he kisses me. Not for long, just enough to leave the taste of a newfound fearlessness on my tongue. "Oh. Yeah. Yeah, that's much better."

"You know," he says, hands moving down to settle around my waist, "I can't kiss you if you taste like nicotine. It's way gross."

"Duly noted." I grin. "I don't taste like it now."

"No," Sigmund says. "You don't." He doesn't return my grin. Instead, his fingers tighten on my hipbones as he says, "Lain, you . . . Yyou *died*. I saw it."

"Nah," I say. "I was dead when you met me. Now I'm better." That's how these things go, the buffer overflow error of the reborn god.

Sigmund closes his eyes, moving closer, cheek over my hearts. "Good," he says. "Stay like that. Please?"

"Yeah. Yeah, that's the plan." When I nuzzle against his forehead, he turns his face up to meet me.

We kiss, and it's better. Better than the last time, better than the first time. Better, always. There's a metaphor in there somewhere, and I'm sure I'll find it one day. Beneath Sigmund's tongue, perhaps, or hiding in his hair. I'll keep looking. I've got time; it's a long way up to the penthouse, after all. When we reach it, there'll be friends and allies, family, explanations. Fantales. One ruffled raven. And the first rays of dawn, exploring the remade world with all the wonder of a child.

Welcome to the Golden Age. An old end, but a new beginning.

Stick around. You'll see.

*Then comes the gloomy
dragon flying,
from below,
from Niðafjöll.
The bodies of men
in his feathers lie.*

—"Völuspá," stanza 66

IT TAKES NEARLY three days to round up all the body parts, even with the memories of where I put them. Or . . . where Baldr put them.

Or Loki.

Whoever.

Look, point being it takes a while, but I do it, and because of that, the Helbleed pulls back from Pandemonium.

On the evening of the third day after the end of the world, I stand on top of my tower—Travis's tower, whatever—with a box of ashes, looking out over the city.

"It's, um. It's a nice view from up here." Sigmund shifts, nervous. He's standing to my left and half a meter behind, anxious about getting too close to the edge.

"Yeah," I say. "Yeah, it is." Pink and orange light glitters off the lake and, in the background, the dark curves of Woolridge roll gently against the sun.

I look down at the box in my hands. Not a lot of ash in a person, as it turns out. Even a tall one like my daughter.

Loki's daughter.

Jesus. I think I need to cry. Someone needs to cry, anyway.

"Are you all right?" I feel Sigmund's hand, cool and gentle, settle against the small of my back.

"No," I manage, voice choked and thready. "No, I'm not."

"I'm sorry." He doesn't know what else to say. What else *is* there to say?

"Do not grieve, husband."

The voice still makes me freeze. It's Sigmund's, but it isn't. Because Sigmund, as far as I'm aware, doesn't know how to speak Old Norse. He also doesn't call me *husband*.

Neither does Sigyn. At least, not *me* me.

"What would you have me do instead?"

I let Loki answer his wife, because it seems like the polite thing to do. The guy's kinda falling apart over the ashes of the daughter he murdered. The least I can do is give him a few minutes of talk time with the ghost of his dead lady.

I feel her—feel Sigmund—close the gap between us, resting her cheek against the skin of my back, tracing one hand across the faintly glowing whorls of the tattoo.

"I would have you rest," Sigyn says. "Do not fret over your daughter's dark designs. She is where she wished to be."

"Dead?" Loki spits, his black heart aching, memories reeling with the feel of the sword as it pierced her breast. The gentle touch of her dying fingers, smooth and soft and pale.

Sigyn just laughs. "Do not underestimate your own, husband. Hel is her father's daughter."

Loki huffs, looking down at the box once more, thinking about an endless, flat gray ocean, and a shore made from the corpses of the dead.

It's windy, this high up above the street, and maybe Loki calls down a little more. Just enough to catch the ashes he throws. To take them off into the night, the first stars of evening as their guide.

When he's done, he tosses the box aside, and turns to face his wife.

It's still Sigmund, of course. A little taller than Sigyn was, and softer, and darker. And we can still see him, with the Wyrdsight. But he's hanging back, and the thing that overlays him now is cold and stern and endless. Victory and compassion, all rolled into one.

When Loki kisses his wife, I look away.

"Sigga . . ." he breathes after a while. Somewhere deep inside, I feel his pain. Resentment, maybe. He's dead—the ghost of an old story, now retold—and he knows it, but . . .

"Hush, husband." Sigyn lays a kiss on his cheek, holding his face between her hands as she looks up with a borrowed smile. "We will meet again."

"Sigga!"

But then she's gone, and it's just Sigmund.

He pulls his hands away, taking half a step back as he says, "Um!"

("*tssch, take him*")

Then I'm me again. Whoever that turns out to be.

"Do you reckon that's gonna happen a lot?" I ask.

Sigmund relaxes at the words, spoken in a language he understands, in idiom he finds familiar. Then he gives an awkward laugh. "Um. Maybe?" He can't quite meet my eyes when he adds, "I mean. I don't mind. Not really. Um . . ." He's oozing fluffy pink clouds of embarrassment but also, I think, a smudge of anxiety. I don't blame him; Loki is a little scary. Definitely a few logs short of a bonfire, if nothing else.

("*better mad than a spoiled, glass-backed fool*")

I guess we'll both get used to it. Whatever it is.

I kiss Sigmund, mostly because I can, then go to fetch the discarded box. Loki might be happy littering my rooftop but Nic will kill me if she finds out.

"Sig?" I ask.

"Yeah?"

Around us, the wind is picking up, and Sigmund has started to shiver. Out in the distance, the fat lazy orb of the sun burns on, uncaring, as the Earth slowly turns its face.

"Take this downstairs and put it in the recycling for me?" I hand him the box. The inside is still smeared with ash. I try not to notice.

"Sure."

"I wanna do something up here for a bit. I'll meet you at the restaurant in ten." Tonight's a date night. Nowhere fancy, just somewhere we can be together.

"Okay. You have fun. See you then." He gives a little wave, I return it, and then he's gone. Off the rooftop and down the elevator, heading toward the ground.

I'm heading down too. Just . . . not that way.

There's a concrete balustrade around the rooftop. To stop people falling off. I jump onto it, claws digging into the concrete, and look over the edge.

It's a very, very big drop.

When I open my wings, they catch the wind and nearly send me falling.

"Woooaa shit!"

I end up crouched on the edge of the wall, all four claws gripping the concrete, heavy tail held out for balance.

Beneath me, the city hums its static hum. Above, the wind dances through an endless, inky sky.

And me?

I let go of the edge, and teach myself to fly.

ABOUT THE AUTHOR

Alis Franklin is an Australian author of queer speculative fiction. She likes cooking, video games, Norse mythology, and feathered dinosaurs. She's never seen a live dropbear, but stays away from tall trees, just in case.

You can find more of Alis at: https://alis.me

www.ingramcontent.com/pod-product-compliance
Lightning Source LLC
Chambersburg PA
CBHW010525100726
47903CB00011B/2898